THE YEAR'S BEST
DARK FANTASY & HORROR

THE YEAR'S BEST
DARK FANTASY & HORROR:
VOLUME ONE

EDITED BY
PAULA GURAN

Other Anthologies Edited by Paula Guran

Published 2020 by Pyr®

Cover image © Shutterstock
Cover design by Jennifer Do
Cover design © Start Science Fiction

Inquiries should be addressed to

Start Science Fiction
221 River Street, 9th Floor
Hoboken, New Jersey 07030
PHONE: 212-431-5455
WWW.PYRSF.COM

10 9 8 7 6 5 4 3 2 1

ISBN 978-1-64506-025-3 (paperback)
ISBN 978-1-64506-026-0 (ebook)

Printed in the United States of America

To all the Essential Workers.
Heroes seldom wear capes and rarely have supernatural powers.

CONTENTS

INTRODUCTION:
STRANGE DAYS

"Fiction reveals truths that reality obscures."
—JESSAMYN WEST

These are unsettling times. The world changed forever as I compiled this anthology, and we don't yet know what it has changed into.

Why, some must be asking, would anyone want to read dark fantasy or horror while a pandemic rages, the economy (and who knows what else) topples, and people are dying and suffering?

I won't attempt to provide any deep thoughts on the subject. But I do have some shallow ones that occurred to me during the process of deciding on the content of this anthology.

Most of these stories begin with a world you can identify with (or the fictional universe is an extension of ours). You are grounded. Then things become disquieting, unnerving, disrupted, intruded upon. The world changes. The normal is subverted. But cleverness, or resilience, or caring, or perseverance still somehow exists. And if doom is inevitable, perhaps we emerge resolved to defy the fictional fate if it ever turns real. At the very least, we can admire those who have faced catastrophe.

For better or worse, these stories will affect you. Make you feel something that reminds you of your own humanity and that of others.

To quote author Ruthanna Emrys:

> Horror as a genre is built around one truth: that the world is full of fearful things. But the best horror tells us more. It tells us how to live with being afraid. It tells us how to distinguish real evil from harmless shadows. It tells us how to fight back. It tells us that we can fight the worst evils, whether or not we all survive them—and how to be worthy of having our tales told afterward.

Dark fantasy? Well, I still will not try to define it, but as China Miéville has pointed out about the genre as a whole: traditional fantasy may only, as Tolkien wrote, offer "consolation," but in the best of modern fantasy "[t]hings are gritty and tricky, just as in real life. This is fantasy not as comfort-food, but as challenge."

Dark fiction isn't escapist, it confronts reality and helps us comprehend it.

I didn't pick these stories with any theme in mind. Certainly not to challenge or provide hope in these days of adversity. Response is always personal, but I think there is a chance you may find a modicum of such in some of these stories.

After ten volumes of the series with Prime Books, this is the first volume with a new publisher, Pyr. I'm grateful to both and hope the Year's Best Dark Fantasy and Horror series has a robust future in the ever-changing world of publishing.

And thanks to you readers, new and old; you, more than anyone or anything, determine its future.

National Burrito Day 2020
Paula Guran

THE FOURTH TRIMESTER
IS THE STRANGEST

REBECCA CAMPBELL

For hours now, the woman across the hall had been screaming. Ten minutes apart, eight minutes, five, and then the long, lonely push through to daylight and silence, and they said nothing about what had happened after that: a child, Jenny hoped, but maybe no child. She could only be sure of the screaming. A needle in Jenny's wrist dripped magnesium sulfate, which dropped a film between her and the world, as if the light that flooded the hospital room was beyond her, and she knocked against it in her permanent twilight.

She only noticed the other woman's screams when she was through her own ordeal, though Greg said it had been going on all along, during the hours when she, turning inward, had drawn her mind deep into her guts and to Max, and had held on to Greg's hand and pulled him down toward them, too. She had heard nothing but her own breathing in the knocking dark of her body, and Max, who made his dark-water journey out.

Before the screaming, hers or the woman's across the hall.

They told her: Curve around your belly, your knees drawn up, your back exposed, and push each vertebra outward. The nurse held her tightly. The anesthesiologist injected a local anesthetic between the second and third lumbar vertebrae before inserting a needle and threading a thin filament between the bones, into the interior of her nervous system, the epidural space where sensation and thought run.

She asked them, "What is that? What's the knocking?" She felt it inside the column of her spine, a shudder with each tap.

The anesthesiologist said, "Knocking? Never heard anyone say that." The knocking ceased. The needle was withdrawn and the filament taped in place at what became, later, the meridian of her experience, below which her body was disobedient and strange to her, constituted not of muscle but of clay, so her legs might have belonged to someone else.

Maybe to the woman screaming across the hall.

They arranged her on beanbags and pillows, maneuvered her like a marionette. Max's head pressed against her right hipbone, delaying his entrance into the world, and in the meantime, Greg listened to the swish-swish of his heartbeat through the electrodes taped to her stomach. He watched her absorb Fentanyl via her spinal column, while out of her sight a machine recorded events in that other realm below her navel, confirming her labor, which her body undertook despite the filamentary intervention in her spine.

When he crowned, she felt no pain, just the trickle of blood, and knew that somewhere on the other side of Fentanyl's meridian, she was torn. "Stop pushing, madam," the doctor said. She obeyed, Max halfway into the world, the ceiling-mounted theater lights illuminating his entrance so bright, she couldn't look at them or the crowd of nurses observing.

"Now you may push, madam," the doctor said, and Max was out in a rush and a gush and the doctor upheld a squalling, shining creature, shocked with hair, and she couldn't tell if that was his face or the back of his head, his little arms and legs stretching for the first time into air and appalled by what they encountered, by variations in texture and temperature that hadn't existed in that other realm, and she ached with love for him and his confusion.

The doctor set him on her belly as the placenta slithered out like Max's malformed twin. She reached toward him with one hand to say, *You are not alone*, and the doctor stopped her, saying, "Do not touch, madam." She obeyed, and could only look at his little reaching hand.

* * *

Thirty-six hours after the doctor called her madam and slit her open to let Max out, she was on the couch, with Max's head pressed up under her chin and her arms wrapped around him. The tenderness inside approached pain, an open wound that would remain open forever and ever, her heart born outside her body. He slept rising and falling with her chest, as though she was his ocean, and he—little innocent—on the raft of his life, pushed out into the unknown, no longer contained by the universe of her body but resting upon it, so she fancied she was any number of things: the world-turtle, or the ocean; the ash tree, or the slope of Parnassus.

Upstairs, Greg was working. She could hear the creak as the two of them paced, the rattle of a door, sometimes the drone of a conference call, Greg's uninflected, professional voice in long discourse. Sometimes she heard them come down the stairs, pausing on the landing to check the scene below. She would speak, but Max startled when she spoke, so better to retreat into silence, which was nevertheless communication of a deep and bodily sort, as she listened for the tick of his heart, little alien, better suited to that other universe, in the dark and the waters, the nutshell world.

"Jenny?" A whisper on the stairs. Max was okay, though, so they didn't need to be concerned. When she looked up at the two of them, she discovered her eyes were closed.

"We're good."

"Sorry I woke you."

"No, I was awake."

"I don't think so."

She opened her eyes. The light changed, afternoon progressed. "Oh. I didn't know."

"It's okay. Text if you need anything."

For a moment, her eyes were open, she was pretty sure, then she blinked and Max stirred awake on her chest with a thin cry like a kitten.

"Am I asleep?" But Greg was gone.

* * *

"Jenny."

What?

"Jenny."

What? What?

"You need to wake up."

She felt Max's warm imprint beside her. He'd gone, though, under the duvet. She felt, briefly, the curve of his back and his strong little legs, but then he slipped further away and he'd be lost in the pillows and sheets and that was against government regulations regarding infant sleep safety.

"Listen to me, Jenny."

Her eyes were definitely open because they ranged around the room: Greg standing over the bed; Max's cot; the window a mirror this early in the morning.

"I'm awake."

"Okay, but you need to wake up."

"He's in here," she explained, but maybe not out loud. She began unbuttoning the duvet where he'd crept inside, careful not to move too quickly and hurt him, but that couldn't be because he was only three days old. Or was it four? Was it Tuesday? She didn't know. He was so small he might be lost in the bedding and then what.

"I've got Max, Jenny."

"Oh," she said, and looking up, she saw that it was true: Max was sleeping in Greg's arms. "Oh," she said again as under her hands the fugitive Max disappeared.

It was night, the velvety summer kind, so dark it was hard to think of more than Max and their dual heartbeats. Sometimes she slept—she thought maybe she slept—and mostly she didn't. They sat outside on the porch together, and Greg was saying something. He finished: "Okay?"

"Okay," she said, though she wasn't sure what she'd agreed to. Something about the public health nurse she'd met with earlier in the pregnancy, about the SSRIs and PPD and things, the annoying one who always called her "hun" because, Jenny suspected, the woman couldn't remember her name. She knew that Greg had been reading since the first trimester, and she had seen the search terms: "postpartum psychosis" among them, which she tried not to take personally. He liked to plan ahead for all possible outcomes.

"Because," he responded, "it's not anyone's fault. It's medical, not moral."

She had, in morose fits during the weeks before labor, searched similar terms and discovered unpleasant truths regarding the damage mothers can do to their children: women who fall asleep with their newborns and smother them; hamsters who eat their young; kangaroos who throw their joeys out behind them to distract predators.

While they sat, the sky darkened but for the strip of dandelion yellow in the west, and between the sunset and the streetlights, there came the brief hour of fireflies darting in and out of green-gold luminescence.

Also mosquitoes. "West Nile," Greg said in the drowsy hour, Max asleep in his arms. "We should get him inside." Greg was a good father. At twilight, he often took Max and she was supposed to have time to herself, but when he wept, her throat swelled shut and it was hard to think, but nevertheless Greg always said, *You should go for a walk.* So even though her feet were still so swollen she had to wear men's Crocs, she walked their block to the busier local street with the stores and coffee shops, like some nocturnal animal dazzled by sunset.

"Sorry," she said for blocking the sidewalk while around her strode determined students talking on cell phones and carrying takeout, in their clean clothes, their hair brushed, probably, and probably their legs didn't feel loose in their hip sockets, nor their belly-skin flaccid and voluminous.

Halfway to the next corner, she passed a baby in a carriage and heard its sleepy evening cry, which triggered the first trickle of foremilk, soaking her T-shirt and running down toward her navel. She turned around and thought of all the undone laundry, how she would wash away the honeyish scent Max left on his clothes, which made her cry if she smelled it and he wasn't in the room. The part of her mind that still sort-of functioned told her it was super weird that she could miss him when he was in the other room, sleeping on Greg's stomach. The first time she left him behind to do something—a follow-up visit to her OB-GYN to inspect the long tear—she had sat on the bus, her eyes leaking tears at the thought of those hours lost, when Max might have slept in the crook of her arm, and she stared at darkness, the pre-birth substance, the shared ylem of their fourth trimester together.

But there was laundry, which meant the basement she had never liked, the concrete pad for the washer and dryer and the rest of it just gravel and dust, and the tracks of animals, maybe the delicate bones of a rat.

She heard them pacing together overhead, worried footsteps as they walked Max. She glanced up at the sound toward the half-open doorway at the top of the old stairs and thought, *If it closed, how would I get out?* Down here in the deeper dark, the before-time dark of a sleep so dense and heavy she thought she might be dreaming, and this could be the moment before she lurched into wakefulness and found herself not in the basement, but in bed, and this dark the dark behind her own eyelids.

The door creaked and swung, until only a thread of light remained.

Max's first doctor's appointment, day twelve. Getting out the door a disaster. Max crying, inconsolable. She stood in the middle of the living room, trying to remember what she didn't have, but how could she think when the sound of his voice wrenched her mind until she couldn't think—

it's okay just a minute don't

what was it—

cry it's okay max boy my max my little guy

sandals she could step into because otherwise she'd have to tie laces and—

just a minute

Such a tiny and desolate sound, it was hard to believe, sometimes, that he was human and not some other sort of creature, so enormous were his eyes, and his head, and his thin little arms and legs braided across his body as though he was still enwombed.

Handbag. No. Phone. Yes. No. Keys?

max my sweet boy my dear please

And? Something else. She need—

baby don't cry im right here im

ed her phone. She grabbed the landline and let it ring until she heard it through the basement door, where a faint light shone through the cracks and

please please max please

—gaps in the lower wall let daylight arrows through the underground dust.

please don't cry

She opened—

please please please please please i cant think please

—the bedroom door and her ears rang with a sudden, miraculous silence, her first numb thought: *Is he dead?* But his chest still rose and fell. She paused on the threshold, rehearsing all the things that happen to newborns left alone in car seats, then she thought of unpacking him and taking him downstairs and *no don't be crazy hypervigilant he's fine.*

The ringing. She descended to find her phone on the floor beside the washer. The light was its screen, and she wondered how she hadn't noticed it falling out of her pocket.

As she touched the phone, two things happened: Max woke up with a shrill and terrified scream she had not yet heard from him; at the same time, the door at the top of the stairs began to close, and—she could not say where the belief came from—she knew she must reach daylight before it shut or something would happen, down here in the dust. Her skin electrified, her heart accelerating, she sprinted up the stairs.

Max screamed and screamed and she wondered why they didn't do something about it, and then she corrected herself, of course they were out, meeting clients. Greg would have rescheduled if he could, he said as he left that morning after doing the five a.m. diaper and carrying Max to her in bed so she could nurse in half-sleep, the two of them drowsy and still but for the deep, hungry pulls he took on her breast.

So Max was alone up there, poor mite, poor stranger in the vast and terrible world, so why shouldn't he cry, abandoned by his mother, who was being swallowed by the prehistoric dark of her own basement, though she sprinted up the stairs.

Three steps from the top, she slapped her hand on the threshold before the latch could catch and as she looked up she thought she saw

—for a moment—the knob turn but this could not be because there wasn't anyone upstairs to turn the knob so why was she sprinting up the stairs? The front door was open, though, and gusts of hot, wet air blanketed the room and the AC was running and that was just irresponsible and

please max stop crying please please i can't think i can't think i can't

Dislike spread from the basement to the narrow stairs, to the door itself, and to the gap beneath it that sometimes emitted a glow like fireflies. A shrinking part of her mind recognized the dislike was stupid, but nevertheless it grew. She began to hear the evening song of a nighttime cicada, in addition to the sudden fade of fireflies clustered in her peripheral as she loaded the washing machine, insects whose lights drew mates or prey.

That felt like something she could safely tell Greg. "There's a cicada in the basement," she said, coherent after three hours of uninterrupted sleep before the three a.m. feeding. She was sitting up in bed, Max in her lap.

After a moment, Greg woke and said, "What?"

"In the basement. A cicada."

"Cicadas don't live in basements," he said. "Cicadas live in . . . in gardens. Not houses."

"I heard one singing. It sounded exactly like evening."

"You were probably dreaming," he said. "I mean, like how you dreamed there was someone upstairs with me. But there's never anyone upstairs with me."

"When did I dream that?"

But Greg was asleep again.

"Hallucinations," the public health nurse had told her, "can actually be a side effect of sleeplessness, hun. Don't be afraid, but don't keep it secret, either. Talk to Greg about it if it happens. Ask for help, hun."

talk to greg sure hun, she had thought at the time. And the public health nurse had looked at her carefully and said, "Promise me you'll talk to someone about it. If it happens."

That sounded like a trap. One should never admit to hallucinations, Jenny was pretty sure, when one had a newborn. She lectured herself on what correct behavior looked like: Carry on as though you know the high song of the cicada and the luminous and deadly glow of hunting fireflies aren't there, because they probably aren't, they're just artifacts of an exhausted body. Ignore the third person in the house, though you have heard her step and seen her descend the stairs behind Greg. Ignore the fact that she hears Greg say her name—"Jennifer"—and who is he talking to? Has he told on her?

In the basement, arms full of clean diapers, she saw the not-real thing move parallel with her oh god was it person-shaped now? It hadn't been person-shaped before. Adrenaline flood, and a new burst of speed on the stairs and she reached the door just as she glanced toward the light, unintended, and saw, yes, a figure racing, also toward the door, but she was faster, she was faster than the yellow-green glide of it, whatever it was. What's worse for your future as a mother with a history of SSRIs and depression/anxiety: To hallucinate a figure in the basement, or for there to actually be a figure in the basement?

Slam the door. Max still asleep in the blessed normalcy of a Tuesday afternoon. When Greg asks how you are, nod and nod and nod because he's already worried that you're crazy with love and sleep deprivation.

Incidents accumulated: She found her keys on a rock on the far side of the basement; she found a cicada's exuvia in her sock drawer; more footsteps upstairs from the two of them but there weren't two of them there was only one, just Greg, and she had to confirm that fact repeatedly lest she slip and say, *You two were pacing a lot today, are you guys worried about something?* And "Jennifer" spoken in low tones, like a secret. The public health nurse had said there were things to watch for, like emotional lability, and a feeling of disconnection from the child, but that was not the case. The public health nurse had told stories about women so exhausted, hun, by the bottomless, unforgiving need of the newborn, who asks all and gives nothing, that they disintegrated. That was silly, though, since Max gave everything in the weight of his strong little body in her arms, the comfort he found in her skin.

The public health nurse never suggested other possible problems, like doors that rattled unaccountably, and too many footsteps overhead. So if you are thinking of things to hide from your husband, consider hiding this:

First, she was in the hospital waiting for the next contraction which, despite the epidural, still surfaced into pain and she thought, *I won't survive it, not this one.* She tried to tell them this, but they only encouraged her to breathe just breathe through it, and she was hung with drips and needles and Max was far away, in a glass box under a heat lamp, and she wasn't allowed to touch him because the doctor said, *Stop, madam. Don't you know what you are? Don't you know what you could do to him?* he asked. *Do you know what polar bears do to their young in times of stress? Is this not a time of stress, hun?*

She struggled up, her breasts full and aching. Greg was out. The third was upstairs, useless, waiting for something but who knew what, and Max was crying, but his voice was muffled as though by shut doors, and as she stood, she realized the sound was coming from the basement. She threw open the door and pelted down the stairs. He was lying on the floor, unblanketed, and around him the cicadas sang and the daytime fireflies lit and darkened and lit again.

But what flickered between them? What shadow intervened? No moment lost, she picked him up and he fit close to her, resting his cheek against her breast. And then—afraid as she was—she decided that Max would not be got, not by monsters, nor the green glow of the fireflies, not by any of it.

It wasn't until wakefulness arrived—halfway through a diaper change, as she washed his little face and dressed him in clean clothes—that she considered it was the first time they, it, or she had moved Max.

"Everything okay while I was gone?" Greg asked, his keys dropping in the dish, his shoes off. Max asleep across her chest where she sat, too far from lamps to turn them on, thinking of a twilit, firefly world.

"Yes." Say it calmly, like it's true.

"You sure?"

"Sure. Sure." Smile, because why would anything be wrong?

Greg sat on the footstool beside her. He did not turn on the lights, which was good of him.

"Because we should think about how things are going. About whether you need to talk to someone."

"I'm talking to you."

"Because there's nothing to be ashamed of." She said nothing. "If you need to talk to someone. That's what the public health nurse said, right?"

You know what they'll do, Jenny, if they find out about you. You must be very careful to not talk about how you found your son in the basement, crying, and you don't know how he got there. Which is why you are very careful not to let on about the third person, the one you hear sometimes, moving around upstairs. Which is why you are careful to remember what the right words are:

"I'm fine, Greg. I'm better than fine. I'm so happy to have him." Greg just looked at her and she asked herself: *What would a regular-type person say?* She added: "But I should probably sleep more."

But what was that? There, in the corner of her eye, rising through the dark? What coalesced in black, betrayed only by a flicker at the curtain's edge, where light seeped in from the street?

A woman—her hair drifting, her feet dragging in the air. One blink and she formed. Another blink—

there by the window—

there by the bed—

there a hand—

there, reaching toward Max who in his sleep still braided his arms and legs across his body—

launched Jenny from the bed, so she brushed the shadow hand of the thing as it—she?—bent over the bassinet, where he was breathing his sweet, milky breath, so deeply asleep he might have returned to that familiar and original darkness within her body. She lifted him and ran for the door.

She might also have been screaming, her throat felt like it, but she couldn't tell yet. She felt the cold on her back, damp like a basement in summer—

She collided with Greg, who stood in the bedroom doorway, and struggled against him, her arms wrapped around Max, who was weighty with sleep in her arms, his silky head knocking against her collarbone where she held him. She could hear him breathing, feel his warmth against her chest and belly, and she felt—against her back—the cold dark of the room from which she fled. Get out. It might already be too late.

She staggered. She heard a woman scream.

Toward the street. Away from the back bedroom and its overhung alleyway of darkness, where branches were fingers, and leaves were hands, and the quick-skittering rats occupied their muddy kingdoms, running from basement to basement and over the garbage of recycling day.

But Greg's arm barred the door.

"Jen, Jen." The room flooded so bright she was blind. "You're asleep."

She would make for the street, through the house and past the door to the basement from which this thing had emerged, she thought. She would stop a car and escape. But as she pushed past Greg to make for the front door, he stopped her, checking her into the wall, and though her arms held Max tightly, Greg was stronger and she felt Max lifted, then gone, and she wailed again as Greg fled from her to the other side of the room, saying, "He's still asleep. That's insane, he's still asleep."

That was wakefulness: "I'm sorry I'm sorry. Give him back!"

"This is why we don't co-sleep," Greg said in a funny, brittle voice. "The way you were screaming, I don't know how he could sleep through that. But he's okay. He's okay."

This time remained unspoken.

After that, they kept him upstairs, sleeping on the floor beside Greg while he tried to work, and the other one watched. When he cried, she sat, immobile, listening, thrumming with love. Greg brought him down every two hours to nurse. When he latched, his sleepy fists pressed against her breast, tears leaked from her eyes and she felt almost okay for a moment. Greg, equally exhausted, said, "You need to sleep."

Yes, they agreed, you must sleep. But she could only sit in the darkness and listen for Max's cries while Greg and the other one walked the floor. And outside the day turned to night and day again and she could not sleep, just wait for dusk and the hour of cicadas and fireflies, and emerge in the nearly cool evening before she took up her place at the foot of the stairs.

"There are fireflies in the basement now," she said when he emerged from his office, Max motionless in his arms. "I saw them when I was doing laundry."

"There aren't any fireflies in the basement. You need to sleep."

She shouldn't have told them about the fireflies that was just stupid because after the firefly comment they must have made an executive decision, and then the public health nurse showed up.

The public health nurse told her she needed extra support, hun. They agreed, and all three of them stood in a circle around her where she lay on the couch, the duvet pulled up to her chin, and the curtains drawn, and the hot wind of a thunderstorm rising, fistfuls of rain clouding the glass.

"Let me hold him," she pleaded, "please let me hold him please."

She was smart, though, she didn't say there were three of them. She pretended there were only two.

"It can't hurt," one of them said, a woman. "She's just tired. And a little bit crazy."

"It's safe enough now," the public health nurse agreed. "We'll just give her a minute."

So they let her hold him and then she cried and cried, and her tears soaked the top of his little head, and he was crying, too, so they said, "You need to sleep."

She went to bed, but she could only lie there and listen for Max, and imagine him curling against her chin and across her chest, his vital body in rest or hunger, in wakefulness or confusion. She should sleep, even if there were fireflies in the basement, because that was the only way back to Max.

When she wakes up, the house is full of thin newborn wails and she thinks, *Greg must have fallen asleep.* She is clear-headed for the first time in years.

She walks through the house and thinks Max's sweet, velvety head might be resting on the floor, or across Greg's lap, and she thinks: *I feel so much better, I'll go get him.* So she pads barefoot while outside the window the cicadas are singing, and the fireflies hunt through the gardens and greens of the neighborhood, and no one but her in all the world is awake. But she stops at the foot of the stairs because the basement door is ajar, and she can hear Max clearly now. She does not stop to think why Max might be down there, nor why they would leave him alone in the night that way, because Greg is a good father. As she descends to Max's voice, her arms ache for him.

Something flickers past her as she reaches the foot of the stairs, where Max is lying on the earth. She crouches to pick him up and he stops crying, while overhead drifts the thing she saw in her peripheral vision—woman-shaped, like a wobbly reflection in a mirror of old glass or a nighttime window. There. Gone.

She looks up to the top of the stairs and sees them—Greg, and Jennifer, and Max—gathered as though for a family photograph. Then the door closes with a soft, incontestable click.

"I've got you," she says to Max—the real Max—who is still asleep, "we're safe now," but that lasts only a moment before he evaporates from her arms, and she is alone.

When Max was a month old, they liked to talk about that first night, how they were afraid to sleep so they just sat awake wondering how they were possibly allowed to take him home, terrified of what might happen if they stopped watching him breathe, even for a minute. Jennifer remembered the night, but had a niggling feeling about it, as if those early hours of love and pain happened to someone else, as if Fentanyl had built a wall inside her more permanent than the anesthesiologist intended. She didn't mention the feeling to Greg— not after the worry of those first weeks, before she started sleeping again.

(When the nurse removed her epidural, she felt something twitch out of her spine. She was shocked at how tiny it was, translucently flexible like the cilia of undersea creatures, residing, temporarily, within her body, the slow-dripping source of poison and stillness that might—how could she think that?—have left some fragment inside her.)

From the basement she hears them talking, Greg and the Other One. She hears them argue and tease and sing to one another. She hears Max's cries coalesce into vowels, then consonants, then syllables, then words, then sentences, then demands, then questions, then knock-knock jokes, then discourses. She hears him thump down the stairs to wash his soccer uniform and she is happy that he brushes past her in the dark, pausing, sometimes, to listen to the incongruous song of cicadas, even in winter.

Upstairs again, he asks about the cicadas and they both listen, then say, "I don't hear anything. Are you sure?"

REBECCA CAMPBELL is a Canadian writer and teacher with a PhD in English (specifically Canadian literature) from the University of Western Ontario, where she worked on landscape and memory as they appear in war literature. (She thinks a lot about battlefields, statues, and poetry.) Campbell also writes speculative fiction. Her work has appeared in *The Magazine of Fantasy & Science Fiction*, Tor.com, *Interzone, Beneath Ceaseless Skies*, and *The Year's Best Science Fiction & Fantasy: 2016*. Her novel *The Paradise Engine*, was published in 2013. "On Highway 18," a haunting tale of teenagers hitchhiking along Canada's Pacific Coast based on events from her own life was reprinted in *The Year's Best Dark Fantasy & Horror: 2018*.

SHATTERED SIDEWALKS
OF THE HUMAN HEART

SAM J. MILLER

S trange that I didn't see who she was when she stood in the street, arm upraised, headlights strobing her like flashbulbs, exactly as she'd appeared in the publicity stills that papered New York City for one whole summer. Only when she got in the cab and told me where she was going and slumped back in the seat, and I looked in the mirror and saw the look of utter exhaustion and emptiness fill her face—only then did it click.

"You're her," I said, breath hitching.

"I'm somebody," she said, weary, clearly gut-sick of having this conversation, but I couldn't stop myself.

"You're Ann Darrow."

"The one and only."

And maybe I *had* recognized her, on some unconscious level, because I hadn't meant to pick up any passengers when I got in my cab and started driving. Friday nights I'd sometimes hit up the Ziegfeld, the Palace, drive in circles to see the movie stars arriving at their premieres, and, later on, leaving, and later still staggering out of their after-parties. Purely recreational, usually, but that night it was downright medicinal. I needed that glamour, those sixty-karat smiles, the wonder in the eyes of the crowd. The lie of a beautiful world.

Bombs were falling, four thousand miles away. Crematoria were being kindled.

I pulled away from the curb. One of her posters was framed on the wall of the room I rented. The only decorative touch that had followed me through all five of the boarding houses I'd lived in since getting kicked out of the house. Ann Darrow, eyes wide with terror, arm upraised to fend off something monstrous. A massive black outline hulked behind her. Art deco lettering beneath her blared KONG: THE EIGHTH WONDER OF THE WORLD.

"You Jewish?" she asked.

"I am," I said, tracing my profile in the rearview mirror. "The nose gave it away?"

"The eyes," she said. "The only people who look really scared today are Jewish."

It took me an awful long time to say, "That's because most people have no idea what horrible things human beings are capable of," and even once I said it it wasn't quite right, didn't quite capture the rich flavor of my fear, my rage.

"Some of us do," she said. "Some of us know exactly."

"I'm Solomon," I said.

"That why your radio's switched off, Solomon?"

"Yeah, sorry. Couldn't stand to hear it one more time. I can turn it back on if you want to listen to something."

"No," she said. "That's one of several things I'm trying not to think about tonight."

September 1st, 1939. At 4:45 that morning, Germany had invaded Poland. Word was, England and France would be declaring war within the week. Not that anyone expected them to lift too many fingers to save the millions of Jews in Poland.

"I'm sorry," I said. "Forgot to ask—where you heading?"

"Just drive," she said. "I'll figure something out."

"You coming from a movie premiere?"

"Yeah," she said. "*The Women*. It had its moments. They love to have notorious floozies and disgraced politicians show up on the red carpet. Who am I to turn down free food and alcohol?"

17

Normally, my New York City cabdriver cool prevailed. Even with only five years' driving under my belt, I'd already had more movie stars in my back seat than there were cross streets in Manhattan. But this was no movie star. No fraudulent sorcerer, whose magic was made up of lighting and makeup and special effects and screenwriting. This was *Ann Darrow*. This was someone who knew what magic was. Who'd been held in its hand. Who'd been lifted high into the sky by it, and then watched it die.

"Let me guess," she said, catching my repeated mirror glances. "You were there that night. You were in the theater. You're a baby, you would have been, what, twelve?"

"Twelve exactly," I said, startled. Most people pegged me for far older. I'd been driving a cab on New York City streets since I was thirteen, and nobody'd ever batted an eyelash at it. "But I wasn't in the theater that night."

"I know," she said. "Somebody tells me they were, I know they're lying. Swear to god, you add up all the people who've told me they were there that night, there were a couple million people in the audience. Place only had a thousand seats, and half of them were empty. People make it seem like Denham was some kind of genius promoter, but that piece of shit was as bad at that as he was at everything else."

I had so many questions. For years I'd dreamed of this moment. Now my words were nowhere to be found.

"Let me guess," she said. "You want to know about . . . him."

"Yeah."

She rolled her eyes.

She wasn't that much older than me. She'd been twenty, when she traveled to Skull Island. But those events, and the six years since then, had accelerated her aging. From her purse, she pulled a bottle and a glass. Not a flask; a glass, in her purse. "You want a drink, Solomon?"

"Not while I'm driving."

"Where are your people from, Solomon?"

"Poland," I said.

She cursed, so softly I couldn't hear which one. "You got people over there still?"

"Three grandparents."

"Oh, honey," she said, one hand reaching forward to touch my shoulder.

She was kind. That much was true. I'd imagined her in the hold of the ship, comforting Kong in his chains and his seasickness. Backstage, calming him down while tiny men flashed cameras in his helpless face. Eighty stories up, pleading with him to pick her back up, trying to tell him that the airplanes wouldn't shoot him while he was holding her. Angry at him for not understanding her, or for understanding and not wanting to put her at risk.

"I never knew them," I said. "My parents came over in 1920. For a while their parents were happy to stay where they were, but since stuff's been getting scary over there we've been saving up money to bring them over. Now I can't really see that happening."

We both watched the next several blocks slide by. Street signals switching, red to green. Crowds throbbing. Laughter. Hunger. None of them carried what she carried, the secrets of something extraordinary.

No sense lying: I wanted something from her. I knew it was wrong, to expect anything of a woman who'd spent six years with everyone clamoring for a piece of her, and I couldn't bring myself to ask, but I could hope. For something—anything—no one else knew. Some piece of him.

Ann Darrow tipped her head back, to down her drink. Saw something high above. "There she is," she whispered.

There she was. I didn't need to crane my neck to look to know what she was seeing. The Empire State Building, showing through the gap between buildings made by 37th Street.

"There were no people living on Skull Island," she said, and chuckled at my shocked expression. "Cannibal natives, that was another one of the lies Denham told the reporters, in the weeks before Kong's debut. He thought it added to the story. Savages menacing the virginal blonde. People eat that shit up, he said. Every time he told the story, it got bigger and crazier. Spiders the size of houses. Pterodactyls. The T. rex was real, but to hear him tell it she had horns and breathed fire and flew. Only Kong stayed the same size."

"Because he was bigger than anything that asshole could dream up."

"Exactly," she said, raising her glass again. "He never hurt me."

"Everyone knows that."

No New Yorker ever accepted the story Denham tried to spin: Kong the Monster. From the moment he fell he was myth, was legend, the hope and hero of everyone who ever tried to climb up from the grit and filth of our streets while the little people tried to drag them back down. He was ours. Every souvenir stand and tchotchke shop in the city sold Kong figurines, Kong toys. Every Halloween, he was the most popular costume. And practically half the city had one of those lockets around their neck, with a tuft of black fur purporting to be his.

All the property damage, all the people who died—no one blamed Kong for that. It wasn't his fault he was bigger than life, bigger than us, made for a better world than ours. You didn't blame the flames that burned down your house. You blamed the man who started the fire.

"Is it true you agreed to be in the movie?"

"Of course not," she said, snorting. "Denham told producers I was on board, but that was a lie."

RKO optioned the story, started preparing to make the movie, but the outcry had been immediate, and immense. The Mayor flat-out refused to let them film in his city. Said it'd be like re-creating the Triangle Shirtwaist Factory Fire for film. People died. Kong died. And so, so did a part of us. Some things were sacred.

"So where were you, Solomon? That night."

"Home. Lower East Side. Six families, thirty people, one apartment. One radio. Everybody glued to it."

Even over the air, even as a thing described by strangers, our hearts were with him. Little boys pounding our chests. Imagining something strong enough to derail a subway car, to shatter the thickest chains . . . but still too small for this city, for its big buildings and its brutal cops, who had bullets where their hearts should be. Which one of us wasn't Kong, a king among ants even as they destroyed us?

When he started climbing the Empire State Building, I slowly backed out of the room. Nobody saw me. They weren't there; they were imagining Kong's ascent. No one heard me scamper down the stairs.

I was a kid. This was my city. I'd sprinted its length more times than I could count. I knew how long it would take me to make it to 34th and Fifth. But how fast could King climb to the top? He'd be slowed down by the beautiful woman he carried.

I never thought he would die. I didn't imagine it was possible.

Thick crowds kept me from getting onto Fifth Avenue, but I could still see him. A tiny spot so high above us. We heard the airplanes, a distant sound, getting nearer. We'd gasped, as one. We heard the gunfire.

I didn't tell Ann any of that. She'd think less of me, if she knew. I'd seen her when she came down to street level again. Bracketed by cops; coat draped over her shoulders. I'd seen the tears streaming down her face, and I'd seen her hate. "What is wrong with you?" she'd shrieked. No one answered. No one knew.

After Kong, Denham spent three years with his back up against the wall. He was still news for a little while, the *Herald-Tribune* running interviews headlined "Most Hated Man in New York City Speaks Out," but before long he was just another one of yesterday's villains, drinking himself to death beside all the other politicians and businessmen who never let a little thing like morality come between them and money. Everywhere he went, someone wanted to take a shot at him, and Denham's crippled manhood wouldn't let him back down from a single one. Until somebody cracked a rib, drove it into some important organ. Even in the hospital he was dialing up journalist numbers he'd committed to memory, offering them exclusives, and even when he told them he was dying they hung up on him.

"I hate this city," she said, watching the after-theater crowds spilling off the sidewalk onto the street.

"Me too," I said. "Even if I also love it."

Her eyes, on mine. "That's it. That's it exactly."

The block where Kong landed—they kept it closed off for weeks. Because of the body, at first—a ten-ton corpse was not so easy to cart off—and then because of the crowds. We came by the thousands. Paupers and newsies and dowager empresses gathered on the shattered sidewalk. We stood, alone with our wonder, and wept.

How much did he change us? Who would we be, if he'd never come blundering into our lives to show us how full of wonder the world could still be, and how full of cruelty we still were? Vegetarianism skyrocketed, it's true—papers said 30 percent of New Yorkers abstained from eating meat now, vs. half of a percent before 1933—and the country passed laws to limit animal cruelty, stop medical testing on mammals, make sure meat animals weren't mistreated. Kong wasn't the only reason, he just made a handy symbol of all that was majestic and worthy of respect in animals.

But we'd changed in bad ways too. Plenty of people hated the big ape, especially after the city voided all lawsuits for injury and property destruction related to his rampage, calling Kong an "act of God." Someone shot the gorilla at the Bronx Zoo through the bars of her cage. Not to mention the backlash to the new laws. Big business laying people off, saying they couldn't make money now that they couldn't cram chickens into tiny cages and feed them shit. Out-of-work slaughterhouse men butchering pigs in the streets in protest.

"I don't wanna take money out of your pocket," she said. "You can drop me off wherever, go pick up some actual passengers, instead of an old drunk feeling sorry for herself."

"No," I said, not wanting it to end, not ever. "I was done already."

Her eyes, on mine again.

"You still on the Lower East Side, Solomon?"

"Upper West," I said.

"You want to take me there?"

I could have said yes. I could have tried to do what she wanted. But I couldn't lie to her, not with my words and not with my body. And if I wanted her to share something meaningful with me, some secret she'd kept from everyone else, I couldn't very well keep any of my own.

"I'll take you wherever you want to go, Ann Darrow. I'd do anything for you—but if it's a lover you want, you could probably find plenty of better ones than me."

"Can't get it up?" she snorted, wounded pride vying in her voice with curiosity, at a man who'd make such an admission.

"Not for women, unfortunately."

She nodded. Looked out the window. An idiotic move, sharing that with her. Stupid of me to think that just because her empathy extended to monsters like Kong, it would reach all the way to monsters like me.

Central Park South; a line of tents that marked the entrance to a Hooverville. Men begged. Women walked up to horse-drawn carriages stopped in traffic, demanded money. Word was, only war would end the Depression, and wasn't that some shit right there? Rich men fucked up so bad they made millions of people poor, and the only way to fix it was to make millions of people dead.

"Go to the Bronx," she said. "Hunts Point. You can start the meter."

"No ma'am," I said. "You'll always ride free in my cab."

For a while we didn't speak. I tried to think of ways to do damage control, but my heart wasn't in it. We were what we were, Ann and I, and people treated us accordingly.

We crossed the Willis Avenue Bridge. Small houses sprouted all around us, and brand-new apartment buildings. Lots of my family members had moved up here. I'd have been able to afford a real place. But doing so would be giving up on any hope of finding love, finding sex, and I was eighteen years old and I wasn't ready to do that yet.

"Everybody wants something from me," she said. "Something I can't give them, because I don't have it myself."

"What's that?" I asked, knowing the answer, because it was what I wanted myself.

"They want Kong."

She guided me—left, then right, then left again. Deeper into the Bronx's weird warped topography, so different from Manhattan's dependable grid. Finally we arrived at blocks and blocks of warehouses. She didn't know the address, and we got lost a couple times looking for the right one.

"Park here," she said.

I did.

"Follow me," she said. And I did. I knew it was stupid. For all I knew her brothers were waiting inside, burly dock worker types who at a word from their spurned sister would gleefully beat me to death. But she was Ann Darrow, and I was as helpless in her hands as she had been in Kong's, and I still held out hope that she could give me what I wanted.

And, anyway, would death be so bad? Who wanted to live in a world like this, anyway? A world getting its revenge on us, for all the damage we did, and damned if we didn't deserve it—dust storms stripping the skin off the country; Oklahoma's entire corn crop mysteriously blighted, according to the radio. A world where Germany invaded Poland and everyone else went about their business. A world that would kill Kong.

"This is where he kept him," she said. I climbed the steps after her. "Before the Broadway debut. Dumbass Denham—he either forgot or never even realized that he bought the whole damn warehouse. He was as bad with his backers' money as he was with his own. And after Kong he was so bogged down in debt and lawsuits that this was the least of his thoughts. He died without a will, without heirs. So I guess it'll stand here until it falls down or the city gets around to foreclosing on it for unpaid taxes."

"Kong was here?" I whispered.

"For three weeks." She rummaged in her purse. "I had a locksmith switch this out. I'm the only one with a key."

The air in the warehouse was rank, mammalian. Wild. The smell of something uncageable, and caged. I shut my eyes. Breathed deep.

"That's him," I said.

"That's him. Not as he was in the wild, of course. Chained, without access to the sea, he couldn't clean himself properly. And his spirit came damn close to breaking. You can smell that, too. A sourness. But he was stronger than us."

I stepped inside, with the same fear and humility as entering synagogue. The walls were blue. So was the floor. And the ceiling.

"What's . . ."

I looked down. The blue was a plant, a vine that had grown to cover every surface.

"Gorillas are vegetarians," she said. "Most people don't know that."

"I did." I'd read a lot about gorillas in the months after Kong fell. Dreamed of being a zoologist, except that you needed to be able to afford to go to college for that.

"Kong ate plants. So he had seeds, in his belly. Nobody but me noticed that something had sprouted from his dung. I potted it, kept it secret."

I nodded.

"I made clippings," she said, and gave me a small terra-cotta pot. "This is for you."

Up close I could see spearhead-shaped leaves. Red veins spread out in curls and ripples. Vines trailed down the side, ending in fat seed pods. At the center of the pot the leaves curled inward, numerous and beautiful as the petals on a chrysanthemum.

A piece of him. Of Kong.

"Watch the center," she said. "And be very quiet."

I watched. I was quiet. I was patient. The pattern of the veins was so intricate. Hypnotic, almost. So much so that I could have sworn I saw one vine growing while I watched. But of course no plant grew so fast.

The leaf-petals parted, suddenly. Like an eye opening. And beneath the petals: an actual eye. Not human, but not far from it, either. All brown iris, and black pupil. It blinked, twice, twitched around as the eye scanned the sky. Then found mine. Held my gaze.

"Is that his?"

Ann nodded. "The plant took something, passing through him."

I held the pot in my hands. Reverent; apologetic. Unworthy.

"I planted some in a vacant lot next to my building," she said. "Near some kudzu. Came back that afternoon and it had totally swallowed up the kudzu. Would have covered the whole lot in a day if I hadn't clipped it back."

Her eyes were on me. Wanting something. "I—I don't . . ."

"We killed him," she said. "We saw him, this god, this king, and the only thing we could think to do was capture and chain and kill it. That's what people are. You see that, don't you? I know you do. It's why I brought you here."

"Yeah, of course," I said, looking back and forth between her eyes and the plant's. "But I don't . . ."

"Skull Island was rough. Anything that evolved to survive there would be the ultimate invasive species. It'd cover the earth, if it got the chance. Choke off all kinds of life."

And—I got it. I nodded. Said, "What a shame that would be."

"The money from my book deal—I spent that on a tour of the USA, and then Europe. Dropped a few seeds wherever I went."

"You spend any time in Oklahoma?" I asked, remembering the news about the blighted corn crop.

"Just enough," Ann said. "Maybe you want to help."

"Thank you," I said, my hands occupied, unable to wipe the tears off my face. Wondering where so many had come from, so fast.

She hugged me. She smelled like alcohol and lilacs and I sobbed into her neck.

I drove back into Manhattan. Headed for the Ziegfeld again. By now the after-parties would be getting out; drunk movie stars needing rides home. Plenty of people hailed me, but I didn't stop. In the seat where Ann sat was a potted plant.

Kong was my passenger. He always had been. I'd carried him in my heart since the moment I watched him fall, felt the earth shake, the sidewalk shatter, my heart with it. All of our hearts.

On the corner of 54th and Seventh, I saw a woman leaning on a streetlamp. Dressed up; holding a high heel under her arm while she rubbed that stockinged foot. Her day had been long, and hard. She was angry. She was going to do something about it. Most people probably wouldn't be able to see it, but I could. Now. How mighty she was. What heights she could climb to. How she could shatter the world with the seeds she carried inside her.

SAM J. MILLER is the Nebula Award–winning author of *The Art of Starving* (an NPR best of the year) and *Blackfish City* (a best book of the year for *Vulture*, *The Washington Post*, Barnes & Noble, and more—and a "Must Read" in *Entertainment Weekly* and *O: The Oprah Winfrey Magazine*). His supernatural thriller *The Blade Between* will appear in late 2020. A recipient of the Shirley Jackson Award and a graduate of the Clarion Writers' Workshop, Miller's work has been nominated for the World Fantasy, Theodore Sturgeon, John W. Campbell, and Locus Awards, and has been reprinted in dozens of anthologies. A community organizer by day, he lives in New York City.

THE SURVIVING CHILD

JOYCE CAROL OATES

1.

The surviving child, he is called. Not to his face—of course.

The other, younger child died with the mother three years before. *Murder, suicide* it had been. More precisely *Filicide, suicide.*

The first glimpse she has of the surviving child is shocking to her: a beautiful face, pale and lightly freckled, darkly luminous eyes, a prematurely adult manner—solemn, sorrowful, wary and watchful.

Sharp as a sliver of glass piercing her heart comes the thought—*I will love him. I will save him. I am the one.*

"Stefan! Say hello to my friend—"

No comfortable way for Stefan's father to introduce her, the father's fiancée, to the surviving child. Presumably Alexander has been telling Stefan about her, preparing him. *I am thinking of remarrying. I have met a young woman I would like you to meet. I think you will like her, and she will—she will like you . . .* No way to express such thoughts that is not painful.

Seeing the apprehension in the child's face. Wondering if, since the mother's death, the father has introduced Stefan to other women whom he has invited to the house; or if Stefan has chanced to see his father with a woman, one who might be expected to take the mother's place.

But Elisabeth is not jealous of other women. Elisabeth is not envious of other women. Elisabeth is grateful to have been plucked from obscurity by the gentlemanly man who is her fiancé, the widower of the (deceased) (notorious) poet N.K.

Stooping to shake the child's small-boned hand. Hearing herself say brightly, reassuringly, "Hello, Stefan! So nice to meet you . . ." Her voice trails off. She is smiling so hard her face hurts. Hoping the child will not shrink from her out of shyness, dislike, or resentment.

Stefan is ten years old, small for his age. It is terrible to think (the fiancée thinks) how small this delicately-boned child had to have been three years before when his mother had tried to kill him along with his little sister and herself.

Alexander told her how the boy stopped growing for months after the trauma. Very little appetite, sleep disturbed by nightmares, wandering the house in the night. Disappearing into the house in broad daylight so that the father and the housekeeper searched for him calling his name—*Stefan! Stefan!*—until suddenly Stefan would appear around a corner, on a staircase, in a corridor blinking and short of breath and unable to explain where he'd been.

Almost asphyxiated by the mother. Heavily sedated with barbiturates as well. Yet somehow: he'd been spared.

Stefan had not cried in the aftermath of the trauma, or not much— "Not what you'd expect under the circumstances."

. *Under the circumstances!* Elisabeth winced at Alexander's oddly unfeeling remark.

The fiancée has been introduced to the child as Elisabeth but the child cannot call her that name of course. Nor can the child call her Miss Lundquist. In time, when Elisabeth and the child's father are married, the child will learn to call her—what? Not Mother. Not Mom. *Mommy?* Will that ever be possible?

(Elisabeth has no idea what the child called his mother. It is very difficult to imagine the elusive poet N.K. as any child's mother let alone as *Mom, Mommy.*)

Those wary, watchful eyes. How like a fledgling bird in its nest Stefan is, prepared to cringe at a gliding shadow. A parent-bird, or a predator that will tear him to pieces? The fledgling can't know which until it is too late.

Yet politely Stefan murmurs replies to questions put to him by the adults. Familiar questions about school, questions he has answered many times. He will not be asked questions which are painful to answer. Not now. When he'd been asked such questions in the aftermath of his mother's death the child had stared into a corner of the room with narrowed eyes, silent. His jaws had clenched, a small vein twitched at his temple but his gaze held firm and unswerving.

Later the father would say he'd been afraid to touch the child's chest, or his throat, at the time—*I was sure Stefan had stopped breathing. He'd gone somewhere deep inside himself where that terrible woman was calling him.*

It is months later. In fact it is years later. *That terrible woman* has disappeared from their lives and from the beautiful old shingle board house in Wainscott, Massachusetts, in which Alexander and N.K. lived during their twelve-year-marriage.

Lived "only intermittently"—Alexander has said. For frequently they lived apart as N.K. pursued her own "utterly selfish" life.

Not in the house but in the adjoining three-car garage, a converted stable, which the fiancée has not (yet) seen, the poet N.K. killed herself and her four-year-old daughter Clea by carbon monoxide poisoning.

And no suicide note. Neither in the car nor elsewhere.

It is true, Alexander acknowledged having found a diary of N.K. kept in the last fevered weeks of her life, in her bedside table.

His claim was he'd had to destroy the diary—without reading it—knowing it would contain terrible accusations, lies. The ravings of a homicidal madwoman, from which his son had to be spared.

For he could not risk it, that Stefan would grow up having to encounter in the world echoes and reflections of the sick and debased mind that had tried to destroy him . . .

Despite the trauma Stefan has done reasonably well at the Wainscott Academy. For several months after the deaths he'd been kept home, with a nurse to care for him—he'd had to repeat third grade—but since then he has caught up with his fifth-grade classmates, Alexander has said proudly. All that one might have predicted—fits of crying, child-depression, "acting out"—mysterious illnesses—seemed not to have occurred, or were fleeting. "My son has a stoical spirit," the father has said. "Like me."

The fiancée thinks, seeing the child—*No. He is just in hiding.*

Elisabeth has calculated that there is almost exactly the identical distance in age between Stefan's age and hers, as between hers and Alexander's: eighteen years. (Stefan is ten, Elisabeth is twenty-eight. Alexander is in his late forties.)

Elisabeth will brood over this fact. It is a very minor fact yet (she thinks) a way of linking her and the child though (probably) the child will never realize.

If she were alive, the sick and debased N.K. would be just thirty-six. Young, still.

But if N.K. were alive Elisabeth Lundquist would not be here in Wainscott in her fiancé's distinguished old family house smiling so hard her face aches.

It is impressive: Stefan knows to stand very still as adults speak at him, to him, above his head. He does not twitch, quiver as another (normal?) child might. He does not betray restlessness, resentment. *He does not betray misery.* His smile is quicksilver, his eyes are heavy-lidded. Beautiful dark-brown eyes. Elisabeth wonders if those eyes, so much darker than the father's eyes, as the child's complexion is so much paler than the father's ruddy skin, resemble the deceased mother's eyes.

Elisabeth has seen photographs of the dramatically beautiful N.K. of course. She has seen a number of videos including those that, after N.K.'s death, went "viral." It would have been unnatural if, under the circumstances, she had not.

The Guatemalan housekeeper Ana has overseen Stefan's bath, combed and brushed the boy's curly fair-brown hair, laid out clean clothes for him. Of course at the age of ten he dresses himself. On his small feet, denim sneakers with laces neatly tied. Elisabeth feels a pang of loss, the child is too old for her to help him with his laces—ever.

It will be a challenge, Elisabeth thinks. To win over this beautiful wounded child.

"Mr. Hendrick?"—Ana appears, smiling and gracious, deferential. It is time now for the evening meal.

Supper is in a glassed-in porch at the rear of the house where a small round table has been set for just three people. At its center, a vase of white roses fresh-picked from the garden.

As they enter the room Elisabeth feels an impulse to take the child's hand, very gently—to allow Stefan to know that she cares for him already though they have just met. She will be his *friend*.

But when Elisabeth reaches for Stefan's hand her fingers encounter something cold and clotty, sticky like mucus—"Oh! Oh God." She gives a little scream, and steps away shuddering.

"What is it, Elisabeth?" Alexander asks, concerned.

What is it, Elisabeth has no idea. For when she looks at Stefan, at Stefan's hand, small-boned and innocent, entirely clean, lifted palm-outward before him in a pleading gesture, she sees nothing unusual—certainly nothing that might have felt cold, clotty, sticky as mucus.

"I just felt—cold . . ."

"Well! Are your hands cold, Stefan?"

Shyly Stefan shakes his head. Murmuring. "Don't know."

Elisabeth apologizes, deeply embarrassed. Must have imagined—something . . .

Alexander has no idea what is going on—unless Alexander has a very good idea what is going on—but chooses to be bemused by his young fiancée, eighteen years his junior: the young woman's fear of harmless insects, her fear of driving in urban areas, her fear of flying in small propeller planes used by commuters from Boston to Cape Cod.

Elisabeth manages to laugh, uneasily. She reasons that it is better for Alexander to express bemusement, impatience, irritation with her, than with the sensitive Stefan.

Quite a beautiful room, the glassed-in porch. White wicker furniture, a pale beige Peruvian woven rug. On a wall a Childe Hassam Impressionist seascape of the late nineteenth century.

As they are about to sit Stefan suddenly freezes. Murmurs that he has to use a bathroom. Over Alexander's face there comes a flicker of annoyance. Oh, just as Ana is serving the meal! Elisabeth is sorry about this.

"Of course. Go."

At the table Alexander pours (white, tart) wine into the adults' glasses. He is determined not to express the annoyance he feels for his son but Elisabeth can see his hands trembling.

Elisabeth remarks that they have plenty of time to drive to the concert in Provincetown for which they have tickets—"It's only six. We have an hour and a half for dinner . . ."

"I'm aware of the time, Elisabeth. Thank you."

A rebuff. Alexander doesn't like his naïve young fiancée even to appear to be correcting him.

Gamely Elisabeth tries again: "Your son is so—beautiful. He's . . . ."

Unique. Unworldly. Wraith-like.

Alexander grunts a vague assent. Somehow managing to signaling *yes* and at the same time *Enough of this subject.*

Elisabeth is one of those shy individuals who find themselves chattering nervously, for conversational silence intimidates them. It is hard for her to remain silent—she feels (she thinks) that she is being judged. Yet, she has discovered to her surprise that it is not difficult to offend Alexander Hendrick, inadvertently. A man of his stature, so thin-skinned? She worries that even a naively well-intentioned compliment about Stefan may remind him of the other child Clea, who died of carbon monoxide poisoning wrapped in a mohair shawl in her mother's arms . . .

Terrible! Elisabeth shudders.

"How is this wine? It's Portuguese—d'you like it?"

Wine? Elisabeth knows little about wine. "Yes," she tells Alexander who is frowning over his glass as if nothing were more important than the wine he is about to drink.

"I'm wondering if I should have bought an entire case. Might've been a mistake."

Is wine important? Elisabeth supposes that it must be, if Alexander thinks so. Her fiancé, to her a distinguished man, director of a wealthy arts foundation established by his grandfather, has a habit of weighing minor acts, innocuous-seeming decisions, as if they were crucially important, and might turn into *mistakes*. At first Elisabeth thought he was only joking since the issues were often trivial but now she sees that nothing is trivial to her fiancé. The mere possibility of a *mistake* is upsetting to him.

Driving to Wainscott, bringing Elisabeth for her first weekend visit to the house on Oceanview Avenue, Alexander said suddenly: "I hope this isn't going to be a mistake."

Elisabeth laughed nervously. Hesitant to ask Alexander to explain for he hadn't actually seemed to be speaking to her, only thinking aloud.

They are waiting for Stefan to return to the table. Ana has lighted candles that quaver with their breaths. Why is the boy taking so much time? Is he hiding from them?—from his father? At Alexander's insistence Ana serves the first, lavish course—roasted sweet peppers stuffed with pureed mushroom. On each Wedgwood plate a red pepper and a green pepper perfectly matched.

Not the sort of food a boy of ten probably likes, Elisabeth thinks.

"Well. Let's begin. We may run into traffic on the highway."

Heavy silver forks, knives. Engraved with the letter *H*. Virtually everything in the house as well as the house itself is Alexander's inheritance; N.K.'s things, which were not many, were moved out after the deaths, given away. Even the books. Especially, books with *N.K.* on the spine.

Not a trace of her remaining. Don't worry, darling!

Wondering another time if Alexander has brought other women to Wainscott, to meet Stefan. To see how they reacted to the surviving child, and the house. Young women, presumably. (Now that he is middle-aged Alexander isn't the type to be attracted to women his own age.) Wondering if, initially drawn to Alexander Hendrick, these women have fled?

When you see the house, you'll understand—why it means so much to me. And why I am not going to move out.

Rarely did Alexander speak directly of N.K. Usually obliquely, and in such a way that Elisabeth was not encouraged to ask questions.

In itself, suicide would be devastating. The suicide of a spouse. But conjoined with murder, the murder of a child—unspeakable.

The dead must present a sort of argument, Elisabeth thinks. The argument must be refuted by the living. The dead who have taken the lives of others, and their own lives, must especially be refuted by the living if the living are to continue.

After several minutes Alexander says sharply to Ana who has been hovering in the background: "Look for him! Please."

Elisabeth winces. The way Alexander gives orders to the house-keeper is painful to her.

Ana hurries away to call, "Stefan! Stefan!"

Elisabeth lays down her napkin. She will help look for the child.

"No. Stay here. This is ridiculous."

Alexander is flush-faced, indignant. With his fork and knife he slides something onto Elisabeth's plate. At first she thinks it is quivering with life, slimy like a jellyfish, then she sees that it is just pureed mushroom, seeping fragrantly from the roasted peppers.

Ana is on the stairs to the second floor. A short stout woman, heavy-thighed. Out of breath. "Stefan? Hello?"

They listen to her calling, cajoling. If only Stefan will answer!

But Ana returns panting and apologetic. Can't find him, she is so sorry—not in his room, not in any bathroom. Not in the kitchen, or the back hall, or—anywhere she could think of.

"God damn. I've warned him, if he played this trick one more time . . ."

Alexander lurches to his feet. Elisabeth rises also, daring to clutch at his arm.

"Maybe he's sick, Alexander. He was looking sad—maybe he just doesn't want to see anyone right now. Can't you let him—be?"

Alexander throws off her hand. "Shut up. You know *nothing*."

He stalks out of the glassed-in porch. Elisabeth has no choice but to follow, hesitantly. Hoping that Ana has not overheard Alexander's remark to her, not the first time her fiancé has told her to *shut up*.

Stomping on the stairs calling "Stefan? Where the hell are you?"

Elisabeth follows into the hall. Not up the stairs. Not sure what she should be doing. Weakly calling, "Stefan? It's me—Elisabeth. Are you hiding? Where are you hiding?"

Where are you hiding. An inane remark, such as one frightened child might ask another.

Desperate minutes are spent in the search for the child. Upstairs, downstairs. Front hall, back hall. Kitchen, dining room. Living room, sitting room. And again back upstairs, to peer into closets in guest rooms. In the master bedroom where (Alexander says grimly) the boy "wouldn't dare" set foot.

Finally, there is no alternative. The distraught father must go to look in the forbidden place: the garage. Telling Elisabeth and Ana to stay where they are. By this time Alexander is very upset. His face is ruddy with heat, his carefully combed hair has fallen onto his forehead. Even the handsome blue silk necktie has loosened as if he'd clawed at it.

Elisabeth hears the man's impatient voice uplifted, at the rear of the house—"Stefan? Are you in there? You had better not be in there . . ."

That place. Where she'd died. And your little sister died.

Anxiously Elisabeth and Ana wait in the hall for Alexander to return. It is not likely (Elisabeth thinks) that the father will easily find the son, and haul him back in triumph.

"Stefan has done this before, I guess?" Elisabeth asks hesitantly. Ana, protective of the child, or not wanting to betray a family secret, frowns and looks away as if she hasn't heard the question.

Saying finally, choosing her words with care, "He is a good boy, Stefan. Very sweet, sad. There is something that comes over him—sometimes. Not his fault. That is all."

To this Elisabeth can't think of a reply. She is steeling herself for Alexander's reappearance. The loud angry voice like a spike driven into her forehead she must make every effort not to acknowledge gives her pain.

And then, almost by chance, Elisabeth happens to glance back into the glassed-in porch, which she knows to be empty, which *has to be empty;* and sees at the table a child-sized figure, very still—can it be Stefan? In his chair, at his place?

Elisabeth hurries to him. So surprised, she doesn't call for Alexander.

"Oh!—Stefan. There you are."

As if he has been running the child is out of breath. Almost alarmingly out of breath.

His face is very pale, clammy-pale, coated in perspiration. His eyes are dilated with excitement, his lips seem to have a bluish cast. And there are bluish shadows beneath his eyes.

Oxygen deprivation? Is that it?

Even as she is profoundly relieved, Elisabeth is astonished. She would like to touch the child—hug him, even—but does not dare. A faint, subtly rancid smell lifts from him, like a sour breath.

Ana hurries to tell Mr. Hendrick that his son has returned safely. Elisabeth approaches the child calmly, not wanting to overwhelm him with her emotion, dares to grasp his hand another time and this time the small-boned hand is pliant and not resistant, a child's hand, slightly cold, but containing nothing repulsive, to terrify.

So relieved to see him, Elisabeth hears herself laugh nervously. She will not allow herself to wonder why he is so breathless, and so pale.

Nor does she accuse the child except she must ask where has he been?—hadn't he heard them calling him, for the past ten minutes or more?—hadn't he heard his father?

Evasively Stefan mutters what sounds like: "Here. I was here."

Nothing sly or mischievous, nothing deceitful about the child. Elisabeth is sure. But how strange!—where had he been? And how had he slipped past her and Ana, to return to the dinner table on the porch?

In the pale freckled face there's a look of adult anguish, cunning. And the skin is still clammy-cold, with the sweat of panic.

As the angry father approaches, footsteps loud in the hall like a mallet striking, Stefan cringes. Elisabeth holds his small weak hand, to protect him.

"You! God damn you! Didn't I warn you!"—for a terrible moment it seems that Alexander is about to strike his son; his hand is raised, for a slap; but then like air leaking from a balloon Alexander's anger seems to drain from him. His eyes glisten with tears of frustration, rage, fear. He drags out his chair to sit down heavily at the table.

"Just tell me, Stefan: where were you?"

And Stefan says in his small still voice what sounds like: "Here. I was here . . ."

Alexander snatches up his napkin, to wipe his eyes. "Well. *Don't* do anything like this again, d'you hear me?"

2.

Bollingen Prize Poet N.K., Child Found Dead in Wainscott, MA
Asphyxiation Deaths "Possibly Accidental"

Bestselling Feminist Poet N.K. Takes Own Life
Four-Year-Old Daughter Dies With Her
"Shocking Scene"—Wainscott, MA

Always Elisabeth will remember: the shocked voice of a colleague rushing into the library at the Radcliffe Institute. ". . . terrible. They're saying she killed herself and . . ."

Lowered (female) voices. Solemn, appalled. Disbelieving.

Glancing up from her laptop as talk swirled around her.

Who had died? A poet? A woman poet? *And* her daughter?

Wanting to know, not wanting to know.

That evening at a reception at the Institute for a visiting lecturer all talk was of the suicide. And the death of the child.

Asphyxiation by carbon monoxide poisoning.

". . . wouldn't have done it. I don't believe it."

". . . herself, maybe. But not a daughter."

". . . not possible. No."

How shocking the news was! The voices were embittered, incredulous. How demoralizing for women writers, women scholars, women who declared themselves feminists. Nicola Kavanaugh—"N.K."—had been a heroine to them, defiant and courageous and original.

"... murder, maybe. Someone jealous ..."

"... that husband. Weren't they separated ..."

"... but not the daughter! I know her—knew her. N.K. would never have done *that*."

Of course they had to acknowledge that N.K. had written freely, shockingly of taboo subjects like suicide—the *unspeakable bliss of self-erasure*.

Elisabeth listened. Grasped the hands of mourners that clutched at hers in anguish. She had not been a fellow at the Institute several years before when N.K. came to give a "brilliant"—"impassioned"—"inspiring" presentation on the "unique language" of women's poetry but she'd heard colleagues speak admiringly of it, still.

At the Institute Elisabeth was researching the archives of the Imagist poets of the early twentieth century. She'd read no more than a scattering of N.K.'s flamboyant, quasi-confessional poetry, so very different from the spare understatement of Imagism; she wouldn't have wanted to acknowledge that she found N.K.'s poetry too harsh, discordant, angry, *unsettling*. Nor had she been drawn to the cult of N.K., that had begun even before the poet's premature death.

What is a cult but a binding-together of the weak. So it seemed to her. The excesses of feminists, she hoped to distance herself from. A certain physical/erotic posturing, needless provocations. Not for her.

Soon then, reading an obituary of N.K. in the *New York Times*, Elisabeth discovered that N.K. had allegedly named herself, or rather renamed herself, as "N.K." in homage to the Imagist poet H.D.; she'd wanted a pseudonym "without gender and without a history."

Names are obscuring, misleading. So N.K. argued. Surnames—family names—have no role in art. Artists are individuals and should name themselves. "Naming"—the most crucial aspect of one's life, the name you bring with you, blatant as a face, should not be the province/choice of others.

Essentially, your parents are strangers to you. It is not reasonable that strangers should name *you*.

And so, Nicola Kavanaugh had named herself "N.K." The poet's vanity would help brand her, help to guarantee her fame.

Soon after, Elisabeth found herself staring at a poster on a wall in Barnes & Noble depicting the gaunt, savagely beautiful N.K. in a photograph by Annie Leibovitz. The poet had been wearing what looked like a flimsy cotton shift, almost you could see the shadowy nipples of her breasts through the material, and around her slender shoulders a coarse-knitted, fringed shawl. Her thick disheveled hair appeared to be wind-blown, her eyes sharp and accusing. Beneath, the caption—*Live as if it's your life.*

3.

"And what did you say your name was, dear?—'Elizabeth'? I didn't quite hear."

"Elisabeth."

Gravely he laughed at her. Leaning over her.

"Is that a lisp I hear?—'Elis-a-beth'?"

"Y-Yes."

By chance, months later, when the last thing on her mind was N.K., Elisabeth was introduced to Alexander Hendrick. A tall gentlemanly man of whom everyone whispered—*D'you know who that is? Alexander Hendrick—N.K.'s husband.*

He was older than Elisabeth by nearly twenty years. Yet youthful in his manner, even playful, to disguise the gravity beneath, even as he had to shave (Elisabeth would learn) twice a day, to rid his jaws of graying stubble, sharp little quills that erupted not only on his face but beneath his chin, partway down his neck.

She'd known something of the man's identity, apart from the disaster of his marriage: he was the director of the Hendrick Foundation, that had been founded by a multi-millionaire grandfather in the 1950s, to award grants to creative artists at the outset of their careers.

Including in 1993, the young experimental poet-artist Nicola Kavanaugh, as she'd called herself then.

Had Alexander Hendrick and Nicola Kavanaugh met before Nicola received the grant, or afterward?—Elisabeth was never to learn, with any certainty.

"Tell me you aren't a poet, my dear Elisabeth."

"No. I mean—I am not a poet."

"You're sure?"—Alexander Hendrick was grimly joking, unless it was his very grimness that joked, that made such a joke possible.

Elisabeth laughed, feeling giddy. Since adolescence she'd been waiting for such a person, who could intimidate her yet make her laugh.

4.

You tell yourself: the new life is sudden.

The new life is a window flung open. Better yet, a window smashed.

Sometimes it is true. The *new life* is flung in your face, you have not the capacity to duck the flying glass.

What was it like, to visit that house? Will you have to live there as his wife—permanently?

Can you—permanently?

Are there traces of her? Is there an—aura?

Oh Elisabeth. Take care.

The (civil) wedding in March is very small, private. Few relatives on either side.

Immediately afterward they leave for a week in the Bahamas. And when they return it is to the house on Oceanview Avenue, Wainscott, where the surviving child awaits, looked after by the housekeeper Ana.

Are you prepared for him? A ten-year-old stepchild whose mother tried to kill him?

In death, N.K.'s notoriety has grown. Articles about her appear continuously in print and online. An unauthorized video titled *Last Days of the Poet N.K.* goes viral. An unauthorized *Interview with the American Medea N.K.*—in fact, a pastiche of several interviews—appears, with photographs of the starkly beautiful woman over the course of years, in *Vanity Fair*. There are Barnes & Noble posters, T-shirts, even coffee mugs—a cartoon likeness of N.K. with an aureole of fiercely crimped dark hair and a beautiful savage unsmiling mouth.

Of these outrages Alexander never speaks—perhaps he is not aware. (Elisabeth wants to think.) The posthumous cult of N.K. is like a cancer metastasizing—unstoppable.

Sylvia Plath, Anne Sexton, and now Nicola Kavanaugh—"N.K." For each generation of wounded and angry women, a deathly female icon.

At first the mainstream media contrived to believe that N.K. had been mentally ill, to have killed her daughter as well as herself. It was known that she'd "struggled with depression" since adolescence, she'd tried to kill herself several times in the past. But then, newer readings of N.K.'s poetry suggest that her horrendous act had been deliberate and premeditated, a "purification" of the self in a rotten world.

It seemed clear that she'd meant to kill Stefan as well, initially. She'd given the seven-year-old a sedative, as she'd given the four-year-old a sedative, and brought him into the garage with her, and into the Saab sedan; then for some reason she'd relented, and carried him back into the house and left him, and returned to the car with the running motor, filling the garage with bluish smoke for the stunned Alexander to discover, hours later.

The dead woman lying in the front seat of the car with the little girl, Clea, in her arms, the two of them wrapped in a mohair shawl.

Was there a suicide note?—Alexander saw nothing.

It would be his claim, he'd seen nothing. Emergency medical workers, law enforcement officers, investigators—suicide note discovered in the car.

Yet, it came to be generally known that there'd been "packets of poems" scattered in the back seat of the car. (As well as the left sneaker of a pair of sneakers—belonging to Stefan.) Not new poems by N.K. but older poems, among her more famous poems, that quickly took on a new, ominous prescience. The posthumous cult of N.K., so maddening to Alexander and his family, quickly fastened upon these poems—*the small bitter apples of extinction*.

Ana had been given the entire day off by Nicola. The housekeeper hadn't been expected to return until eight o'clock in the evening by which time Nicola and Clea had been dead for several hours.

Stefan, missing, was eventually found by searchers inside the house, partially dressed, and shoeless, at the rear of an upstairs closet. (The mate to the child's sneaker in the rear of the Saab would be discovered in a corner of the garage amid recycling containers, as if it had been tossed or kicked there.) He was curled into a fetal position, so deeply asleep he might have been in a coma. His blood pressure was dangerously low. His skin was deathly white, his lips had a bluish cast. Emergency medical workers worked to revive him with oxygen.

The surviving child was slow to come to consciousness. Not only carbon monoxide poisoning but barbiturate would be discovered in his blood. He would remember little of what had happened. Except— *Mummy gave me warm milk to drink, that made me sleepy. Mummy kissed me and told me she would never abandon me.*

Yet, the child's mother must have changed her mind about killing him with his sister. A short time after she'd started the Saab motor, when the seven-year-old was unconscious, but before she herself had lapsed into unconsciousness, she'd pulled him from the back seat of the car, dragged or carried him all the way upstairs to a hall closet . . .

Elisabeth ponders this. Why did N.K. relent, and allow one of her children to live? The boy, and not the girl? *Did* in fact this happen, as it's generally believed?

Elisabeth wonders if the seven-year-old might have crawled out of the car, and saved himself. Yet, why would he have hidden upstairs in a closet? And he'd been deeply unconscious, when his father discovered him.

More than three years after the deaths the Wainscott police investigation is closed. The county medical examiner issued his report: homicide, suicide. Carbon monoxide poisoning. Heavy barbiturate sedation. Still, no one knows precisely the chronology of events of that day. The surviving child cannot be further questioned. The surviving husband will never speak again on the subject publicly, he has declared.

And privately? Elisabeth knows only what Alexander has chosen to tell her, which she has no reason to disbelieve. N.K. had suffered from manic-depression since early adolescence, she'd been a "brilliant poet" (Alexander had to concede) afflicted by a strong wish to harm herself, and others unfortunate enough to be caught up in her emotional life. She'd been coldly ambitious, Alexander said. Always anxious about her reputation, jealous of other poets' prizes, publicity. Ultimately she'd cared little for a domestic life—though, for a few years, she'd tried. Perversely the children had adored her, Alexander said bitterly.

And yet, what is it we cannot know? Though the heart breaks, the great sea crashes, crushes us. We must know.

Since becoming Alexander's wife Elisabeth has resisted reading N.K.'s poems. Yet, it is difficult to avoid them for often lines from the poems, even entire poems, are quoted in the media. Quickly Elisabeth looks away but sometimes it is too late.

. . . crashes, crushes us. We must know.

Very still Elisabeth has been sitting, fingers poised above the laptop keyboard. How many minutes have passed she doesn't know but her laptop screen has gone dark like a brain switching off. By chance she hears a quickened breath behind her—turns to see, in the doorway, the beautiful child, her stepchild, Stefan.

"Oh—Stefan! Hello . . ."

Elisabeth is so startled by the sight of him, something falls from the table—a ballpoint pen. Clattering onto the floor, rolling.

"H-Have you been there a while, dear? I didn't hear you . . ." Rises to her feet as if to invite the elusive child inside the room but already Stefan has backed away and is descending the stairs.

Like a wild creature, she thinks. A wraith.

If you reach out for a wraith he shrinks away. Oh, she is so crude!—so yearning, the child sees it in her face and retreats.

5.

"Certainly not! We live here. We are very happy here. It's *ordinary life* here." Declaiming to visitors Alexander laughs with a sharp sort of happiness.

A steady procession of visitors, guests at Hendrick House. In the summer months especially, on idyllic Cape Cod.

No aura. Not her. That one is dead, gone. Vanished.

On the wide veranda looking toward the ocean, in the long summer twilight. Drinks are served by a young Guatemalan girl who is helping Ana tonight, cut-glass crystal glitters and winks. Elisabeth is the new wife, shy among her husband's friends. He has so many!—hopeless to try to keep their names straight.

Perhaps these are not friends exactly. Rather, acquaintances and professional associates. Visitors from Provincetown, Woods Hole. House guests from Boston, Cambridge, New York City connected with the Hendrick Foundation.

In summer the house on Oceanview Avenue is particularly beautiful. Romantically weathered dark-brown shingle board with dark shutters, stone foundation and stone chimneys. Steep roofs and cupolas, a wrap-around veranda open to the ocean on bright windy days. Fifteen rooms, three storys, the converted stable at the rear. Not the largest but one of the more distinctive houses on Oceanview Avenue, Wainscott. Originally built in 1809, and listed with the National Landmark Registry. Beside the heavy oak front door is a small brass plaque commemorating this honor.

Of course, Alexander has an apartment elsewhere, on Boston's Beacon Street, near the office of the Hendrick Foundation. In the years of his marriage to N.K. he was obliged to rent an apartment in New York City, on Waverly Place, to accommodate her.

". . . well, yes. We 'took a chance' on her at the Foundation—though after Allen Ginsberg that sort of wild feckless quasi-confessional poetry was fashionable—riding the crest of the 'new feminism' . . ."

Elisabeth marvels at the coolness with which at such times Alexander is able to speak of N.K. So long as the subject is impersonal; so long as the subject is poetry, and not *wife*.

Coolness, and condescension. (Male) revenge on the (female) artist. Yes she is, or was, brilliant—"genius." But no, I am not so impressed.

Most of these guests had known Nicola Kavanaugh. This, Elisabeth gathers. You see them frowning, shaking their heads. Pitying, condemning. Allowing the widower to know that they side with him of course—the bereft, terribly wronged husband.

Monstrous woman. Deranged and demented poet.

"... yes, I've heard. It will be 'unauthorized'—of course. The last thing we need is a biography of—her. Fortunately, copyright to her work resides with me, and I don't intend to give permission for any sort of use—even 'the'—'and'—'but' ..."

Laughter. As he is famously stoical so Alexander is so very witty.

A *biography?* This is the first Elisabeth has heard.

Not from Alexander but from other sources Elisabeth has learned how the poet Nicola Kavanaugh was reluctant to marry—anyone. How she'd suffered since early adolescence from mania, depression, suicidal "ideation"—and suicide attempts. Love affairs with Nicola were invariably impassioned, destructive. And then, at last, after a most destructive relationship with a prominent woman artist living in New York City, to the astonishment of everyone who knew her, and against their unanimous advice, Nicola suddenly married the older, well-to-do Alexander Hendrick, who'd been one of her ardent courters for years.

For solace she'd married, it was said; for financial security, and to pay for therapists, prescription drugs, hospitalizations; as a stay against the wild mood swings of manic-depression; for peace, comfort, sanity. *Because a sexually rapacious young woman took advantage of a besotted well-to-do older man with literary pretensions.*

Though in her poetry N.K. scorned the conventional life of husband, children, responsibilities, bourgeois property and possessions yet in her life she'd behaved perversely, taking all these on.

Elisabeth has heard that Nicola loved the house in Wainscott—at first. A romantically remote place on Cape Cod to which she could retreat, and work. A place where she could be alone when she wished, in solitude.

And she'd loved her children, as well—at first.

Yet, it would turn out that the poet wrote some of her most savagely powerful poems in this house, in the final year of her life. Sequestered away in an upstairs room, barring the door against intruders—her own children.

Terrible things Elisabeth has heard about the predecessor-wife. Terrible things she is reluctant/eager to believe.

In her extreme emotional states N.K. mistreated, abused both children. Screamed at them, shook them. Locked them in a closet. *Sight of babies appalls. Doubling myself. Sin of hubris. Stink of pride. Bringing another of myself into the world: unforgiveable.*

And *How will they remember their mother?—little lambs of sacrifice, shall their eyes be opened?*

Alexander would testify at a police inquiry into the deaths that his wife had wanted children to save her life and then, after their births, she'd resented them. She'd loved them excessively (it seemed) but had been fearful of hurting them. She couldn't bear them around her often but claimed not to trust nannies or the housekeeper. She didn't want them near windows for fear they would fall through the windows, piercing themselves on the glass. Didn't like to take their hands to lead them upstairs or across a street, there was the terror of losing the grip of their hands. Could not bear to bathe them for fear of scalding them, or drowning them. Several times she'd wakened Alexander in the middle of the night (in Alexander's bed: for the two did not share a room) crying she'd cut the children's throats like pigs, tried to hang them upside-down but couldn't, they fell to the floor and were bleeding to death. Alexander had to take the sobbing hysterical woman into the children's rooms to show her that they were untouched and then for a long time she stood disbelieving by their beds until saying at last in a flat voice. "All right then. For now."

Is madness contagious? Elisabeth shivers in the perpetual wind from the Atlantic.

"... Stefan? Reasonably well. Thank you for asking. There's a girl looking after him tonight, upstairs."

"How has he adjusted, in this house? It must be ..."

"No. Stefan is very happy here. I've told you. He cries if he's made to leave even overnight."

"Really! Is that so."

"Yes. Strangely so. As I think I've told you—all of you."

"He must be very happy then, with his new stepmother ..."

New stepmother. Elisabeth has been only half-listening as talk swirls about her head but she hears this, distinctly.

A rude remark, cruel and insinuating, or an entirely sincere remark, made by an old friend of Alexander's who wishes him and family well?

"Really, we are all very happy here. Elisabeth has been 'settling in'—wonderfully. She and Stefan are making friends. So far, the summer has been . . ."

Feeling the visitors' eyes on her. Sensing their disappointment in her, so plain-faced, dull and so *ordinary* after Nicola Kavanaugh.

Like a dun-feathered bird holding herself very still, not to attract the attention of predators. Very still among these strangers seeming to listen to their sharp witty voices while hearing in the wind from the Atlantic the throaty voice intimate as a whisper in her ear.

But you know that I am not gone, Elisabeth. You know that I have come for you and the boy.

6.

"This house is not 'poisoned'—not by *her*."

Not to Elisabeth has Alexander uttered such words but she has overheard him on the phone, speaking with Wainscott relatives. His tone is vehement, contemptuous. *Who has been spreading such rumors of—hauntings . . .*

He will not be driven away from this property, he has said. Hendrick House will endure beyond individual lives. It will endure long after *her*.

Elisabeth never has to wonder who *her* is. Sometimes, the contemptuously uttered pronoun is *she*.

Bitterly Alexander says: "Nicola came here, with a pretense of wanting a 'quiet' life, and she never made a home here. Her clothes were in suitcases. Her books were in boxes. Ana did most of the unpacking, shelving books. Nicola couldn't be bothered. She was immersed in her poetry, her precious career. She had her lovers, women and men. She'd promised that she had given them up when we were married but of course she lied. Her entire life was a lie. Her poetry is a lie. When she

47

was sick with depression her lovers abandoned her. Where were they? Hangers-on, sycophants. And her 'fans'—they were waiting for her to die, to kill herself. The promise of the poetry. But they hadn't anticipated that their heroine would take her own daughter with her. *That,* they hadn't expected." Alexander speaks defiantly. Elisabeth listens with dread. Like holding your breath in the presence of airborne poison. She doesn't want to breathe in hatred for the deceased woman, she doesn't want to feel hatred for anyone.

How beautiful the house is, Elisabeth never tires of marveling.

But beware. Beauty's price.

Sucking your life's blood.

Strange, wonderful and strange, and uncanny, to live in a kind of museum. Classic Cape Cod architecture, period furnishings. Especially the downstairs rooms are flawlessly maintained.

Of course such maintenance is expensive. Much effort on the part of servants, and on the part of the wife of the house. Polished surfaces, gleaming hardwood floors. Curtains stirring in the ocean breeze. High, languidly turning fans. (No air conditioning in any of the landmark houses of Wainscott, so close to the Atlantic!) Long corridors with windows at each end looking out (it almost seems) into eternity.

Rot beneath, shine above. Rejoice, love. Lines from one of N.K.'s chanting poems—"Dirge"—Elisabeth hasn't realized she'd memorized.

Does the door lock? No?

Still, the door can be shut. Though no one is likely to follow her here, except (perhaps) the child Stefan, who is away at school on this rainy, windy autumn day.

Alexander is in Boston for several days and even if he were home, it isn't likely that he would seek her out in this part of the house in which he has little interest.

On the third floor, up a flight of steep steps, Elisabeth has discovered a small sparely furnished room in what had been, in a previous era, the servants' quarters.

Here there is no elegant silk French wallpaper as in the downstairs rooms. Not a chandelier but a bare-bulb overhead light. A single window overlooking sand hills, stunted dun-colored vegetation, a glittering silver of the Atlantic.

In the room is a narrow cot, hardly a bed. A bare plank floor. No curtains or shutters. Not a closet but a narrow cupboard opening into the wall, rife with cobwebs and a smell of mildew.

At a table in this little room at a makeshift desk Elisabeth sits leaning on her elbows, that have become raw, reddened. Much of her skin feels wind-burnt. For here at the edge of the ocean there is perennial wind: gusts rattling windowpanes, stirring foliage in tall pines beside the house.

Elisabeth has brought her laptop here but often leaves it unopened. Her work on the Imagist poets beckons to her as if on the farther side of an abyss but—she is afraid—she is losing her emotional connection with it. Reading and rereading passages of prose she'd written with conviction and passion as an eager young scholar at the Radcliffe Institute and now she can barely remember the primary work, let alone her enthusiasm for it. The spare impersonal poetry of H.D. seems so muted, set beside a more impassioned and heedless female poetry.

Elisabeth strains her eyes staring toward the ocean. Wind-stirred waves, pounding surf frothing white against the pebbly shore. Overhead misshapen storm clouds and in the pines beside the house what appear to be the arms, legs of struggling persons—naked bodies . . .

Promiscuous life rushes through our veins. Unstoppable.

An optical illusion of some sort. Must be.

Elisabeth can see the thrashing figures in the corner of her eye but when she looks directly at the agitated foliage she can't decipher the human figures but only their outlines. The impress of the (naked) bodies in the thrashing branches, where they struggle like swimmers in a rough surf.

Turning her head quickly to see—if she can catch the figures in the trees.

"No. You can't catch them."

Behind her, beside her a throaty little laugh. It is Stefan who has crept noiselessly into the room.

Very quietly, though very quickly, like a cat ascending the steep steps to the third floor of the house Stefan must have come to join her. Hadn't she shut the door to the little room? He'd managed to open it, without her hearing.

Elisabeth is startled but tries to speak matter-of-factly. For she knows, children do not like to see adults discomforted.

"Catch—what?"

"The things in the trees. That never stop."

Stefan speaks patiently as if (of course) Elisabeth knows what he is talking about. "You can see them in the corner of your eye but when you look at them, they're gone. They're too fast."

But there is nothing there. In the trees, in the leaves. We know that.

Elisabeth's heart is pounding quickly. Almost shyly she regards the stepchild who so often eludes her, seems to look through her. Stefan seems never to grow, has scarcely grown an inch in the months since Alexander first introduced them.

My new, dear friend Elisabeth. Will you say hello to her? Smile— just a bit? Shake her hand?

Oh, Stefan's curly hair is damp from the rain! Elisabeth would love to embrace him, press his head against her chest.

Droplets of rain like teardrops on his flushed face and on the zip-up nylon jacket he hasn't taken time to remove. Something very touching about this. Has Stefan hurried home from school, to *her*?

"Stefan! You're home early . . ."

Stefan shrugs. Maybe he hadn't gone to school at all but simply hid in the house somewhere, in one or another of the numerous unused rooms. Or in the forbidden place, the garage.

Stefan ignores his stepmother's words as he often does. Knowing that the words that pass between them are of little significance, like markers in a poem, mere syllables.

He is at the window, peering out. Wind, rain, thrashing pine branches, an agitation of arms and legs almost visible . . .

Convulsed with something that looks like passion we tell ourselves, Love.

Whose words are these? Elisabeth wonders if Stefan can hear them, too.

It is true, she thinks. The convulsions in the trees. Our terrible need for one another, our terror of being left alone. To which we give the name, *Love*.

"She taught me how to see them—Mummy. But they always get away."

Elisabeth isn't sure that she has heard correctly. This is the first time that Stefan has uttered the word *Mummy* in her hearing.

"Now Mummy is one of them herself. I think."

For the remainder of the long day feeling both threatened and blessed.

The child had come unbidden to *her*.

A wraith may not be approached, for a wraith will retreat. But a wraith may approach you. If he wishes.

Stefan darling. Try to forget her. I have come to take her place, I will love you in her place. Trust me!

7.

Certainly it is true as Alexander has said, there is nothing *poisoned* or *haunted* about the Hendrick family house.

For how could there be anything wrong with a house listed in the National Landmark Registry and featured in the fall 2011 issue of the sumptuous glossy *Cape Cod Living* . . .

Yet, things *go wrong* in the house. Usually these are not serious and are easily remedied.

For instance: sometimes after a heavy rain the water out of the faucets tastes strange. There is a faint metallic aftertaste, in full daylight you can see a subtle discoloration like rust. And there are mysterious drips from ceilings, actual pools of water, bulges in wallpaper like tumors. Unsettling moans and murmurs in the plumbing.

The water is well water, claimed to be "pure"—"sweet tasting." The well is a deep natural well on the Hendrick property that has been there for generations, fed by underground springs.

Ana tells Elisabeth that, perhaps, she should make an appointment with the township water inspector to come to the house for a sample of their well water. To see what, if anything, is wrong.

Drips in the ceilings, bulges in wallpaper, groaning pipes—Elisabeth should call the roofer, the plumber as well. Since the fancy silk wallpaper in the dining room has been discolored she had better call a paperhanger too. And there are several cracked windowpanes, after a windstorm, that will have to be replaced—sometimes shards of glass litter the downstairs foyer, though no (evident) window panes have been broken. Ana can provide local numbers for (Elisabeth gathers) these repairmen are frequently called.

"All the old big houses in Wainscott are the same," Ana says adamantly, "—all my friends, they work in them, they tell me. It is nothing special to this house."

Nothing poisoned or haunted in this house. We know.

It has fallen to Elisabeth to make such appointments since Alexander is often in Boston on business. Indeed Elisabeth is eager to shield her husband from such mundane tasks for he is easily upset by problems involving his beloved house, and it is increasingly difficult to speak to him without his taking offense.

Also, Elisabeth is the wife of the house. As Mrs. Alexander Hendrick she feels a thrill of satisfaction, she is sure that her emotionally unstable predecessor took no such responsibility.

The new wife is nothing like—her! Alexander didn't make a mistake this time. This Elizabeth—"Elisabeth"—is utterly devoted to him and the child and the household, she is a treasure . . .

Listening, but the voice trails off. Always she is hoping to hear *And Alexander is devoted to—her!*

Methodically, dutifully calling these local tradesmen and (oddly) no one is available to come to the house on Oceanview Avenue just then. All have excuses, express regret.

But we can pay you—of course! We can pay you double.

Calling a local plumber and the voice at the other end expresses surprise—"Hendrick? Again? Weren't we just there a few months ago?" and Elisabeth stammers, "I—I don't know, were you? What was wrong?" and the voice says, guardedly, "Anyway, there's no one available right now. Better try another plumber, I can give you a number to call."

But it is a number that Elisabeth has already called.

"Try Provincetown. They'll charge for coming here, but . . ."

None of this Elisabeth will mention to Alexander. It is only results he cares to be informed of.

So much to do each day. Like a merry-go-round that has begun to accelerate.

Vague thought of *having a baby of my own, someday, a little sister for Stefan.* About this she feels excitement, hope, dread, guilt.

So many distractions, Elisabeth has (temporarily) set aside her scholarly work she'd been doing at the Radcliffe Institute. Research that once fascinated her. Elusive and shimmering as a mirage in the desert, her PhD dissertation on the experimental verse of H.D. and H.D.'s relationship to Ezra Pound and T.S. Eliot. She has written drafts of the (seven) chapters but must revise, add footnotes, update the already extensive bibliography.

No end to fascinating research! But she must be careful that she does not stray from H.D. to N.K. She does not intend to *snoop.*

It is uncanny, some lines of poetry by H.D. echo lines of poetry by N.K. Or rather, some lines of poetry by N.K. echo lines by H.D.

A case of plagiarism? Or—admiration, identification?

I have had enough.

I gasp for breath.

When they were first married and Elisabeth came to live in her husband's family home in Wainscott it was with the understanding that Elisabeth would return to her scholarly work when things "settled down." The director of the Hendrick Foundation is a feminist—of course. In the past most Hendrick fellowships went to male artists, but no longer.

No one has urged Elisabeth to complete her PhD at Harvard more enthusiastically than Alexander. When Stefan is older, and doesn't require so much attention, Elisabeth might find a teaching position at a private school on the Cape . . .

It is true, Stefan requires attention. The fact of Stefan, the surviving child. Elisabeth knows that she must be indirect in watching over the elusive child, not obvious and intrusive. She must never startle him by a display of affection. And she must never intervene between father and son.

If Alexander is chiding Stefan, for instance. It is painful to Elisabeth to hear but she must not intervene.

As she sometimes overhears Alexander speaking harshly on the phone, so she overhears Alexander speaking harshly to Stefan. Chiding him for being dreamy, distracted—*other-minded*. For sometimes Stefan is surprisingly clumsy—slipping on the stairs, spraining an ankle; falling from his bicycle, badly cutting his leg. Objects seem to twist from his fingers—cutlery, glassware that shatters on the floor. He is often breathless, anxious. Nothing annoys the father so much as an *anxious* child who shrinks from him as if in (ridiculous!) fear of being struck.

At such times Elisabeth bites her lower lip, straining to hear. She should not be eavesdropping, she knows. If Alexander caught her . . . .

She rarely hears Stefan's reply for the boy speaks so softly. If there is any reply.

Yet it is true as Alexander has boasted: Stefan appears to be happy in the house on Oceanview Avenue. At least, Stefan is less happy elsewhere.

Indeed he is reluctant to leave on short trips, even to Provincetown. It is all but impossible to get him to stay away overnight. If forced he will protest, sulk, weep, kick, suck his fingers. Even Ana is shocked, how childish Stefan becomes at such times.

The house is an epicenter, it seems. Stefan will allow himself approximately a mile from this center before he becomes anxious.

From her third-floor aerie Elisabeth has observed Stefan pedaling his bicycle to the end of the block, turning then to continue around the block. Though he quickly passes out of her sight Elisabeth understands that Stefan must keep the house at the epicenter of his bicycling. Soon then, he will reappear, coming from the other direction along Oceanview, pedaling fast, furiously, as if his life were at stake.

Once waiting for Stefan to reappear, waiting for—oh, how long?—an hour?—an *anguished hour?*—Elisabeth can bear it no longer and hurries downstairs, rushes out onto the front walk to look for him; and stands in the avenue waiting for him—*where is he?* Until finally she glances behind her and sees Stefan hovering at the front door watching her.

She is embarrassed, and blushes deeply. When she returns to the house Stefan has disappeared, damned if she will look for him.

8.

Convulsed with something that looks like passion we tell ourselves, Love.

A high, skittering sound as of glass shards ringing together. Unless it is laughter. Steps back and in the next instant the cut-glass chandelier in the front hall loosens, falls from the ceiling, crashes to the floor narrowly missing her.

In the aftermath of the shattering glass, that high faint laughter so delicious, you want to join in.

Surfaces, and beneath. Elisabeth is learning not to be deceived by the elegant polished surfaces of the house.

A place of sickness. Don't breathe.

Walls look aslant. Doors stick, or can't be closed. Doorknobs feel uncomfortably warm when touched, like inner organs.

Light switches are not where Elisabeth remembers them to be— where Elisabeth *knows* them to be. Fumbling for the switch in her own bedroom.

You will never find the light nor will the light find you but one day the light will shine through you.

Finally, her fingers locate the switch. Blasting light, blinding.

In the mirror, a blurred reflection. Wraith-wife.

No: she is imagining everything. In the mirror there is nothing.

For several days her skin has felt feverish. A sensation of heaviness in her lower belly, legs. No appetite and then ravenous appetite and then fits of nausea, gagging. The worst is dry heaving, guttural cries like strangulation.

The most peaceful blue sleep. Hurry!

* * *

Midway in the shower in Elisabeth's bathroom fierce sharp quills springing from the showerhead turn scalding-hot with no warning.

Elisabeth cries out in surprise—and pain—and scrambles to escape before she faints . . .

A previous time, the shower turned freezing cold.

Slipping and skidding on the tile floor, whimpering in pain, shock.

In fear of her life—almost. Hearing in the pipes in the walls muffled derisive laughter.

Safer to take a bath. Always in the morning and (sometimes) before bed as well if she is feeling *sullied, bloated.*

Fortunately there is, in another adjoining bathroom, an enormous bathtub in which she might soak in hot (not scalding) sudsy water curling her toes in narcotic pleasure, letting her eyelids sink shut.

Tub is too crude and utilitarian a word for such a work of art: a marble bathtub. Faint blue veins in the marble like veins in flesh. Ancient, stately, six feet long, and deep. Eagerly Elisabeth tests the water, lowers herself into it taking care not to slip, not to fall. It is such pleasure, pure sensuous delight. Almost at once she begins to sink into a light doze. Her hair straggles into the steamy water, her pale soft startled-looking breasts begin to lift . . .

Hurry! We have been waiting.

Finds herself thinking of an Egyptian tomb. Mummified corpses of a young wife and her baby wrapped in swaddling laid solemnly in the tomb side by side.

Sinking into the water, the enervating heat. Her mouth, nose beneath the water . . . Too much effort to breathe . . .

I have had enough.

I gasp for breath.

Waking then. With a start, in shock. No idea where she is, or how much time has elapsed in this place.

Hovering above the naked female body. The body is white, wizened. The fingers and toes are puckered, soft. In panic she must return to this body . . . .

The bath water has turned cold and scummy and smells vile as turpentine. The marble has become freezing cold and slippery. In her desperation to climb out of the deep tub Elisabeth's feet slip and slide, her strength has been sucked away. Loses her balance and falls onto the floor nearly striking her head on the marble rim.

Oh!—pain has returned, and humiliation. For she is trapped inside the wizened white naked female body again.

In the winter many nights Alexander is away. Bravely, Elisabeth is the *wife of the house*. Elisabeth is the *stepmother* of the surviving child.

Dining together, evenings by the fireplace. Like something animated the child will speak of school, books he is reading, or has read. Safe topics for stepmother and stepchild to navigate like stepping stones in a rough stream.

The father forbids television in the house on Oceanview Avenue. No internet for Stefan. No video games! He will not have his son's mind (he knows to be a brilliant and precocious mind like his own at that age) polluted by debased American culture.

(Alexander watches television in his Beacon Street apartment but the sort of television that Alexander watches is not debased.)

As if he has just thought of it Stefan says, "That room—where you are—that was Mummy's, too."

Elisabeth is surprised. *That room?*—she'd chosen because it is so spare, so unattractive. Two flights of stairs, the second flight to the old servants' quarters steep and narrow.

She'd assumed that N.K. had worked in another room. *Her* room shows no signs of human occupancy.

"Oh, Stefan. I—I didn't know . . ."

"Mummy wouldn't let us in, mostly. Not like you."

Is this flattering? Elisabeth wants to think so.

But who is *us*, she wonders. Little Clea, also?

The remainder of the meal passes in silence but not an awkward silence and when Elisabeth undresses for bed that night she finds herself smiling, a frothy sensation in the area of her heart of uplift.

Not like you like you like you. Not!

And later, as she is sinking into a delicious sleep—*Live like it's your life.*

Solemn ticking of the stately old Stickley grandfather clock in the hall.

Yet Elisabeth begins to hear the ticking accelerate, and hesitate; a pause, and a leap forward; a rapid series of ticks, like tachycardia. (She has had tachycardia attacks since moving into the house, but in secret. Never will she voluntarily confide in her husband that she has what is called a *heart murmur*.) In the night she hears the clock cease its ticking and lies in a paroxysm of worry, that it is her own heart that has ceased. A whisper consoles her—*Quick if it's done, is best. Most mercy. Blue buzz of air, the only symptom you will feel is peace.*

Ignores the whisper. Very quietly descending the stairs barefoot to check on the clock, to see why it has ceased ticking; why the silence is so loud, in the interstices of its ticking.

The clock face is blank!—there is no *time* . . . .

It has already happened, Elisabeth. That is why time has ceased. It is all over, and painless.

But no: when she switches on the light she sees that the clock is ticking normally. (Elisabeth is sure: she stands barefoot in the hallway shivering, listening.) And there is the clock face as always, stately Roman numerals, hour hand, minute hand, a pale luminous face with a lurid smile just for her.

The wife of the house.

The well water has been diagnosed by the township water inspector: an alarmingly high degree of *organic and fecal material*. Decomposing (animal?) bodies. Excrement. Contaminated water leaking into the well and until the well can be dredged and the water "purified" it is recommended that the Hendrick household use only bottled water for drinking and cooking purposes.

Informed of this humiliating news Alexander flushes angrily. Elisabeth steels herself to hear him declare *This house is not poisoned*. But he turns away instead as if it Elisabeth who has offended him.

9.

The next evening meal with Stefan. Elisabeth has given Ana the day off, wanting to prepare the meal herself.

Though she takes care to prepare only a variation of one of the few meals that Stefan will consent to eat, that doesn't involve chewy pulpy meat in which muscle fibers are detectable, or anything "slimy" (okra, tomato seeds), or small enough (rice, peas) to be mistaken by the child for grubs or insects. To Ana's vegetarian egg casserole Elisabeth has added several ingredients of her own—carrots, sweet peppers, spinach.

But Stefan isn't so talkative as he'd been the previous night. When Elisabeth brings up the subject of her third-floor room, and the view of wind-shaken trees outside the window, Stefan says nothing. Almost, Elisabeth might wonder if he'd ever spoken to her about the struggling figures in the trees or she'd imagined that remarkable exchange. Just slightly hurt, that Stefan is suspicious of the casserole she has prepared, examining forkfuls before lifting them to his mouth. And he is taking unusually small bites as if shy of eating in her company, or undecided whether he actually wants to eat the food she has prepared.

Yet he'd once nursed. Imagining the child as an infant nursing at the mother's breast.

Or, at Elisabeth's breast.

She feels a flush of embarrassment, self-consciousness. What strange thoughts she has! And she is not drinking wine with the meal, as Alexander often urges her to do, to keep him company.

Tugging at the breast of life we must devour.
Helpless otherwise, for dignity's not enough.
Surrender dignity and in return royally
Sucked.

In person, when N.K. read this abrasive poem, or recited it in her smoky, throaty voice, audiences laughed uproariously. (Elisabeth has seen videos.) The enormous wish to laugh with the woman declaiming such truths, like a tidal wave sweeping over them.

Since Alexander has been spending more time in Boston, Elisabeth has been on the internet watching videos of N.K. Doesn't want to think that she is becoming obsessive. Knows that Alexander would disapprove and so has no intention of allowing him to know.

Fear of being sucked and fear
Of sucking.

Stefan's silence is not hostile nor even stubborn but (Elisabeth thinks) a consequence of shyness. Stefan may have felt that at their last meal he'd revealed too much to her, and betrayed his mother.

No betrayal like loving another.
No betrayal like love of the Other.

Distracted by such thoughts Elisabeth has taken too much food into her mouth. Trying to swallow a wad of clotted pulp in her mouth. Her casserole is lukewarm and stringy, unlike Ana's. Something coarse-textured like seaweed—must be the damned spinach. Chewing, trying to swallow but can't swallow. Horribly, strands of spinach have tangled in her teeth. Between her teeth. Can't swallow.

Trying to hide her distress from Stefan. Not wanting to alarm the child. (Oh, if Alexander were here, to witness such a sight! He'd have been dismayed, disgusted.) A deep flush rises into Elisabeth's face, she can barely breathe. This clump of something clotted, caught in her throat— horrible! The harder she tries to swallow, the more her throat constricts.

"Excuse—"

Mouth too full, can't enunciate the word. Desperate now, staggering from the table knocking something to the floor with a clatter. With widened eyes Stefan stares at her.

Must get to a bathroom, thrust a finger down her throat, gag, vomit violently into a toilet . . . .

And then you die. And then
it is over.
So much struggle so long—why?

At last in a bathroom, no time even to shut the door behind her as she manages to cough up the clotted pulpy mash, stringy spinach, in a paroxysm of misery gagging as she spits it into the toilet bowl. Though able to breathe again she is distressed, agitated. Too weak to stand, sinks to her knees. Her face is flaming-hot and the heaviness in her bowels like a fist.

In the aged plumbing a sound of faint laughter.

Then, Stefan is standing beside her. Without a word soaks a wash-cloth in cold water from the sink and hands it to Elisabeth to press against her overheated face.

Too frightened, too exhausted even to thank the child. His small-boned hand finds hers, his fingers in her fingers clasped, tight.

Oh Stefan thank you. Oh I love you.

10.

Impossible to sleep! Bile rising in her throat. That which she has bitten off, she cannot swallow. The muscles of her throat gag involuntarily, recalling. Cannot believe how close she'd come to choking to death.

What an awful death—gagging, choking. Unable to swallow and (at last) unable to breathe.

Days have passed. Nights. She is losing track of the calendar.

Her eyelids are unnaturally heavy. Yet she cannot sleep. Or if she sleeps it's a thin frothy sleep that sweeps over her like surf. Briefly her aching consciousness is extinguished and yet flares up again a moment later.

A brain is dense meat. Yet, a brain is intricately wired, billions of neurons and glia. The wonder is, how do you turn the brain *on?* How do you turn the brain *off?* An anesthesiologist can put a brain to sleep but can't explain why. And only the brain can make itself conscious.

Falling on the stairs, stumbling. *But the stairs moved. It was not my foot that tripped, stumbled. The stairs moved.*

Finds herself at the rear of the darkened house where the throaty voice has brought her. Not sleepwalking but there is a numbness encasing her that suggests the flotation-logic of sleep. Hand on the doorknob. Why?—she has no wish to look into the garage which is the forbidden place. Still less to step into the garage where it is perpetual twilight and smells still (she believes) of the bluish sweetly-toxic gas that killed the mother and daughter.

Alexander has said, stay away. No need. Do you understand, Elisabeth?

Yes, she'd said. Of course.

I will be very, very unhappy with you if.

Briefly he'd considered (he said) shutting up the garage, securing it. But then—*why?* Whatever danger the garage once threatened is past.

Yet, the door to the forbidden place is opened. In the doorway shy as a bride Elisabeth stands.

Dry-eyed from insomnia. Aching, oversensitive skin.

Shadowy objects in the gloom. One of the household vehicles—an older BMW, belonging to Alexander but no longer used.

Like any garage this garage is used for storage. Dimly visible lawn furniture, gardening tools, flower pots, shelves of paint cans, stacks of canvas. Shadowy presences in the periphery of Elisabeth's vision.

The Saab in which *the deaths* occurred is gone of course. Long banished from the property. Elisabeth has never been told, has never inquired, but surmises that it was towed out of the garage, hauled away to a junk yard.

For no one would wish to drive, or to be a passenger in, a *death car.*

(Would the interior of the car continue to smell of death, if it still existed? Or does the odor of death fade with time?)

In the doorway Elisabeth stands. It is strangely peaceful here, on the threshold. Gradually her eyes become adjusted to the muted light and she has no need to grope for a switch, to turn on overhead lights.

The garage door is closed of course. You can see light beneath it,

obviously you must stuff towels along the entire length of the door to keep the sweet-poison air *in* and the fresh air *out.*

Blue buzz of air. The only symptom is peace.

Come! Hurry.

She is hurrying. She is breathless. On her knees on the bare plank floor in front of the narrow cupboard in the third-floor maid's room she reaches into the shadowy interior. Cobwebs in hair, eyelashes.

Wrapped inside a beautiful heather-colored mohair shawl riddled with moth holes.

Her hands shake. This must be one of N.K.'s diaries, unknown to Alexander!

The diary he'd found after her death, he'd destroyed. *To spare my son.*

Feminists had angrily criticized the husband's actions but Alexander remained unrepentant. Insisting it was his right—the diary was disgusting and vile (though he'd claimed not to have read it), and it was his property. His right as a father to spare his son echoes and reflections of the mother's *sick and debased mind.*

But Alexander is not here now, Elisabeth thinks. Alexander will not know.

The diary appears to be battered, water-stained. It is only one-quarter filled. The last diary of N.K.'s life.

At the makeshift desk Elisabeth dares to read in N.K.'s sharply slanted hand, in stark black ink. The low throaty voice of the poet echoes in her ears intimate as a caress.

fearful of harming the children
fearful of harming the children entrusted to her
begins with "the"—not "her"
telling herself they are not THE children, they are HER children

she does not want to carry the new baby on the stairs
fearful of dropping her slipping, falling
fear of injuring loving too much

(not the husband's child)
(does he know?—must know)

of course the husband knows a man must know
pillow over my face, he says so the children will not hear
will win custody you will never see them again
your disgusting poetry will be my evidence in a court of law
you are not a fit mother
not a fit human being

he has struck me with his hand. the back of his hand. hits me on the
chest, torso, thighs where my clothing covers the bruises. he says he will

take the children from me if I tell—anyone. if I tell my doctor. I must say, I am clumsy, I drink too much, take too much medication (even if I do not—not enough).

I must declare legally, I have invented these accusations against him.

I am a poet/I am a liar/I am sick & debased/I have loved others, not him/I am one who makes things gorgeously up.

days of joy, now it is a dark season
days of happiness I can hear echoing at a distance
he says I am not the beautiful young woman he married
I am another person, I am not that woman

to be a mother is to surrender girlhood
to be a mother is to take up adulthood

he says I am sick, finished unless I slash my wrists I am of no interest to anyone

knowing how I am vulnerable, wanting to die (sometimes)
welcomed me back, forgave me (he said) even as I forgave him (his cruelty)
his lies, he'd so adored me
but then it has been revealed, he has not forgiven me he will never love the baby he guesses is the child of another

as in Nature, the male will destroy the offspring of other males

(why does this surprise me? it does not surprise me)
a mistake to have confided in him, in a weak mood my fear of harming the children & he pretended to sympathize
then later, laughed at me in his eyes, hatred like agates

last night daring to say do it & get it over with

Elisabeth is so shocked she nearly drops the diary. For a long time she sits unmoving, staring at the page before her.

At last, hearing a sound outside the room, a tentative footstep. It is Stefan, is it?—the surviving child.

Stefan enters the room though Elisabeth has not invited him inside, nor even acknowledged him. Asks her what is that, what is she reading, and Elisabeth says it is nothing, and Stefan says, his voice rising, "Is it something of Mummy's? Is that what it is?" and Elisabeth starts to reply but cannot. Wraps the diary in the shawl to hide it, leans over the makeshift desk and with her body tries to shield it from the child's widened eyes.

11.

So very easy. Sinking into sleep.

Position yourself. Behind the wheel of the car, so calm.

First, you swallow pills with wine. Not too many pills, enough pills for solace. And the child, you must tend to him.

Dissolved in milk. Warm milk. Who would suspect? No one!

Start the motor. Lay your head against the back of the seat. Shut your eyes. The child's eyes. Wrap him in the shawl, in your arms.

Soon, you are floating. Soon, you are sinking. Soon, you are safe from all harm.

For days, unless it has been weeks, Elisabeth has been feeling feverish. Sick to her stomach. A fullness in her belly as if bloated with blood. Gorged with backed-up blood.

One day ascending the stairs she loses her balance, slips. It is a freak accident. It is (certainly not) deliberate. A sharp, near-unbearable pain in her right ankle, that has twisted, sprained. In her lower belly a seeping of blood, then a looser rush of blood, hot against her thighs, clotted. At first she thinks that she has wetted herself, in panic. She calls for help. Weakly, faintly, doesn't want to upset her husband, doesn't want to upset the child, so very lucky that Ana comes hurrying—"Oh, Mrs. Hendrick!"—and in the woman's eyes compassion, concern.

You may warm yourself in the shawl. That is for you.

Just seven weeks old. The tiny creature—"fetus." Not a pregnancy exactly—you wouldn't have called it.

Elisabeth is astonished, disbelieving. She'd been *pregnant?* How was that possible?

When he learns of the miscarriage (which is what Elisabeth's doctor calls it) Alexander is stunned. His face is gray with shock, distaste. "That's ridiculous. That couldn't be. You *were not pregnant.* The subject is closed."

12.

In her *Paris Review* interview N.K. said in jest, "The best suicides are spontaneous and unplanned—like the best sex.

"No more should you plan a suicide than you'd plan a kiss, or laughter."

True of N.K.'s earlier suicide attempts but not true of the actual suicide in a locked and secured garage in the house on Oceanview Avenue, Wainscott. *Life catches up with you, taps you on the shoulder.*

Towels stuffed beneath doors, a plotted and meditated death, motor of a car running, bluish toxic exhaust filling the air. Stink of exhaust, having to breathe it in order to breathe in precious toxic carbon monoxide; the child beside her sedated, too weak to resist; the child in the rear of the Saab less cooperative but too groggy to resist . . . Beautiful Clea, beautiful Stefan, children the mother hadn't deserved. In her deep unhappiness *calling us back, the kiss of oblivion.*

In the dimly lighted garage Elisabeth finds herself groping her way like a sleepwalker.

A powerful curiosity draws her. As water draws one dying of thirst.

Though Elisabeth has never been and is not suicidal.

This BMW, the older of Alexander's cars, seems to have been abandoned in the garage. Elisabeth is concerned that the battery might have died.

She will see! She will experiment.

The key to the BMW Elisabeth found after searching the drawers in Alexander's bureau. Loose in her pocket is the key now, and a handful of sleeping pills. Consoling!—though she has no intention of using the pills.

And in her hand a bottle of Portuguese wine, she'd struggled to open.

And the moth-eaten heather-colored mohair shawl that is yet beautiful, like wisps of cobweb.

Envy is the homage we pay to those whose hearts we don't know.
Envy is ignorance raised to the level of worship.

Just to enter the (forbidden) garage. To sit in the (forbidden) car. To turn on the ignition—the motor is *on!*

(If the ignition hadn't turned on, that would be the crucial sign. *Not now not you not for you.* But the ignition has turned on.)

Just to listen to music on the car radio. (But all Elisabeth can get is static.)

Just to drink from the bottle. Solace of wine, that might numb the ache between her legs where blood still seeps, nothing dangerous, no hemorrhage but more like weeping. *Not a real pregnancy, not for you.*

Like a woman with no manners drinking from the bottle. Hardly the wife of the house on Oceanview Avenue.

Homeless woman. Reckless, harridan. Alexander would be appalled but in her distracted state she'd forgotten a—what, what is it—wineglass . . .

The BMW motor is quiet. Loud humming, could be a waterfall. Bees at a distance. Oh, but Elisabeth has also forgotten—in her pocket, a handful of green capsules.

Turns off the staticky radio. Leans her head back against the top of the seat. *A mood is music.*

Very sleepy, tired. Even before the drone of the engine, the smell of the exhaust, tired. Weight of the air. Can hardly move.

One day. You will know when.

In the mohair shawl she is warm, protected. Warmth like a woman's arms. *Airy lightness. Like a kiss, or laughter.*

13.

Elisabeth?—*the first time the child has uttered her name.*

And the sound pierces her heart, so beautiful.

Small fists on the window of the car door close beside her head. Her heavy-lidded eyes are jarred open. With the strength of panic Stefan has managed to open the heavy car door, he is shouting at her—No! No! Wake up!

Pushing away her hand. Fumbling to turn off the ignition. Coughing, choking.

In that instant the motor ceases. Hard hum of the motor ceases.

Elisabeth is groggy, nauseated. Hateful stink of exhaust, the garage has filled with bluish fumes. Yet: Elisabeth wishes to insist that she is not serious, this has not been a serious act.

If she were serious she would not have behaved in such a way in the presence of the child. (In fact, she'd assumed that Stefan was at school. Why is Stefan not at school?)

Only a single capsule swallowed down with tart white wine. Just to calm her rapidly beating heart. No intention of anything further.

Wrapped in the beautiful moth-eaten mohair shawl. Shivering in delicious dread, anticipation. But now comes the frightened child crouching beside her. Pulling at her, clawing at her. With all the strength in his small being dragging her out of the car. As she stumbles he runs to press the button open the garage door.

A rattling rumbling noise like thunder . . .

Pulling at Elisabeth. On drunken legs, coughing and choking. Pleading with her—Get outside! Hurry!

Together staggering out of the garage into wet cold bright air smelling of the ocean.

Don't die, Elisabeth—*the child is begging.*

Don't die. I love you. *The child is begging.*

Never has Elisabeth heard her stepson speak to her in such a way. Never seen her stepson looking at her in such a way. Never such concern for Elisabeth, such love in his eyes.

And now that they are outside in the fresh clear air Stefan will tell Elisabeth a secret.

The most astonishing secret.

Not Mummy who'd pulled Stefan from the car three years ago, carried him out of the poisonous garage and upstairs in the house to (just barely) save his life. For Mummy had been unconscious, her head back at an angle as if her neck was broken, and little Clea unconscious wrapped for warmth in Mummy's shawl and Mummy's arms and no longer breathing.

Not the mother. Not her.

Stefan will explain: it had been the father who'd come home, who had saved him.

Alexander had entered the garage, he'd smelled the stink of the exhaust billowing from the rear of the car. Seen the hellish sight knowing at once what the desperate woman had done. And in that instant made his decision to let her die.

Do it! Do it, and be done.

There is no love in my heart for you. Die.

Alexander's decision not to rescue the mother and not to rescue the little girl wrapped in the shawl in the mother's arms. Only just the boy in the back seat of the Saab who was his son.

Blood of my blood, bone of my bone. My son.

Choking, coughing as he pulled the semi-conscious child out of the car. Seeing that the boy was still breathing, sentient. Not knowing if it was too late and the child's brain had been injured irrevocably but frantic to save him, the son. His son. Gasping for breath as he carried the seven-year-old out of the garage and kicked shut the door behind him.

Upstairs and in a panic hiding the boy in a closet. Not knowing what he was doing but knowing that he must do something. And not understanding at just that moment that he would claim to have discovered the boy in the closet, in his search for his son. And not understanding yet that the story would be, it had been the mother who'd carried the son upstairs, laid him on the closet floor, and shut the door.

The father's hands badly shaking. Still he'd have had time to return to the garage, to rescue the mother and the younger child if he had wished but he had not wished. Had not even turned off the motor, in his haste to save his son.

A brute voice urged, in terrible elation—Let them die, they are nothing to you. They are not of your blood.

Elisabeth will be stunned by this revelation. Elisabeth will grasp at the child's hands, to secure him.

You have never told anyone this, Stefan? Only me.

Only you.

And so it was murder, yet not murder. The father had only to wait as the garage filled up with poisonous haze, until the death of the woman was certain.

His excuse could be, he was agitated, confused. He was not himself. Had not planned—ever—to do such a thing. Never would he have murdered N.K. with his own hands. Never would he have wished the little girl Clea dead, though Clea was not his but another man's daughter.

One of the wife's lovers. Forever a secret from Alexander for in her diary he would discover and destroy there were codified names, obvious disguises. Would not know the identity of the little girl's father though he'd been rabid with jealousy for this unknown person and in his passion would have liked to murder him as well.

And so, it had happened. The deaths that were (the father would tell himself) accidents.

Yet, he'd taken time to arrange the towels beneath the door to the garage, as the woman had arranged them. For it was crucial, the poisoning should not cease until it had done its work.

Gauging the time. Though his thoughts came careening and confused. How many minutes more, before the woman he'd come to hate would be poisoned beyond recovery.

Twenty, twenty-five minutes . . . By then, he believed that the woman and the child must be dead, and their deaths could not be his fault. For the hand that had turned on the ignition was not Alexander's but the woman's.

In astonishment Elisabeth listens. Yet she is not so surprised for she has known the father's heart.

Stefan has saved her. It is wonderful to Elisabeth to learn that he has loved her all along, these many months of the most difficult year of her life.

Returning from school to save his stepmother. Daring to enter the garage, that was forbidden to him. Daring to yank open the heavy door of the BMW, to shut off the ignition. Daring to scream into her slackened face—No! No! Wake up.

In confusion and fright she'd flailed at him. Thinking at first that he was the furious husband.

Then, he'd hurried to open the garage door. Like rumbling thunder above her. Tugging at her, urging her from the death-car. Together staggering outside into the bright cold air of March.

In this bright cold air Elisabeth will run, run. Strength will flow back into her legs, her lungs will swell. Never has Elisabeth run so freely, alone or with another. She is suffused with joy. Light swells inside her, in the region of her heart. In her throat, into her brain. Behind her eyes that swell with tears. It is not too late, the child has not come too late to save her. Running hand in hand away from the shingle board house on Oceanview Avenue. Hand in hand away from the Hendrick family house and along the coarse pebbly shore wet from crashing froth-bearing surf Elisabeth and Stefan run. Giddy with relief for the cold Atlantic wind has blown the poisoned air away as if it had never existed. Rising on all sides now are gray sand dunes beautifully ribbed and rippled into which they can run, run and no one will follow.

JOYCE CAROL OATES is a recipient of the National Medal of Humanities, the National Book Critics Circle's Ivan Sandrof Lifetime Achievement Award, the National Book Award, the PEN/Malmud Award for Excellence in Short Fiction, and has been several times nominated for the Pulitzer Prize. She has written some of the most enduring fiction of our time, including the national bestsellers *We Were the Mulvaneys*; *Blonde,* which was nominated for the National Book Award; and the *New York Times* bestseller *The Falls*, which won the 2005 Prix Femina. Her most recent novel is *Night. Sleep. Death. The Stars.* She is the Roger S. Berlind Distinguished Professor of the Humanities at Princeton University and has been a member of the American Academy of Arts and Letters since 1978.

THE PROMISE OF SAINTS

ANGELA SLATTER

In the Church of Mary's Mercy, which sits upon a hill overlooking the sea, there lies a bejeweled saint, attended by nuns of various vintages. Girls and women come to her to pray or beg (some would say there's little difference) for one thing or another. Sometimes she hears, sometimes she does not. Or perhaps life simply takes its path without her attention or otherwise.

Back when she died and was laid here—so very long ago—her attendants, the sisters-that-were, dressed her in the richest of robes, a cloak with an ermine collar as if to keep the chill from her bones. There's no flesh on her, merely a fragile canvas of thin-thin skin, so she's also been wrapped in fine netting to keep all her component parts together and in roughly the right order and shape. Her organs were purportedly removed by her first curators and kept in jars, but no one's found them in many a year, so possibly they were carried off by someone with strange tastes, or simply thrown out by a careless sacristan.

Her teeth are fitted with braces made of rubies set in a gold framework; sapphires that might or might not echo the missing eyes sit in the sockets; and her skull is covered in a bonnet that looks like a constellation of diamond daisies. Epaulets made up of a rainbow of gems sit on the shoulders of her cloak, and beneath is a cloth-of-gold vest over her dress that helps keep her ribcage intact. The bony hands protruding from the bottom of the sleeves are encased in items that are a combination of rings and bracelets. Her legs are covered and if anyone's ever lifted her red woolen skirt (the hem worked with silver embroidery) to see if there's any adornment there, no one is admitting to it; indeed, no nun has any memory of her being moved for several lifetimes. The skeletal feet have been hung with silver chains dangled with tiny engraved foxes and bells.

She's been here a long time, the Sainted Maiden, lying on a bier in the tiny alcove to the left of the altar.

Tales are told, as they often are when the truth is lost, and they say she moves around at night. They say she dances across the green and purple marble squares of the nave as if at a wedding. Some say her dance is one of exultation, some say of defiance. But the fact is that no one knows anything about her, what her name was, who her people were (for no one in the town claims kinship), or even how she came to be venerated so.

Unprotected by barriers of any kind, the dust settles freely upon her, but no one's game to touch her—everyone's aware that disturbing the holy dead with anything more than entreaties is never a good idea—not even the Sisters who tend to her as the years of their lives march away. Certainly none of the supplicants, and there are many, can bring themselves to offer her the slightest contact. All they bring are demands, generally marital in nature.

The Hallowed Girl, it's said, was once a bride herself—although no one knows if the marriage was completed and consummated, or aborted, so her titles are varied and perhaps contradictory—and that's why these others come to beg what she may or may not have had.

Adalene first brought Elspeth to see the Saint when she was five. The child had shown no interest, no gratitude nor enthusiasm for her mother's hopes, but kept her eyes downcast, stepping deliberately on the cracks in the floor for all she was worth, little bitch. Adalene's grip on her daughter's hand was desperate and hard even to her as she pulled Elspeth along. Finally, they halted and Elspeth still didn't look up.

Not until Adalene said, "That'll be you, one day."

The girl raised her eyes then, took in the skeleton caught in its cocoon of tulle and wool and fur and gold. The gems encrusting it sucked in the light of the torches but threw out less than they ate, it seemed. Elspeth looked at the skull with its jaw slightly askew, slightly ajar, no eyes except those gleaming sapphires hard as hearts, and she screamed.

Elspeth thought her mother meant she'd be dead. That someone would stick her with shiny pins and make her into an exhibit, as pretty and useless as a butterfly under glass. She took it for a threat, and it was a long while before she calmed. A long time before her mother could get her to listen that they were there to ask for a blessing: that Elspeth was to beg the Sainted Maiden for a good husband.

Elspeth had no such desire and couldn't imagine ever wanting a husband. At that very moment all she truly wished and wanted was to never lay eyes on the hallowed, hollowed girl ever again.

It was then that one of the nuns—the youngest of them but already nearing fifty—drawn by Elspeth's screech, came over from whatever task she'd been attending to in the shadows to place a broad palm against the girl's cheek. The woman was terribly tall, her face gentle and her smile absent-minded, but there was something about her touch that leeched away much of Elspeth's fear, or at least enough that she could ask a question.

"What's her name?"

"She has none, only titles."

"Everyone should have a name," said Elspeth.

The nun looked at the girl properly this time, actually focused on her and the smile was different, not simply something she aimed at everyone. "And yet she has none."

It made Elspeth terribly sad and she wished aloud for the Bride to be named and loved; she wished with the same strength as her mother had wished for her to be well-married. Such very different things, one propelled by a kind of greed, the other by a sort of kindness. And that latter desire removed whatever vestiges of fear might have remained, so that Elspeth did something no one had done in untold years: she touched the Hallowed Girl.

Small fingers to skeletal digits, the most glancing of contacts—soft flesh against dusty bones, a small shudder of shock—but it was a touch nonetheless. The first in so very, very long. Whether it was that or the sort of magic stirred up by wishes no one will ever know. Whatever the cause, something was woken.

That night, the Maiden visited Elspeth for the first time.

It would not be the last.

Perhaps it was in her sleeping or perhaps her late waking—it was so difficult to tell, but Elspeth could have sworn she felt the tender touch of bony hands, felt the shifting of her bedclothes and mattress beneath a weightless weight, felt the breath that was not breath flowing across her face as the Maiden whispered to her. The Hallowed Girl, the Sainted Maiden, the Immaculate Bride told Elspeth that she would be her one and only. That Elspeth was her truest love and would tend to the Saint as lovingly as any wife. Elspeth would require no husband for, in return, all of her needs would be met in the Church of Mary's Mercy. And that the Saint would, on their wedding day, offer her the highest of bride prices.

In the moonlight that flooded the room the Hallowed Girl touched a finger to Elspeth's, the one that leads straight to the heart, and in her dream or waking she saw a silver ring—tiny foxes chasing each other, nose to tail—form on that finger and glint. It soon sank into her flesh, but the following morning she could still feel it there beneath the skin. A promise and a chain.

Adalene took her daughter to the Saint all those years ago and hasn't she had reason to regret it ever since?

What she'd hoped would result in a profitable match had seemed to simply have developed into a religious mania. From that time forward Elspeth had spent part of her days (and some of her nights, if Adalene did but know it) in the Church, tending the shrine of the Hallowed Girl.

Frankly, Adalene had despaired. It's tremendously hard to matchmake if one of the parties has a tendency to not appear when they are meant to. Numberless days was Adalene left clutching a damp scone and rapidly cooling cup of tea in the sitting room of some other mother-on-the-make, while Elspeth failed to arrive for a meeting with a potential suitor and his dam. Nothing Adalene said or did made a whit of difference.

But then, ridiculously, one of those potential suitors found her daughter's lack of interest appealing. Fascinating, apparently. He pursued her in spite of his own mother's warnings—oh, Adalene knew there'd been warnings, she'd seen the woman's expression as her son's questioning about Elspeth became positively fervid.

"Can she weave?"

"Yes." *Barely.*

"Can she manage a household?"

"Of course." *An outright lie that would only be discovered too late.*

He'd nodded. "She carries herself well, I have seen her around town and her posture is notable. She will wear finery beautifully, that is an important thing for a rich man's wife."

"Yes." *A truth at last.*

Elspeth's husband-to-be is prosperous, precisely the sort Adalene would have wished for herself if she'd got another chance, but her combination of ill temper—which renders discontent as her constant companion—and plain face closed that avenue. Had she been sweeter of one or the other, she might well have had suitors lining up at her cottage door. As a widow, she was regarded with pity by the young women of the town; the older ones, knowing better, called her blessed. She views them all with contempt though she smiles politely at them in the market square and when she takes in their mending, or whenever she'd offered her daughter to wife.

But this oncoming son-in-law pleases her for the moment—he will no doubt disappoint in time, but for now he is sufficiently unknown a quantity to furnish a sort of contentment for Adalene. He'll furnish some financial stability too and that will smooth over a multitude of sins.

Adalene only knows she'll be as close to happy as she's likely to get when Elspeth is wed, and that day cannot come too soon, before the girl ruins even that.

* * *

The Saint had promised so many things.

In the silent space between the shadows of the Church, and in the dim twilight of her visits to Elspeth's bedroom, words had come like covenants on a breath that smelled like nothing from the living. *Freedom. Love. Eternity.*

Some days, when sunlight brings clarity, Elspeth wonders if she is mad. If that moment all those years ago when fear burned through her like wildfire hadn't consumed her sanity. Her mother certainly thinks so, what with her refusals to marry, her defiance. Though Adalene can be unpleasant, Elspeth loves her mother. She believes her mother loves her despite the terrible things she says. The girl knows her mother wants to provide for both their futures, but Elspeth's was mapped out sixteen years ago, wasn't it? And through Adalene's own actions did she but know it.

Her mother's despair was what caused Elspeth's silence when the suitor appeared at the door, avid and ardent and determined. That and the promises her Saint had made, that there'd be no wedding, no matter what Adalene coaxed or cajoled or threatened. That and the knowledge that skeletal saints are notoriously bad at providing a dowry or portion for a widowed mother's old age. That and the suspicion that perhaps she was addled, holding onto the promise of a fever dream long stale. So she'd remained silent when the proposal was made and accepted; she behaved like a girl about to be wed to the man who sought her.

But she clung, too, to a thin thread of hope. To the fact that the Saint on one of those long-ago nights of shadows and breaths and caresses, also promised the one thing that no one else has ever had, or at least not in the longest time, so long ago it wasn't recorded or remembered.

Ultimately Elspeth knew that the vow she'd held most dear was the promise of the Saint's very own name.

Jasque is a wool merchant, or rather the son of a recently deceased one. His mother still holds the reins of enterprise, but Jasque is free to act as though he makes important decisions. He's quite happy to live with a heavy purse and light responsibilities.

He could have chosen a better bred, but less beautiful bride—indeed his mother, Ernestine, had urged him in the direction of a girl whose left eye turned but a little, and whose family owned many flocks of sheep. But he decided the lovely Elspeth was for him precisely because it seemed he could not have her.

Ernestine knows how troublesome beautiful girls can be (she was one herself), what with wills of their own and everyone falling over themselves to please in hope of their favors, or even just a glance, kind or indifferent it matters not. But her son's a fool for a pretty face and all she can do is love him anyway and shrug. Oh and tie up whatever parts of the business she can in legal machinations, and hide profits so it's hard for her boy to fritter them away on expensive offerings, and harder still for a girl to extract gold from the spinning of wool like some voracious fairy-tale princess.

But this girl, this Elspeth, doesn't seem to want anything; she makes neither demand nor request; she's nothing like that grasping parent of hers. She's polite when given a gift, but there's seemingly no greed in her; and she's pious, too, spends part of every day at the Church, helping the last aging nun to tend the shrine. This makes Ernestine, quite naturally, suspicious. She's never known a girl to look at her very fine son with his very fine robes and very fine face (which, admittedly, will go to fat soon enough just like his father so she'd best get him married off quickly), and the heavy coin purse at his belt and not want *something*. Therefore there must be, she reasons, something that rides beneath the surface, some need or desire that cannot be seen by daylight.

She doesn't say this to her son, for her mother's heart is soft, no matter that her mind is practical and wary. Besides, fewer things drive a man into another woman's arms than a mother's displeasure and, though her son's already made his decision, there's a tiny hope in her breast that something will happen to make the machinery of this match fall apart. Tomorrow her boy will marry and that will be the end of it, and Ernestine will have plenty of time to discover her daughter-in-law's faults and flaws.

Jasque, however, has his own concerns though he'd never voice them to his mother.

Tomorrow his bride is to walk barefoot along the path from her home to the Church of Mary's Mercy. She'll be dressed in a dress heavy with seed pearls and silver thread (paid for from Jasque's pocket). Then they'll stand in front of the altar and say their vows before the priest. Jasque knows that the source of his disquiet will be lying not so many feet away, just out of sight, but there all the same, like some mote in his eye that cannot be removed.

Another thing he's never mentioned to Ernestine: Elspeth's acceptance of his proposal was made by *her* mother. He'd had to propose in front of Adalene for the woman protected her daughter's virtue like a dragon on a mound of gold, and Jasque has no good reason to claim she was wrong to do so. But when he'd offered his suit, it was the older woman who'd said *yes*. The girl had looked over his shoulder as if there was someone standing behind him, someone else to whom she might answer.

She'd smiled, batted her lashes, and seemed to acquiesce.

But she has ever refused to meet him at night, no matter how he's pressed her, and she's also refused to stop her devotions at the Church. She did so gently and politely as she does everything, but her refusal was no less adamant. The last of the Sisters would soon be gone, she'd said, and someone must be there to take her place.

He had been displeased, but was smart enough not to press. Yet, spoiled only child of too-indulgent parents as he was, Jasque was not one to take "no" for an answer.

And Jasque was certain that she could not serve what no longer existed.

Elspeth wears her wedding dress to church the next day, although the Hallowed Girl has promised there is to be no wedding, at least not to Jasque. The gown is beautiful and it seems perfect for the occasion. When will she get a chance to wear it again? Besides, it seems only right to come to the Bride in such finery.

As she walks, barefoot, she notices that there's no one by the side of the road and a weight lifts from her shoulders. This is good: she takes it to mean the Saint's promise is true—otherwise there would be crowds, waiting and watching, throwing flower petals and wishes for happiness, fertility and long life. Her steps become much lighter, swifter. But when Elspeth turns into the last windy street, the one that runs up to the hill upon which Mary's Mercy sits, it is *there* that she sees a crowd, and the breath in her stops for long seconds.

She continues on, however; she cannot turn tail and run, not now. And as she approaches the congregation she realizes there's no sense of revelry and no one looks happy; this gives her courage. Townsfolk cluster in the churchyard, gossiping in groups.

Elspeth keeps walking. At the great double doors with their bands of silver engraved with a series of skeletal figures dressed in funereal finery are Adalene and Ernestine, both wailing in the arms of the remaining nun—the one whose touch first brought Elspeth's heart to the Bride. Ernestine's howls are renewed as she sees the daughter-in-law-to-be, but the energy is mostly spent, the emotion behind them is broken. Adalene echoes her much as a cat does another, trying to outdo a rival. Elspeth wonders how long they have been here.

The elderly nun, expression serene, makes no effort to stop Elspeth as she enters the church. Whatever lies inside is meant for her gaze. Around her finger, she feels the ghostly ring shifting, moving up through her flesh, strangely painless.

Light comes in through the colored glass of the windows, painting the aisle and pews in a rainbow, yet the Maiden's bier remains in shadow, so it takes some moments for Elspeth to make out the details of the scene.

On the floor are some gems that have fallen off the corpse, and a thick wooden cudgel too, as if dropped by a careless hand. The Hallowed Girl still reclines in her place, skeletal head on the red velvet pillow, jewels catching the light and eating it.

But Elspeth's Bride does not lie alone.

Jasque is in her arms, held tight as a lover, his head tilted to rest on her shoulder as if he sleeps, though his eyes stare. There is blood, quite a lot of it, dripping down and pooling and seeping through the cracks between the purple and green tiles; some of the spatters look like flowers blooming. As Elspeth draws nearer she can see that the Bride's ribs have broken through her fine netting and have entwined with Jasque's just as lovers' fingers might.

Elspeth's first duty as a wife will be to unlock them.

The promise of saints is expensively bought.

But soon she will know her beloved's true name.

ANGELA SLATTER is the author of the supernatural crime novels *Vigil*, *Corpselight*, and *Restoration*, as well as ten short story collections, including *The Girl With No Hands and Other Tales*, *Sourdough and Other Stories*, *The Bitterwood Bible and Other Recountings*, and *The Heart Is a Mirror for Sinners & Other Stories*. Two gothic fantasy novels set in her Sourdough and Bitterwood worlds, *All These Murmuring Bones* and *Morwood,* are forthcoming. She has won a World Fantasy Award, a British Fantasy Award, a Ditmar, an Australian Shadows Award and six Aurealis Awards. Slatter's short stories have appeared in Australian, UK, and US "best of" anthologies. Her work has been translated into Bulgarian, Chinese, Russian, Italian, Spanish, Japanese, Polish, French, and Romanian. She has an MA and a PhD in Creative Writing.

BURROWING MACHINES

SARA SAAB

T here was a strange agitation to London that summer from the
very beginning, a hormonal moodiness, a belly heat, if cities
could be said to go through such things. We had enough sunshine to
roll around in, but twilight snapped to dark between one sentence and
the next, like someone'd tossed a quilt over the giant lamp of the sun.
They'd found all those new fossils while digging up the duck pond at
Hampstead Heath and they shut the footpath the whole way round.
People like me who were barely getting themselves out the door for a jog
in the park in the late afternoon haze gave up on exercise entirely.

By May I was sleeping from the end of my night shift all the way
through to my final cut-the-bullshit alarm at eight p.m. I'd crawl out
of bed feeling like death warmed up. I'd put on my orange hi-viz and
cargoes, and a stripe of lipstick, God knows who for, and walk down to
Camden Town Station with my hard hat's suspensions pushing against
the blood-beat of a headache at my temples.

The drilling work in the tunnel, at least, started miraculously on
schedule. I lost myself for underground hours that summer planning
the reroute of London's Victorian water mains around the burrowing
machines' trajectory, the construction of temporary wall struts and the
boring of holes for soil samples. I spent most of my waking hours fifteen

meters below ground in a dark punctuated by machine headlights, flashlight beams, and shadows, and on the rare occasions I met Adarsh at the Old Man's Arms for a fish supper and a dry cider before work, he'd give me that look that told me he thought I was in urgent need of rescue from my life.

"No one but you would be this into *burrowing*, Jo," he said when I met him in early June.

"We haven't had a new tunnel for the Northern Line in three decades," I reminded him around a tartar-sauced chunk of battered cod.

"How filthy is that dirt you're shoveling anyway? All London's millennia of shite, and bones, and bubonic plague, and *more* shite."

"It doesn't bother me. If you saw these giant tunneling machines do what they do, I think you'd appreciate it."

Adarsh sipped his craft ale, eyebrows high enough on his forehead that they almost skimmed his turban.

"And you hear the river through some of the walls," I added.

"The Thames?"

"No, you numpty. The River Fleet."

"The underground stream." Adarsh poked a stuffed olive with a toothpick. Made me think of Fran, who'd hated all foods that didn't belong in sandwich bread.

"Proper river. High and low tides. Currents. Everything. At high tide it vibrates in the stone."

The River Fleet—London's geologic minotaur, winding North to South, fallen out of favor, diminished and trapped underground in its labyrinth of sewers back in the eighteenth century. The tourist-friendly experience was the faint hush of it through a tiny sewer grate on Ray Street in Clerkenwell. Being separated from the Fleet by just an underground tunnel wall in the small hours of morning was an entirely different thing.

But that was just trivia. None of it would matter until later.

In late June, we started to slip behind on the tunnel expansion project.

When I looked at Annabel's Gantt charts, it all seemed minor—engineers taking unexplained sick days, a pervasive anxiety that stretched ten-minute breaks to twenty. Like that same out-of-sortsness that had been weighing on me was spreading.

The first really observably weird thing happened on a Saturday night, two hours after the last Northern Line train. We were doing a tunnel walkthrough when one of our junior engineers, Philip, noticed a hole punched in the wall of the existing southbound Tube tunnel.

Gray moon rocks of concrete and a pile of dust dampened in the maintenance crawlspace beside the train tracks. We stuck our flashlights through the hole, wide as a crockpot, to the void on the other side. Our beams spotlighted the adjoining space. Glaze and slime on old brickwork. Water babbled along well below the level of the hole.

"I didn't know the Fleet flowed right alongside here," Philip said, and ran a hand round the hole's ragged edge. "That's maybe half a meter of concrete."

"Are there burrowing machines on the other side? In the Thames Water tunnels?" I asked no one in particular. I knew there weren't. There shouldn't be.

"Nah," said Philip.

"Structural weakness," I said. But the concrete around the hole was sound. No sagging, no hairline cracks, no subsidence.

What it looked like to me? Like someone had battered through the tunnel wall—from the River Fleet's adjoining tunnel, into ours.

They filed a police report and launched the obligatory Health and Safety investigation, but by mid-July, nothing. After another week, Thames Water's guys patched up the hole. We bolted in some steel mesh to reinforce the concrete along that segment of the Northern Line.

The tunnel expansion was finding its feet again. We had a thirty-meter span of freshly excavated tunnel we could walk into upright, arms outstretched, and more importantly, we hadn't burst a single Thames Water pipe under my watch.

Privately, I tried to adjust myself out of my funk.

Adarsh talked me into a deal on twenty hot yoga passes at a studio in Chalk Farm. I stupidly showed up for the first lesson in tracksuit bottoms and a cotton sweater (Adarsh hadn't told me what hot yoga was), and left so dehydrated I barely went to the loo for two days. I gave Adarsh nineteen passes back. Then I got together with his friend Aman a few times—awkward daytime rendezvous because of my flipped schedule. I bought myself an urban spa retreat, booked a week off in autumn, signed up for a wine delivery service. Cheap screw-top bottles of picpoul. The crates took over my tiny kitchen, but what do you do.

Did it help? I thought so. I did. I felt cared for, if only by my own self. But the world wasn't done with me, and neither was my brain.

So, I suppose, first, the dreams. About Fran. Dream-Fran. Fish-Fran.

That July she turned up night after night, carrying the blue fishing rod, our Christmas gift to our father, the one I'd been toying with when she wandered off. Glossy as a brand-new car, that rod, and I can still see the polish of it nearly three decades on. In dream-Fran's other hand was the tin bucket we used for treasure unearthed on mudlarking adventures along the bank of the Thames.

When I remember my sister, I remember her with her braids and wellies, her missing teeth. But dream-Fran wasn't like that. She was indistinct—not like she'd been rubbed out or sun-faded, but sort of like she was made of squid skin. Her eyes were black dots in jelly flesh, her nose two upward punctures you'd miss if you weren't looking. The bucket and rod were what tipped me off that it was her.

Fish-Fran didn't do anything in the dreams, just hung around me. I couldn't see where we were exactly, but it felt like we were in the tunnels, that same cozy swaddled feeling and layering of shadows.

"Where did you go?" I asked her, every night.

"I went to find the mouth of the Thames that daddy talked about," she said.

Or, "I was hunting for rubies and sapphires in the mud."

Or, "I went to look for something important in the water."

"Are you alive?" I asked her.

But instead of assortments of answers, I got nothing, or once, the touch of her jelly skin on mine.

London is so rammed with stories it's hard to connect the dots across the width and depth of it. But now that I've pieced it all together, something else happened in July, the first clue to really hang onto. A piece of a puzzle no one wanted to see completed.

The fossils from Hampstead Heath went to the paleontologists. They measured and prodded them and said: an ancient organism, amphibious, big, really big. We don't have a name for it yet.

Anyway. That's what there was. Dad had let us fish with the glossy blue rod, but said we couldn't eat anything we caught in the Thames: too sickly, too poisoned. Throw it back, he'd say.

London and its millennia of shite and history, like Adarsh said.

On the night of Saturday, July 23rd, the red LED of the station clock showing a half hour to midnight, I was an endless up-escalator away from both the trains and engineering crew, chatting to the station supervisor in the ticket hall over a cup of Darjeeling and a pack of chocolate digestives. It was some banter about the new line, how convenient it would be to have a direct route from Camden Town to Luton Airport once our work was done.

There was a slight rumbling beneath my work boots and then a metallic scraping sound. More rumbling. A short time later a ruffled announcement rang out on the Tannoy.

"Inspector Sands to Northern Line southbound platform four." *Inspector Sands*: code for an emergency at a Tube station, among Londoners an open secret.

We were already on the escalator, taking the steps as nimbly as our boots would allow, my stomach a bony fist.

Downstairs, pandemonium. It was the last southbound service on a Saturday night. Drunk passengers hammered wildly on the windows of the train from within and from the platform; its doors were still closed. The train driver had abandoned her cab, was shouting *I don't know* at the platform supervisor, then, louder, at the station supervisor who arrived along with me.

Below the periodic shattering of glass under blows from the train's emergency escape hammers, there was a sound like a faint waterfall, and a stench like a swamp. The waterfall noise was loudest at the dark maw of the tunnel where the train had been holding at a red signal.

The rails flooded in a minute. Gray water began to rise toward plat-form level. We had engineering crews not far away reviewing plans and prepping the night's work, as well as passengers onboard the stricken train. There weren't enough people at that time of night for a crush, but I remember a lot of panicked milling and a nervous kind of shouting that reminded me of the animal pens at my aunt Calista's dairy farm. After we got the train's doors open, we focused on the most critical thing: getting everybody the hell out of the station.

Upstairs, after every passenger had been evacuated and emergency services had arrived, it was Philip who was first to realize it.

"Jo, can I talk to you for a minute?" He pulled me aside. "Hope-fully I'm all muddled up, okay? But that was a nine-car service. The last service is always nine cars. I left the excavation as soon as I heard it. Ran down to see. Counted the carriages." He counted idly on his fingers now, hesitated on the second set of five. "The eighth carriage I could see was still sort of in the tunnel, it hadn't come all the way out, and it was dark behind." Philip could barely look at me. There was an awful look in his eyes, a burden I could tell he was about to pass to me, a live grenade.

"There were only eight. Only eight cars."

"Where was the ninth?"

Philip shook his head. He was two years out of apprenticeship, a competent, honest kid from South London whose mother had forced him into the vocational program when all he wanted was to record drill albums and chase his sliver of fame from club to club.

"No ninth carriage back there, Jo," he said. "Just water and stink and fucking darkness."

Within a week there were names and pictures: fifteen souls who'd made the mistake of choosing the wrong carriage, the wrong train, the wrong bloody night. I scrolled past the news story because I couldn't look at their faces. Most were university students; there were two cousins on a stag night; a pensioner coming back from the theater with his grandson.

There was a protracted search: divers, the Fire Brigade, daily press briefings. They'd keep looking, they said. They wouldn't give up. But they found nothing. The ninth carriage had disappeared.

The Northern Line was out of service citywide, our worksite off-limits. I made sure to take no pleasure from rejoining the world of the living. I barricaded myself in bed with the curtains drawn and experimented with sleeping pills that would stop me from dreaming of fish-Fran.

Adarsh called enough times that I switched my mobile off. I didn't have the stomach for him, for anyone. Or, not quite: I would have talked to my father if he were still alive. I would've done anything to speak to him.

Another week and an emergency dam was put into the River Fleet's tunnel. This allowed an engineering team—thankfully not mine—to drain the southbound Northern Line track.

In early August, they'd drained enough water and shifted enough rubble that they found the hole.

It was massive, a breach tall and wide as a Routemaster. It was in the same section as the last hole, an implosion of concrete that'd torn through our mockery of a reinforcement mesh like a tongue through a sheet of tissue. Measurements confirmed the hole was well big enough to let through a train carriage, if you could get around the logistics of a twenty-five ton block of metal detaching from train and track and maneuvering through to a parallel tunnel.

The search operation scoured as much of the underground river as it could. And found nothing. All of London turned its attention to the River Thames, especially where the Fleet let out into its postcard-perfect sibling through the embankment wall beneath Blackfriars Bridge.

"How can a whole train car of people go missing underground?" asked Adarsh, when he'd insisted on a fish supper enough times that I had to oblige or risk him attempting some kind of intervention.

"I don't know." Speech tasted wooden. I couldn't touch my dinner, nursed a double vodka soda even though the late daylight was obscenely cheerful. "It doesn't make sense."

But of course I speculated—all I did lately was speculate—trying out ideas too laced with impossibility to be anything but thoughts I had in private. I wondered how many of us had made the same leap, sensed the same wrongness about the city in spite of the smiling glare of its streets.

I wondered what we'd upset. What history we'd woken.

No brand of sleeping pills was strong enough to make Fran go away.

By the muggy middle of August I was becoming accustomed to her following me around the subterranean tunnels of my dream world.

"Where are we going, Jo?" she asked one night in her five-year-old voice, skipping ahead of me down a tunnel, the flashlit shadow of the fishing rod extending long and black and hook-ended before her.

"Anywhere. Shall we go and find you?"

She reached a gray, oozing hand toward me. "I'm right here."

"And other times?" I asked. "Where are you when I'm awake?"

"I'm nowhere there. I don't live there. It's too wet." I took my sister's hand. We walked side by side. The feel of her repulsed me, but I clung to my memory of real Fran as hard as I could.

"And I like swimming, but not *that* kind of swimming," said Fran.

"What kind of swimming?" I asked. The tunnel was tight. My shoulders scraped wet brick.

"Swimming until you can't see *London Bridge Is Falling Down*. Till you can't see Jo or Daddy. Swimming until you get hurt."

"But there's none of that bad swimming now," I said.

Fran stopped. She set down the mudlarking bucket and put steamed-dumpling fingers to the damp wall of the tunnel.

"Yes there is, Jo. I feel it. It's back. You and daddy can't make it go away."

"Can you?" I asked.

"No," said Fran in a singsong. "Nobody can."

We went back to work on the tunnel that week. It was almost too somber to bear. Not a single joke, not a sloppy innuendo, not a crack about the weather, not even the reliable no-daylight vampire analogy. Not once. But the vibrations of the burrowing machines still soothed me, I suppose. I felt more myself than I had in a long time.

The project was two months behind, but no one mentioned it. Not even Annabel-of-the-Gantt-charts dared breathe a word about deadlines after what had happened.

And late was better than never. Our fresh thirty-meter excavation was soon double that. We were doing good work.

One night we got a little careless, detonated a badly calibrated blasting emulsion to loosen stubborn bedrock too close to the soft side wall. And we had on our hands another breach between Tube tunnel and river tunnel, this time a small one, fist-sized, likely harmless.

Philip brought me over to assess the damage.

"The Fleet must be at low tide," I said.

"How do you want to fix it?" he asked.

"I reckon cement, this time," I said. Ancient brickwork on the Fleet's side had been damaged by the blast, chunks of it missing. There was a peephole gap clear through. I put my ear against it as if it were a subterranean conch shell.

The dirge of the buried river, soft and insistently there.

"Jo?"

"Go get the drilling crew and Thames Water's engineer, please."

"Yes boss." Philip's flashlight beam bounced away toward the mouth of the excavation.

I was alone.

I knelt in front of the breach, waterlogged rock and silt cool against the padded knees of my cargoes.

I can't describe why I got so close. I felt turned around, turned upside down, like the furniture of my life was hanging from the ceiling. I wanted to sleep in the sunshine and rave all night. Wanted to compress London to a snow globe, then to a point. Wanted to swim in the Thames and take that impure brown water into my lungs.

There was dripping and burbling and my breathing overtop, a symphony.

I shone my flashlight through. On the other side, a blinding, slick, prismatic reflection, no depth. Bulk, right up close.

I took a work glove off. And I touched. Felt the give and muscle of an enormous living thing.

I suppose all stories are passed along with cheap words, tinsel and streamers. I know there's nothing I can really say. And maybe the moment you touch a monster and don't draw back is the moment you become one, molt your humanity. But I'd never felt so old and I'd never felt so buried alive. The expanses and alleys and green spaces of London were at that moment barely pockets of oxygen, barely enough for a day's survival in a very, very long life.

And then it was gone. And Philip was back.

"You probably have this under control," I said, because I didn't, and I hurried toward the industrious snake of the up-escalator, my body a bundle of broomsticks wrapped in leather.

We completed the tunnel in the autumn of the following year. I attended the ribbon cutting ceremony for the new Northern Line service— Camden Town to Luton Airport—in a pinstripe jacket and pencil skirt I'd dry-cleaned for the occasion. They stood me somewhere near the back, which was fine by me. I'd been offered a plus-one but didn't invite Adarsh. I wanted to be there by myself.

Then, around Christmas, under a frosted Blackfriars Bridge, curls of metal chassis still glossy with the livery of a Northern Line train began to let out into the Thames where the mouth of the Fleet was. They ran dragnets at the outlet for a month or more. No human remains were recovered.

Around the same time a new species of amphibian was discovered in the shallows of the Thames. The Royal Society wanked and self-congratulated for weeks. The specimens were thought to be juveniles, or, crazy as it sounded, larvae. They were proper big babies, long as a human arm.

The tabloids published an exposé, all of them printing the same pixelated photo of an alleged specimen alongside a strip of measuring tape. It had hundreds of needle teeth and kind of sad, mopey, monochrome eyes and a keratin knob on its forehead and—most importantly—what appeared to be the yellow strap of a carriage handle embedded in its eel-like, translucent flesh. But tabloids are tabloids, and London is chock-full of stories. So people forget.

Oh, and the fossils in Hampstead Heath's duck pond had a name now. They called the prehistoric beast the Dendan, after a mythical fish in the *Arabian Nights*. Said it was likely king of the aquatic food chain in its time, being bigger than a galleon, with a carnivore's teeth and a stomach the size of a hotel room. A good one. A penthouse suite.

You'd think more people would have made the connection. Maybe I find it easier to believe impossibilities than others do. I don't know.

I climbed out of my funk, little by little. The dreams mostly stopped. I like to think Fran had told me all I needed to know.

Now when I think about our terrible last day with Fran on the bank of the Thames, I can't help but see it differently. Less like me being distracted and losing my little sister when our father went to fetch a pail of bait from the car. Less like her being picked up by a dirty and depraved pervert. More like Fran seeing the prismatic writhe of fish in the shallows, wading out to try to catch one, or to play.

I force myself to imagine it was quick after that, the bad swimming, the hurt.

Anyway, it's all guesswork and fantasy. I don't see the harm in building a sand fortress that protects your heart a little better.

That's that. They asked me to work on the eastbound expansion of the Central Line, but I said no thanks. I enrolled in a paleozoology diploma course. Lectures at nine a.m. every other day. I'd forgotten how frantic London is during rush hour, how many lives there are to be shuttled along its roads and its bridges and tunnels. Deaths, births, seasons. How many stories the city can absorb like a sponge.

SARA SAAB was born in Beirut, Lebanon. She now lives in North London, where she has perfected her resting London face. Her current interests are croissants and emojis thereof, amassing poetry collections, and coming up with a plausible reason to live on a sleeper train. Her fiction has been published in venues including *Clarkesworld*, *The Dark*, *Anathema*, *Shimmer*, *Beneath Ceaseless Skies*, and *The Year's Best Science Fiction: Thirty-Fifth Annual Collection*. She is a 2015 graduate of the Clarion Writers' Workshop.

ABOUT THE O'DELLS

PAT CADIGAN

I was just a little girl when Lily O'Dell was murdered.

This was before everyone was connected to the internet and people posted things online straight from cell phones. Infamy was harder to achieve back then but Lily O'Dell's murder qualified. It was the worst crime ever committed in the suburb of Saddle Hills, or at least the goriest. One night in June, Lily's abusive husband Gideon finally did what he'd been threatening to do for the two years they'd been married, using a steak knife from the set her sister had given them as a wedding present.

The police had already been regular visitors to the O'Dell house. Lily had pressed charges the first couple of times. Then a woman officer mentioned a restraining order and a jail term instead of probation and community service. After that, Lily always gave the cops some prefab story, like she'd fallen down the cellar stairs and hit the cement floor face-first and when Gideon had tried to help her up, she'd been so dizzy she'd fallen *again*. Was she a klutz or what? Maybe she needed remedial walking-downstairs lessons, ha, ha, but not cops coming between her and her lawfully wedded husband, no way, José!

Anywhere else, Lily O'Dell's murder might have been predictable but people didn't get murdered in Saddle Hills. They didn't leave their doors unlocked—that era was long gone—but the streets were safe, the schools were topnotch, and all the parks had the newest playground equipment and zero perverts lurking near the swings. This was the true-blue suburban American dream and the O'Dells didn't fit in.

For one thing, they didn't have kids and for another, they weren't even homeowners—they lived in one of the neighborhoods' few rental properties. No one expected they'd last long. Sooner or later, one of them would leave the other, who would skip out on the lease. Or they'd decide to start over somewhere else and skip out together. The company that owned the place would keep their damage deposit, shampoo the carpets, and rent to people who didn't need the police to break up their fights.

Instead, Gideon O'Dell chased his wife around the block and through several backyards before catching her in front of our house. He stabbed her so many times, the knife broke and he was too blind with rage to notice—he just kept pounding with the handle until it slipped out of his grip. Everybody said when the cops arrived, he was crawling around looking for the blade.

And I slept through the whole thing. At four, I slept like the dead.

Mr. Grafton in the house across from ours had some kind of special power attachment for his garden hose. From my bedroom window, I watched him using it on the spot where the O'Dells had played out the final scene of their marriage. It didn't look to me like there was anything left. When the FOR SALE sign appeared on his front lawn, I figured he was tired of power-spraying the road, which he'd started doing at least twice a week.

It was more than that, as I learned from my favorite hiding-place behind the living room sofa. My father told my mother and my older sister Jean (who at thirteen enjoyed the privilege of *adult conversation*) that Mr. Grafton's wife forced him to go to the doctor. Now he had medicine that was supposed to make him stop power spraying the road. He told my father he didn't like how it made him feel. Besides, he wasn't a *nutjob*. He hadn't *hallucinated* the O'Dell killing, it had *really happened.* So it wasn't *his* fault that when he looked out his window at night, he could see it *again,* as clearly as if it were happening right that very moment.

My mother said Mr. Grafton was such a gentle man, he could barely bring himself to pull a weed. Jean said that explained why Mrs. G did all the gardening but not why Mr. G had lost his marbles.

I expected my parents to jump on her for that. But to my surprise, my father said, "No, honey, Gideon O'Dell lost his marbles, and one of the worst things about people like him is the effect they have on everyone around them."

"Yeah, I bet Lily O'Dell would be the first to agree with you," Jean said.

That got her a scolding. My father told her what had happened to Lily O'Dell was a tragedy, not a joke; my mother said it was bad luck to disrespect the dead. Then Jean peered over the back of the sofa and found me. "Hey, what do you call a little pitcher with big ears?" she said.

"Gale," my parents said in unison. My father reached over, picked me up by the back of my overalls, and sat me on his lap. He started lecturing me about sneaking around and listening to private conversations. But I knew he wasn't really mad because he did it as the Two-Hundred-Year-Old Professor with his glasses pushed far down his nose, which always made me giggle till I hurt.

The Graftons sold their house a month later. Jean asked if we were going to move, too. My father said just thinking about having to pack everything up made him want to run screaming into the street. It was supposed to be funny but none of us laughed.

"I'm sorry," he said after a moment. "I wasn't thinking. Maybe without Joe Grafton power washing the street every two days, we can finally put it behind us."

"Stains like that don't wash out so easily," my mother said.

My parents split up the summer I turned fourteen. I was surprised although I shouldn't have been. Watching them grow apart hadn't been much fun, and I'd had to do it alone. Jean went through high school in such a whirlwind of activities, she was never home even before she left for college.

I knew something was wrong but I thought they'd fix it; they fixed everything else. My parents were *good* people. We'd never had the police at our house, nor would my father ever chase my mother through the street with a steak knife. If there was a problem, they'd solve it.

Only they didn't. They sat me down between them on the sofa to explain that my father was moving into a condo closer to his job downtown. My mother and I would stay in the house. I wouldn't see as much of my father as before but all I had to do was call and we were still a family bullshit bullshit bullshit.

It was all so polite and calm, as if they were talking about something normal, like a dental appointment. Finally, they wound down and asked if I had any questions.

"Yeah," I said. "What the *fuck?*"

They didn't even have the decency to look shocked by the f-word. After a long moment, my mother said, "We know how upsetting this is, Gale—"

"You don't know *shit!*" I yelled, wanting them to feel like I'd slapped them. Then I ran up to my room and slammed the door so hard it should have shattered into a million pieces, or at least cracked down the middle. I felt even more betrayed when it didn't.

My first impulse was to call Jean and scream at her. She'd already know—yet another betrayal. Parents were on one side and kids were on the other, that was the natural law. She was supposed to be on *my* side, not *collaborating* with *them*.

I put down the phone on my desk. My parents would come up to try talking to me; if they heard me on the phone with my traitor sister, they'd put their traitor ears to my traitor door. I waited to hear the telltale creak in the hallway. I said loudly, "Dear Diary, I wish my parents would drop dead."

They didn't even knock. "That's *horrible!*" my mother said. All the color had gone out of her face except for two pink spots on her cheeks. "How can you talk like that?"

"Because she knew we were listening," my father said, although he didn't look too sure of himself. "It's completely normal for her to be angry. Even Jean's p.o.'ed at us."

"Oh, well, as long as everything's *completely normal,* we can all relax," I said. "It's not like anyone's getting stabbed in the middle of the street."

My parents looked at each other. "Maybe we *should* move," my mother said.

But we didn't. My parents talked to a couple of realtors but there was nothing available nearby. We'd have had to move farther away, which was out of the question. My parents wanted to keep me in the same school.

I could have screwed that up by acting out. It would have been their worst nightmare and I spent hours fantasizing in my room. Drugs or booze would get me suspended but for immediate expulsion, I'd need a weapon, ideally a gun. With my luck, though, I'd end up shooting my own ass off. A knife would do, we had plenty of those.

Or I could just ditch school—that would actually create more legal problems for my parents than for me. My fleeting moment of guilt was drowned out by a rush of anger.

So what? Screw them. They do whatever they want, never giving a crap about my *feelings. They don't have to, they're grown-ups. They can get away with* fucking murder.

Except Gideon O'Dell—he hadn't, and Lily hadn't even gotten away with her own life. My mother's words came back to me: *Stains like that don't wash out so easily.* I thought it was odd she'd put it that way, as if she didn't think whatever Mr. Grafton saw had been all in his head.

Which made me wonder for the zillionth time how the hell I could have slept through something like that. I was still a sound sleeper. One night not long before the O'Dell murder, lightning struck a nearby transformer during an especially violent storm, and there were fire engines and police cars all over the place. The commotion kept everyone in a six-block radius up all night, but if the power hadn't still been out the next morning, I'd never have known.

* * *

At first, I thought I was dreaming. Then I heard more pounding and a male voice demanding someone answer the door. When my parents went downstairs, I almost went, too, before I remembered I was still mad and I didn't want them to think I cared.

I raised the screen on my bedroom window so I could lean out and see what was going on. Two police officers were on our steps with my parents; they had on their silly matching robes, like they were just regular and my father wasn't sleeping in Jean's old room until he moved out next week.

Another police car pulled up in front of the Graftons' old house. I could see the people who lived there huddled close together on their front steps but I couldn't tell if any of their robes matched.

". . . bed between eleven and eleven-thirty?" one cop on the steps was saying.

"I went to bed shortly after eleven." My mother's voice sounded draggy and plaintive. "Don was watching a news program."

"Were you asleep when your husband came to bed, ma'am?" the second cop asked.

"She usually is," my father said coolly.

"I usually am," my mother said, echoing his tone.

I couldn't blame them for not wanting to tell the cops they were sleeping separately; it wasn't like they were the O'Dells.

"Now, your daughter Gale—is *she* all right?" asked the other cop.

"*Of course* she's all right." My mother was suddenly wide awake and pissed off.

"We'd like to confirm that."

"It's four a.m.!" my father snapped. "She's asleep."

"Well, actually . . ." The second cop turned to look directly at me. So did everyone else.

I glared at everyone for a long moment before I pulled my head in. Lowering the screen, I saw the third cop talking to the people across the way. One was pointing emphatically at the street. Or rather, at a particular spot on the street.

I went downstairs. One cop was in the living room with my father and the other was in the kitchen with my mother. *Sexist much?* I thought; good old Saddle Hills. The cops asked me if I'd seen or heard anything unusual, like screaming. I told them the way I slept, I wouldn't have heard a rock concert.

I thought they'd leave when it became obvious we'd all been asleep till they'd woken us up, but they didn't. Apparently cop-obvious was different from obvious-obvious. They went through the entire house and my parents admitted that despite their matching robes, they weren't happily married after all. It got boring; I stretched out on the sofa with a paperback.

The next thing I knew, the police were telling my parents they were sorry for the inconvenience in that way they have that's somehow both sincere yet totally detached. It was getting light when I stumbled back to my room and dropped dead.

A few hours later, my father's angry voice woke me. Were the cops back? I rolled out of bed and raised the screen.

It took a few moments before I realized the guy on the front steps was from across the street. He was trying to explain something but my father wasn't having any, telling the guy to get the hell off our property if he didn't want to find himself on the wrong end of a lawsuit.

The guy gave up. But as he started down the steps, he looked up and saw me. I drew back, hoping he wasn't stupid enough to try talking to me. He wasn't.

Or rather, not then. He waited until my father moved out and rang the doorbell right after my mother left for the supermarket. I considered not answering, then decided if he got weird, I could call the cops. Or my father.

"Yes?" I asked stiffly through the locked screen door. He was a bit younger than my father and not much taller than I was, with a round face, thinning blond hair, and the kind of pale skin that burns even when it's overcast. The shadows under his puffy brown eyes made him look like he'd been up all night.

"I knew exactly what I was going to say before I came over here," he said unhappily. "Now I can't remember."

"Oh." I had no idea what to do with a helpless adult. "Retrace your steps, maybe it'll come back to you." I started to close the door.

"It's not that," he said quickly. "It's—I don't know how to begin."

So what did he expect *me* to do? "Maybe you should talk to my parents. Well, my mother." I started to close the door again.

"Have you ever seen a ghost?" he asked desperately.

I still didn't let him in.

His name was Ralph Costa and he was why the cops had visited us in the middle of the night. He'd seen a man stabbing a woman in the street and thought it was my parents.

"Why would you think *that?*" I asked, thinking maybe I should have shut the door on him after all.

"She ran up your front steps and tried to open the door," Ralph Costa said. "I thought she lived here. But *he* dragged her into the street and . . ."

"Stabbed her a lot?" I suggested.

He looked sick. "At first, I couldn't even move. Then I was on the phone, yelling for the cops to get here now. I woke May and the kids and made them stay in the back of the house so they wouldn't see. But when the cops came, there was no body, no blood, just . . . nothing. But I *know* I wasn't dreaming or hallucinating. *I saw a man kill a woman.*"

I'd heard every variation of the story—whoever told it would say Gideon almost caught Lily in *their* backyard—but this was new. "Was she screaming?"

"Of course—she must have been, I heard her—" he cut off, looking puzzled, and I could practically see him replaying it in his mind. "I *heard* her." He shook his head. "I tried to apologize to your father but he was pretty irate."

"Yeah, the cops tromped around for hours looking for bloody knives and dead bodies. It was pretty bad." I couldn't help rubbing it in; it *had* been pretty bad. Worse, the cops had asked the neighbors if my father ever beat us and now they were all looking at us funny.

"I really *am* sorry," Ralph Costa was saying. "If it makes you feel any better, the cops stayed at our house a lot longer, asking about my mental health. They didn't mention the O'Dells until just before they left. My wife looked it up later on microfiche at the library. No one ever told us."

"You're still pretty new," I said. "And it *was* a long time ago."

"Not even ten years," Ralph said, which reminded me time was different for grown-ups. "Did anyone else ever see—well, what I saw?"

I considered telling him about Mr. Grafton and decided against it. The house had changed hands twice before the Costas had moved in, which was pretty unusual. But my parents said the first people had moved to be closer to a sick relative and the second ones got a sudden job transfer. No ghosts.

"I'm a kid," I said finally. "Nobody ever tells me anything." It wasn't a total lie. Mr. Grafton hadn't told *me* about seeing the O'Dells. "Hey, I got stuff to do before my mother gets back. Have you talked to the neighbors?"

He looked unhappy. "Asking people if they've ever seen ghosts replaying a gruesome murder is no way to make friends."

I almost said I was sorry, then thought, why should *I* apologize? *He* was the one seeing things. He thanked me for listening and left, and I went to sort laundry in the basement, where I couldn't hear the doorbell.

I didn't tell my mother about Ralph Costa right away but the longer I put it off, the harder it would be to explain why. And if she heard about it from Ralph first, she'd have a cow: *A stranger has to tell me what you're doing—do you know how that makes me look?* Divorce had made her touchy.

But what could I say? *Hey, Mom, that guy who thought Dad murdered you dropped by while you were at the supermarket. Turns out he saw Lily O'Dell's ghost. But wait, it gets better—did you know Lily ran up our front steps and Gideon dragged her into the street by her hair?* I couldn't even imagine *that* shitstorm but I was pretty sure it would end up being all my fault.

God, grown-ups had *no idea* of the trouble they made for kids just by running their big fat mouths. *Damn them*, I thought, feeling angry, miserable, and cornered. *Damn them all, even the ones who* didn't *stab their wives to death in the street.* How the hell was a kid supposed to deal?

Finally, a couple of nights later, fortified by takeout beer-battered fish and chips, I decided I'd just go for it. Only what I heard myself say was, "Mom, did I *really* sleep through Lily O'Dell getting killed?"

For a moment, I didn't think she was going to answer. Then: "Actually, I'm pretty sure you saw the whole thing."

I felt my jaw drop. She watched me gape at her for a few moments, then sighed. "If I tell you about that night—and I can only tell you what *I* saw—promise me you won't obsess about it."

"Okay, I won't."

"I mean it. And *don't* go blabbing to all your friends."

Before I could answer, her hand was clamped around my wrist, not tightly enough to be painful but it wasn't comfortable, either. "Seriously. If I find out you're trying to impress your friends with this, the consequences will be"—she paused for half a second—"*severe.*"

What are you gonna do, kill me? I suppressed the thought, hoping her mom ESP hadn't picked it up. "I give you my word."

Like that, she let go and was back to casual. "You were sleepwalking that night."

"You never told me I sleepwalked!" I was flabbergasted.

"Only a few times, and it never happened again after that night." She shrugged.

"Did you take me to the doctor?"

"Of course we did," she said, almost snapping. I opened my mouth to say something else and she glared at me. "Gale, do you want to talk about sleepwalking or Lily O'Dell? I'm too tired for both."

I was on the verge of telling her I was sorry motherhood was such a burden but caught myself. Her lawyer had phoned earlier. Those calls seldom put her in a good mood.

"That night?" I said in a small voice.

"It was a Saturday," my mother said. "After you and Jean went to bed, your father and I stayed up to watch a movie on cable. You got up three times, first wanting a glass of water, then to ask for a PB&J. The third time, you were sleepwalking."

My mother sighed. "We didn't think you could open the front door.

103

Even if you managed to work the bottom lock, you weren't tall enough to reach the deadbolt or the chain. But we didn't know how resourceful you could be even asleep. You got your stepstool from the front closet."

Now she chuckled a little. "The chain lock was still a few inches out of reach, though, so you used the yardstick. It was in the corner right beside the front door. Moving the chain with it wasn't easy—I tried it myself later—but you were on a mission to get that door open.

"You'd have been out on the steps with Lily O'Dell if not for the fact that the screen door lock kept sticking. I oiled it, your dad tried axle grease, and Jean even put mayonnaise on it once but that only made it *stink* and stick.

"So when Lily O'Dell came up the front steps and begged you to let her in, there was nothing you could do. Except maybe wake up."

My mother's face turned sad. "When I got to you, Gideon O'Dell was dragging Lily into the street. He might have already stabbed her a few times or maybe he'd just beaten her bloody—" my mother stopped and shuddered. "*Just* beaten her bloody. Jesus wept.

"Anyway, there was so much blood on your face and your pajama top, I was afraid Gideon O'Dell had hurt you, too. But it was all Lily's— she'd pushed in the screen and grabbed at you. I cleaned you up, changed your pajamas, then put you to bed in our room and told you to stay there. Naturally, you didn't. I found you asleep by the window in your room.'"

I waited, but she didn't go on. "Then what?"

"We let you sleep in. You woke up around noon and as far as we could tell, you didn't remember a thing."

"I don't see how that's possible." I was picturing Lily O'Dell on the other side of the screen door, beaten and bloody and begging for help.

"You were very young," my mother said for what must have been the millionth time. "The doctor said your mind was protecting you from trauma."

"But wasn't Jean traumatized?"

My mother smiled a little. "I wouldn't let her put on her glasses. Your sister was so nearsighted she couldn't see past the end of the driveway." She finished the last bit of wine in her glass. "If you've got questions, ask now—after this, the subject is closed. Forever."

"But I need to think," I said, wincing inwardly at how whiny I sounded.

"Think faster, kid." There was a hard, all but pitiless edge in my mother's voice I'd rarely heard before. Sometimes she sounded like that with her lawyer, and most of the time with my father. But she was supposed to show she loved me no matter what. Those were the rules, she was my mother.

Correction: she was my *getting-divorced* mother, she made her own rules.

She put her hand on the base of her empty wineglass and I blurted, "Did you take me to another doctor? Like a psychologist or a shrink?"

"We didn't need to," she said. "Dr. Tran said you were perfectly healthy and suggested we consider the kind of deadbolt that needs an indoor key. Or put a bell on your bedroom door." My mother laughed a little. "We tried that. But not for long—your singing 'Jingle Bells' out of season drove us all crazy. You never sleepwalked again anyway."

That explained a vague memory of singing Christmas carols in an inflatable kiddie pool in the backyard. "Did you talk to Dr. Tran about my repressed memory?"

My mother glanced up at the ceiling. "It's not a repressed memory."

"But—"

"You've forgotten plenty else in your life and those aren't repressed memories," my mother said. A hard little line appeared between her eyebrows and I knew I was pushing it. "Nobody remembers *every* detail of their lives."

"But something like *that?*" I said.

"I told you, your brain was protecting you," my mother replied. "Probably saved you years of therapy, if not decades. But if you drive yourself crazy because you *weren't* traumatized, I'll go upside your head."

"Is that why you and Dad are getting divorced?" I asked. "Because *you're* traumatized?"

I expected her to snap at me but she only shrugged. "I'll have to ask my shrink."

"*You* have a *shrink?*"

"Yeah. I'm getting divorced." She gave me a sideways look under half-closed eyelids. "Thought you knew."

"*Mom*! Seriously—"

"That's private." She got up and started clearing the table.

"Wait," I pleaded, "I have more questions."

She leaned against the kitchen counter. "Give it a rest, will you? It was horrible but it's over. You have no good reason to bring it up."

"Actually, someone else brought it up," I said. "A few of days ago."

My mother didn't march over to Ralph Costa's house immediately, or even the next morning, which surprised me. I asked her what she was going to do but all she said was, "I'm thinking," and warned me not to ask again. I thought the suspense was going to kill me, but then something unbelievable happened.

Gideon O'Dell came back.

He looked completely different without the long hair, beard, and mustache but I recognized him immediately.

I was reading a book under the redbud tree in the front yard. My mother had said it would have to go this summer. I was sulking about it when a truck with a crew of tree men from Green & Serene pulled up in front of the house next door and Gideon O'Dell hopped out of the driver's side. For a second, I thought he actually *was* a ghost, except he was wearing Green & Serene overalls and cap.

I froze.

Everybody had said he'd be in prison for the rest of his life. Had he escaped? If so, wouldn't he have tried to get as far away from here as possible?

Sure—unless he was hiding in plain sight to throw everyone off. Only he didn't act like someone in hiding. He and the rest of the crew went to work trimming the trees in the Coopermans' front yard like they were all just guys and none of them had killed his wife in the middle of this very street. *Because they didn't know*, I thought; if they had, they wouldn't have given him any tools with sharp edges.

Eventually, they went into the Coopermans' backyard and I bolted for the house.

I didn't tell my mother. She was an office manager now for a small law firm (a different one than her lawyer's) and the job had really perked her up. New wardrobe, new hairstyle, even new friends she went out with on the weekends. It made me realize how little I'd seen her smile or heard her laugh in the last few years, even before the divorce. The last thing I wanted to do was spoil everything. Maybe it wouldn't have but I was pretty sure she wouldn't think it was good news. At the same time, I was bursting to tell her because maybe someone at her job would know why he was walking around free.

Telling my father during one of our weekend visits was even more out of the question. I'd never told him about Ralph Costa because I was afraid he'd drive up on the guy's lawn and take a swing at him. Plus, he wasn't doing as well as my mother, morale-wise, although I thought that was the condo. It felt more like a long-stay hotel than a real home. I asked my father if he were going to look for something else once the divorce was settled.

He was actually surprised at the question. "Of course not. I got a good deal on it. This is home for the foreseeable future." He gave a short laugh that didn't have much humor in it. "Assuming any part of the future *is* foreseeable."

Oh, Dad, I thought, *you have* no *idea.*

Nobody did, just me. And Gideon O'Dell. Like we were the only two people on the planet.

Whenever the Green & Serene crews were around, I stayed in, which was a lot, since everybody in the neighborhood used them. Every so often, I'd peek out a window to see what they were doing (what *he* was doing). But what really happened was, every so often, I *didn't* peek out a window. I watched Gideon O'Dell like a hawk and to be honest, it was pretty boring. All he did was work hard.

Well, so far. Just because he only cut branches now didn't mean he was reformed.

And he looked so *criminal*. The saggy tank tops he wore didn't cover much; using binoculars, I could see how crappy his tattoos were. On the left side of his chest, there was a wide rectangular patch that looked like several layers of skin had been scraped off.

He'd had a tattoo removed, I realized; probably something with Lily's name. His second try at cutting her out of his life like she'd never existed. If so, she'd left a pretty big scar.

Not just on him, either. I thought of Mr. Grafton and Ralph Costa, and even my parents. And me, of course, with the only scar no one could see.

Dammit, how the *fuck* was Gideon O'Dell out of prison?

Strangely enough, a cop show rerun gave me the answer. A guy who had killed someone in a fit of rage took a plea bargain for manslaughter instead of murder and got ten years instead of life. I almost fell off the sofa.

"Does that really happen?" I asked my mother as she came in from the kitchen with a bowl of popcorn. She looked puzzled so I gave her a quick summary. "But that's just TV, right? Or just in big cities, right?"

"Not always," she said and my heart sank. "One of our lawyers just had a murder case. She got the client a plea bargain, although I can't remember offhand what it was."

"Do people know that?"

She frowned slightly. "It's a matter of public record."

"That doesn't mean anyone *knows*," I said. "I mean, if it didn't make the news."

"Most things don't, unless they're high profile."

"Like the O'Dell murder?" I said, before I could think better of it.

I expected her to give me grief for bringing it up again but she only nodded. "They moved the O'Dell trial to a different venue. His lawyer said it wasn't possible to get an impartial jury. He was probably right. It was so lurid, the town was glad to be shut of it."

"You sure picked up a lot since you got that job," I said.

"I'm a quick study." She pushed the bowl at me. "Don't make me eat all this myself. Because I can and I will. Unless *you* save me."

It seemed like that was all I ever did.

* * *

Two days later, I saw Ralph Costa talking to a couple of Green & Serene guys, including Gideon O'Dell. It was all very ordinary, a man talking to tree service guys about the hackberry tree beside his house. No earth tremors, no thunder and lightning, no frogs falling from the sky, or fire, or blood. No apparitions and no ghosts, either. Ralph Costa obviously had no idea.

The discussion was short and friendly—Gideon O'Dell actually patted Ralph on the arm before he walked away. Ralph didn't suddenly cry out in horrified recognition. But then, Ralph had never seen him except as—

As what—a ghost? But Gideon O'Dell wasn't dead. So how could Ralph Costa or Mr. Grafton have seen him murdering Lily?

Maybe it was the ghost of his old life? That sounded stupid even just in my head.

Unbidden, my mother's words came to me: *Stains like that don't wash out so easily.*

Maybe that was it—Lily was a ghost, Gideon was a stain.

That should have sounded just as stupid, but it didn't.

Even at this point, I didn't consider talking to my friends. The few who weren't away spending two months with a divorced parent had soccer or swim team or were in summer school. That's what I told myself, anyway. In reality, I just didn't want to tell them about my parents. They'd have understood; a lot of them had already been through it. It seemed like most of the kids I knew lived either with single parents or in what the magazine called blended families, because that made step-parents and step-brothers and step-sisters sound sweet like a smoothie rather than something out of the Brothers Grimm.

My friends would all be very sympathetic. Then they'd start rehashing their own horror stories along with the ones they'd heard secondhand. Talk about Grimm. But they were actually supposed to make you feel better about your own shitstorm. *See how much worse it could be?*

Except I *did* know. My friends all knew about Saddle Hills' worst-ever crime. But none of them had grown up within sight of Lily O'Dell's murder, or seen Mr. Grafton trying over and over to wash it off the road. And none of them had a murderer for a tree man.

Then it occurred to me while I was brooding up in my room one afternoon: what if I told them I did?

Hey, guys, you're never gonna believe this—

They'd all be in such a rush to tell everyone else, they probably wouldn't even notice my father had moved out.

But then what?

Would people call the police? Cancel their tree service? Would there be emergency neighborhood watch meetings? Would everyone march on City Hall? Or would the villagers simply descend on Green & Serene with pitchforks and torches to drag the monster out and throw him over the cliff themselves?

It was entirely possible, I thought uneasily, that if people did know, Gideon O'Dell might not be safe. For real.

Yeah, ask his wife how that *feels,* a voice in my head whispered nastily. *Screw him. He's a murderer who should be doing life in prison, not pruning elms. He got off easy, not even ten years. You know who* didn't *get a deal? Lily O'Dell—she's dead forever. He deserves whatever he gets. If he's not a real ghost, he ought to be.*

After a bit, I realized I'd been sitting with my fists balled up so tightly my palms were starting to cramp. It was one of the few times I was glad I was a nail-biter because otherwise my palms would have been bleeding. Gideon O'Dell had made me that angry.

Gideon O'Dell had made me *that* angry?

Well, not *just* him—my parents and their divorce bullshit and every other grown-up who just tromped around only caring about themselves. My parents probably thought I was *adjusting* and maybe sometimes I thought so, too. As if anything could really be that easy! Like fucking up my life was no big deal. They were as bad as Gideon O'Dell.

Part of me knew the comparison was out of proportion but that was more mature than I wanted to be just then. It was *grown-up* thinking, and seeing as how I couldn't do anything else they did like drink or drive or join the army or just fuck shit up for the hell of it, I wasn't going to be an adult about this, either.

"What's going on next door?" I asked, looking out the dining room window at all the G&S trucks pulling in. "Are the Coopermans having a party for the tree men? Or are they just luring them in for a mass baptism?" The Coopermans left pamphlets in our mailbox about the joys of being baptized once a month.

"They're cutting down the elm in their backyard," my mother said. "Deborah Cooperman asked if I wanted any for firewood."

"Oh, *shit*." I moved to the patio doors to watch the tree men setting up "I *love* that tree. How *could* they?"

"Language," my mother said but without any real feeling. She was engrossed in a computer magazine. "All elms in this country have Dutch elm disease and eventually, there's nothing you can do."

"Theirs still looks okay to me," I grumbled.

"G&S gave them an estimate of what the upkeep would cost. They decided to keep their kids instead." She chuckled. "If I had to choose between our elm tree and you, I'd choose you."

I glared at her, suppressing a remark about grown-ups' choices.

"Probably," she added, smiling with half her mouth. "On a good day, for sure. But I also have bad days. You have been warned."

I couldn't help laughing. All of a sudden, I was tired of being mad at her and my father, fed up with being fed up. I sat down next to her on the sofa and let her tell me about the computer she'd learned to use at her job and how it was changing everything. She was talking about the office network when I suddenly felt cold, like the temperature had dropped from eighty-five to fifty-five, and I knew Gideon O'Dell had arrived. I got up and went to the patio door.

"Gale?" my mother asked, puzzled. "What's wrong?"

"Everything," I said.

Why would Gideon O'Dell come back here instead of going just about anywhere else? For all the happy memories? To find himself? To find *America?*

Christ, why did grown-ups do *anything*?

Because it was the worst possible idea, of course.

Made sense.

It took three days for them to reduce the Coopermans' elm to firewood and toothpicks and I watched pretty much the whole thing. Or rather, I watched Gideon O'Dell while I sat out on the patio pretending to read *A Tale of Two Cities*. I'd already read it for school so if anybody asked what section I was pretending to be on, I could answer. Not that anyone would—my mother was at work all day and none of the tree men were going to wander over to the fence on a break and ask me what else I'd read by Dickens. There was a small risk of the Coopermans sending over one of their kids with a pamphlet; if so, I'd pretend to use it as a bookmark and toss it later.

But no one bothered with me. Mrs. Cooperman was busy making lemonade and iced tea for the G&S guys and even gave them lunch. I suppose it was a good Christian thing to do since killing the elm was such hard work. She smiled and waved at me a couple of times and I waved back, fantasizing about telling her who was in her backyard. If Mary had been outside, she'd have probably been telling all the tree men how great Jesus was. *Jesus loves you. Jesus loves everybody.*

But did Mrs. Cooperman? How much Christian charity would she have for Gideon O'Dell? Would she judge not or cast the first stone? I was tempted to find out, except I had a very strong feeling it would somehow backfire. Either my parents would be furious with me for not telling them right away or it would turn out the guy wasn't really Gideon O'Dell after all.

Or worst of all, he *was* Gideon O'Dell with a fake ID, and he'd come back later to shut me up.

Right now, he was high up in the tree with a chain saw. All of the leafy branches had been cut away and now they were starting on the thicker arms. He seemed to be having a good time. Guys with power tools were basically kids with toys. But it was more than that, I thought. He was killing a live thing.

That's *why he came back*, I thought suddenly. My heart was

pounding like a jackhammer in slow-motion: Bang . . . bang . . . bang. *Because secateurs and machetes and chain saws are more fun than a cheap steak knife.*

I walked over to lean on the fence. I'd been so worried about him seeing me but now I wanted him to. I wanted him to know I was onto him.

But when he did finally look in my direction, his gaze slid away without interest before I could even hold my breath. Talk about an anti-climax. I actually felt cheated. Disrespected, even.

But maybe he'd been too busy killing his wife to notice me that night. Now he was too busy killing a tree. Or trying to; the chain saw jammed suddenly, then cut out altogether. Was that as frustrating as a broken steak knife?

Lily O'Dell had still been alive when the blade broke off but she hadn't been screaming. She'd had no breath left. Her left lung had collapsed and the right one was about to. The adrenaline that had powered her desperate sprint was gone. She'd used the last of her energy to punch through the top of the screen door and grab at me. Then Gideon O'Dell dragged her away by her hair into the street, where he stabbed her and stabbed her and stabbed her until the handle of the knife was so slippery with blood it slid out of his hand.

My head cleared and I found myself sitting on the ground beside the fence with the sun in my eyes. I went back to my chair on the patio wondering what the hell had come over me. Some kind of vivid waking dream? Not a memory—or rather, not *my* memory. What I had seen in my mind's eye had all been from Lily O'Dell's point of view.

It only took one day for Gideon O'Dell to cut down the redbud tree in our front yard, working alone. Two other guys deep-watered the elm beside the house and the walnut tree in the backyard and explained how to harvest the walnuts. We couldn't just pick them off the tree like apples, which was disappointing. It all sounded like a lot of tedious effort for a few nuts. Even having a murderer in our front yard didn't make it less boring.

I sat on the carpet a couple of feet back from the screen door pretending to read Poe's *Tales of Mystery and Imagination*. As usual, Gideon O'Dell worked away like nothing had ever happened here, like he wasn't twenty feet away from the very spot where he stabbed his wife to death.

How could he not feel weird being here?

Maybe he had amnesia. Maybe he got beaten up so many times in prison he had brain damage.

Abruptly, he put down the chain saw, looked directly at me. I stared back; the book resting on my folded legs fell shut. If he hadn't seen me before, he had now. Hadn't he? No, he hadn't; his eyes weren't focused on me at all, I realized, watching as he took the bandanna around his neck off, wiped his face with it, then tied it around his head.

What are you doing here? What do you want? I asked him silently. His face gave nothing away. The only thing I could read was the name tag pinned to the front of his overalls: GO. What kind of a name was that?

His initials, of course, what his buddies used to call him. Also his family, including L—

I shook my head to clear it. Gideon O'Dell, aka GO, was now staring thoughtfully at the roof. I went up to my room.

I stayed back from the window, watching the rest of the redbud's destruction with binoculars. Occasionally, I turned to the forever-unclean spot on the road, like I might see something besides old dirty asphalt. Like Lily O'Dell's blood might come bubbling up out of the ground in outrage.

Nothing happened, of course, except GO finished demolishing the redbud.

The son of a bitch came back on Sunday afternoon. Parked his truck in our driveway, trotted up the stairs, and rang the doorbell. I stayed in my room, wondering if he'd finally decided to force his way in and kill us. It was broad daylight, everyone in the neighborhood was home and kids were outside playing, but a mad killer might not care.

I couldn't hear what my mother said when she answered the door but she sounded friendly. So did Gideon O'Dell, friendly and a little subservient before he got a ladder and climbed up onto the roof with a toolbox.

My mother came up to tell me not to use the front door for a while. "If you want to go out, use the patio door. I've got a guy fixing loose tiles on the roof."

"One of the G&S guys," I said accusingly. "The one that cut down the redbud."

She nodded. "He saw them while he was here. He said he'd done that kind of work and he'd charge less than a roofer so I told him to come back today."

"What if he does a lousy job?" I asked.

"He guaranteed his work, and if he couldn't fix something, he'd tell me."

"What if he's lying? For all we know, he's a burglar casing the joint."

"Then he'll know there's lot better pickings next door. Assuming he can fence a collection of ugly silver and tacky Nelson Rockwell plates." She chuckled.

"What if he's *worse* than a burglar?" I said as she turned to leave. "Like, a murderer?"

She turned back to me, eyebrows raised. "Like what—an IRS agent?"

"What do you know about him?" I persisted. "What's his name? Where does he live?"

"You know, when most parents have this conversation, it's the other way around." She came over and sat down next to me on the bed. "He's just fixing some roof tiles, Gale. We're not going out on a date. And he's not a *total* stranger, he works for our tree service. I'm paying cash so I only know his nickname, which is—"

"Go," I said. "Do you know his *real* name?"

All at once, she went serious. "Did this guy ever try anything *inappropriate* with you?" she asked. "Or one of the neighbor kids?"

That lie was too evil to tell, even about him. "No, definitely not," I said. "But who knows what kind of person he really is?"

"Who knows what kind of person *anybody* really is?" My mother gave me a hug. "You don't like the guy, stay away from him. No fault, no foul, everybody wins. Okay?"

He's not just a guy, he's a murderer, he's Gideon O'Dell, I tried to say. But when I opened my mouth, all that came out was, "Okay."

She kissed me on the forehead and went back downstairs, leaving me to wonder what the hell was wrong with me. It *wasn't* okay. Gideon O'Dell was up on our roof, exuding poison from his wife-murdering soul and somehow I was the only one who could feel it.

Because Lily O'Dell had touched me, I realized. I couldn't remember but I didn't have to. I had *her* memory—it was in her blood.

"Pizza for supper?" my mother asked. She'd just made another gallon of iced tea to replace what Gideon O'Dell had drunk. I had ice water instead.

When I put away the ice cube trays and closed the freezer door, I saw a fridge magnet holding a slip of paper with a phone number on it and underneath, *Go's cell, call anytime, leave message.*

"That's just in case he has to repair his repair job," my mother said.

"You think he'll have to?" I asked.

"We'll see. They're predicting heavy thunderstorms tonight." My mother chuckled. "Don't worry, I'm sure it's nothing that'll keep you awake."

"We'll see," I said, mimicking her. She didn't notice.

We ate pizza from Valentino's in front of the TV. Talking her into having a glass of wine wasn't hard and she didn't protest when I suggested a second, but then, it was an Australian Shiraz. I told myself that was why she'd poured such a full glass and drunk it more quickly than usual. But so what? She wasn't *drunk,* just very relaxed. She'd get a good night's sleep and no hangover.

Or maybe just a little one, I thought as she had a third glass, which killed the bottle. There was no more wine in the house but she wouldn't have opened another bottle anyway—she was too relaxed to use a corkscrew. She'd also get part of her good night's sleep in front of the TV but that suited me just fine.

My mother was snoring softly even before the first warning rumble of thunder. I threw Grandma's hand-crocheted afghan over her and waited to see if she'd stir. More thunder, louder this time; she didn't even twitch. I went into the kitchen to get Gideon O'Dell's phone number, started to go up to my room, then stopped. Not because I was having second thoughts but because I wanted to make sure my mother wasn't about to wake up. I tiptoed into the living room to check on her.

As if on cue, thunder boomed, seemingly right overhead. It wasn't loud enough to rattle the windows but I thought if anything would wake her, that would. She didn't even twitch. I turned out all the lights, started to go up to my room again and then paused, looking at the front door. The TV threw just enough light so I could see it was locked.

Unlock it.

The words were so distinct, it was like someone had actually whispered in my ear. But I could hear my mother still snoring under the babble of the latest hot cop show. If I was hearing voices, they weren't too bright; opening the door would wake my mother for sure.

Not open it—not yet. Just unlock it.

It crossed my mind even as I did so that this alone would be enough to wake my mother, because you never, *ever* left anything unlocked after dark. But any disturbance in the Force this might have caused was no match for three glasses of Shiraz. Or for Lily O'Dell, who I realized was in charge of this party.

Good. Now you can go upstairs.

I felt like I should say thank you but at the same time, I understood Lily O'Dell didn't care how well-mannered I was.

Lightning flickered like a strobe; a few seconds later, thunder cracked like the sky was breaking apart. Maybe it was. My room was dark except for the nightlight in the wall outlet beside my bed, an owl and a pussycat sitting in the curve of a crescent moon. I unplugged it and opened the window. There was a streetlight about halfway between our driveway and the one next door but it seemed dimmer than usual and I couldn't see the street very well. As I raised the screen and leaned out, it started to rain.

It was the kind of rain that comes straight down and very hard, like it's real pissed-off at everything it's falling on. Tonight, I could actually believe it was. It slapped leaves off trees, smashed down the geraniums lining either side of our driveway, pounded the pavement hard enough to bounce.

Had it rained the night Lily O'Dell got killed? I was pretty sure it hadn't—

Yes, it did. It rained blood. You got caught in the storm.

I reached out as far as I could, palm up, just to make sure but it was plain old rainwater. Still coming down hard, enough to make my hand sting.

The lights in the Graftons' old house went out. Was it that late already? Maybe I should check to see if my mother was still asleep—

Time to make that call. That's what you came up here for.

Yes, but now that it was time to do it, I was starting to feel shaky.

You think you're shaky? Try sprinting around the block and hopping fences in backyards. Your knees'll knock like castanets.

I could see a form in the straight-down sheets of rain, someone in the street, waiting while tiles slid off the roof and smacked wetly on the front steps.

Call him and tell him to come over immediately. Give him hell or sob your heart out but get him here now. Now.

I picked up the phone and dialed.

I started by sobbing my heart out but Gideon O'Dell didn't want to come over. There was nothing he could do while it was still raining and even if it stopped, he certainly couldn't work in the dark. I kept sobbing and he kept being reasonable, so I tried getting mad. The way he answered made me think he'd had a lot of anger management classes in prison.

"You just get your ass over here right now and give me back all the money I paid you," I said, "or I tell everyone on the block who you *really* are, *Gideon.*"

He practically choked. "You—you *what?*"

"If you think people here want a murderer taking care of their trees—"

"Okay, please, stop. I'm coming now, all right? I'll be there in ten minutes. Not even that. Just don't—please, I've got all your money—"

I slammed the receiver down, shaking all over. Thunder rumbled but without much power as the rain began to lessen. Lily O'Dell was walking slowly up the incline of our lawn, toward the front door. I knew she'd want me to open it now.

My mother was still fast asleep, hugging a throw pillow. The cop show had been replaced by old reruns of a different cop show, one that only came on very late. How long had I been upstairs? And had it been raining hard and angry the whole time?

Open the door.

That would wake my mother for sure, I thought. Just in time for Gideon O'Dell to show up apologizing and begging her not to tell anyone. She'll have no idea what he's talking about but maybe she'll be too distracted by the tiles that fell off the roof to care—

Open the door now. *Before the doorbell wakes her.*

The rain had stopped.

Lily O'Dell wasn't covered with so much blood that I couldn't see what Gideon O'Dell had done to her face. One eye was swollen shut and the other was getting there; her nose wasn't just broken but so smashed that it didn't look anything like something to breathe through. One side of her face was caved in, her lower lip was badly split and she'd lost some teeth. I could see distinct finger marks in the bruising around her neck.

Only I shouldn't have been able to. All the lights were out and the TV wasn't bright enough. And yet, I *could* see her, could see her struggling to breathe, seemingly unable to gulp in enough air. But I didn't hear it until she punched both hands through the screen door.

Suddenly I was small, looking up at her in horror and confusion, tasting blood as she smeared her hands over my face. Her voice was barely audible as she begged for help, and when Gideon O'Dell yanked her away, she couldn't make a sound.

Gideon O'Dell, however, was yelling and cursing as she dragged him down the lawn by his hair, past his truck parked at the curb. I don't think he knew it was her until they got to that very specific spot on the street, but when he did, he went completely hysterical. I thought for sure his screaming and begging would wake up the entire neighborhood.

But he didn't. No lights went on in any of the neighbors' houses or across the street; my mother slept on, undisturbed and unaware. And all the while, I was trying to get the screen door open but the stupid lock wouldn't budge.

I don't know where the knife came from—maybe it was a ghost, like Lily. But also like Lily, it hurt him for real. I didn't want to watch but I couldn't look away, couldn't yell for my mother, couldn't even move. All I could do was stand there and watch Lily pay Gideon back stroke for stroke, slash for slash, stab for stab.

It took a very long time. When she was finally done, she turned to look at me and bowed her head a little, like she was saying thanks.

Then it began to rain again, pounding straight down like before. I closed the door and went to bed.

In the morning, the truck was still parked in front of our house but there was no trace of Gideon O'Dell, nothing to show why he had come here or where he had gone, not even a stain on the asphalt. It had rained that hard.

PAT CADIGAN sold her first professional science fiction story in 1980 and became a full-time writer in 1987. She is the author of fifteen books, including two nonfiction books on the making of *Lost in Space* and *The Mummy*, one young adult novel, and two Arthur C. Clarke Award–winning novels: *Synners* and *Fools*. She has won the Locus Award three times and the Hugo Award for her novelette, "The Girl-Thing Who Went Out for Sushi," which also won the Seiun Award in Japan. Cadigan lives in North London with her husband, the Original Chris Fowler, where she is stomping the hell out of terminal cancer.

A CATALOG OF STORMS

FRAN WILDE

The wind's moving fast again. The weathermen lean into it, letting
it wear away at them until they turn to rain and cloud.

"Look there, Sila." Mumma points as she grips my shoulder.

Her arthritis-crooked hand shakes. Her cuticles are pale red from
washwater. Her finger makes an arc against the sky that ends at the dark
shadows on the cliffs.

"You can see those two, just there. Almost gone. The weather
wouldn't take them if they weren't wayward already, though." She *tsks*.
"Varyl, Lillit, pay attention. Don't let that be any of you girls."

Her voice sounds proud and sad because she's thinking of her aunt,
who turned to lightning.

The town's first weatherman.

The three of us kids stare across the bay to where the setting sun's
turned the cliff dark. On the edge of the cliff sits an old mansion that
didn't fall into the sea with the others: the Cliffwatch. Its turrets and
cupolas are wrapped with steel cables from the broken bridge. Looks
like metal vines grabbed and tethered the building to the solid part of
the jutting cliff.

All the weathermen live there, until they don't anymore.

"They're leaned too far out and too still to be people." Varyl waves
Mumma's hand down.

Varyl always says stuff like that because . . .

"They *used* to be people. They're weathermen now," Lillit answers.

. . . Lillit always rises to the bait.

"You don't know what you're talking about," Varyl whispers, and her eyes dance because she knows she's got her twin in knots, wishing to be first and best at something. Lillit is always second at everything.

Mumma sighs, but I wait, ears perked, for whatever's coming next because it's always something wicked. Lillit has a fast temper.

But none of us are prepared this time.

"I *do too know.* I talked to one, once," Lillit yells and then her hand goes up over her mouth, just for a moment, and her eyes look like she'd cut Varyl if she thought she'd get away with it.

And Mumma's already turned and got Lillit by the ear. "You did what." Her voice shudders. "Varyl, keep an eye out."

Some weathermen visit relatives in town, when the weather is calm. They look for others like them, or who might be. When they do that, mothers hide their children.

Mumma starts to drag Lillit on home. And just then a passing weatherman starts to scream by the fountain as if he'd read Mumma's weather, not the sky's.

When weathermen warn about a squall, it always comes. Storms aren't their fault, and they'll come anyway. The key is to know what kind of storm's coming and what to do when it does. Weathermen can do that.

For a time.

I grab our basket of washing. Mumma and Varyl grab Lillit. We run as far from the fountain as fast as we can, before the sky turns ash-gray and the searing clouds—the really bad kind—begin to fall.

And that's how Lillit is saved from a thrashing, but is still lost to us in the end.

AN INCOMPLETE CATALOG OF STORMS

A Felrag: the summer wind that turns the water green first, then churns up dark clouds into fists. Not deadly, usually, but good to warn the boats.

A *Browtic*: rising heat from below that drives the rats and snakes from underground before they roast there. The streets swirl with them, they bite and bite until the browtic cools. Make sure all babies are well and high.

A *Neap-Change*: the forgotten tide that's neither low nor high, the calmest of waters, when what rests in the deeps slowly slither forth. A silent storm that looks nothing like a storm. It looks like calm and moonlight on water, but then people go missing.

A *Glare*: a storm of silence and retribution, with no forgiveness, a terror of it, that takes over a whole community until the person causing it is removed. It looks like a dry wind, but it's always some person that's behind it.

A *Vivid*: that bright sunlit rainbow-edged storm that seduces young women out into the early morning before they've been properly wrapped in cloaks. The one that gets in their lungs and makes them sing until they cry, until they can only taste food made of honey and milk and they grow pale and glass-eyed. Beware vivids in spring for the bride's sake.

A *Searcloud*: heated air so thick it blinds as it wraps charred arms around those it catches, then billows in the lungs, scorching words from their sounds, memories from their bearers. Often followed by sorrow, searclouds are best avoided, run through at top speed, or never named.

An *Ashpale*: thick, gathering clouds from the heights, where the ice forms. When it leaves, everything in its path is slick and frozen. Scream it away if you can, before your breath freezes too.

The Cliffwatch is broken now, its far wall tumbled half down to the ocean so that every room ends in water.

We go up there a lot to poke around now that we're older.

After that Searcloud passed, Mumma searched through our house until she found Lillit's notes—her name wasn't on them, but we'd know her penmanship anywhere. Since she's left-handed and it smears, whether chalk or ink. My handwriting doesn't smear. Nor Varyl's.

The paper—a whole sheet!—was crammed into a crack in the wall behind our bed. I rubbed the thick handmade weave of it between my fingers, counting until Mumma snatched it away again.

Lillit had been making up storms, five of them already, mixing them in with known weather. She'd been practicing.

Mumma shrieked at her, as you could imagine. "You *don't* want this. You don't *want* it."

I ducked behind Varyl, who was watching, wide-eyed. Everyone's needed for battle against the storms, but no one wants someone they love to go.

And Lillit, for the first time, didn't talk back. She stood as still as a weatherman. She *did* want it.

While we ran to her room to help her pack, Mumma wept.

The Mayor knocked when it was time to take Lillit up the cliff. "Twice in your family! Do you think Sila too? Or Varyl?" He looked eagerly around Mumma's wide frame at us. "A great honor!"

"Sila and Varyl don't have enough sense to come out of the rain, much less call storms," Mumma said. She bustled the Mayor from the threshold and they flanked Lillit, who stepped forward without a word, her face already saying "up," even as her feet crunched the gravel down.

Mumma left her second-eldest daughter inside the gates and didn't look back, as is right and proper.

She draped herself in honor until the Mayor left, so no one saw her crying but me and that's because I know Mumma better than she thinks I do.

I know Lillit too.

Being the youngest doesn't have many advantages, but this one is worth all the rest: everyone forgets you're there. If you're watchful, you can learn a lot.

Here are a few:

I knew Lillit could hear wind and water earlier than everyone else.

I know Varyl is practicing in her room every night trying to catch up.

I know Mumma's cried herself to sleep more than once and that Varyl wishes she were sleet and snow, alternately. That neither one know what Lillit will turn into when she goes.

And I know, whether Lillit turns to clouds or rain, that I'll be next, not Varyl. Me.

And that maybe someone will cry over me.

I already started making lists. I'll be ready.

Mumma goes up to the Cliffwatch all the time.

"You stay," she says to Varyl and me. But I follow, just close enough that I see Lillit start to go all mist around the edges, and Mumma shake her back solid, crying.

Weathermen can't help it, they have to name the storms they think of, and soon they're warning about the weather for all of us, and eventually they fight it too.

While Mumma and I are gone, the Mayor comes by our house and puts a ribbon on our door. We get extra milk every Tuesday.

That doesn't make things better, in the end. Milk isn't a sister.

"The weather gets them and gets them," Mumma's voice is proud and sad when she returns. From now on, she won't say "wayward," won't hear anyone speak of Lillit nor her aunt as a cautionary tale. "We scold because of our own selfishness," she says. "We don't want them to change." Her aunt went gone a long time ago.

We all visit Lillit twice, early on. Once, sweeping through town after a squall. Another time, down near the fishing boats, where the lightning likes to play. She saved a fisherman swept out to sea, by blowing his boat back to safe harbor.

We might go more often, but Mumma doesn't want us to catch any ideas.

A basket of oysters appears outside our door. Then a string of smoked fish.

When storms come, weathermen name it away. Yelling works too. So does diving straight into it and shattering it, but you can only do that once you've turned to wind and rain.

Like I said, storms would come anyway. When we know what to call them, we know how to fight them. And we can help the weathermen, Mumma says after Lillit goes, so they don't wear themselves out.

Weathermen give us some warning. Then we all fight back against the air.

"The storms got smarter than us," Varyl whispers at night when we can't sleep for missing her twin, "after we broke the weather. The wind and rain got used to winning. They liked it."

A predator without equal, the weather tore us to pieces after the sky turned gray and the sea rose.

Some drowned or were lost in the winds. Others fled, then gathered in safe places and hunkered down. Like in our town. Safe, cliffs on all sides, a long corridor we can see the ocean coming for miles.

Ours was a holiday place, once, until people started turning into weather too. Because the sky and the very air were broken, Varyl says.

Soon we stopped losing our treasures to the wind. Big things first: Houses stayed put. The hour hand for the clock stayed on the clock tower. Then little things too, like pieces of paper and petals. I wasn't used to so many petals staying on the trees.

The wind hadn't expected its prey to practice, to fight back.

When the weather realized, finally, that it was being named and outsmarted, then the wind started hunting down weathermen. Because a predator must always attack.

But the weathermen? Sometimes when they grow light enough, they lift into the clouds and push the weather back from up high.

"And through the hole they leave behind," Varyl whispers. Half asleep, I can barely hear her. "You can see the sky, blue as the denim our old dress might have been, once."

The Cliffwatch is broken now, its roof gaping wide as if the gray sky makes better shelter.

We climb over the building like rats, looking for treasure. For a piece of her.

We peer out at the ocean through where the walls used to be. We steal through a house that's leaned farther out over the water since the last time we came, a house that's grown loud in asking the wind to send its emptied frame into the sea.

Varyl stands watch, alone, always now. She's silent. She misses Lillit most.

Mumma and I collect baskets of hinges and knobs, latches and keyholes. People collect them, to remember. Some have storms inscribed around their edges: a Cumulous—which made the eardrums ring and then burst; a Bitter—where the wind didn't stop blowing until everyone fought.

"She learned them for us, Mumma," I whisper, holding an embroidered curtain. My fingers work the threads, turning the stitches into list of things I miss about Lillit: her laugh, her stubborn way of standing, her handwriting. How she'd brush my hair every morning without yanking, like Varyl does now.

Mumma doesn't shush me anymore. Her eyes tear up a little. "Sila, I remember before the storms, when half the days were sunny. When the sky was blue." She coughs and puts a gray ribbon in my basket. "At least, I remember people talking like that, about a blue sky."

I'm wearing Varyl's hand-me-down dress, it's denim, and used to be blue too; a soft baby blue when it belonged to my sister; a darker navy back when it was Mumma's long coat.

Now the gray bodice has winds embroidered on it, not storms. Varyl did the stitching. The dress says: *felrag, mistral, lillit, föhn*, in swirling white thread.

The basket I hold is made of gray and white sticks; my washing basket most days. Today it is a treasure basket. We are collecting what the weather left us.

Mumma gasps when she tugs up a floorboard to find a whole catalog of storms beaten into brass hinges.

We've found catalogs before, marked in pinpricks on the edge of a book and embroidered with tiny stitches in the hem of a curtain, but never so many. They sell well at market, as people think they're lucky.

Time was, if you could name a storm, you could catch it, for a while. Beat it.

If it didn't catch you first.
So the more names in the catalog, the luckier they feel.
We've never sold Lillit's first catalog. That one's ours.

After Lillit goes, I try naming storms.

A *Somanyquestions*: the storm of younger sisters, especially.
There is nothing you can do about it.

A *Toomuchtoofast*: that storm that plagues mothers sometimes.
Bring soothing cakes and extra hands for holding things and
folding things.

A *Leaving*: that rush when everything swoops up in dust and
agitation and what's left is scoured. Prepare to bolt your doors
so you don't lose what wants to be lost.

When I sneak up to the Cliffwatch to show my sister, she's got rain
for hair and wind in her eyes, but she hugs me and laughs at my list and
says to keep trying.
Mumma never knows how often I visit her.

"Terrible storms, for years," Varyl tells it, "snatched people straight
from their houses. Left columns of sand in the chairs, dragged weeds
through the bedding."
But then we happened, right back at the weather. I know this story.
And the battle's gone on for a while.
Long before Lillit and Varyl and I were born, the Mayor's
son shouted to the rain to stop before one of her speeches. And
it did. Mumma's aunt at the edge of town yelled back lightning
once.
The weather struck back: a whole family became a thick gray mist
that filled their house and didn't disperse.
Then Mumma's aunt and the Mayor's son shouted weather names
when storms approached. At first it was frightening, and people stayed

away. Then the Mayor realized how useful, how fortunate. Put them up at the Cliffwatch, to keep them safe.

Then the news crier, she went out one day and saw snow on her hand—a single, perfect flake. The day was warm, the sky clear, trees were budding and ready to make more trees and she lifted the snowflake to her lips and whirled away.

The town didn't know what to think. We'd been studying the weather that became smarter than us. We'd gotten the weather in us too, maybe.

Mumma's aunt turned to lightning and struck the clouds. Scattered them.

Right after that, the ocean grabbed the bluff and ripped it down. Left the Cliffwatch tilted over the ocean, but the people who'd got the weather in them didn't want to leave.

That was the battle—had been already, but now we knew it was a fight—the weathermen yelling at the weather, to warn us before the storms caught them too. The parents yelling at their kids to stay out of the rain. Out of the Cliffwatch.

But I'd decided. I'd go when my turn came.

Because deciding you needed to do something was always so much better than waking up to find you'd done it.

Mumma's aunt had crackled when she was angry; the Mayor's son was mostly given to dry days and wet days until he turned to squall one morning and blew away.

The storms grew stronger. The bigger ones lasted weeks. The slow ones took years. At market, we heard whispers: a few in town worried the storms fed on spent weathermen. Mumma hated that talk. It always followed a Searcloud.

Sometimes, storms linked together to grow strong: Ashpales and Vivids and Glares.

I lied when I said Mumma never looked back. I saw her do it.

She wasn't supposed to but the Mayor had walked on and she turned and I watched her watch Lillit with a hunger that made me stomp out the gate.

Returning to the Cliffwatch is worse than looking back. Don't tell anyone but she does that in secret. All the time.

She doesn't visit then. She stands outside the gates in the dark when she can't sleep, draped in shadows so no one will see her, except maybe Lillit. I sneak behind her, walking in her footsteps so nothing crunches to give me away.

I see her catch Lillit in the window of the Cliffwatch now and then. See Lillit lift a hand and curl it. See Mumma match the gesture and then Lillit tears away.

Mumma doubles her efforts to lure Lillit back. She leaves biscuits on the cliff's edge. Hair ribbons, "in case the wind took Lillit's from her."

She forgets to do the neighbors' laundry, twice, until they ask someone else. We stay hungry for a bit, then Varyl goes after the washing.

Up in the old clock tower in town where a storm took the second and minute hands but left the hour, a weatherman starts shouting about a Clarity.

Mumma starts running toward the cliff, but not for safety.

Varyl and I go screeching after her, a different kind of squall, beating against the weather, up to the Cliffwatch.

A Secret Catalog of Storms

A Loss That's Probably Your Fault: a really quiet storm. Mean too. It gets smaller and smaller until it tears right through you.

A Grieving: this one sneaks up on mothers especially and catches them off guard. Hide familiar things that belong to loved ones, make sure they can't surprise anyone. A lingering storm.

An I Told You Not To, Sila: an angry storm, only happens when someone finds your lists. The kind that happens when they burn the list so that no one will know you're catching wayward.

The biggest storm yet hits when we're almost done running.

We're near the top of the cliff, the big old house in our sights, and bam, the Clarity brings down torrents of bright-lit rain that makes the insides of our ears hurt. Breathing sears our lungs and we can't tell if that's from the running or the storm. And then the storm starts screeching, tries to pull our hair, drag us over the cliff.

We try to shelter in the Cliffwatch.

The wind hums around us, the ice starts blueing our cheeks, Varyl's teeth start chattering and then stop, and oh let us in, I cry. Don't be so stubborn.

Varyl pounds on the door.

But this time, the door doesn't open for Varyl. The door doesn't mind Mumma either, no matter how hard she pounds.

Only when I crawl through the freeze, around to the cliff's edge and yell, something turns my way, blows the shutters open. I pull my family through, even Mumma, who is trying to stay out in the wind, trying to make it take her too.

We get inside the Cliffwatch and shake ourselves dry. "That Clarity had an Ashpale on the end of it," I say. I'm sure of it. "There's a Bright coming."

So many storms, all at once, and I know their names. They are ganging up against us.

I want to fight.

Varyl stares at me, shouts for Mumma, but Mumma's searching the rooms for Lillit.

"We can't stay here and lose Sila too," Varyl says. She turns to me. "You don't want this."

But I *do*, I think. I want to fight the weather until it takes me too.

And maybe Mumma wants it also.

Varyl clasps my hand, and Mumma's, the minute the weather stops howling. She drags us both back to our house, through the frozen wood, across the square, past the frozen fountain. Our feet crunch ice into petals that mark our path. Varyl's shouting at Mumma. She's shaking her arm, which judders beneath her shirt, all the muscles loose and swingy, but the part of Mumma at the end of the arm doesn't move. Because she saw what I saw, she saw Lillit begin to blow, saw her hair rise and flow, and her fingers and all the rest of her with it, out to face the big storm, made of Ashpale and Vivid and Glare and Clarity.

That was the last time we saw Lillit's face in any window. Mumma had brought ribbons but those blew away. Now sometimes she scatters petals for Lillit to play with.

Climbing the remains of the Cliffwatch later, we find small storms in corners, a few dark clouds. You can put them in jars now and take them home, watch until the lightning fades.

Sometimes they don't fade, these pieces of weather. The frozen water that doesn't thaw. A tiny squall that rides your shoulder until you laugh.

They're still here, just lesser, because the weather is less too.

That day, all the storms spilled over the bay at once, fire from below and lightning and the green clouds and the gray. That day, the weathermen rose up into the wind and shouted until they were raw and we hid, and the storms shouted back—one big storm where there had been many smaller ones—and it dove for the town, the Cliffwatch, the few ships in the harbor.

And the weathermen hung from the cliff house and some of them caught the wind. Some of them turned to rain. Some to lightning. Then they all struck back together. The ones who already rode the high clouds too.

We wanted to help, I could feel the clouds tugging at my breath, but some of the winds beat at our cheeks and the rain struck our faces, pushing us back. And the terrible storms couldn't reach us, couldn't take us.

Instead, the Cliffwatch cracked and the clouds and the wind swept it all up back into the sky where it had come from long ago.

Later, we walked home. A spot of blue sky opened up and just as suddenly disappeared. A cool breeze crossed my face and I felt Lillit's fingers in it.

A hero is more than a sister. And less.

The milk keeps coming, but the fish doesn't.

The weathermen are in the clouds now. Varyl says they keep the sky blue and the sea green and the air clear of ice.

We climb into the Cliffwatch sometimes to find the notes and drawings, the hinges and papers and knobs. We hold these tight, a way to touch the absences. We say their names. We say, *they did it for us. They wanted to go.*

With the wind on my skin and in my ears, I still think I could blow away too if I wished hard enough.

Mumma says we don't need weathermen as much anymore.

Sometimes a little bit of sky even turns blue on its own.

Still, we hold their catalogs close: fabric and metal; wind and rain.

We try to remember their faces.

At sunset, Mumma goes to the open wall facing the ocean.

"You don't need to stay," she says, stubborn, maybe a little selfish.

But there she is so there I am beside her and soon Varyl also.

All of us, the sunset painting our faces bright. And then, for a moment before us out over the sea, there she is too, our Lillit, blowing soft against our cheeks.

We stretch out our arms to hug her and she weaves between them like a breath.

FRAN WILDE's novels and short stories have been finalists for six Nebula Awards, three Hugo Awards, and a World Fantasy Award. They include her Andre Norton and Compton Cook winning debut *Updraft*, its sequels, *Cloudbound* and *Horizon*; and the middle-grade novel *Riverland*; Her short stories appear in *Asimov's*, Tor.com, *Beneath Ceaseless Skies*, *Shimmer*, *Nature*, *Uncanny*, *The Year's Best Dark Fantasy and Horror: 2017*, and elsewhere. She is the recipient of the 2018 Eugie Foster Memorial Award.

THOUGHTS AND PRAYERS

KEN LIU

*E**mily Fort:*

So you want to know about Hayley.

No, I'm used to it, or at least I should be by now. People only want to hear about my sister.

It was a dreary, rainy Friday in October, the smell of fresh fallen leaves in the air. The black tupelos lining the field hockey pitch had turned bright red, like a trail of bloody footprints left by a giant.

I had a quiz in French II and planned a week's worth of vegan meals for a family of four in family and consumer science. Around noon, Hayley messaged me from California.

Skipped class. Q and I are driving to the festival right now!!!

I ignored her. She delighted in taunting me with the freedoms of her college life. I was envious, but didn't want to give her the satisfaction of showing it.

In the afternoon, Mom messaged me.

Have you heard from Hayley?

No. The sisterly code of silence was sacred. Her secret boyfriend was safe with me.

"If you do, call me right away."

I put the phone away. Mom was the helicopter type.

As soon as I got home from field hockey, I knew something was wrong. Mom's car was in the driveway, and she never left work this early.

The TV was on in the basement.

Mom's face was ashen. In a voice that sounded strangled, she said, "Hayley's RA called. She went to a music festival. There's been a shooting."

So much data, so little information.

The rest of the evening was a blur as the death toll climbed, TV anchors read old forum posts from the gunman in dramatic voices, shaky follow-drone footage of panicked people screaming and scattering circulated on the web.

I put on my glasses and drifted through the VR re-creation of the site hastily put up by the news crews. Already, the place was teeming with avatars holding a candlelight vigil. Outlines on the ground glowed where victims were found, and luminous arcs with floating numbers reconstructed ballistic trails. So much data, so little information.

We tried calling and messaging. There was no answer. Probably ran out of battery, we told ourselves. She always forgets to charge her phone. The network must be jammed.

The call came at four in the morning. We were all awake.

"Yes, this is . . . . Are you sure?" Mom's voice was unnaturally calm, as though her life, and all our lives, hadn't just changed forever. "No, we'll fly out ourselves. Thank you."

She hung up, looked at us, and delivered the news. Then she collapsed onto the couch and buried her face in her hands.

There was an odd sound. I turned and, for the first time in my life, saw Dad crying.

I missed my last chance to tell her how much I loved her. I should have messaged her back.

Gregg Fort:

I don't have any pictures of Hayley to show you. It doesn't matter. You already have all the pictures of my daughter you need.

Unlike Abigail, I've never taken many pictures or videos, much less drone-view holograms or omni immersions. I lack the instinct to be prepared for the unexpected, the discipline to document the big moments, the skill to frame a scene perfectly. But those aren't the most important reasons.

My father was a hobbyist photographer who took pride in developing his own film and making his own prints. If you were to flip through the dust-covered albums in the attic, you'd see many posed shots of my sisters and me, smiling stiffly into the camera. Pay attention to the ones of my sister Sara. Note how her face is often turned slightly away from the lens so that her right cheek is out of view.

When Sara was five, she climbed onto a chair and toppled a boiling pot. My father was supposed to be watching her, but he'd been distracted, arguing with a colleague on the phone. When all was said and done, Sara had a trail of scars that ran from the right side of her face all the way down her thigh, like a rope of solidified lava.

You won't find in those albums records of the screaming fights between my parents; the awkward chill that descended around the dining table every time my mother stumbled over the word *beautiful*; the way my father avoided looking Sara in the eye.

In the few photographs of Sara where her entire face can be seen, the scars are invisible, meticulously painted out of existence in the darkroom, stroke by stroke. My father simply did it, and the rest of us went along in our practiced silence.

As much as I dislike photographs and other memory substitutes, it's impossible to avoid them. Co-workers and relatives show them to you, and you have no choice but to look and nod. I see the efforts manufacturers of memory-capturing devices put into making their results better than life. Colors are more vivid; details emerge from shadows; filters evoke whatever mood you desire. Without you having to do anything, the phone brackets the shot so that you can pretend to time travel, to pick the perfect instant when everyone is smiling. Skin is smoothed out; pores and small imperfections are erased. What used to take my father a day's work is now done in the blink of an eye, and far better.

Do the people who take these photos believe them to be reality? Or have the digital paintings taken the place of reality in their memory? When they try to remember the captured moment, do they recall what they saw, or what the camera crafted for them?

Abigail Fort:

On the flight to California, while Gregg napped and Emily stared out the window, I put on my glasses and immersed myself in images of Hayley. I never expected to do this until I was aged and decrepit, unable to make new memories. Rage would come later. Grief left no room for other emotions.

I was always the one in charge of the camera, the phone, the follow-drone. I made the annual albums, the vacation highlight videos, the animated Christmas cards summarizing the family's yearly accomplishments.

Gregg and the girls indulged me, sometimes reluctantly. I always believed that someday they would come to see my point of view.

"Pictures are important," I'd tell them. "Our brains are so flawed, leaky sieves of time. Without pictures, so many things we want to remember would be forgotten."

I sobbed the whole way across the country as I re-lived the life of my firstborn.

Gregg Fort:

Abigail wasn't wrong, not exactly.

Many have been the times when I wished I had images to help me remember. I can't picture the exact shape of Hayley's face at six months, or recall her Halloween costume when she was five. I can't even remember the exact shade of blue of the dress she wore for high school graduation.

Given what happened later, of course, her pictures are beyond my reach.

I comfort myself with this thought: How can a picture or video capture the intimacy, the irreproducible subjective perspective and mood through my eyes, the emotional tenor of each moment when I *felt* the impossible beauty of the soul of my child? I don't want digital representations, ersatz reflections of the gaze of electronic eyes filtered through layers of artificial intelligence, to mar what I remember of our daughter.

When I think of Hayley, what comes to mind is a series of disjointed memories.

The baby wrapping her translucent fingers around my thumb for the first time; the infant scooting around on her bottom on the hardwood floor, plowing through alphabet blocks like an icebreaker through floes; the four-year-old handing me a box of tissues as I shivered in bed with a cold and laying a small, cool hand against my feverish cheek.

The eight-year-old pulling the rope that released the pumped-up soda bottle launcher. As frothy water drenched the two of us in the wake of the rising rocket, she yelled, laughing, "I'm going to be the first ballerina to dance on Mars!"

The nine-year-old telling me that she no longer wanted me to read to her before going to sleep. As my heart throbbed with the inevitable pain of a child pulling away, she softened the blow with, "Maybe someday I'll read to you."

The ten-year-old defiantly standing her ground in the kitchen, supported by her little sister, staring down me and Abigail both. "I won't hand back your phones until you both sign this pledge to never use them during dinner."

The fifteen-year-old slamming on the brakes, creating the loudest tire screech I'd ever heard; me in the passenger seat, knuckles so white they hurt. "You look like me on that roller coaster, Dad." The tone carefully modulated, breezy. She had held out an arm in front of me, as though she could keep me safe, the same way I had done to her hundreds of times before.

And on and on, distillations of the 6,874 days we had together, like broken, luminous shells left on a beach after the tide of quotidian life has receded.

In California, Abigail asked to see her body; I didn't.

I suppose one could argue that there's no difference between my father trying to erase the scars of his error in the darkroom and my refusal to look upon the body of the child I failed to protect. A thousand "I could have's" swirled in my mind: I could have insisted that she go to a college near home; I could have signed her up for a course on mass-shooting-survival skills; I could have demanded that she wear her body armor at all times. An entire generation had grown up with active-shooter drills, so why didn't I do more? I don't think I ever understood my father, empathized with his flawed and cowardly and guilt-ridden heart, until Hayley's death.

But in the end, I didn't want to see because I wanted to protect the only thing I had left of her: those memories.

If I were to see her body, the jagged crater of the exit wound, the frozen lava trails of coagulated blood, the muddy cinders and ashes of shredded clothing, I knew the image would overwhelm all that had come before, would incinerate the memories of my daughter, my baby, in one violent eruption, leaving only hatred and despair in its wake. No, that lifeless body was not Hayley, was not the child I wanted to remember. I would no more allow that one moment to filter her whole existence than I would allow transistors and bits to dictate my memory.

So Abigail went, lifted the sheet, and gazed upon the wreckage of Hayley, of our life. She took pictures, too. "This I also want to remember," she mumbled. "You don't turn away from your child in her moment of agony, in the aftermath of your failure."

Abigail Fort:

They came to me while we were still in California.

I was numb. Questions that had been asked by thousands of mothers swarmed my mind. Why was he allowed to amass such an arsenal? Why did no one stop him despite all the warning signs? What could I have—should I have—done differently to save my child?

"You can do something," they said. "Let's work together to honor the memory of Hayley and bring about change."

Many have called me naïve or worse. What did I think was going to happen? After decades of watching the exact same script being followed to end in thoughts and prayers, what made me think this time would be different? It was the very definition of madness.

Cynicism might make some invulnerable and superior. But not

everyone is built that way. In the thralls of grief, you cling to any ray of hope.

"Politics is broken," they said. "It should be enough, after the deaths of little children, after the deaths of newlyweds, after the deaths of mothers shielding newborns, to finally do something. But it never is. Logic and persuasion have lost their power, so we have to arouse the passions. Instead of letting the media direct the public's morbid curiosity to the killer, let's focus on Hayley's story."

It's been done before, I muttered. To center the victim is hardly a novel political move. You want to make sure that she isn't merely a number, a statistic, one more abstract name among lists of the dead. You think when people are confronted by the flesh-and-blood consequences of their vacillation and disengagement, things change. But that hasn't worked, doesn't work.

"Not like this," they insisted, "not with our algorithm."

This is the way Hayley deserves to be remembered, I thought.

They tried to explain the process to me, though the details of machine learning and convolution networks and biofeedback models escaped me. Their algorithm had originated in the entertainment industry, where it was used to evaluate films and predict their box-office success, and eventually, to craft them. Proprietary variations are used in applications from product design to drafting political speeches, every field in which emotional engagement is critical. Emotions are ultimately biological phenomena, not mystical emanations, and it's possible to discern trends and patterns, to home in on the stimuli that maximize impact. The algorithm would craft a visual narrative of Hayley's life, shape it into a battering ram to shatter the hardened shell of cynicism, spur the viewer to action, shame them for their complacency and defeatism.

The idea seemed absurd, I said. How could electronics know my daughter better than I did? How could machines move hearts when real people could not?

"When you take a photograph," they asked me, "don't you trust the camera A.I. to give you the best picture? When you scrub through drone footage, you rely on the A.I. to identify the most interesting clips, to enhance them with the perfect mood filters. This is a million times more powerful."

I gave them my archive of family memories: photos, videos, scans, drone footage, sound recordings, immersiongrams. I entrusted them with my child.

I'm no film critic, and I don't have the terms for the techniques they used. Narrated only with words spoken by our family, intended for each other and not an audience of strangers, the result was unlike any movie or VR immersion I had ever seen. There was no plot save the course of a single life; there was no agenda save the celebration of the curiosity, the compassion, the drive of a child to embrace the universe, to become. It was a beautiful life, a life that loved and deserved to be loved, until the moment it was abruptly and violently cut down.

This is the way Hayley deserves to be remembered, I thought, tears streaming down my face. *This is how I see her, and it is how she should be seen.*

I gave them my blessing.

Sara Fort:

Growing up, Gregg and I weren't close. It was important to my parents that our family project the image of success, of decorum, regardless of the reality. In response, Gregg distrusted all forms of representation, while I became obsessed with them.

Other than holiday greetings, we rarely conversed as adults, and certainly didn't confide in each other. I knew my nieces only through Abigail's social media posts.

I suppose this is my way of excusing myself for not intervening earlier.

When Hayley died in California, I sent Gregg the contact info for a few therapists who specialized in working with families of mass shooting victims, but I purposefully stayed away myself, believing that my intrusion in their moment of grief would be inappropriate given my role as distant aunt and aloof sister. So I wasn't there when Abigail agreed to devote Hayley's memory to the cause of gun control.

Though my company bio describes my specialty as the study of online discourse, the vast bulk of my research material is visual. I design armor against trolls.

Emily Fort:

I watched that video of Hayley many times.

It was impossible to avoid. There was an immersive version, in which you could step into Hayley's room and read her neat handwriting, examine the posters on her wall. There was a low-fidelity version designed for frugal data plans, and the compression artifacts and motion blur made her life seem old-fashioned, dreamy. Everyone shared the video as a way to reaffirm that they were a good person, that they stood with the victims. Click, bump, add a lit-candle emoji, re-rumble.

It was powerful. I cried, also many times. Comments expressing grief and solidarity scrolled past my glasses like a never-ending wake. Families of victims in other shootings, their hopes rekindled, spoke out in support.

But the Hayley in that video felt like a stranger. All the elements in the video were true, but they also felt like lies.

Teachers and parents loved the Hayley they knew, but there was a mousy girl in school who cowered when my sister entered the room. One time, Hayley drove home drunk; another time, she stole from me and lied until I found the money in her purse. She knew how to manipulate people and wasn't shy about doing it. She was fiercely loyal, courageous, kind, but she could also be reckless, cruel, petty. I loved Hayley because she was human, but the girl in that video was both more and less than.

I kept my feelings to myself. I felt guilty.

Mom charged ahead while Dad and I hung back, dazed. For a brief moment, it seemed as if the tide had turned. Rousing rallies were held and speeches delivered in front of the Capitol and the White House. Crowds chanted Hayley's name. Mom was invited to the State of the Union. When the media reported that Mom had quit her job to campaign on behalf of the movement, there was a crypto fundraiser to collect donations for the family.

And then, the trolls came.

A torrent of emails, messages, rumbles, squeaks, snapgrams, tele-vars came at us. Mom and I were called clickwhores, paid actresses, grief profiteers. Strangers sent us long, rambling walls of text explaining all the ways Dad was inadequate and unmanly.

Hayley didn't die, strangers informed us. She was actually living in Sanya, China, off of the millions the U.N. and their collaborators in the U.S. government had paid her to pretend to die. Her boyfriend—who had also "obviously not died" in the shooting—was ethnically Chinese, and that was proof of the connection.

Hayley's video was picked apart for evidence of tampering and digital manipulation. Anonymous classmates were quoted to paint her as a habitual liar, a cheat, a drama queen.

Snippets of the video, intercut with "debunking" segments, began to go viral. Some used software to make Hayley spew messages of hate in new clips, quoting Hitler and Stalin as she giggled and waved at the camera.

I deleted my accounts and stayed home, unable to summon the strength to get out of bed. My parents left me to myself; they had their own battles to fight.

Sara Fort:

Decades into the digital age, the art of trolling has evolved to fill every niche, pushing the boundaries of technology and decency alike.

From afar, I watched the trolls swarm around my brother's family with uncoordinated precision, with aimless malice, with malevolent glee.

Conspiracy theories blended with deep fakes, and then yielded to memes that turned compassion inside out, abstracted pain into lulz.

"Mommy, the beach in hell is so warm!"

"I love these new holes in me!"

Searches for Hayley's name began to trend on porn sites. The content producers, many of them A.I.-driven bot farms, responded with procedurally generated films and VR immersions featuring my niece. The algorithms took publicly available footage of Hayley and wove her face, body, and voice seamlessly into fetish videos.

The news media reported on the development in outrage, perhaps even sincerely. The coverage spurred more searches, which generated more content . . .

As a researcher, it's my duty and habit to remain detached, to observe and study phenomena with clinical detachment, perhaps even fascination. It's simplistic to view trolls as politically motivated—at least not in the sense that term is usually understood. Though Second Amendment absolutists helped spread the memes, the originators often had little conviction in any political cause. Anarchic sites such as 8taku, duangduang, and alt-websites that arose in the wake of the previous decade's deplatforming wars are homes for these dung beetles of the internet, the id of our collective online unconscious. Taking pleasure in taboo-breaking and transgression, the trolls have no unifying interest other than saying the unspeakable, mocking the sincere, playing with what others declared to be off-limits. By wallowing in the outrageous and filthy, they both defile and define the technologically mediated bonds of society.

But as a human being, watching what they were doing with Hayley's image was intolerable.

I reached out to my estranged brother and his family.

"Let me help."

Though machine learning has given us the ability to predict with a fair amount of accuracy which victims will be targeted—trolls are not quite as unpredictable as they'd like you to think—my employer and other major social media platforms are keenly aware that they must walk a delicate line between policing user-generated content and chilling "engagement," the one metric that drives the stock price and thus governs all decisions. Aggressive moderation, especially when it's reliant on user reporting and human judgment, is a process easily gamed by all sides, and every company has suffered accusations of censorship. In the end, they threw up their hands and tossed out their byzantine enforcement policy manuals. They have neither the skills nor the interest to become arbiters of truth and decency for society as a whole. How could they be expected to solve the problem that even the organs of democracy couldn't?

Over time, most companies converged on one solution. Rather than focusing on judging the behavior of speakers, they devoted resources to letting listeners shield themselves. Algorithmically separating legitimate (though impassioned) political speech from coordinated harassment for *everyone* at once is an intractable problem—content celebrated by some as speaking truth to power is often condemned by others as beyond the pale. It's much easier to build and train individually tuned neural networks to screen out the content a particular user does not wish to see.

The new defensive neural networks—marketed as "armor"—observe each user's emotional state in response to their content stream. Capable of operating in vectors encompassing text, audio, video, and AR/VR, the armor teaches itself to recognize content especially upsetting to the user and screened it out, leaving only a tranquil void. As mixed reality and immersion have become more commonplace, the best way to wear armor is through augmented-reality glasses that filter all sources of visual stimuli. Trolling, like the viruses and worms of old, is a technical problem, and now we have a technical solution.

To invoke the most powerful and personalized protection, one has to pay. Social media companies, which also train the armor, argue that this solution gets them out of the content-policing business, excuses them from having to decide what is unacceptable in virtual town squares, frees everyone from the specter of Big Brother–style censorship. That this pro–free speech ethos happens to align with more profit is no doubt a mere afterthought.

I sent my brother and his family the best, most advanced armor that money could buy.

Abigail Fort:

Imagine yourself in my position. Your daughter's body had been digitally pressed into hard-core pornography, her voice made to repeat words of hate, her visage mutilated with unspeakable violence. And it happened because of you, because of your inability to imagine the depravity of the human heart. Could you have stopped? Could you have stayed away?

The armor kept the horrors at bay as I continued to post and share, to raise my voice against a tide of lies.

For the faceless hordes of the internet, it became a game to see who could get something past my armor, to stab me in the eye with a poisoned videoclip.

The idea that Hayley hadn't died but was an actress in an anti-gun government conspiracy was so absurd that it didn't seem to deserve a response. Yet, as my armor began to filter out headlines, leaving blank spaces on news sites and in multicast streams, I realized that the lies had somehow become a real controversy. Actual journalists began to demand that I produce receipts for how I had spent the crowdfunded money—we hadn't received a cent! The world had lost its mind.

I released the photographs of Hayley's corpse. Surely there was still some shred of decency left in this world, I thought. Surely no one could speak against the evidence of their eyes?

It got worse.

For the faceless hordes of the internet, it became a game to see who could get something past my armor, to stab me in the eye with a poisoned videoclip that would make me shudder and recoil.

Bots sent me messages in the guise of other parents who had lost their children in mass shootings, and sprung hateful videos on me after I whitelisted them. They sent me tribute slideshows dedicated to the memory of Hayley, which morphed into violent porn once the armor allowed them through. They pooled funds to hire errand gofers and rent delivery drones to deposit fiducial markers near my home, surrounding me with augmented-reality ghosts of Hayley writhing, giggling, moaning, screaming, cursing, mocking.

Worst of all, they animated images of Hayley's bloody corpse to the accompaniment of jaunty soundtracks. Her death trended as a joke, like the "Hamster Dance" of my youth.

Gregg Fort:

Sometimes I wonder if we have misunderstood the notion of freedom. We prize "freedom to" so much more than "freedom from." People must be free to own guns, so the only solution is to teach children to hide in closets and wear ballistic backpacks. People must be free to post and say what they like, so the only solution is to tell their targets to put on armor.

Abigail had simply decided, and the rest of us had gone along. Too late, I begged and pleaded with her to stop, to retreat. We would sell the house and move somewhere away from the temptation to engage with the rest of humanity, away from the always-connected world and the ocean of hate in which we were drowning.

But Sara's armor gave Abigail a false sense of security, pushed her to double down, to engage the trolls. "I must fight for my daughter!" she screamed at me. "I cannot allow them to desecrate her memory."

As the trolls intensified their campaign, Sara sent us patch after patch for the armor. She added layers with names like adversarial complementary sets, self-modifying code detectors, visualization auto-healers.

Again and again, the armor held only briefly before the trolls found new ways through. The democratization of artificial intelligence meant that they knew all the techniques Sara knew, and they had machines that could learn and adapt, too.

Abigail could not hear me. My pleas fell on deaf ears; perhaps her armor had learned to see me as just another angry voice to screen out.

Emily Fort:

One day, Mom came to me in a panic. "I don't know where she is! I can't see her!"

She hadn't talked to me in days, obsessed with the project that Hayley had become. It took me some time to figure out what she meant. I sat down with her at the computer.

She clicked the link for Hayley's memorial video, which she watched several times a day to give herself strength.

"It's not there!" she said.

She opened the cloud archive of our family memories.

"Where are the pictures of Hayley?" she said. "There are only place-holder Xs."

She showed me her phone, her backup enclosure, her tablet.

"There's nothing! Nothing! Did we get hacked?"

Her hands fluttered helplessly in front of her chest, like the wings of a trapped bird. "She's just gone!"

Wordlessly, I went to the shelves in the family room and brought down one of the printed annual photo albums she had made when we were little. I opened the volume to a family portrait, taken when Hayley was ten and I was eight.

I showed the page to her.

Another choked scream. Her trembling fingers tapped against Hayley's face on the page, searching for something that wasn't there.

I understood. A pain filled my heart, a pity that ate away at love. I reached up to her face and gently took off her glasses.

The trolls had trained my mother's armor to recognize *Hayley* as the source of her distress.

She stared at the page.

Sobbing, she hugged me. "You found her. Oh, you found her!"

It felt like the embrace of a stranger. Or maybe I had become a stranger to her.

Aunt Sara explained that the trolls had been very careful with their attacks. Step by step, they had trained my mother's armor to recognize Hayley as the source of her distress.

But another kind of learning had also been taking place in our home. My parents paid attention to me only when I had something to do with Hayley. It was as if they no longer saw me, as though I had been erased instead of Hayley.

My grief turned dark and festered. How could I compete with a ghost? The perfect daughter who had been lost not once, but twice? The victim who demanded perpetual penance? I felt horrid for thinking such things, but I couldn't stop.

We sank under our guilt, each alone.

Gregg Fort:

I blamed Abigail. I'm not proud to admit it, but I did.

We shouted at each other and threw dishes, replicating the half-remembered drama between my own parents when I was a child. Hunted by monsters, we became monsters ourselves.

While the killer had taken Hayley's life, Abigail had offered her image up as a sacrifice to the bottomless appetite of the internet. Because of Abigail, my memories of Hayley would be forever filtered through the horrors that came after her death. She had summoned the machine that amassed individual human beings into one enormous, collective, distorting gaze, the machine that had captured the memory of my daughter and then ground it into a lasting nightmare.

The broken shells on the beach glistened with the venom of the raging deep.

Of course that's unfair, but that doesn't mean it isn't also true.

"Heartless," a self-professed troll:

There's no way for me to prove that I am who I say, or that I did what I claim. There's no registry of trolls where you can verify my identity, no Wikipedia entry with confirmed sources.

Can you even be sure I'm not trolling you right now?

I won't tell you my gender or race or who I prefer to sleep with, because those details aren't relevant to what I did. Maybe I own a dozen guns. Maybe I'm an ardent supporter of gun control.

I went after the Forts because they deserved it.

RIP-trolling has a long and proud history, and our target has always been inauthenticity. Grief should be private, personal, hidden. Can't you see how horrible it was for that mother to turn her dead daughter into a symbol, to wield it as a political tool? A public life is an inauthentic one. Anyone who enters the arena must be prepared for the consequences.

Everyone who shared that girl's memorial online, who attended the virtual candlelit vigils, offered condolences, professed to have been spurred into action, was equally guilty of hypocrisy. You didn't think the proliferation of guns capable of killing hundreds in one minute was a bad thing until someone shoved images of a dead girl in your face? What's wrong with you?

And you journalists are the worst. You make money and win awards for turning deaths into consumable stories; for coaxing survivors to sob in front of your drones to sell more ads; for inviting your readers to find meaning in their pathetic lives through vicarious, mimetic suffering.

We trolls play with images of the dead, who are beyond caring, but you stinking ghouls grow fat and rich by feeding death to the living. The sanctimonious are also the most filthy-minded, and victims who cry the loudest are the hungriest for attention.

RIP-trolling has a long and proud history, and our target has always been inauthenticity.

Everyone is a troll now. If you've ever liked or shared a meme that wished violence on someone you'd never met, if you've ever decided it was okay to snarl and snark with venom because the target was "powerful," if you've ever tried to signal your virtue by piling on in an outrage mob, if you've ever wrung your hands and expressed concern that perhaps the money raised for some victim should have gone to some other less "privileged" victim—then I hate to break it to you, you've also been trolling.

Some say that the proliferation of trollish rhetoric in our culture is corrosive, that armor is necessary to equalize the terms of a debate in which the only way to win is to care less. But don't you see how unethical armor is? It makes the weak think they're strong, turns cowards into deluded heroes with no skin in the game. If you truly despise trolling, then you should've realized by now that armor only makes things worse.

By weaponizing her grief, Abigail Fort became the biggest troll of them all—except she was bad at it, just a weakling in armor. We had to bring her—and by extension, the rest of you—down.

Abigail Fort:

Politics returned to normal. Sales of body armor, sized for children and young adults, received a healthy bump. More companies offered classes on situational awareness and mass shooting drills for schools. Life went on.

I deleted my accounts; I stopped speaking out. But it was too late for my family. Emily moved out as soon as she could; Gregg found an apartment.

Alone in the house, my eyes devoid of armor, I tried to sort through the archive of photographs and videos of Hayley.

Every time I watched the video of her sixth birthday, I heard in my mind the pornographic moans; every time I looked at photos of her high school graduation, I saw her bloody animated corpse dancing to the tune of "Girls Just Wanna Have Fun"; every time I tried to page through the old albums for some good memories, I jumped in my chair, thinking an AR ghost of her, face grotesquely deformed like Munch's *The Scream*, was about to jump out at me, cackling, "Mommy, these new piercings hurt!"

I screamed, I sobbed, I sought help. No therapy, no medication worked. Finally, in a numb fury, I deleted all my digital files, shredded my printed albums, broke the frames hanging on walls.

The trolls trained me as well as they trained my armor.

I no longer have any images of Hayley. I can't remember what she looked like. I have truly, finally, lost my child.

How can I possibly be forgiven for that?

KEN LIU is the winner of the Nebula, Hugo, and World Fantasy Awards; he wrote The Dandelion Dynasty, a silkpunk epic fantasy series (starting with *The Grace of Kings*), as well as *The Paper Menagerie and Other Stories* and *The Hidden Girl and Other Stories*. He also authored the *Star Wars* novel, *The Legends of Luke Skywalker*. Prior to becoming a full-time writer, Liu worked as a software engineer, corporate lawyer, and litigation consultant. Liu frequently speaks at conferences and universities on a variety of topics, including futurism, cryptocurrency, history of technology, bookmaking, the mathematics of origami, and other subjects of his expertise.

LOGIC PUZZLES

VAISHNAVI PATEL

The daughter hates this new country with its methodical streets and packed supermarkets, hates the way every inch of space has been scrubbed clean of character, hates her teacher who speaks to her slowly and loudly as if she is deaf instead of merely unfamiliar with a language that follows no logic. America is devoid of the chaotic magic of her homeland, devoid of any kind of magic. She tells her father, I would rather die than stay here one more day. Please can we go back to India.

The father barely hears her plea through the fog of exhaustion that has settled over him like a shroud. He drives two hours every morning to a small factory, where he crawls inside devices that churn out plastic bags while his fellow workers taunt him for the color of his skin and leave him in the maw of the machinery if he complains. He tells his wife, This is all for a better future. I may not see our daughter, but at least she will have a good life.

The mother hoardes gold, hiding every piece of jewelry she received as a wedding gift and converting her family's meager savings to bars. In India, gold could turn to silver turn to iron turn back to gold, a strange alchemy of the air that twisted plans as they were made. But here she buys as much gold as she can and slips them into boxes filled with packing peanuts in the crawlspace and clothbound covers of books of Hindi poetry. She tells her daughter, When I die, check the whole house. You never know where you might find treasure.

The mother is right. Her daughter discovers real treasure in the dead of a Midwestern winter, when the snow has lost all novelty and the memory of warmth is failing. Her mother has brought back a paper grocery bag filled with books from the library's bag sale, tattered copies of trade novels published decades ago with perfect white children on the cover, and cookbooks yellowed and warped with age worshipping someone named Betty Crocker.

But near the bottom, the daughter's hand brushes against something soft and unmarred, and her fingers close instinctively around the prize. The cover has a glossy finish, and the pages are thick with the dream-like scent of new books. Inside lie beautiful puzzles, the clean black grids printed against stark white paper, each puzzle a self-contained story far more interesting than her sixth-grade reading materials, with clearly spelled out rules and right answers. These are the first things to make sense in this godforsaken country. She immediately senses magic in these pages, a different sort of magic than that of her childhood, but magic nonetheless.

Tulips are pushing out in the small front yard of the townhouse by the time the daughter finishes the book. As she pencils in the answers to each puzzle, power washes through the page and she begins to understand the logic that governs her new world. Her teacher praises her growth on the second trimester report card, writing, Integrating nicely with other students and, Great progress toward normalizing speech patterns.

What she means, of course, is, Assimilating well. The teacher's pride in her own tutelage drips from every word, an ode to her ability to scrub color from voices and culture from minds. Perhaps, as the teacher believes, it will help the daughter. Perhaps it will buy her an American job, a Caucasian husband, a white-picket fence. Or perhaps, unmoored from the people that look and sound like her, the daughter will waste away into nothing at all, a soft sigh in the ripping wind of progress.

But the daughter is not unmoored. She spends her evenings sitting in a hot pink plastic chair and drawing puzzles of her own with a thick

No. 3 pencil onto wide-ruled notebook paper, all bought on discount at the local dollar store, a haven for the Indian community. She usually hates going there, watching her mother socialize while she waits impatiently by the cart, but now she brings paper and pencil and hopes her mother runs into another friend. She writes clues, painstakingly spelling out, The daughter preferred the black socks, or, The daughter went to bed after the mother. Her favorite clues are grouped, the family together and separated at the same time: Out of the mother, the daughter, and the father, one likes striped socks, one goes to bed last, and one is not a parent.

And if, the next day, her mother goes to bed before her and wears striped socks around the house, the daughter thinks nothing of it. Her mother has a headache from the sharp antiseptic supplies she uses to clean the homes of demanding white ladies, and she has not had time to do laundry, so striped socks are the only clean ones left. In India, the daughter could never use magic. She was simply an observer of the fleeting transformations that emerged from the chaos and slipped away again, watching with delight as a snake became a branch or a flock of birds materialized from thin air. It does not occur to her that here, a place steeped with the magic of stability and rules, she can harness it herself.

She loves making puzzles perhaps more than solving them. When she writes, the imaginary blurs into reality blurs into the imaginary in a gently pleasing manner, and an American normalcy seeps into her life. She makes friends, swaps lunches, watches Disney. Her puzzle about group project partners at school comes true, and she snickers at the tears her white classmates shed at being separated from their best friends. To her the pairs are perfectly balanced—orderly—so mean must be paired with nice, good with bad, smart with dumb. Every puzzle she writes makes instinctive sense, and she can barely remember the process of thinking up clues. They appear to her fully formed.

Her mother asks questions in stilted English, bemused by this new hobby, but the daughter cannot voice how it feels to create order in her puzzles. It's a different order than the perfectly square yard of their home, or the perfectly lined homes on their street, or the perfectly clean streets in their town. This order does not wrap its hands around her throat and suffocate all life's joy; it takes her by the hand and leads her away from her American hell.

She tries to explain anyways because she loves her mother. But the words, House, hands, choking, I love, I hate, do not come out quite right. It does not cross her mind to speak in anything other than English. That is the language of these puzzles.

Once her mother loses interest in the conversation, the daughter starts writing another puzzle. Out of the mother, the father, and the daughter, one is very smart, one is very stupid, and—

She has not seen her father in days. Her mother makes excuses for the fact that since moving to America her husband has barely seen his child for three hours a week, describing in great detail the sacrifices he makes to keep a roof over their head, food on the table, and other clichés taught in English learning programs. The daughter understands her parents' division of labor, her father covering the essentials while her mother works to build up the all-important American Savings, but when her mother provides yet another justification for her father's absence, all she can picture is him trapped comically within the factory, unable to come home. She imagines his belt tangled impossibly with a piece of machinery and giggles.

Out of the mother, the father, and the daughter, one is very smart, one is very stupid, and one is stuck inside a plastic-bag-maker.

The father comes home to find the kitchen table a mess, sheets of paper strewn about. His wife holds one such paper in her hand, shaking her head and sounding out unfamiliar words. What is this? he asks. What happened? His wife hands him the paper. An L-shaped grid and his daughter's precise handwriting swim in and out of his blurring vision.

She's writing, his wife says. I just don't understand what it means. His muscles ache. He has been awake twenty hours. Children, he replies, shrugging his shoulders. He has not seen his daughter for far too long, pulling overtime at the factory, but this weekend he will. Just a few more shifts until then. How wonderful, this American concept of a weekend, a day off. He never once regrets moving his family here.

The following afternoon, as the daughter tries to trade her dry cheese sandwich with another classmate's lunch, a tinny voice on the classroom loudspeaker calls her down to the principal's office. She takes a notebook and pencil with her, and when she reaches the office, a woman in a tight blue skirt and white blouse says, Oh Hon, have a seat.

The daughter's name is not Hon, but she obeys anyways. She begins drawing up another puzzle, naming her favorite character Hon. She includes the woman in the blue skirt, naming her Peacock. She adds her teacher and mother to round it all out. Today's puzzle will be about favorite classes and favorite lunches.

Just as she writes her first clue—Hon does not like sandwiches—her mother rushes into the office. Tears pour down her face, eyeliner streaking grotesque black fingers onto her cheeks. She babbles in halting, gasping Hindi. The daughter flinches away. If anyone overheard them speaking in this foreign tongue, her friendships, written into tenuous existence like so much erasable pencil, would dissolve.

Why are you crying? she asks, enunciating each syllable so even her mother can understand.

Your father, her mother says in thick-accented English, and then the word that will follow them forever: dead.

At the funeral service, nobody from the father's factory attends. Why would they? It was a freak accident for which they bear no responsibility, not the spotter who forgot to pull him out on time and left for his lunch break, trapping him inside the machine, or the newcomer who turned on the machine, not bothering with the lengthy safety procedures, or the rest of the staff that used to spend happy hours making fun of the stuffy immigrant. The company pays for the funeral, gives the widow a modest sum and even more modest condolences, and replaces the cog it lost.

After the ceremony, when the body has been taken for cremation, the mother goes home and tears through the house in a frenzied haze, unearthing gold jewelry and gold bars and silver pots given as farewell gifts by well-meaning relatives in India. The daughter trails her mother from room to room, already composing another puzzle in her head about each object, its age, and its value. The mother loads their life savings into the car and drives, slowly and carefully, to the strip mall's Cash for Gold store.

She goes inside, leaving the daughter in the car. The daughter patiently draws herself a grid, then writes clues about gold earrings worth hundreds and gold bars worth ten times that. The numbers don't look quite right, lopsided and alien, so she erases the numbers and pencils in larger ones, smaller ones, for fun. The changes are nearly as unruly as the transmutations of her homeland, and a pang of longing shoots through her. The puzzle comes together quickly, so she covers her answers and re-solves it to stave off boredom. Her mother comes out after an hour of haggling with huge stacks of cash and a cashier's check worth far more money than she has ever seen in her life.

The store owner had not wanted to give in, but against the onslaught of this intermittently crying brown woman citing prices and rates and sums in fractured English, he slowly caved. As they were nearing a final price, he found himself suddenly moved by her plight. He emptied his store of money, withdrew his store's reserve accounts, and handed all of it over to her. He will remember this experience for the rest of his life, and after the store has shuttered due to that day's catastrophic loss, he will rant to his friends about entitled immigrants stealing from honest, hardworking Americans. Not one friend will point out that he used to swindle old people out of their gold for a living.

They will laugh at him for being tricked by a woman, and he will never reveal the truth: she did not trick him.

The mother enters the car and her daughter does not acknowledge her. Her daughter has not cried this whole time, too absorbed in her games to care that her father is gone forever. She slams the door, shouts, You value those puzzles more than your father's life!

The daughter ignores her, embarrassed by the outburst although nobody else can hear them. How much did her mother really value his life? Her father was eaten by a machine, a death he could have easily died in India. What was the point of coming to America? she wants to ask her mother. You are stupid. Father was stupid. Let's leave now while we still can. I am going to die here. But her mother has extended her hours at the cleaning company, opened a bank account, and become ever more determined to maintain this life.

When they get home, the daughter sits at the kitchen table as her mother orders pizza, one American experience that even she finds it difficult to hate. She picks up her pencil, wondering what puzzle she will construct next. She moves to draw a grid, but instead her hand writes, Consider the mother, the father, and the daughter: one alive; one dead—

She hesitates, uncertain what her clue will be. A shiver passes through her. She knows what she wants to say, but she finally suspects the power in her puzzles and fear bubbles inside her. The puzzles demand absolute truth, and the words are dragged out of her before she can stop them. Her pencil scratches against paper.

Consider the mother, the father, and the daughter: one alive; one dead; one dying.

VAISHNAVI PATEL is a Chicago native attending Yale Law School. She spends most of her time reading casebooks and writes fiction to unwind.

A STRANGE
UNCERTAIN LIGHT

G. V. ANDERSON

Anne twirled the thin, dull wedding band around her finger, quite loose. In their rush to be married, they'd failed to have it fitted properly. And there were scores layered in the metal, old scrapes and nicks from its previous owner that appeared when the light from the train window hit it just so. No one else sitting in the compartment noticed its poor quality, or they simply pretended not to. They hid behind the latest broadsheets instead, the front pages still reporting on the Munich Agreement despite it having been some weeks past.

"New bride, are you?" one middle-aged woman wreathed in shabby fur asked her, somewhere past Thirsk. "I can always tell."

"Just yesterday," Anne replied, swaying slightly as the train hit a switch track.

Opposite, beneath his trimmed graying mustache, the corner of Merritt's mouth twitched. He still wore the same dark double-breasted suit he'd put on that last morning in Kent, rumpled now by almost two days' travel, and there was a trace of liquor about him underneath the smell of bedsheets, cigarette smoke, and coffee. Anne knew she must fare no better: She'd had no time to pin her hair properly that morning, nor smear her usual scoop of talcum under her arms.

She caught the eye of the middle-aged woman again and saw now her knowing expression, the discerning brow. Her face grew hot.

"My husband and I honeymooned in the South of France," the woman said wistfully. "Lovely place. I'm not sure what I'd have made of Yorkshire—it can be rather grim, this time of year."

"I grew up in Yorkshire," replied Merritt, watching the embankment alongside the train fall away. "The best of the season's passed, it's true, but we should catch the last of the heather." He sat a little straighter and held out his hand to Anne. "Darling, look—"

Purple, Merritt had told her when she'd asked him about his home county, and what a poor preparation that was for the bristling mat of ling spread out before them. Anne sprang up and unhooked the catch on the window, sending the men's newspapers flying.

"For Heaven's sake, young lady—"

"My *hair*—!"

But Anne wouldn't shut the window on that patchwork of heather and cotton grass, those banks of soft green bracken. She slung one arm out of the window and let the vibrations of the engine rattle her teeth. It hardly felt real that, until yesterday, she'd never set foot outside her little Kent town, let alone seen London. Her whole world had been contained within the walls of the schoolhouse, or her bedroom, or her father's surgery. And now here she was, almost as far north as it seemed north could go.

"And there's Rannings," said Merritt, who'd caught her mood and stood with her, pointing across the moor to the elegant redbrick country house-turned-hotel. His body warmed her back.

"Oh," Anne breathed, "it's—"

She jerked away blinking—some grit in her eye, some spark of coal—and looked down in time to see the colorless shade of a man caught between the rails and the wheels, to be sliced through like brisket, splashing his blueish guts up the side of the train, and the window, and her face; and Anne's own guts turned cold. *Please, God, not here, too.* The strength went out of her legs and she slumped against Merritt, who hadn't seen a thing, of course, and who laughed a little as if she were a child who'd overexcited herself. Then he saw how pale she'd gone. "Darling, what's the matter? Here, sit down, we'll be arriving soon."

All along the train, passengers were standing to check their bags stowed on the overhead racks, to put away a book or a bundle of knitting, to adjust their coats and fish gloves out of pockets. Amidst the hubbub, Anne shrank back into the badly sprung seat. Her eyes flicked to the red walls of Rannings before another embankment rose up and hid them from view.

These aberrations had been with her since late childhood. Silhouettes swinging in the orchards at night; shadows lurking solemnly around the churchyard on Sundays. "Brought on by stress," her father had decided, after consulting the latest journals from London: A nervous disorder resulting from overstimulation, to be treated with ice baths and, later, shock therapy. How she could possibly be overstimulated in a town like Penshaw, miles from anywhere important, he never thought to ask. The intrusions had worsened, passing through London, but that was different. A sudden elopement and its subsequent wedding night would overstimulate anyone.

There was nothing to strain her nerves in Yorkshire, nothing to worry about now that she was free, was there? And yet, they'd followed her anyway.

Merritt was smiling mildly at her. She couldn't smile back. She'd never found the right moment to tell him, in the two weeks of their acquaintance and their whirlwind departure, and had hoped she'd never need to. He seemed a respectable sort of person. Respectable people, in her experience, recoiled from lunacy. He might wash his hands of her completely and leave her ruined. After all, she was quite mad, and—and this scraped at her in particular—how well did she know him, really?

She picked at the dry skin beneath her new wedding band. It calmed her.

I come upon the moor at dusk and quickly lose my way. A band of moormen point out the path of exposed shale ahead, clutches of auburn-breasted grouse swinging from their fists. They're curious of me; it's not often you see a girl in a fine dress traveling alone.

"You're a long way from home," one of them jokes.

"Liverpool's not so far as you think, sir," I say.

"You don't sound like a Scouser." His smile turns to scowl. "You sound right proper."

The stays of my corset—and this twit—are chafing me raw. I turn away from them and allow myself a grimace.

"It'll be dark soon and, beggin' your pardon, you're not from round 'ere," another deep voice calls to me as I climb the loose shale. "These moors can be treacherous. You'll come back with us and set out again when there's light to see by, if you know what's good for you."

From my vantage point, I scan the way ahead. The shadows pool like pitch in the mossy hollows and it's a cloudy night—there'll be no moon, no stars. Already, my breath expels as mist and hoarfrost lends its sheen to my coat. It's tempting to accept their offer. The grouse look plump, full of fat and flavor. But these men are strangers whose stares grow bolder the longer I stay, and I've tested my employer's generosity far enough. I promised to return to Missus Whittock within the week or consider my position lost. I cannot spare even one night.

"Thank you for your concern, sir, but I'm in haste."

"Then," says the youngest, quietly but firmly, stepping forward and raising his lamp, "let me escort you." He peels away from them and joins me atop the shale.

"See you're back home before chime hours," the deep-voiced moorman calls to him. The lad nods and leads the way to the path.

The lamplight drives away the shadows, exposing the frost-rimed bog asphodel pushing up through the rag-rug of sphagnum. Somewhere off to our right, a vole startles and darts away, too quick to catch. My guide doesn't notice. He looks to the horizon, charting the contour of the darkening moors' silhouette against the bloody sky like a seaman charts his stars. It looks featureless to me, but he must recognize some dale or other because he turns to me and says, "We're some ways off yet. I've heard the house keeps early hours. They might not answer the door this late to someone like—I mean, unless you're expected." He hesitates, scanning the cut of my coat, the stitching of my boots. "Are you expected, miss?"

"No," I admit.

A few steps, and then, "Where's Liverpool, miss?"

He's looking at me like I've come from another world. I suppose I have. On Liverpool's docks, you can hardly hear yourself think. Ships laden with spoils from the West Indies bring free men and officers' servants with them; and immigrants from Glasgow and Belfast, such as my parents, come looking for work. Lascars and Chinamen haul ashore crates stamped with the East India Company crest—crates heavy with silk, salt, and opium—and for all their labor, their captains often leave them behind.

Liverpool's rough mixture of language and color and cloth may seem strange here, but it's familiar to me. It's this numbing quiet, this cold, the moormen's slow burr that I will not forget.

But Yorkshire can't be as cut off as all that. My guide's coloring is dark and reddish, yet his lashes frame stark olive eyes. Even here, his face is poured from the melting pot of the world.

"It's to the west," I tell him. "At the mouth of the Mersey."

We trudge on.

"Begging your pardon, miss, but what's your business at Rannings? If you're looking for a position, I should warn you—"

"It's nothing like that," I snap, and then twist my mouth; he's only being kind. "An old friend of mine called on the doctor at Rannings last winter and hasn't sent word home. I've come to fetch him. You haven't seen him, have you? He's tall, taller than you, and walks with a limp." What a poor description for someone I'd know from the back of their head! God knows I fell asleep facing it often enough as a child.

He chews his lip. "I think I'd remember a stranger like that. But I hope you find him." He hesitates now, his warm skin giving off vapor in the lamplight. "We hear talk, sometimes, from the groundsmen . . . about the doctor."

I reach for his arm, grip the corded muscle there. He stops and looks at my hand in alarm. "What sort of talk?"

The lad squirms. "I don't know, I don't like to say." I squeeze and he concedes, tightly, "That he's unkind, and Godless. That he pays well for babies born during chime hours."

"Chime hours—your companion said that, too. What does it mean?" He wrenches his arm away. "When the church bells ring at midnight, the door to Hell opens."

I know instantly what he's referring to, but Hell? What superstitious nonsense!

I don't get a chance to correct him, though, because a blast of bitter wind hits my back like a swell smashing against a breakwater and throws us together. "Don't!" a distant voice pleads. "Don't go in there!" I push away from him and turn into the cold to see what the spirits have sent me: a young woman, pale as egg whites. She's staring past me, as these apparitions often do—no. No, not past. At.

She's staring at me, purposefully, with recognition. I've never known such a thing—I keep my mind and heart open to them like my father taught me, but the spirits have never truly made contact—and then she's gone. The cold wind still stings, but there's nothing chimerical about it.

My guide lifts the lamp high to better fix me with a stare that would melt wax. "You're one of them. Why'd you ask about chime hours, then? What did you see?"

I twist around and hold up my palms. "I told the truth before: I want to find my friend. He's like me. That is, he's gifted, too, and now I worry he's come to some harm."

"What did you see?" he repeats more forcefully.

"Nothing that'll hurt you. Just a woman on the moor. Some poor soul who died here, no doubt."

He's fighting to stay put, shifting his weight from one foot to the other. I expect him to run. I reach out my hand to ask for the lamp at least, but he grits his teeth and surprises me. "What's your name?"

"Mary," I reply. "Mary Wells. What's yours?"

"James," he says. Then he turns and continues along the path to Rannings.

Before I chase after him, I glance back to where the spirit appeared. *Don't!* she'd said. *Don't go in there!* With a stricken face, as if she knows what awaits me at the house. Easier said than done. As Missus Whittock's paid companion, I'm little more than a doll. The old friend I've come to find, Benjamin, the boy from the docks—he represents everything about myself I've forgotten. The hard-won scran shared between our families; the pride in our own survival. Between the elocution lessons, carriage rides, and empty conversations, my past is the only part of me that still feels warm, like flesh. I can't let it die.

The spirits wouldn't possibly understand.

They disembarked near Middlesbrough where Merritt hired a motorcar. They had to double back a few dozen miles, following the railway south, but eventually he took a sharp left, plunging them into untamed moorland. Two follies and a gatehouse later, Rannings was rising before them in all its symmetrical beauty. Its front elevation measured fifteen sash windows across and three high, with four Palladian columns framing the twisting entrance steps leading to the door. Merritt kept checking Anne's expression and smiling at what he found there.

An old porter hobbled forward as the motorcar crunched to a stop, to help with their luggage. "Poor chap," Merritt muttered; such men were a common sight since the war. They followed him to reception, which was just as palatial as the exterior and gloriously warm. Limestone quarried from the moor paved the entrance hall. Behind the reception desk, a staircase unfurled into a mezzanine, and to the left and right Anne glimpsed parlors, dining rooms, gaming tables, all humming with lazy, aristocratic conversation.

"Mister and Missus John Merritt Keene," Merritt told the receptionist, while the porter managed their bags. His hooded eyes lingered on Anne a fraction too long.

Her fingers worried at her wedding band. As a doctor's daughter, her position in society—especially Kent society—was assuredly middle class; and hadn't Merritt told her his father was a lecturer at York? The social season was winding down and their fellow guests might only be the dregs that remained, but nevertheless the porter's attention made her feel uncomfortably out of place. At any moment, the manager might come along and refuse them, casting his eye over the uneven hem of Anne's woolen skirt as if it affronted him and his guests personally.

As the receptionist checked them in, Merritt said, "We'll freshen ourselves up and take a late lunch in the room, won't we, darling?" Here, he looked at Anne. "I'm afraid we're not fit to be seen about the place." The receptionist smiled. She had a bit of lipstick on her teeth which made Anne feel better. "I'll have something sent up." She handed him a key. "Room thirty-two, on the second floor. It's just been refurbished. We do hope you'll enjoy your stay, Mister Keene. Missus Keene."

"Yes, yes, splendid," Merritt said.

Despite the porter's apparent frailty, their luggage had already arrived by the time they climbed the two flights of stairs and located number thirty-two. Inside, they found a beautiful suite warmed by natural light from a window overlooking the front drive.

Merritt shucked off his shoes and collapsed into a chair while Anne explored the bedroom, dared to run her fingers across the silk bedspread. Someone had placed a vase of fresh roses atop the dresser with wet hands: A few droplets warped the pattern on the porcelain.

"Merritt?" Anne sidled up to the connecting doors. To his distracted, "Mm?" she said, "Can we afford this?"

He raised an eyebrow and smiled at her, his head tipped back against the chair exposing his unshaven throat. "Well, I wouldn't say you should get used to it. We shan't be off motoring and staying in hotels every week. But yes, I have a little put by for special occasions." He sighed and tilted his head. "Tell me, do you like it?"

"Oh yes," Anne gushed. "It's lovely. I imagine it must be just like Monte Carlo."

"Hah! You'd loathe Monte."

"You shall have to take me, so I can decide for myself."

Merritt fished out his cigarette case and patted his pockets. Anne had the matches. She struck one for him. "We'll take a grand tour of Europe for our first anniversary, like the fashionable people do," he said when his cigarette was lit, "and utterly bankrupt ourselves on the tables."

"How foolish of us."

"How foolish indeed."

Merritt took her hand—only her fingers, really—stroked them with his thumb. He parted his lips, and Anne wondered if he meant to voice what she was already thinking: Look how foolish we've been already. Perhaps he wanted to kiss her. Isn't that what married couples did when they reached their honeymoon suite? Was there something else he expected of her, something she didn't know to do?

The bed lay empty behind them.

A knock at the door diffused the moment: their food, delivered on a rolling table. Finger sandwiches and small pastries, pots of tea and coffee, cheese and warm bread, slices of salty ham. They ate with their hands, dropping crumbs all over the upholstery, which felt terribly naughty. "And what would the young lady like to do with her afternoon?" Merritt teased, spreading pâté across a cracker.

"I don't know. What is there to do?"

"Oh, we could go for a drive? I'm sure there's cards downstairs, or a bar, if you'd like me to get you drunk." His look turned wicked.

"You know I'd hate that. No, I'm sick of sitting down. I long to stretch my legs. Can we go for a walk? I'd like to see the grounds."

He sucked pâté off his thumb. "Of course, darling."

But even in that short time, the moor had transformed. Everything had taken on a queer blue quality, with the sun so low and obscured by fog. Moisture beaded in the warp and weft of Anne's coat and darkened her unruly fringe. "Sun sets at six, sir," called the porter from the front steps. Merritt raised his hand to show he'd heard.

"Perhaps we should stay inside after all?" Anne said, adjusting her collar and gazing out over that bleak hinterland.

"Don't be silly," Merritt said, holding out his arm. Together they wandered west around the side of the great house. Sodden pockets of moss squelched underfoot, expelling water like blood, and the cries of lonely pipits—juveniles that had yet to migrate south—pricked Anne's mind. It had been easy, in the warm and dry, to forget about the shadow sliced beneath the train; now, she could think of nothing else.

"Tell me about Rannings," she said, just for something to say, and Merritt obliged.

It had been built, he recalled, in the mid-eighteenth century by the Sixth Earl of Hythe who, like so many nobles with interests in the Caribbean, could think of nothing better to do than squander his wealth on a show home. The family estates in Barbados and Grenada, the dark bent backs of slaves, the foreman's whip—all were well taxed to fund this venture. One by one, the red bricks settled into their mortar. Until the flow of money stopped.

"Oh," Anne said. They'd reached the back of the house where the foundations and a few half-finished walls remained. Rannings was laid out like a horseshoe with two flanks that would have joined together at the rear to enclose an inner courtyard, but construction had ceased before the earl got his way. Someone had attempted to make a feature of the foundations by turning them into flower beds, but the cold and the wet, and exposure to the vicious Yorkshire wind, had made a mockery of that. "The slaves rebelled, burning hundreds of acres," Merritt said. "The earl was ruined. He sold Rannings around, oh . . . 1810, 1812? But the new owners didn't stay. I heard there was some legal trouble. The house lay empty right up till the turn of the century; a few tenants here and there, that's all." He nodded ahead, to the plume of smoke from a faraway train. "We used to see it from afar as boys, my brothers and I, and wonder what it was like inside. It was a barracks during the war. It's been a hotel ever since."

The petering walls, the weed-choked foundation stones and the gaping abyss between them: All of it pulled Anne's nerves taut as wire. Reminded her of wounds, of weeping bedsores. Cold sweat slid down her back like dead finger trails. "Why don't they finish what's left of it?"

"Some clause in the freehold." He shrugged, leading her away.

They walked in silence, and the further they went from Rannings, the easier Anne's mind turned to other concerns. The revelation of Merritt's having brothers, for example. He'd never mentioned them. They were, she thought, yet another thing to add to the long list of things she didn't know about her husband. Suddenly, his arm felt alien under her hand, the scruff of growth along his jaw perilously male.

She'd happened to be at her father's surgery the day they met. Merritt had brought in a friend who'd broken his ankle jumping a stile. With the man howling in pain and the doctor on his rounds two miles away, Anne had pushed up her sleeves and set and splinted the ankle herself. She'd seen her father do it enough times; had held down patients before, when there was no one else to be found.

Afterward, Merritt called in to praise her quick actions. He called in the next day, too, even when his friend had been sent home and he had no reason to stay. His graying temples betrayed his age and the townsfolk called him a fool, chasing after a girl so young. But Anne allowed their trysts. Encouraged them, despite her father's protests. Penshaw was a confined place where everyone knew everyone else's business, no matter how intimate, and the young people whose friendship she'd depended on as a child had married and moved away. She was desperately lonely.

And Merritt knew nothing about her other than what she chose to present to him. That fresh start—it was too intoxicating to resist.

Perhaps Merritt felt the same way.

He felt her stiffen and pressed his hand to her back, steadying her. She tried not to balk at that steering touch. She had not escaped the grasp of one father only to fall into the hands of another.

They came upon a small village called Haxby three miles from the house, no more than a rough square overlooked by cottages and a church with a crooked spire. The old vicar was closing the door for the night. He waved cheerfully to them as if they'd worshipped there all their lives. Anne waved back shyly and leaned toward Merritt. "Is this your parish?"

"No, this is still part of the estate," Merritt replied. "My family live north of here. We'll stay at Rannings a few days more, then I suppose I should take you to meet them."

He stopped at the sight of the memorial in the square. Newly erected and yet already stained with mildew, it listed the local war dead in cold iron letters.

"Will your brothers be there?"

Merritt's lips thinned. "No. My brothers are here." Anne's eyes picked them out in the dark.

William Keene
20 December 1895 – 2 August 1917

Clarence Henry Keene
4 July 1898 – 3 August 1917

"We've walked too far," Merritt said coldly.

They returned to Rannings as the last of the light fled. Merritt said nothing to her over supper, throwing back brandy by the fire until late. And when he finally came to bed, just like their wedding night, the sheets lay quite flat and undisturbed in the space between them.

The wailing starts before I see the house and grows louder as we pick our way across the incomplete foundations. James raises the lamp and I catch sight of the walls, dark as dried blood. Almost every great house in England's been built with sugar money. I burn at the thought of the lives that paid for these bricks, these window frames, the furnishings inside.

"What sort of doctor lets his patients cry like that?" I hiss.

James shudders beside me. "Who knows what he does to 'em first." Then he passes me the lamp; it seems he's reached his limit. "Look, I said I'd bring you and I have, but I won't get no closer than this, miss. The house is touched." He glances at the walls as if they might be listening and lowers his voice further. "The doctor took someone from us, too, a long time ago. You're a braver lass than me, standing up to him. Be careful, miss."

I nod solemnly. "Thank you."

James melts into the darkness beyond the lamp's reach, leaving me to climb the coiling steps and ring the bell alone. The housekeeper—or matron, I suppose she'd be better called—answers the door in her housecoat and slippers. She looks at me meanly. "We're not hiring. Clear off!"

I push past her. "Actually, I'm here for Mister Benjamin Walchop. A year is quite long enough for someone who doesn't even need treatment, don't you think?"

The entrance hall's Baltic, the limestone flags beneath my feet gritty with dirt. I'd expected to find rugs and hangings, perhaps a varnished sideboard lit by gas lamps like the ones Missus Whittock has in her drawing room, but the space is bare and lifeless, as are the dim rooms leading off from either side. In a far corner, a gleaming cockroach scuttles away from the lamplight and disappears through a hole in the skirting board.

A hospital, Benjamin had reassured me when he'd come to the

Whittocks' back stoop to say goodbye; he'd been warped with hunger, in body and sense. A sanatorium. Well, perhaps I'm ignorant, but to me, Rannings looks and sounds like an asylum taken wholesale from those silly novels my employer likes so much. I'd laugh if I wasn't so angry.

I turn on the matron. "Where's Benjamin?"

"You should've made an appointment." She closes the door, trapping me inside.

"Oh yes," I scoff, gesturing around, "this is clearly the sort of place where one must write ahead. You're quite run off your feet, I'm sure. But, see, I've been asking after Benjamin for months now, with no response. Is the doctor in?"

She stiffens at my tone and narrows her eyes distrustfully. Looks over my attire and my hale figure beneath, evaluating where I've come from. Missus Whittock clothes and feeds me well; anything less would reflect badly on her husband's income. The matron sniffs. "You're in luck, Miss . . . ?"

"Wells," I say.

She leads me to the right, through a high-ceilinged room with heavy drapes that mute the echoing clip of my boots. A few moths flicker around my lamp, casting erratic shadows on the walls. I shoo them away.

From behind me, I hear the rattle of dice in a cupped palm, the clatter as they land. I stop and turn, but there are no tables. I can't imagine there ever having been any, though I suppose there must have been, once. And—is that the taste of champagne? It burns my tongue, sharp and painful. Yes, I'm sure it is. Missus Whittock let me have a sip last year. For a girl raised on beef scouse and farl, it's a difficult flavor to forget.

The matron is staring at me. "Seen something interesting, Miss Wells?"

"No."

Her lips tighten like they're holding in a smile, and for the first time I'm afraid.

Cold, clammy hands pushed up between the floorboards like couch grass, splintering the wood. Anne recoiled from the edge of the mattress as fingers plucked at her through the sheets.

Help! Help us!

She started awake and then lay still, unsure; the pale morning light had left the room as spectral as the moor, and the ghost of a too-firm grip ached on the inside of her upper arm. The skin there was discolored, a bruise just forming. Her heart started to pound until she remembered that Merritt had marched them both back to Rannings last night, his hand like a vise.

He was awake, too, sitting by the open window with his head in his hands. His shins, exposed by shrunken pajamas, had pimpled with gooseflesh.

Anne curled up tight and tried to doze, but true sleep was long gone. She sighed. The floorboards were unmarked and cool against her soles as she padded over to the swelling curtains.

Merritt's brandy-laced breath swirled like brume. He swallowed stickily. She reached past him and pulled down the sash. Placed a hesitant hand on his shoulder. "Merritt?"

He blinked and took her hand. "Sorry, darling. Bit of a shock, that's all."

"Your brothers."

"I should've expected a memorial, of course. They're setting them up all over."

Anne sank into the seat beside him and together they looked out over the carriage sweep, the lawn, and the dale beyond. The sun was poised on the brink of the horizon, lightening the eastern sky like a spill of bleach. Rannings had been a barracks during the war, she remembered Merritt saying, and now that she looked, she fancied she could see the scars on the lawn where drills had churned the grass. "Did they train here?"

"Briefly—just long enough to learn how to hold a pistol. I was stationed in Scarborough. In 1917, we were sent to the front, to Belgium. . . ." He looked at her blearily; he was still drunk. White sputum had collected in the corners of his mouth. "You don't know what I'm talking about, do you? You've never known wartime. Christ. When were you born?"

"1916."

His eyes unfocused, and the little color left in his cheeks drained away. "You're barely half my age. What must people think of me?"

Anne gave Merritt's fingers a small, nervous squeeze. "I don't see how that's anyone's business."

"Then what must *you* think of me?" Merritt ran a shaking hand through his hair, still slick with yesterday's oil. "I never got to be a young man, y'know. My youth died with my brothers, in the mud of Passchendaele. I thought I'd put it all behind me, but then I came to Penshaw and met you. You reminded me of everything I'd missed." He dragged his hand down his face, peering at her through greasy fingers. "And now there's talk of another bloody war in every newspaper, every morning. I can't face it—I can't bear it again!"

Anne's breath caught. No one had ever been so honest with her, never bared themselves so raw, not even her parents; what did he want her to say?

She opened her mouth, but so did he, to retch. The vase of roses was still on the dresser nearby. She snatched out the flowers, thorns biting into her palm, and thrust the vase under Merritt's chin in time to catch a dribble of bile.

"You need rest," said Anne, back on familiar ground, "and plenty of water." She poured out a tumbler and cupped the back of his head as he gulped it down, the sharp bulge in his neck bobbing grotesquely. With a groan and a lot of morose muttering, he returned to bed. Anne tucked him in. It felt too awkward to stay there in the semi-dark, serenaded by phlegmatic snores, so she dressed and went downstairs. Other guests nodded to her as they passed, all following the smell of frying bacon. The receptionist greeted each one in the detached, polite way Anne knew well from operating the telephone in her father's surgery. "Good morning, Missus Keene. Breakfast is through here."

"Thank you, yes," Anne said, hovering by the desk. "Um, my husband is sleeping in. Could something plain be sent up to him in an hour? Perhaps some toast?"

"Of course," the receptionist said smoothly, noting it down. Her fingernails matched her red lipstick, her perfectly pinned hair that elusive shade of auburn no dye could replicate. Anne tucked a loose, wiry curl of her own hair behind her ear.

"How have you found your room, Missus Keene?"

"Oh, fine."

"I'm glad to hear it." The receptionist underlined her note and looked up to greet the next guest.

"That sounded rather dismissive, didn't it?" Anne twisted her hands together, recapturing the receptionist's attention. "It really is lovely. I've—I've never stayed anywhere like this before. I don't know how to behave."

The receptionist smiled at that—a real, warm smile, rather than the too-wide, toothy show she'd put on for their arrival yesterday. "You'd be surprised how many people say that. There's nothing to it, honestly. I'd say you're a natural."

Anne blushed. "Well, anyway, I'd never guess it was a barracks, and empty before that."

"Never empty for long," she replied. "Rannings has had quite the history. It's even been a hospital. Well, asylum."

"An asylum?"

The receptionist inclined her head, misinterpreting Anne's appalled expression. "A private institution. Shut down about a hundred years ago, but we keep that quiet. I'm sorry, I shouldn't gossip."

As Anne ate the breakfast she no longer had the appetite for, she wondered: Did Merritt know about that particular piece of Rannings history? Was he the sort of person to think it a talking point, an object of interest, like the lords and ladies who'd once paid to see the inmates of Bedlam?

Her father had considered sending her to one or two institutions when she was younger, before deciding to attempt treatment himself. She'd found the brochures in his desk drawer. Modern therapies were nothing like the crude ministrations of the previous century, they reassured their reader, but Anne couldn't stop imagining the worst: manacled inmates, hair shorn for wigs, rolling in their own filth. Such wretched conditions were common before the reforms of the mid-nineteenth century. A privately run asylum in the 1830s must have been Hell on Earth.

Her fellow diners ate on, oblivious, but Anne couldn't stomach any more. The sound of cutlery scraped in her ears. So too the wet click of people's mouths as they chewed. A vulgar flash of mulched sausage when someone laughed, slimy debris coating their tobacco-stained tongue.

Out in the entrance hall, away from the noise, it was better. The porter had left the door ajar while he assisted with a guest's departure. The cool air lifted her fringe and wicked the sweat away from her neck. Tickled her numb lips. She rubbed them hard.

Help! Help us!

Hand frozen over her mouth, she stared down the long parlor opposite. It was furnished with damask sofas and oak reading desks now, but yesterday afternoon, tables had been arranged for craps and baccarat. Someone had tucked a champagne flute into a bookcase and it had been missed by the staff. Anne only noticed it because the morning light caught the glass exactly right.

At the far end of the room stood the whisper of a girl in early nineteenth-century dress. Her posture was bold, totally at odds with her finery. She turned away as if called, and then disappeared through a door that didn't exist.

"Miss Wells to see you, Doctor."

He removes his spectacles and stands as I enter, offering me a shallow bow. I curtsy, studying him from beneath my lashes. The doctor is thin and ropy, a sick tree in winter, with meatless jowls that quiver as he shoots the matron a hard glance. "It's rather late," he says. "I was about to retire."

"You'll want to stay for this one, Doctor. She has a lot of . . . questions." The matron smiles. The light from my lamp picks out her eyes.

"Questions about what?"

"Mister Benjamin Walchop," I say, raising my chin. "He came to you a year ago. I bid you release him from your care so that he can return home immediately."

The doctor leans in. "And you are a relative?"

"A friend, representing Mister Walchop's family. I have their authority here." I pull a sealed letter from my skirt pocket and hand it to him. Benjamin's mother has scratched her mark within, but the rest is by my hand since she never learned how.

The doctor skims it and casts it aside. "I'm afraid that will not be possible. Mister Walchop's is an interesting case and his treatment is not yet complete."

"Treatment for what, exactly? He is not ill." I glance between them. When it's clear an answer isn't forthcoming, I go on, "I saw the contract you sent him. It specified a period of six months in exchange for payment. You've broken your own terms. If you intend to keep him here longer, the least you could do is compensate his family properly."

The doctor chuckles. "How mercenary."

I grip the back of the chair facing the desk. "It's as he would wish it. But now that I've seen your sanatorium for myself—if you can possibly call it that—such terms simply won't do. I've already contacted the authorities with my concerns. I'm sure the magistrate would like to know where you earned your doctorate. So would I, for that matter."

"Oh," the doctor says slowly, baring dull, gray teeth, "I like her. The door, Matron."

She slams it shut. I glare at her, my fist tightening on the back of the chair. The room's both too hot and too cold. Beneath my dress, sweat has left a crust of salt on my skin.

He replaces his spectacles and opens a drawer in his desk, fingers through the files within. "You shouldn't threaten legal action if you cannot take the consequences. I must protect my interests." He peers over the rim of his spectacles and tuts. "Where does a low creature like you find the gall for such threats, I wonder?"

I prickle at that, but finally hold my tongue. For all the time I've spent with Missus Whittock and her set, I can't scrub away the lilt, the brass. What a lady may get away with, a poor girl cannot. How much I've forgotten. How fat I've grown on privilege.

"The treatment, since you ask, is more a series of tests." He withdraws a file and opens it. "I've studied many children, Miss Wells. There was a girl, once, who could talk to birds—just called them out of the sky on a whim. Another could detect lies. One boy could hear my very thoughts, fancy that. But none of them hold a candle to your friend. The boy who cannot die, despite my very best attempts."

My legs tremble beneath my skirts.

When we were ten, Benjamin was mauled by a terrier. I battered it around the head with a brick but the dog held on, shaking Benjamin's leg viciously. A ratter, obeying its breeding. His mother came out with a glowing poker and burned it till it let go, but not before his cries had called the whole neighborhood down upon us. A hundred pairs of eyes watched as his torn calf knitted itself together right there in the street. It didn't knit neatly enough, though: He was left with a nasty limp, and it's hard to find a dock-master who'll give you work when there's fitter pickings to be had. His mother tried to shrug off the rumors by telling people the bite hadn't been so bad, that the truth had got twisted in the telling, but by then the story had spread. Who knows how quickly it reached the ear of this doctor, and for how long he watched unemployment slide into desperate poverty, waiting for the right moment to bait his line.

We stare at each other, and I know I'm right. He must see it in my expression, too, because he laughs with delight and throws the open file he'd fished out onto the desk. The notes are minimal. The insert bears my name. Mary Margaret Wells.

"Mister Walchop has a rare gift that could change the world, and they say birds of a feather flock together," he leers. "So answer me one question, Miss Wells: What is it that you can do?"

I lunge for the door. Terror's already buckling my knees, but the matron strikes the back of my head with a candlestick for good measure. I fall hard, smashing James's lamp. Voices rumble thickly above me, then she takes me by the armpits and drags me through the doorway. Lord, she's strong. We go down a staircase; my heels thud on every step. I'm drooling a bit. I can hear someone crying.

I'm just getting my wind back, just finding the strength to struggle, when she throws me into a dark room and locks the door. I lie on the floor, listening to her receding footsteps and the whimpering from the next room over.

"Hello?" I croak.

The whimpering stops. Rough scratching comes from my left and then the reply, "Who're you?"

"Mary," I say.

"I can't hear nowt. Come closer to the wall. There's a hole."

I crawl toward the voice and run my hands over the damp stone. My palms bump against a protruding finger. A chunk of mortar has been chipped away, I realize, leaving a gap between our cells. I link my warm finger into their cold one. "I'm Mary," I repeat. "Who are you?"

"I'm Martha."

I squeeze Martha's finger. It's missing its nail. "How long have you been here, Martha?"

"I dunno, few weeks."

Her accent is broad. The same ruse, then: taking chime children from the poor where they won't be missed. I grind my teeth at the thought.

The darkness thins and I look up: A narrow, barred window above me lets in a little light as the moon slides out from its cover of cloud. I release Martha's finger and reach up to grasp the bars.

It's been but minutes since James left me; I pray he lingered despite his fear. I suck down the freezing air, each breath as painful as pressing a bruise. "James?" I bellow, fit for a dockhand. "If you're there, help! Help us!"

"No one ever comes this way," says Martha.

"I did," I shoot back.

Ice suddenly blooms on the iron like mold. I pull my hands away before they can stick and look over my shoulder. The ghost from the moor, the one who cried the warning, is in my cell. Her gray eyes are wide with shock. Her hand grasps the doorframe for balance. She must have perished here; tortured, perhaps, by the doctor's twisted tests. But her clothes are strange. I've never seen skirts that fall straight and stop at the shin. I don't have time to question it. "Please, help us."

"Who're you talking to?" asks Martha.

Anne had never hallucinated a person who wasn't in pain, at the point of death. Sometimes, the morbidity of her own mind was worse than seeing visions altogether. This girl, though, had looked whole and healthy, with a calculating, determined expression that endeared her to Anne immediately.

The porter was curling his fingers around the edge of the front door. Instinctively, Anne darted behind the reception desk and through the staff entrance beneath the staircase. There, in the dark, she hiccuped a laugh and held it in with her hand. Why had she hidden from him like a child? A porter wouldn't question a guest standing in the hall, nor would he challenge her if she'd decided to explore the parlor. But then there'd been that stare of his when they arrived—too long, too intimate.

Through the gap in the door's hinge, she took her turn to watch him in the hall. Why did he linger? He might have been waiting to serve another guest, but she fancied he was listening for her, could hear her shaking breath.

He looked directly at her hiding place. Began to make for it. Her breath caught. She ran lightly down the staff corridor, past linen cupboards and offices, hoping she was faster. Eventually she reached a door that opened onto the inner courtyard. Three kitchen boys were huddled by the water pump sharing a cigarette. They glimpsed her as she backtracked, one of them calling out in surprise. She panicked and dashed right, the windows flashing past, until she was forced to turn into the east wing.

Clearly, this part of the ground floor was unused. Someone had wallpapered once, and laid down carpet, but the sprucing ended there. One room still boasted its old gas fittings. Another's plaster was rotting away.

Anne slowed to a stop and leaned against an empty doorframe to catch her breath, the playground fear that had driven her this far melting away, leaving her feeling more than a little silly. She tugged her sleeves down to cover her wrists and wrapped her arms around her middle. The ceiling creaked, its bare lightbulb swinging gently: a guest moving around their room. On the floor above that, her husband lay sprawled in the bed of number thirty-two.

She'd grown up watching her father tear people's bodies apart and stitch them back together, but the mind was a different beast—she knew that better than most. The loss of his brothers on the very same battlefield he'd survived had left Merritt with particular scars that no amount of ice baths or shock therapy could heal—God knew, they'd done nothing for her—but those were the only tools she understood. And drink, it seemed, was his.

How was she supposed to stitch her husband back together with nothing but words?

Her soles had left footprints in the dusty carpet. Breadcrumbs leading the way she'd come. As her eyes followed them, even as her foot tensed to take a step, a draft from farther down the hall swept them away. A door at the far end, hung badly, wavered, scraping against its frame. From the sliver of darkness beyond, Anne heard the rasp of saw on bone.

Help! Help us!

The cry sounded so close, so real, that she hesitated. It was easy to ignore the intrusions when no one else reacted to them. When she was alone, there was no way to tell if they were genuine or not. She'd left her mother lying on the kitchen floor for hours with a concussion once, unsure whether she'd imagined the shriek and smack of a head hitting the black-and-white tiles. If someone really was stuck and calling for help and she turned away, just as she'd turned away that day, she'd never forgive herself.

She approached the door, pulled it wide, the brass handle so cold it burned her palm. A belch of stale, sour air came up from the staircase beyond, chased by a drawn-out sob that might have been the wind keening through some broken window. The steps demanded she take them one at a time, hewn as rough as they were and slick with mold.

Merritt's matchbox still bulged in her cardigan pocket. She got it out and struck one, peering around a forgotten wine cellar. The racks were empty now, though the vinegary tang of wine gone bad lingered. A leak from some unseen pipe had left a film of water on the floor, so that the walls seemed to extend for infinity in the reflection, and her tiny matchlight, her own pale face, stared up at her from below.

There was a door leading farther into the basement. She pushed it open and advanced into a corridor, similarly flooded. The match was burning low. She shook out the flame and lit another, edging toward the first room on her right. The rasping returned, louder.

"Hello?" she said meekly.

That word, and then her gasp, echoed back.

A boy was laid out on a table within—ashen except where the skin of his chest had been peeled aside in lapels of red, exposing white ribs.

Anne reeled, dropping the match. The light guttered out, but she could still see him branded on the inside of her eyelids. Her breath wouldn't come. "It's not real," she whispered, and the whispers flew back at her. *It's not real, not real, not real.*

Help!

She fumbled with the matches, lost one, lit another.

A lean man with his back to her, pate shining. He was standing over another body, another child, viciously pumping his arm back and forth, and the rasping of the saw was in her bones. She gulped down bile and left the room.

"Is—is there anyone here?"

The second room she looked in on was blessedly empty. She clasped the doorframe and sighed. The calls for help had been in her head after all. But—what was that? Scratching from the next room over, and a wretched sniveling. She bit her lip and sloshed along, the water deeper here and starting to flood her shoes. The third door had slumped free of its upper hinge, its bottom corner jammed into the floor. She squeezed through the gap and held up the remaining sliver of matchstick. "H-hello?"

A little girl with her back to Anne, clawing at the far wall in an attempt to reach a high-set window. She turned to look at something over Anne's shoulder, and the sight of whatever she saw there brought on a fresh, frantic attempt at the wall.

The flame reached Anne's fingers and she yelped with pain. She lit another—her last—and waded toward the girl, but she was gone now, despite having looked and sounded so solid.

The wallpaper where she'd stood was sloughing away in thick, fatty strips. There, on the bare stone beneath . . . white scratch marks, in sets of four and five. Anne placed her own fingers on them, in the grooves.

"No," she moaned, "it's not real."

Not real, not real, real, the echoes replied. *Real, real, real.*

She dropped the match and fled the cell. Twisted in the dark to find the way out. The staircase was through the wine cellar door on her left; she could see the light on the steps. Out of the depths of the basement to her right, a woman was charging toward her, yanking cord from around her neck. "Get back here, you little bitch!"

She screamed then and dived for the exit, throwing herself up the steps and through the deserted rooms of the east wing with abandon, fear clinging to her like a net of spiders. She yanked open a door to the courtyard, alarming the staff working there—"Miss? Miss, you can't be here!"—and ran through the sucking mud of the foundations, drawn to the open moor and fresh air beyond.

Something cold grabbed her calf. She looked down: The ground had sprouted a dozen flailing cadaverous arms. One partially buried face, an accusing eye.

She kicked out, too terrified to feel it connect. When her feet finally met hard gray shale, they slid around in her shoes, her socks sodden and the leather stretched; she slipped and fell down the incline, scraping her palms on the rock. She got up, but her side was hurting now and she was fighting the urge to cry. She risked a glance back at Rannings. The girl from the parlor, almost invisible in daylight, was walking toward the house.

A gust of wind, or perhaps the strength of Anne's gaze, jostled her and she turned. Their eyes met. Anne bit back a sob. She was so young, no more than seventeen. "Don't!" she yelled at the apparition, for all the good it would do, since she couldn't be real. "Don't go in there!"

When the vision faded, Anne put a bloody hand to her forehead and took a deep breath. Stress, her father had said. Overstimulation. It was clear that Rannings was causing exactly that, and the only way to settle her nerves was to put as much distance between herself and that awful building as possible. Anyway, she couldn't bear the thought of going back; she'd only bring the smell of the cellar with her and taint everything. So she walked on, one hand pressed to the stitch in her side, the other guarding her face from the worst of the lashing wind.

As she tramped through the heather she'd so wanted to see, her spirit unraveled. Penshaw seemed like Eden now, a bucolic paradise as untouchable and as improved by nostalgia as childhood. She'd telephoned her parents from King's Cross just yesterday morning and already her mind had muddied the exact intonation of her mother's voice, had softened her father's outrage as he told his daughter, and then Merritt, exactly what he thought of them. The simplicity of that life suddenly appealed to her as it hadn't before, the march of time marked by service on Sundays, reliably followed by a joint of beef and potatoes, hot from the oven.

Haxby lay beyond the next dale. Anne made for the church as the sky darkened and booms of thunder vibrated in her chest. The church-yard gate opened with a squeal. The first fat drops of rain hit the nape of her neck and slithered down between her shoulder blades as she heaved the door open and stepped inside where it was dry. The deluge came down behind her like a final curtain at the theater.

In the murky light from the diamond-grid windows, Anne saw empty pews knocked slightly askew. A dark pulpit. Quite different from the church in Penshaw, where the secretary took great pains to refresh the flowers and notices, and there was always someone, if not the vicar, tending the vestry and lighting candles in the chapel. Still, the door had been unlocked and she had seen the vicar just yesterday.

Anne's hands were chalk-white, her nails lilac with cold. She stuffed them into her armpits and walked stiffly up the nave, leaving muddy footprints on the memorial slabs. Somewhere in the rotting beams above, a pigeon cooed and defecated, a falling white smear joining the many others splattering the chancel steps. She skirted the mess and wandered along the north transept, knocking on a discreet little door to what she assumed must be the vestry. Each rap echoed, reminding her horribly of the wine cellar, so she opened the door with an apology on her lips only to find it empty apart from a few chests. They were filled with blankets. She shook out a tartan one and wrapped herself in it, coughing and sneezing at the dust. Returning to the nave, she picked a seat far from the pigeon and clumsily removed her saturated socks and shoes. Tucking her feet up under her, she fell into a lethargic, shivering stupor.

Rain shimmered on the windows. The roof had a leak, an insis-tent drip coming from the south transept. The pew was hard enough to numb her back and behind. And yet she did sleep, fitfully, for a few hours, while the storm battered the moor and drowned the graves in the churchyard.

Until she sensed movement. Her eyelids fluttered open, her chapped lips peeled apart. The angle of the sun, the shadows, had changed. The vicar squinted at her from the end of the pew, bent almost double with his hands clasped behind him. He beamed at the sight of her stirring.

"Reverend." Anne licked her lips and rubbed her eyes. The blanket fell from her shoulders. "I'm sorry," she said, tugging it back. "I couldn't find you, and I was so cold. I took this. I hope you don't mind."

"Nay, 'tis nowt." His ears were so overgrown with age, so soft and cartilaginous, that they waggled when he shook his head. He sucked at his own lips in such a way as to imply several missing teeth. "It's good to have company. It's been twenty year since anyone new's come by."

"You waved to me yesterday. I was standing by the memorial."

"Ah," he said, nodding blandly. He didn't remember her in the slightest. "Well, you can stay as long as you like. What's your name?"

"It's . . . Keene," replied Anne. "Missus Keene."

He worked his gums, wet bottom lip protruding thoughtfully. "You don't sound right sure. Newly married, eh?"

"Yes. The day *before* yesterday." Anne sighed, buried herself deeper into the blanket. "I'm afraid we've made a terrible mess of things."

"Oh?" The vicar chuckled. "What's troubling you, then, Missus Keene?"

Anne looked at her wedding band. For the first time since she'd put it on, she'd completely forgotten about it. "He's a drunk. The war's left him with some sort of shell shock. And I—I—"

"Go on, lass, spit it out."

"Well, I see things, people, that aren't there."

The vicar raised his brows at this. His eyes emerged from the crumpled folds of his face, startlingly blue.

"I didn't want to tell him, but I don't see how it can be avoided now I've made such a spectacle of myself." Anne showed him her palms, grazed during her fall. He tutted sympathetically. "My God, he'll be so ashamed of me," she whispered, the details of her flight coming back to her: the mad scramble through the mud, the shrieking, the bewildered staff. Her heart thumped against her ribs. "What will I do? I can't go home."

"You're seeing apparitions?" He came closer, turning one waxy ear her way. "Tell the good reverend all about it, lass."

So she told him about the hanging men in the orchards of Penshaw, the shadows that drifted formlessly in the churchyard, the bleeding woman she'd sometimes seen slumped on the bench outside the green-grocer's. And then in London, where her madness became difficult to hide: the crawling man in the alleyway, his fingertips blackened with plague. The one who stepped off the Embankment into the Thames. The burnt child. And then the man caught beneath the train, the cries for help that had tricked her into investigating the bowels of Rannings, and what she'd found there.

The vicar made an inquisitive audience. Unlike the numerous doctors to whom she'd described her visions, he pushed for more detail, more description, and yet his questions never felt prying. By the time she finished, he'd taken a seat beside her, brooding like a particularly ugly gargoyle. "I've heard of the doctor afore but it's worse than I thought. Summat must be done for them poor souls." He cocked his fluffy head. "Tell me, when was you born?"

Anne groped for a reply. The question had caught her off guard. "The third of F—"

"The *time*, lass, the *time*."

She frowned. "Oh, I don't know. My father always says he delivered me on the dinner table. Supper, I suppose you'd call it. Why?"

"Vespers," the vicar said to himself. His eyes popped out again like blue winkles emerging from their shells. He leaned in conspiratorially, his bulbous, arthritic hands clasping his knees. "Nah then, have you ever heard of chime children?"

Anne gave him a tired, indulgent smile. "No, I haven't."

"Chime children are what's born when the bells toll. They can do owt—commune with God's creations, heal the sick, even pierce the veil of Heaven. Folk up here say they're born at midnight, and folk down your way might say morning or evening, but it's the bells what matter." He pointed up to the tower where the transept and nave intersected, where presumably a bell now hung, silent. "I'll bet the bells was ringing out when you came into this world. Powerful thing, bell-metal. . . . You still with me, lass? You look right flayt."

Anne was on her feet, hugging the blanket tight. "There's no such thing as ghosts, Reverend," she said coldly. "My delusions are caused by stress, and in the last two days I have estranged myself from my only family and married a man I barely know. Our minds are extremely susceptible to suggestion. We all learned about the Black Death and the Great Fire of London in school. I was told of Rannings' history, the asylum. I've read anatomy books. I've heard my father perform amputations. All I had to do was fill in the blanks."

"What about the scratches in the wall? You said they felt real."

"Everything I see feels real, Reverend, but there must be a rational explanation."

The vicar smiled at her as if she were a marvel and spread his arms. "If you wanted rational, why seek shelter in a church?"

She had no answer to that. "But this bell nonsense—it sounds so pagan. It's hardly appropriate for a vicar."

"The Bible tells us God created the world, so I say chime children are His work. Nowt can exist that He did not intend, Missus Keene."

Anne buried her face into the musk of the scratchy blanket and exhaled. Her tongue pulsed against her bottom teeth. A part of her willed it to be true: It explained so much about where and in what state her visions appeared. She had never been a morbid child, had suffered no early grief, so there seemed no reason for her illness to fixate on churchyards, on pain and terror.

She lifted her head and gazed at the ceiling, the roosting pigeon. How could she be sure this wasn't simply another delusion? But then the vicar was here, wasn't he? She wasn't alone?

"Can it be true?" She gazed at him. "I'm not mad?"

"You've no control over what you see or when." He lifted a finger. "Intrusions is still intrusions, sane or no. You must find a way to bear them."

"But I've seen others, other people who aren't suffering. The girl I saw today, she looked fine. Does that mean even she's . . . dead?"

"Maybe, maybe not." The vicar shrugged, resting his hands on his gut. "Some folk leave impressions, not just where they died, but where they made a difference." He looked around his church with such serene pride that Anne found herself looking as well. At the crooked pews, the broken memorial slabs. A candelabrum knocked to the floor, draped in cobwebs, and a bare altar. A leaking roof. A pigeon and its excrement. A vicar who, despite his unwashed appearance and gummy mouth, was strangely odorless.

Anne felt sick. She went to the front door and pushed it open, but the rain was thick and driving sideways, pulping the shrubs. The path to the churchyard gate was underwater, and she could barely make out the war memorial twenty feet away. She would easily get turned around in this, without the sight of Rannings to guide her back. Thunder growled, and between the dark clouds, lightning flickered.

The vicar walked through her and out into the storm, unaffected by the rain. He stooped especially low to read one gravestone and then another, until he found what he was looking for. "Aye, here's me."

Anne's skin tingled. "Please don't walk through me again, Reverend." But she held the blanket over her head, trusting the stiff weave to keep out the worst of the rain, and plunged barefoot into the churchyard to read the stone.

Rev. Jonah Rolfe
28 June 1771 – 5 December 1855

"Fifty year," the vicar said. "I poured my heart and soul into this parish for fifty year. I were happy here, lass, right happy I were. You should've seen it in its prime." A frown, a return to the present moment. "I remember you now. Yesterday means nowt to me, but I do remember you." His voice was fading. Anne stepped closer, protecting him from rain he could not feel. "Help them poor souls up at the house, if you can. They'll want to talk—that's why they come to you. Our bell will make it easier. Purest bell-metal an earl can buy."

"Good luck, lass."

And then he was gone.

* * *

"Who're you talking to?" asks Martha.

"A ghost," I say—a ghost who's already gone, her eyes the last of her to fade. I can't be sure she even heard me.

Martha moves behind the wall. I imagine her pressing her ear to the hole. "What?"

"Never mind." I rub the back of my head where the matron struck me and my fingers come away wet and dark. A headache forms there, as if a gentle press was all it needed. I ease back down beside the hole and we link fingers again.

"Can you find things, too?" she whispers. "Is that why you're here?"

"I seem to be much better at losing them. . . . Why, what can you find?"

"Owt," Martha replies, and there's a note of quiet pride in her voice. "When I were little, folk used to say I must've stolen things, to know where to find 'em. They chased us out of town. Where we live now is better. Now folk pay me, sometimes, to help find stuff."

I smile, understanding her pride. As children, any coins Benjamin and I could contribute to our families were precious, whether they'd been earned honestly or lifted out of a loose purse. Every coin meant our mothers could afford to put one less neighbor's shirt through the backbreaking mangle, make one less matchbox when we'd all gone to bed. Our fathers could come home from the docks one hour earlier, live one more day before their bodies gave out. It's why the damage to Benjamin's leg was such a blow. But I also smile because her gift gives me hope.

"Listen, Martha, does it work for people, what you can do?"

She's quiet for a moment. Perhaps the doctor's asked her the same thing, and now she regrets saying as much to me. "Sometimes."

I give her finger a little squeeze. "You see, I came to find my friend. He's here somewhere, locked up, just like us. Have you heard anyone crying out?"

"I think so," she whispers back. "They're somewhere dark, some-where . . . down there." I can barely hear her as she draws away from the wall, a dowsing rod for Benjamin. Then she yanks on my finger and says, her voice pitched high with sudden panic, "Please don't leave me here! I know you didn't come for me, but I wanna go home, too."

I soothe her as best I can, pressing her poor exposed nail beds to my lips. Guilt stings my eyes. I came for Benjamin and Benjamin alone, but I don't have the heart to abandon this child. I'm not a monster. Will Missus Walchop ever forgive me, if I'm forced to choose? This girl can die and Benjamin cannot—is that what I must tell his mother, what I must tell myself, in leaving Benjamin to his torture?

The peal of a faraway bell ripples through me. I look up to the window.

Fog slithers in like water. "What's that?"

"It's coming from the church at Haxby," says Martha. "It must be midnight."

"Chime hours," I breathe.

Every clang strikes me like a smith's hammer. White dots blister my vision, expanding and joining together until I can't see, and everything—the chill bleeding through my skirts, the vise of my stays; even Martha, noticing something's wrong—comes to me as if from a great distance. I turn obligingly inward like I was taught, into the light.

An old bell appears above me, scabbed with turquoise verdigris. Below, pulling the rope, is the ghost. I watch the bell's clapper connect with the rim. As the vibration stretches impossibly long, pinning us in a moment, our eyes meet. Her left eyelid distorts when she smiles.

"It's you," she says.

Suddenly she's right here, or I'm there—space has ceased to matter— and she's all loud, chromatic flesh. Blood springs from the fissures of her chapped lips, coloring them a shocking red and infusing her breath with iron. She's reaching gently for my hand. Hers are as soft as a gentlewoman's, until I turn them over and find her palms flecked with cuts. I close my callused fingers over hers.

"You were right, wise spirit," I tell her. "I should've listened to your warning."

Her brows draw together. "You know me?"

"Of course," I say slowly. "You told me not to go to the house."

This shakes her in a way I can't understand. Do spirits not remember their own actions? But then something resolves. Her mouth presses into a straight, serious line. She breathes deeply, her exhalation quivering.

"All right. Is there something you wanted to tell me? Is there some message?"

Now it's my turn to be shaken.

Chime folk are rare, and my gift is rarer still. Everything I know about spirits comes from hand-me-down talk, filtered through a dozen mouths. A woman from a village called Hale, some dozen miles from Liverpool's docks, was said to see the dead, and the crux of her parting advice which finally found its way to me was this: Listen to them. Let them impart their wisdom or last words so they can rest.

They don't ask us for messages.

"I don't understand you, spirit," I say, letting go of her hands. "It's usually the other way around."

"Is it?"

"Don't you have a message for *me*? Another warning? I'll heed you this time." I step back and take her in, the thrill of making contact giving way to sober clarity. Her accent, her clothes, are alien. I can't place her lack of corset, her narrow skirt, the lumpy spencer that extends down to her waist. Her hair, tawny as a barn owl's hood, escapes from pins set above her ears. "When did you die?"

Her eyes widen. "I'm not dead! I'm . . . I'm on my honeymoon. Today is the twenty-second of October, 1938. I saw it on a newspaper someone was reading at breakfast."

I find myself on the floor, such as it is in this place, knees bent inward like a child. 1938. An incomprehensible date. The future. I must be seeing the future. I'm snatching glimpses of people not yet born, tasting champagne made from grapes that are yet to grow. Suddenly, I understand why history hasn't recorded the incidents I see—they haven't come to pass. The spirits never speak to me because they don't even know I'm there. But if this woman can see me. . . .

"Oh God, do I die here?" I cover my eyes. "Don't tell me, I don't want to know."

"I'm sorry," she whispers, and she's at my level, prizing my hands from my face. "All I know is that I've seen dreadful things all my life.

I thought I was mad. I think I still am mad." She laughs weakly. "But I saw you in the parlor at Rannings today, and on the moor. You were intact and . . . simply perfect. For the first time, I wasn't scared." She smiles again giddily, her left eyelid taut. "I'm not scared."

I'm younger than she, but I feel a tug of responsibility. I palm her cheek and fix her with a steadying look. "There is nothing to fear from the dead. They may frighten you, they may come when you want to be alone, but they won't harm you." I draw our foreheads together. Benjamin did this for me, when my gift first manifested and I couldn't sleep. It's my dearest memory of him. Tears drip into our laps. I can't tell which are mine.

"So," I say, and we draw apart, "what else did you see in the house, besides me?" She describes as best she can the flayed boy. The girl in the cell, who can only be Martha, clawing her fingernails off trying to escape. As she speaks, I feel the resonance of the bell fading. Our time grows short. "Did you see a boy? Scrawny and tall, with a limp? He doesn't heal completely—he might have other scars, too."

"A boy—?"

"In 1938, is there any record of him," I push, "of us being held against our will?"

"I don't know." She hides her face in her hands. "After Rannings was sold, there was some talk of legal trouble, and I think the receptionist said the asylum was shut down about a hundred years ago, which would be—"

"Now," I finish viciously. "Tell me, was the doctor tried? The missing children, the flayed boy—were they found?"

"No, no, I don't know. . . ."

I close my eyes, holding my anger in. The doctor targets poor, hungry families, mothers like Benjamin's, like Martha's, who can't afford to turn down money even at the expense of a child. He trusts that the world will turn without stopping for them. Sickeningly, he's right: There will be no accounting for this in his lifetime.

"What is it now, the house?" I ask bitterly.

"It's a hotel. A very expensive hotel."

A hotel! I can't help but laugh, but there's no joy in it. "Mark me:

Children have died here far from home, and they deserve justice. My friend, Benjamin, deserves justice. God knows what he's been through. I don't know the limits of his gift; perhaps the doctor has already found a way to break him." I grip her arm and she flinches. "Avenge us. That is what the spirits want. That's what I want, if I'm to die here."

"I will, I promise," she says, her voice faint.

"Goodbye. God bless you." I kiss her cheeks as they turn translucent. Even if I survive this night, my bones will be dust by the time she walks the Earth. I don't even know her name.

I'm released slowly back to my senses, as if recovering from a faint. Barely a second has passed. Martha is crying my name. She's heard me collapse, convulsing, and her terror has attracted the matron's attention. Those are the soles of her slippers I hear, flapping against the steps.

Martha's crying falters when she hears me stir, but I grunt at her to keep going as I prop myself up. I tear at my bodice and the damp silk parts easily—fashionable clothes, like fashionable people, aren't made to withstand much of anything at all. My fingers fumble at the laces of my corset as the matron barks from outside our cells, "What's going on in there?"

The laces slither free. I wait behind the door where it's darkest, wrapping them around my fists into a makeshift garrote. Martha's listening. She's not stupid. "There's summat wrong with Mary," she wails. "She won't wake up!"

Keys jingle. The matron enters, holding a candle aloft. I don't give her time to clock the bare floor: I throw my crossed hands over her neck and jerk them home. She drops the candle and flails, gurgling. Her elbow drives into my side, cracks a rib, drawing a gasp. But I'm a Belfast girl raised in Liverpool; I can give as good as I get, and right now I've got nothing to lose.

One more squeeze of the garrote and she goes down with a thud.

Her keys are still dangling from my door. I unlock Martha's cell and she flies to me, burying her face in my soft belly. "Ah," I gasp, "not too hard." Every breath burns and my back aches now without the support of my stays. Unlaced for the first time since I was a young child, my middle's as cold as a shucked mollusk.

I stare down the corridor. For a moment, the path to Benjamin is clear. But I can't draw a painless breath deep enough to shout his name, and anyway, Martha's shaking her head at me desperately, unsure of her gift, and the matron's storming toward us, her purple face twisted with rage. I mustn't have held on long enough. I've never tried to strangle anyone before.

"Get back here, you little bitch!"

Martha shoves her, giving us room to sprint past and up the stairs, to lock her in behind us. The matron's ham-sized fists batter the door, but it holds.

"What now?" Martha says, clinging to me.

"We get out of here," I reply, stroking her head, "but I need something first. A letter that I brought with me. Is it still on the doctor's desk?"

She nods.

My heels left twin trails in the dust where the matron dragged me. We follow them to their source, the keys jutting between my fingers to make a spiked fist. The doctor's door is ajar and the room is still. He must have retired for the night. But even here, a faint banging makes its way up from the basement, and even now he may be descending the stairs to investigate.

I snatch up Missus Walchop's letter and rifle through the files in his desk, my hands shaking so much I almost can't pinch out the one I want.

"Drop them."

Martha flinches. The doctor's blocking the doorway. The barrel of a revolver's pointing at her head. I pull her behind me as he fires, blasting a hole in the paneling. As precious as we are to him, he'd kill us to cover his tracks? Selfish coward! I grit my teeth and lunge, ready for the bullet to punch through me if it means sparing Martha, but my unexpected offensive sends his second shot wide, the third jams, and by then I'm close enough for a right hook that would make my mother proud. One key skewers his cheek. Another lodges in his eye. The revolver, and the doctor with it, falls to the floor.

I stand over him, wheezing, with one hand pressed to my rib. His unscathed eye rolls in agony, and when it settles on me I hunker down, baring my teeth in a grin. "You wanted to know what I can do, Doctor?

I can see what is yet to pass, and I've seen the future for this place—for you. Your work will come to nothing. No one will remember your name. And these"—I hold up the file, the letter—"will ruin you, I'll make sure of that." He whimpers. I straighten and take Martha's hand, and together we leave.

Where the crunching drive gives way to soft moss, I hear light foot-steps ahead and hold my breath, but it's only James, praise God. I can smell the grouse and lamp oil on him. He must sense more than see the ruin of my bodice and corset, revealing the thin, secret shift beneath, because he passes me his coat without comment, tells me instead how my cries for help echoed over the moor and that he couldn't bear to go home still hearing them.

And of Martha, he says, "Who's this?"

"That can wait." I groan, leaning heavily against him. "Take me to the magistrate. Or the nearest lawman who'll hear me out."

Martha turns her face up to mine. "What're you gunna do?" Missus Walchop's letter and a broken contract press against my side.

I look up at the dark bulk of Rannings. My employer, if she'll still be my employer after this, with all her hollow frivolities, will have to damn well wait.

If you're still in there, Benjamin, you better hold on.

"I'm going to tear it down. Tear it all down."

"Good God." Broad hands stroked her face, wiped away strands of wet hair. "You rang the bell, didn't you? Good girl, clever girl, I heard you, I'm here now." Merritt tried to rub warmth into her numb legs, her feet, so rough it hurt.

"Stop," Anne mumbled. She'd seen a hypothermic man die from such rubbing. "Your coat."

"Easy, easy. All right." He wrapped her in his coat, damp but still warm from his body and better than nothing. He scooped her up with a grunt and carried her out of the bell tower.

"There's . . . something . . . something I need to tell you—"

"Whatever it is can wait, darling. Over here! I've got her!"

The groundsman's cart pulled up outside the church, escorted by police in shimmering waterproof cloaks. Merritt laid her inside and wrapped her in dry blankets, tried to pour warm tea into her mouth. She spluttered when the cart began to move.

"I can see ghosts," she told him while he mopped her chin.

"Don't talk nonsense," he said.

"It's true. My parents thought I had a—a nervous disorder. When we met, I'd just come back from the hospital. Shock treatment. It didn't help. Nothing does." She had his full attention. She licked her lips. "Penshaw must have seemed a pretty sort of place to you, but for me it was a prison. The more anxious I felt, the more I hallucinated. I thought it would stop when we left, but it's been worse."

There it was, the look of disgust she'd been so afraid of. She reached for his hand but he wrenched it away. "It's dead people I see, Merritt, dying people, all the time. I think they're ghosts. They have messages for me, things they want me to do—"

"Stop," he snapped. "If you want to be free of me, just say so."

"Telephone my parents, they'll tell you everything."

He glared at her. Anne gripped the blankets. The moment was slipping its tracks in a way she hadn't expected.

"Are you trying to get back at me for this morning? Am I not the husband you hoped for, after that? Can you not stand a little real life?"

"Says the man who drinks because he can't bear his own grief!" Too late, the words were said. She could see she'd hurt him.

The cart jolted and suddenly the dark pit in her stomach opened, the gorge rising in her throat. They were approaching the foundations of Rannings, where everything felt rotten. Anne flung off the blankets and jumped out of the cart before Merritt or the policemen could stop her. She ran through the rain and mud until she found the epicenter, the ugly heart of it all. There, she began digging with her hands. The arms of the dead pushed up around her like daisies. "I know," she told them, "it'll be over soon."

"Stop, Anne! Stop this!" Merritt shouted as he jogged toward her, lost his footing. "You'll catch your death!"

"Will you just listen to me for once?" she flung back. "Dig, for God's sake!"

Merritt watched helplessly as she scraped out great clots of mud. Policemen surged past him, hands reaching out to grab her, when her fingernails broke against something hard. She'd uncovered a crescent of discolored bone, a tiny pelvis. They hauled her away, but the bone lay stark against the black sludge, glowing in the light from the criss-crossing torch beams.

Seventeen skeletons in total. The deepest at eight feet, the shallowest at just three.

Rannings was forced to close immediately, so they settled the bill and drove north to Middlesbrough that night, before the press descended upon the area to seek out her photograph. Anne stayed briefly at the hospital. The nurses said she was lucky to be alive.

Merritt sat by her bedside, and when she had the strength to sit up, they talked frankly at last. Neither had married for love. They'd symbolized something to each other—escape for her, lost time for him—and they hadn't looked any deeper than that because there was nothing more they wanted to find.

"Was this a mistake?" he asked.

At a loss, she turned her palm upward and he grasped it gently.

He looked so broken, though there was no alcohol on his breath. She bit her lip and twisted her wedding band, still loose. It came off readily with only the slightest resistance at the knuckle, and she held it out to him, scuff marks and all.

They looked at each other for a long time, the bustle of the ward filling the silence. "It's either divorce or annulment," he said at length. "Both options leave you high and dry. I assume you don't want to go back to Kent?"

"Never," she whispered.

They watched the nurses on their rounds for a while. Somewhere, a voice on the wireless was relaying every gory detail of the unfolding scandal. Anne requested it be turned off, but the silence was somehow worse.

"I wondered . . . Have you—could you—my brothers?"

She smiled sadly, expecting the question. The hope. "Perhaps. Truly, I don't understand how this works."

Merritt rubbed his cheeks. "I can't promise to be a good husband, Anne, but I can listen, I can do that. We rushed into this, but we needn't rush out of it. And maybe someday, we'll understand it together."

The hospital discharged her the next day. Anne waited on a bench while Merritt brought the motorcar around, the breeze blowing her hair into her eyes. She tucked it behind her ear and caught the eye of an old man across the street. He nodded to her and crossed the road, the morning newspaper tucked under his arm. He favored his right leg.

Without the Rannings' uniform, she hardly knew him. The porter.

When he reached her, he smiled with more gums than teeth. "You look just like Mary said you would. I'm sorry if I gave you a scare, before."

Anne stood to meet him, her jaw slack. Of course. A boy with a limp. "Are you—?"

"She found me, in the end, like. Well, Martha did. That was her gift."

In a daze, Anne extended her hand and he shook it warmly. "How is this possible? You must be over a hundred years old." With a glance at his bad leg, she said, "I suppose it can't be a war wound, then?"

He patted his thigh. "Not from the war you're thinking of, but I got plenty of those, too. I fit right in." He untucked the newspaper and showed her the front page. The headline declared Rannings' reputation to be in tatters. "Mary would've wanted me to thank you for this in person, like. We tried our best, but it couldn't happen yet because you hadn't happened yet, or something; she always explained it better. After she died, I had to come back and see it through by myself, hard as it was. Thank God it's done."

"She died?"

"Aye, as do we all, I hope," he said, and then laughed at her shock. "But don't worry: She held on a bloody long time. Saw in the new century. You must've just missed each other."

He handed her a small photograph, folded so much that the very center had worn away. In it, an elderly woman reclined on a sunbed, caught in a blurry roar of laughter. Her bathing suit and style of her hair placed her sometime in the early twenties, and the beach could have been anywhere, but Anne liked to think it was Kent.

The motorcar came purring around the corner and stopped at the curb. Merritt slung his arm across the back of the seat. "Anne, is this chap bothering you?"

Benjamin flipped the photograph over. There was an address written on the back. "Look me up next time you're in Bootle," he said with a wink, then he turned up his collar and walked on. Anne watched him go, quite breathless, until Merritt tooted the horn and made her jump. She strode to the motorcar and got in. "He wasn't a journalist, you know."

"Can't be too careful." He pulled into the traffic. "Well, shall we start over?"

"I don't know where to begin."

He sucked on a cigarette. "My parents' house is over two hours away."

Anne smiled. She rolled down the window to let out the blue smoke and let in the sounds of the city, and rested her chin in one hand. She gripped the photograph tight with the other. She'd do it properly, this time. She'd tell him everything. No more secrets; no more shame. Bold, like Mary.

In 2017, **G. V. ANDERSON** won a World Fantasy Award with her professional debut, "Das Steingeschöpf." Since then, she has won a British Fantasy Award and had her work selected for anthologies such as *Best of British Science Fiction* and *The Year's Best Dark Fantasy & Horror: 2019*. Her short stories can be found in *Strange Horizons*, *The Magazine of Fantasy & Science Fiction*, *Lightspeed*, and elsewhere. She lives and works in Dorset.

CONVERSATIONS WITH THE SEA WITCH

THEODORA GOSS

In the afternoons, they wheel her out on the balcony overlooking the sea. They place her chair by the balustrade. Once there, the queen dowager waves her hand. "Leave me," she says, in a commanding voice. Then, in the shrill tones of an old woman, "Go away, go away, damn you. I want to be alone."

They, who have been trained almost from birth to obey, leave her, bowing or curtsying as they go. After all, what harm can come to her, an old woman, a cripple? They do not call her that, of course. One does not call a queen dowager such things. But their mothers and fathers called her that long ago, when she was first found half-drowned on the sea shore—the crippled girl.

"A poor crippled girl," they whispered, incredulous, when the prince emerged from her room and told his father, "I'm going to marry her. She saved my life in the storm. She has no name—not as we have names. I'll call her Melusine."

Elsewhere in the castle, the king, her son, is issuing orders, perhaps about defending the northern borders, perhaps just about the education of the young prince, his heir. The queen is walking in the garden with her ladies-in-waiting, gathering roses. The young princess, her granddaughter, has stolen into the garden, where she is playing by the water-lily pool with her golden ball. In a moment, it will fall in. She has always been fascinated by water. She takes after her grandmother—her fingers are webbed. There are delicate membranes between each finger.

In the chapel, the former king, her husband, lies in his grand tomb of black-veined green marble. Next to it is another tomb, where she will someday lie. Now, it is empty like a promise unfulfilled. She knows it is there—she can feel it patiently waiting, and she knows it will not have to wait much longer. After all, did she not exchange five hundred years of life in the sea for one human lifetime? Once she lies beside him, completely surrounded by stone, she will have left the sea permanently at last.

But she is not thinking of that now. She is waiting for company.

She does not have to wait long. Soon after they leave—the servants, who have lives about which she knows nothing, about whom she thinks no more than she would of the white foam on a wave—the sea witch rises.

"Greetings, princess," says the witch. That, at least, is the closest we can get in translation, for she speaks the language of the sea, which is not our language. In the air, it sounds strange and guttural, like the barking of seals. In the water, it is higher, more melodious, like the song of the sleek gray dolphins that sometimes visit our waters. It carries far.

"Greetings, witch," says the queen dowager. It is obvious, from her tone, that this is an honorific. "How goes it beneath the water?"

And then the sea witch tells her: all is well at court. Her eldest sister is a beloved queen. There have been storms along the southern coast, causing shipwrecks. Which is good—that stretch of the coast was suffering from over-fishing, and this will keep the fishermen away for a while. The whales that were trapped in the main harbor of the capital city have returned to the open sea. When Melusine became queen, it was forbidden to harm a whale, and her son continues that tradition. Her middle sister's second child has recently emerged from his father's pouch. The sea-folk, although mammalian, reproduce like sea-horses: a child, once born, is deposited in the father's pouch and emerges only to suckle its mother's breast until it can fend for itself. The sea is a dangerous place. The sea-folks' children must be strong to survive.

"And how is your throat?" asks the sea witch. "Have you tried the poultice I recommended?" It is made of seaweed, boiled down into a paste.

"Better," says the queen dowager. "But I feel death coming close, witch. Coming on human feet, soft and white and tender."

"May it not come for a few years yet," says the sea witch. She herself will likely live for another hundred years. "Who will I talk to after you are gone?"

The queen dowager laughs—the situation is, after all, ironic. And then she puts her hand to her throat, because it aches.

Two old women—that is what they are. Two old women who have lost the ones they loved, whom the world has left behind. All they have now is these conversations. Do not pity them. They get more enjoyment out of these talks than you imagine.

It was, the queen dowager thinks, a fair bargain: her voice, the voice that produced the beautiful songs of the sea-folk, like dolphins calling to one another, for a pair of human legs. Of course they were useless. A witch can split a long, gray, flexible tail into a pair of legs, pink and bare, but she cannot make them functional. What is inside them will not bear a body's weight. The crippled girl, lying on the sea shore, in love with the prince she had saved from the storm, hoping against hope that somehow she could make her way to him, perhaps by crawling higher among the rocks, knew she might die there, among the pools filled with barnacles and snails. She knew the crabs and seagulls might eat her soft white flesh. The rest of her might dry up in the sun.

Was it luck or some vestige of the sea witch's magic, or true love, which has its own gravitational power, that he was walking on the shore at exactly the right time?

As soon as he saw her, he said, "You're the girl I saw among the waves. The one who rescued me."

She tried to answer—she had lost her song, not her voice—but he could not understand what she was saying, and her voice tired quickly, trying to speak through this new medium. The sea-folk learn to understand human speech, from listening to sailors in their boats and children playing along the shore. They must guard the sea from us, so they learn about us what they can. But we, proud and ignorant, thinking there is no intelligent life but that of the air, do not learn about them, and so only a few of us speak their language. Those who do are often considered mad. They spend their lives gathering things the tide has thrown up, living as they can on the detritus of the sea.

The prince carried her to the castle, put her in the grandest of guest bedrooms, and announced to his mother and father that this was the girl he was going to marry. When asked who she was, this girl with nothing—no clothes, no voice, no name—he said she was the daughter of the sea king himself. When his father asked about her dowry, he said it was safety among the waves. If she were queen, their ships would be safe—at least from the sea-folk, who often sank ships for their cargoes of furniture and figurines, which were to them the finest of trinkets, decorating their underwater caves.

In a seafaring nation, which had made its fortune from trade with distant lands—in spices, printed fabrics, hand-painted porcelain—this dowry was judged to be better than gold or jewels. And it is a fact that the fishing boats of that country had luck with their catches once the prince married the girl he had found among the tidal pools. After their marriage, the old king abdicated in favor of his son. The county had never been so prosperous as under King Cedric and Queen Melusine.

It took a few years, working with speech therapists and vocal coaches, for her to communicate clearly with her subjects, to sound merely foreign rather than outlandish and otherworldly. When she laughed, it still startled the palace staff—it sounded so much like barking. She could never learn to walk—she did not have the internal structure for locomotion on dry land. Sometimes she missed the ease of movement under water. Often in dreams she would be swimming, and she would feel the smooth movement of her tail, the strong forward thrust through water, with pleasure. But she loved the prince, later the king, who treated her with such tenderness, carrying her himself anywhere she wished to go—trying to compensate for the loss of her watery kingdom. She loved her children, with their strange pink feet and tiny toes, kicking and waving in the air as their nappies were changed or they threw tantrums. And we all make difficult choices.

The strangest thing about life on land, she told the sea witch once they started holding these conversations, was reproduction. The monthly cycle of blood, as though she were expelling a red tide. Incubating a child herself instead of depositing it in her mate's pouch, to develop safely in that second womb, coming out only for lactation. She did not understand the concept of a wet nurse. When her children were brought to her for feedings, she laid them beside her and imagined moving through the water, with them swimming alongside, latched to her breast. That is how a child of the sea-folk feeds beneath the waves.

Eventually, she taught them to swim in the palace baths, which dated to Roman times. Her legs could not give her the thrust of her lost gray tail, but with a strong breast stroke, she could pull herself through the water and recapture, for a while, what it had been like to swim through the depths of the sea.

She still swims sometimes. And she makes lace—the most delicate, intricate lace. Her fingers have grown crooked, but this is an ancient art of the sea-folk, which they learn as children: they knot strands made of seaweed, pounded and pulled into long fibers. It is a strong thread that shimmers in sunlight. Into her lace, she weaves patterns of starfish and cuttlefish and stingray. When she is too tired to do either, she reads poetry or stares out the window—the king, her husband, made sure that her bedroom window overlooked the sea. She has had a full life. She could, if she wished, spend every moment remembering it. Her childhood in the palace of her father the sea king, swimming through rooms on whose walls grew coral and anemones, coming up to the surface only to breathe the necessary air, although the sea-folk can hold their breath for hours at a time, then diving down again into her natural element. Hunting and foraging with her sisters through algae forests, for the children of the sea-folk have the freedom of the sea from a young age. Rescuing her prince from the storm after his ship went down, dragging him back to shore on a broken spar through turbulent waves. Going to the sea witch, making the fatal bargain. The years of being a wife, mother, widow.

Once a day she is wheeled out to the balcony. The sea witch comes, rising from the waves, and they speak.

Usually, their conversation follows a familiar pattern. But on this day, the queen dowager asks a question she has never asked before. It has never, before, seemed the right time to ask. "Do you regret your decision?" she asks the sea witch, wondering if she is being rude or too personal. But surely between old friends? After all this time, they must consider themselves that.

The sea witch is silent for a moment, then shakes her head. "No, at least I tried. You were not the only one, you know. I traded for your voice, the hair of another maiden, the soft gray skin of yet another. He would not love me, no matter how I tried to please him. He loved no one but himself."

He lived in the deepest, darkest abyss in those parts, an underwater crevasse that seemed to descend to the center of the earth. None of the sea-folk knew how old he was. Four hundred years? Six hundred? Older yet? He had filled himself with the magic of those dark spaces, and did not seem to age.

"He taught me so much," says the sea witch. "From him, I learned a magic that allowed me to stay under water for days at a time. A magic that raised the waves and created storms. The magic that took your voice. For years, I studied spells and potions under his tutelage. But when I told him that I loved him, he called me a silly guppy, no wiser than an infant, and told me to go away, that I was interrupting his studies. I did not go away—I moved to the edge of the crevasse in which he lived, and there I stayed, living in the cavern in which you found me. I hoped that if he saw my devotion, he would come to love me in time. But it merely irritated him.

"He cared only for knowledge—only for discovering the secrets of that dark abyss and the power it would give him. At first he would go to the surface periodically. But after he drove me out, he began to stay beneath the water for weeks at a time. He told me he no longer needed to breathe air. His eyes grew larger, his once-muscular body thinner. He developed a permanent look of hunger. I do not think he ate, except when krill or small shrimp floated by and he could catch them without interrupting his studies. He became hunched, as though curled up on himself. I did not care. I had not loved him for his beauty, which was considerable, but for his intellect, his desire for knowledge. I thought he might admire those things in me as well, so after my attempts to charm him failed, I studied the darkest of arts, the most potent of potions.

"One day, I perfected a spell that was beyond even his power. It was one he had attempted many times himself: a way of turning our tails into the tentacles of a squid, with the squid's ability to darken the water with its ink. I cast it, triumphant, knowing that he must love me now, or if not love, then at least respect me. At last, feeling the reverberations of that spell in the water, he came to my cavern.

"I thought he would be pleased that I had discovered this secret— that he would praise me and want to learn it from me. But no—he hurled himself at me with the full thrust of his tail and struck me across the face. Then, with his hands, he attempted to strangle me. But you see, I had eight new tentacles that I had not yet learned to control . . ."

The sea witch pauses for a moment, then says, "I tore him limb from limb. I could not even see—the water was dark with my ink. When it cleared, there were pieces of him scattered among the coral. The small fish were already nibbling at his flesh."

Then they are both silent, the queen dowager in her wheeled chair on the balcony, the sea witch floating among the waves, her body half out of water, a woman above, an octopus below.

What are we left with in the end, but old women telling stories? The first old women who told stories were the Fates. What else could they do, sitting in their chairs all day, spinning, measuring, and cutting the threads of our lives? Each thread was also a story, and as they spun it, they told it. They are telling our stories still.

Once upon a time, says Clotho as she spins the thread on her spindle. There was a king with three sons, the youngest of whom was called Dumbling, or the prettiest girl you have ever seen who was born with the feathers of a swan, or a queen who could not bear a child until a white snake told her that she was pregnant. And then, says Lachesis, the lass lived happily with her bear husband until she wanted to see what he looked like at night, or the prince found a castle in the forest inhabited entirely by cats, or the cook was so hungry that she took a spoonful of soup and all the sudden she could understand the language of animals. Finally, says Atropos, the loyal servant chopped off the brown bull's head and there stood the prince he had been searching for, or the maid spun linen so fine that it could fit through the eye of a needle so the Tsar took her back to his palace, or the false princess was put in a barrel filled with nails drawn by two white horses, and did she regret her treachery! They lived happily ever after, or not, and they are feasting still unless they have died in the interval. Every story has a beginning, middle, and end. After that end, there are only old women sitting together in the sunshine.

"And were you happy?" asks the sea witch.

"Very happy," says the queen dowager. "I'm still happy, even when I lie awake at night in a bed that is too large for one shrunken old woman, remembering tenderness that will never come again. Even when I know that soon my body will lie in a dry, dark place. My granddaughter, the youngest, Eglantine—I think someday she will come find you and ask to return to the sea. When she does, I hope you will give her my tail."

She pauses a moment. "And were you happy?" she asks the sea witch, for everyone deserves a little happiness in life, even witches.

The sea witch thinks for a moment. "No, I cannot say that I was. But I learned a great deal. No one in the sea, or perhaps even on land, has the knowledge I do. If I wished to, I could send a storm to destroy all the ships in this harbor, like a boy breaking sticks. Of course I would not do that, out of courtesy to you . . ." She bows to the queen dowager, who bows in return. "But I could, and that is something. Knowledge and power—those count for something when one is old."

"As do the memory of loving and being loved," says the queen dowager.

And then they are silent for a while, enjoying the sunshine and the lapping of waves.

"Well, until tomorrow," says the sea witch, finally. She knows the queen dowager's attendants will be coming soon.

"Of course," says the queen dowager.

The thread is spun, measured, and snipped, whether it be gold or hemp or sea silk. And afterward, the old women sit in the sunshine.

THEODORA GOSS is the World Fantasy and Locus Award–winning author of the short story and poetry collections *In the Forest of Forgetting*, *Songs for Ophelia*, and—most recently—*Snow White Learns Witchcraft*, as well as novella *The Thorn and the Blossom*, debut novel *The Strange Case of the Alchemist's Daughter*, and its sequels *European Travel for the Monstrous Gentlewoman* and *The Sinister Mystery of the Mesmerizing Girl*. She has been a finalist for the Nebula, Crawford, Seiun, and Mythopoeic Awards, as well as on the Tiptree Award Honor List. Her work has been translated into twelve languages. She teaches literature and writing at Boston University and in the Stonecoast MFA Program.

HAUNT

CARMEN MARIA MACHADO

Two months into my time as Fred and Elsie's ghost, they wake up in the middle of the night to find me at the kitchen table, staring at the Ouija board unfolded over the unfinished pine. I didn't mean to be staring at the board when they came down the stairs. I'd snuck down after they'd gone to bed to skim from their leftovers and it was already there, waiting.

They come into the room slowly, but not out of fear—they're used to me now. They're just old, the kind of old where you always look like you're moving around underwater.

"Now you can talk back to us," Elsie says. She burns a little incense, for effect. She sits down across from me, touches the heart-shaped planchette, and waits. I drop my fingertips onto the wood, not touching Elsie, but able to move it just the same. T-H-A-N-K-Y-O-U, I spell, the curved glass window amplifying each letter like a raindrop.

After that, Elsie and Fred watch *Law & Order*, and I doze in the recliner. When the cops run after the suspect, Elsie sits forward in her chair and hollers. I wake a little and watch her through my lashes, then drift away again. It feels safe to sleep in this house. No one is going to hurt me. Common sense dictates you don't just go about touching ghosts.

* * *

I'm not really a ghost. I'm just a runaway, a broken-home girl whose home broke for good. When Fred and Elsie first found me, I was sitting on the floor of their warm kitchen, soaked from an autumn storm. My curls plastered to my forehead like leeches, my clothes vacuum sealed to my skin. I had no way of knowing that this house—the one whose back door had been so helpfully unlocked—belonged to a couple whose teenage daughter had drowned in their pool years ago after hopping the fence in the dark, a teenager who looked a little like me. They drew their own conclusions.

I would tell them I was real, if I could. I would run to Elsie and press my fingers into the soft meat of her cheek and say, "I'm real, I'm real, I have a name and a heartbeat and I used to be afraid but I'm not anymore, because I'm here." But what if they call the police? What if they send me away or, worse, back? It's better for them to think I'm dead. Everyone else does anyway. And it's pleasant, to be able to listen and observe, to not have to talk to anyone. It's probably a good thing I don't believe in ghosts myself, or else this old house would seem really creepy.

Elsie sings to me. I think she thinks it placates me, keeps me from doing—I don't know. Whatever ghosts do to people they're mad at. For the first week Elsie kept a vial of table salt with her, in case she needed to fend me off. In case I had wicked intentions. But now the salt lives next to the pepper and Elsie belts country songs at me all night. Patsy Cline, Loretta Lynn, anything by Dolly Parton.

They're retired now, but Elsie was once a math teacher, and Fred an engineer. Sometimes they go to a local bar for karaoke. On their way out, Elsie sings back into the darkness, "We'll see you soon, sweet girl." They always return laughing. I can hear Elsie's voice even when she's blocks away, tripping down the last few notes of "Walkin' After Midnight," asking Fred if he remembers a moment of their shared past. His voice is low. I can only identify it by the spaces in between hers.

Nowadays, they love the night. They love that they can sleep all day and visit with me when the sun goes down. They love that the night has brought them back what they lost.

* * *

Then one night, Fred doesn't wake up.

I can hear Elsie saying his name, and there's a moment when it changes. Her voice sort of bends over, like it's given up on something. I resist the urge to run, because ghosts never run. In the doorway, I see Elsie sitting up in bed, her hand pressed flat to Fred's chest. She isn't crying, just holding her hand there. She sees me in the doorway.

"Where is he?" she asks. I must look confused, because her hand begins to gesticulate wildly, like she is shooing away a bee. I realize she is referring to the world I can see and she can't, the other room inside this room, where the dead live. Where I live.

But he is nowhere, except on the bed, not moving.

Elsie kneels in front of me and I can smell her body, and it is human and confusing. She doesn't touch me but her hands come so close.

"Can you see him?" she asks.

I back out of the doorway and run down the stairs, breaking my own rule. Elsie follows me, slowly. In the kitchen, she sits down at the table and flips open the Ouija board.

"Please," she says. "Talk to me. Tell me where he is."

I do not want to. I want to run to the back door, shove it open into the moonlight, and tear across the lawn and find some other place to be a teenage runaway, somewhere less safe and kind, somewhere less haunted. But then Elsie would know. She would realize I was real and, soon after, realize I was abandoning her.

So I sit. She runs the planchette over hello and then she writes F-R-E-D-F-R-E-D-F-R-E-D. I place my fingers outside of hers and push.

N-O-W-H-E-R-E, I spell.

"Now, here?" she whispers.

I do it again.

"Nowhere?" she says.

I gather her fingers in my own. "Just us now," I tell her, in my own voice. "Just us."

CARMEN MARIA MACHADO is the author of the bestselling memoir *In the Dream House* and the short story collection *Her Body and Other Parties*. A finalist for the National Book Award, she is the recipient of the Bard Fiction Prize, the Lambda Literary Award, the Brooklyn Public Library Literature Prize, the Shirley Jackson Award, and the National Book Critics Circle's John Leonard Prize. In 2018, the *New York Times* listed *Her Body and Other Parties* as a member of The New Vanguard, one of "15 remarkable books by women that are shaping the way we read and write fiction in the 21st century." Machado's essays, fiction, and criticism have appeared in the *New Yorker*, the *New York Times*, *Granta*, *Harper's Bazaar*, *Best American Science Fiction and Fantasy*, and elsewhere. She holds an MFA from the Iowa Writers' Workshop and is the Writer in Residence at the University of Pennsylvania. Machado lives in Philadelphia with her wife.

NICE THINGS

ELLEN KLAGES

After the memorial service, Phoebe Morris returned to the beach-front townhouse where her mother had lived for the last twenty years, and prepared to cope. There was nothing of Mother's that she particularly wanted, but there were papers to sort and clothing to donate, and it was her responsibility. She was an only child, an orphan now, with just an aging aunt in assisted living. Rose had sent flowers and a nice note, apologizing for her absence and invoking her hip.

Phoebe stood by the door. The living room seemed sterile: pale carpet, beige furniture, sliding glass doors leading to a patio and the beach beyond. The only color came from a single shelf of dust-jacketed books, bestsellers all, and a few displays of fragile knickknacks on the mantel and polished side tables.

Drawing her arms in close to her body was instinctive. She might accidentally knock one of the little figurines over, as if her very proximity was enough to shatter them into bits. A bull in a china shop, Mother had called her. She'd hold the dustpan and glare accusingly at her curious, clumsy daughter. "This is why I can't have nice things."

Phoebe took off her good jacket and draped it over the back of the couch. Now that all of Mother's precious things were hers, she didn't know where to start. Part of her wanted to lay claim to her inheritance by sweeping them all off onto the floor, being that bull, smashing each and every one of them. Experimentally, she picked up a little Dresden shepherdess with a skirt of frilly, prickly ceramic lace. She raised it, arm cocked and—

She couldn't.

It was as if any minute her mother would come through the doorway and catch her in the act of—of what? Of touching Mother's things. But they weren't *hers* anymore. Still, permission had not been granted by the one person whose approval had always been required. The back of Phoebe's neck tingled: watched, judged, and found guilty.

That old familiar feeling.

The little Dresden doll went back in its place and the bottle of Pinot Grigio from the supermarket down the street went into the fridge. Upstairs, she changed into jeans and a sweater, and dug a pen and her notebook out of her carry-on bag. What she needed was a to-do list.

The sensible thing was to appraise first, smash later. Most of the little figures were porcelain, and some of them might be valuable. People collected that sort of thing, didn't they? Phoebe didn't know; she'd shared little of her mother's taste. She'd been told that was a flaw. She wrote *Appraiser—Estate Sale?* at the top of the page, and that made her feel a bit more settled, in control.

Her day job was creating order out of chaos. A senior copy editor for the university press, she went through academic verbiage and noted what needed further research, queried questionable statements, and ensured that every fact was accurate. She was thorough and efficient, a professional nitpicker. A skill learned at her mother's knee.

For an hour she walked idly from room to room, opening drawers and cabinets and looking through the contents as if she were at an estate sale herself, browsing, not searching. Getting the lay of the land, like an archaeologist going through the remains of her own culture.

Her childhood had been privileged and uncomfortable, full of small, continual battles. "Do you *have* to slouch?" "Can't you find something better to read?" "Phoebe! Don't bite your nails." Rarely constructive, the comments became an accretion of minutiae that eventually grew around Phoebe like a coral reef, encasing her small soft self, bit by chalky bit, yet barely blunting their sting.

She felt guilty for feeling more relief than grief. She'd shed a few tears when the inevitable phone call had finally come, but knew she would not miss her mother. No more awkward visits, no more read-between-the-lines letters expressing disappointment, but signed "Love," and then, formally, "Your Mother." She had brought a few of those with her from home, hoping they would provide an emotional nudge, but they remained in her suitcase.

On a shelf in a hall cupboard, she found a brown cardboard box marked FAMILY. Maybe that would help. A way to reclaim her own history, try and make sense of it, knit some frayed ends together. Dangerous territory, though. Best to tackle it before her energies were exhausted by dozens of mundane tasks. She carried the box to the glass-topped table between the kitchen and the living room; she planned to sell that as soon as possible. It was too big for her bookshelf–lined Ann Arbor dining room, and was steeped in the remains of lessons in how young ladies should behave themselves, intertwined with the invariable battles over food.

A wooden lazy Susan held salt and pepper shakers, paper napkins, and a ceramic dish of Sweet'N Low packets. She moved it to the counter, next to the blender and the three nearly identical gold-tone canisters: FLOUR. SUGAR. MOTHER.

None of them were actually labeled. They all looked like coffee cans, complete with airtight plastic lids. The contents of two were smooth and white, the third gray, with a few unpalatable lumps of bone.

The funeral home had tried to sell her a fancy eight-hundred-dollar urn to put on her mantel. Decorating with a dead relative's ashes? No, thank you. For the time being, this cut-rate funereal object held what was left of Mother. Phoebe wasn't sure if she'd have approved of not wasting money, or been annoyed at the lack of pomp.

Mother had left no instructions about what to do with her—after. She'd had an appointment with her lawyer, but the disease had spread too quickly. For months, Mother had dismissed Death as if it were an inconvenient sales call: "I'm sorry, but this isn't a good time for me. I'm really not interested. Please take me off your list." She had slipped into that final coma with the conviction that this could not be happening to *her*. No time left to make plans or make peace.

Phoebe opened the bottle of wine.

Loose photographs in a variety of sizes filled the top six inches of the box, in no particular order: Daddy as a soldier, photos of Cleveland in the 1950s, Phoebe's first grade class picture. She leafed through deckled edges and pink-tinted Kodachromes, throwing away unidentified relatives, skimming off photos of her mother as a girl, arm in arm with the now-aged aunt. Vivian and Rose, in ruffled dresses and pin-curls. Children Phoebe had never known. She would put those in a manila envelope and mail them off with a thank-you note for the flowers.

She lifted off a heavy, framed photo of her parents as newlyweds, then stared in disbelief at the red folder it had uncovered. She flinched, pale gold droplets of wine scattering across the glass. Suddenly she was nine years old again, her eyes prickling with tears, her hands clenched in long-buried outrage.

Mrs. D'Amico had assigned the project the first week in March. A report on an animal of their choice, ten pages, with pictures. They would have a whole month, because they were not little children anymore, they were fifth graders, and this was preparation for junior high and high school, which would not be easy, no-siree.

Phoebe chose dinosaurs, and spent her afternoons at the library, taking pages and pages of notes. The centerpiece of her report was a sheet of heavy art paper, folded and three-hole-punched to fit the folder. She'd made a tab from a white index card, PULL TO OPEN, in her neatest printing. That revealed a colored-pencil drawing, two notebook pages wide: a brontosaurus surrounded by spiky prehistoric foliage.

Art was not her best subject. She'd spent a whole weekend hunched over her little desk, fingers cramping with the effort. The dinosaur's legs were longer and skinnier than the picture in the encyclopedia, but it was still the best drawing she had ever done. The night before the report was due, she'd gotten out of bed three times to make sure it was still there, to admire what she had made.

The report came back a week later with a red-inked *A* and a *Very Good!* in Mrs. D'Amico's perfect penmanship. Phoebe hurried home though a soft drizzle, the folder under her slicker, and nearly skipped through the kitchen door.

Her mother sat smoking at the glass-topped table, an ashtray and a coffee cup at her right elbow, her silver Zippo lighter and a green pack of Salems stacked neatly beside them. A crescent of red lipstick smeared the edge of the cup. She shuffled a deck of cards and laid out a complex game of solitaire, finishing the array before she looked up.

Phoebe held out the red folder. "It's my dinosaur report," she said. "I got an *A*."

"Let me see." Mother put the cards down and took the report. She opened the cover, nodded, and leafed through in silence. Phoebe stood on tiptoe, her slicker hanging open. She leaned forward when her mother got to the centerfold, watched in anticipation as her drawing was unfurled, then rocked back when it was folded up again and the page was turned without comment.

Her mother closed the folder. "We should save this one. I'll put it in the cupboard by my desk with the rest of my papers." She smiled as if Phoebe should be pleased.

She wasn't. Her stomach did flip-flops. "It's mine," she said, almost a whisper "I want to keep it in *my* room."

"Your room?" Mother shook her head and crushed her cigarette into the ashtray. "But it's so messy, dear. What if this gets lost? Or ruined? Better to put it someplace safe. Then we'll always know where it is." She stood, the report in one hand, and patted Phoebe on the shoulder. Then she left the kitchen and locked away the brontosaurus.

Phoebe stared at the doorway for a minute before slowly taking off her slicker, hanging it on its hook. She knew where her brontosaurus was, but she would not be allowed to visit. Rummaging in her mother's cupboard was forbidden.

And somehow her brontosaurus had just become one of Mother's things.

* * *

Decades later, Phoebe Morris downed her wine in one long swallow, then wiped her damp cheek with the back of her hand and cradled the red folder to her chest. It was as if she had found her Grail, a relic from her childhood so unattainable that it had become legendary in her personal mythology. A long-missing piece of her true self.

She opened the folder, turning pages of her neatest childhood cursive, blue Bic pen on wide-lined notebook paper, pulling out the center, folding it back again with a sigh. It really wasn't a very good drawing, the proportions all wrong, not the masterpiece she'd enshrined in her memory palace.

Her longing for this particular bit of treasure had been huge and fierce, but now what? Take it home and put it in a box of her own? Buy a scrapbook? Unearthed, the legend had become another ordinary object.

She laid the folder on the tabletop, next to a small, worn brass rabbit that had anchored a stack of monogrammed notecards and envelopes on her mother's desk. Phoebe's secret pet. She'd always had to be careful to put it back *exactly* as she found it, so Mother wouldn't demand an explanation of why she'd picked it up in the first place and deliver another lecture.

For a moment, Phoebe held it in her hand, reveling in the cool contours of the cast metal, the surprising heft of it, and even more in the radical idea that she could now put it anywhere she chose and there would be no consequences.

She got up, stretched, and returned to browsing. After an hour, the rabbit was joined by a handful of similarly forbidden objects that had nostalgic resonance: her mother's ornate desk scissors; an angular art deco perfume bottle, a few gelid amber drops at its bottom; and a small leather-bound album with black-and-white photos detailing the first six months of Phoebe's life.

At dusk she ordered Chinese delivery from the menu next to the wall phone. Dumplings and shrimp toast and sizzling rice soup. She was always surprised how expensive Chinese food was for one person—thirty dollars for a few appetizers—when it was so cheap for a group. She shook her head and reminded herself that she no longer needed to pinch pennies, at least not on the level of dumplings. Once she sold Mother's townhouse, she could pay off the mortgage on her cozy little bungalow at the edge of campus and have enough left over for a nice nest egg.

She felt a new wave of guilt as she realized that, if they had been prizes in a game show, she'd have chosen the money over Mother without a second thought. Mother had never brought much comfort at all.

The dumplings did, along with a second glass of Pinot Grigio.

Phoebe finished the soup, put the other leftovers in the fridge, and scribbled more items on her to-do list. She'd tackle the clothes in the morning, bagging the bulk for Goodwill. She was pretty sure Mother had purged any vintage things when she downsized after the divorce and moved to Sarasota.

The rest of the evening she spent inventorying the kitchen drawers and cupboards. No emotional landmines. Nothing of any importance either, but why toss perfectly good cans of tomato soup or a box of Minute Rice? She checked her email, wrote back to the friend who was housesitting for her, and RSVP'd to her book club. Then she went to bed.

It was full light, after 8:00, when she woke. She showered and went downstairs. The sound of the surf was rhythmic and soothing. She stood by the patio door, watching the waves roll in along the white sand beach, then returned to the kitchen and put the kettle on for tea. Electric stove. It would take forever. She opened the refrigerator and took out the carton of dumplings. Two left. She speared one of them on a fork and held it upright like a Popsicle, biting into one crimped edge. It was cold but delicious, the dark sauce a tangy sheen. She wolfed it down, put a teabag into a flowered mug, and started on the second.

Leaning against the faux-marble counter, waiting for the kettle to boil, she looked down at the array of objects. The brass rabbit sat on a stack of photos. The scissors lay across the leather album.

She paused in mid-nibble.

Where was the red folder?

She looked under the table, on the seats of the chairs, and finally opened the flaps of the cardboard box. There it was. But she hadn't moved—She shrugged. She must have. Just didn't remember. As she lifted the folder, a single piece of paper slid out and fluttered to the floor. Not a blue-lined notebook sheet, its three-punched holes coming loose from the binding after all these years. It was heavy, cream-colored stationery, the monogram VRM embossed in slate blue capitals across the top: Vibby Reynolds Morris. In the center, in Mother's distinctive script, was a single word:

Mine.

Phoebe gasped and dropped the fork, dumpling and all, noting with dismay the brown stain it left on the white carpet. The kettle whistled insistently.

After a long moment, she turned it off, laid the note on the counter and retrieved the dumpling. She sat, finishing it slowly, savoring each flavorful morsel until she felt more like a competent, practical woman than a scared child.

There had to be a reasonable explanation.

"Look," she said to herself. "Mother was a real piece of work. But she's gone. She must have written that years ago. Sorting through pictures herself. Some to keep, some to give to cousin what's-her-name. I just didn't see it yesterday."

There. Nice and logical.

So why was her hand shaking?

Shit.

Phoebe ripped the note in half, again and again until it was confetti, tipped it into the trash, and made a cup of tea. She sipped, grimaced. No milk. She added MILK to her list, then stood up. Time to get out of here, get busy. Start *doing* the things on her list, not just making it longer. It was a beautiful fall morning, and she really needed a change of scenery. She put on her shoes, grabbed the keys to the rental car, and left the townhouse.

Three hours later, after a hearty, grounding IHOP breakfast, she returned with milk and packing supplies. Garbage bags and manila envelopes and a five-pack of shipping boxes. Bubble wrap, two rolls of tape. Phoebe was armed and ready to pillage and purge.

The downstairs bedroom first. Musty, sickroom smell. She opened the French doors for a gulf breeze, and turned to the closet that took up most of one wall, sliding apart the mirrored doors. My god, there was a lot of stuff. No wonder Mother had always looked like Jackie Kennedy on casual Friday—perfectly coiffed dark hair, pearls, in trim slacks or a Lilly Pulitzer skirt. One side had built-in shelves and drawers. The other was hung with pastel dresses, skirts, and blouses, arranged by color. Mother was a Spring.

Phoebe didn't have a season. Hibernation? Her own wardrobe ran to blacks, grays, and dark blues. Early on she had drabbed herself out of harm's way; safer not to call Mother's attention. A lifetime of protective coloration.

Mother's repeated attempts to dress Phoebe in her own image had ultimately failed. She owned no pastels. Or lipstick or three-inch heels. Very little jewelry. Clearing the closet would be swift and ruthless.

She pulled out two of the Hefty bags, shaking the black plastic free with a little more force than necessary. One for trash, one for Goodwill. She slid open a drawer and tossed out nylon panties, slips, and bras. Another drawer held a tangle of scarves, still scented with Chanel. Phoebe threw those on the bed for a more careful inspection later. Cashmere, silk—maybe Hermès? Those she would set aside for the estate sale people.

The bottom drawer surprised her: a stack of neatly folded plaid wool shirts in various shades of greens and rusts and yellows. All in beautiful condition, all vintage 1960s. When Phoebe was little, her parents had season tickets to the Browns, which involved tailgate parties and other "sporty" weekend events. Pendleton and pearls.

She smiled, picturing her mother in one of these shirts, remembering one afternoon with a warm nostalgia rare for her childhood. She must have been about five. Her parents had taken her along to an afternoon party. Someone's huge backyard, views of Lake Erie, bright autumn leaves, a real popcorn machine. Phoebe had a hot dog and a Hires root beer. Mother and Daddy sat on the stone patio together, laughing. Phoebe got to run around. When it got dark, Daddy carried her piggyback to the car.

What beautiful soft wool. She stroked the top shirt, tempted to try it on, then looked at the label. Size six. She wouldn't even get an arm in. Mother had weighed 108 pounds the morning Phoebe was born, full-term. She had taken after her father's side of the family: sturdy and solid. Another memory surfaced, not warm and fuzzy, a trip to the department store downtown, sixth grade, Mother frowning at the size 12 tag on a dress as if Phoebe were the Incredible Hulk.

With a sigh, Phoebe lifted the stack of shirts and set them on a chintz-covered chair. They looked distinctly out of place. Did Sarasota have a vintage clothing store? *Some*one would drool over these. She turned back to close the bottom drawer, and saw a small bag tucked into a corner. Fist-sized, blood-red velvet. She'd never seen it before.

As a child, Phoebe had occasionally, secretly, looked in her mother's dresser when she knew she was alone in the house, curious about what went under grown-up women's clothes. Mysterious garments that her Barbie hadn't come with, full of hooks and clasps and odd bits of rubber, scary and fascinating.

She picked up the sack. It was full of—what? Spare pearls? No, not round. Loose diamonds? Yes, please. She loosened the satin drawstring, opened the sack wide, and tipped its contents into her palm. She stared down at a dozen blunt whitish objects. "Jesus," she said aloud. They were teeth.

Well, of course Mother had kept her baby teeth long enough to do the pillow thing, but saving them? Phoebe shuddered and tipped her hand over the trash bag. The teeth rattled like tiny hailstones against the black plastic, followed by the velvet bag.

Body parts. Remains. She thought about the canister in the kitchen. What *was* she going to do with Mother? Maybe a road trip, scattering her along the way? She'd always wanted to travel. Perhaps a spoonful in each of those logo-stamped ashtrays they had at fancy hotels, next to the elevators? A smidgen in the planters of the smoking lounge of the golf club? Vibby and "the girls" had played bridge in that room every Wednesday for the last twenty years. She ought to feel right at home there.

On second thought, the ashtray thing was probably a little too irreverent. Phoebe didn't want to be any more haunted than she already was. What about their old house, back in Shaker Heights? No. Mother hadn't been happy there. Had she been happy here? Phoebe wasn't sure.

She threw a tangled nest of pantyhose into the trash and began dragging pairs of dainty shoes out of the closet, putting them into the second bag. Size six here as well. Black heels, low; black heels, high; white heels, satin; pink and white running shoes; a pair of buff-colored bowling shoes. Bowling shoes? When had Mother ever *bowled*?

When the bag was full, she tied its handles shut and put it by the hall door. Getting rid of shoes was satisfying and easy. Figuring out the appropriate way to dispose of Mother's ashes, not so much. She needed to say goodbye. Forgive her? Tell her off? The memorial service had been lovely, but formal. Very high Episcopal, which had suited the white-haired mourners much more than Phoebe.

Her therapist had encouraged her to spend as much time as she needed, to find closure and a way to move on. Phoebe wanted to call her, get some sensible advice, except Patricia was at a conference all week. Another woman was covering the practice, but it wasn't like she'd lost a filling and any old dentist would do. Patricia had been seeing her for years, knew all her pillow-thumping, Kleenex-soddening stories and secrets.

Phoebe took a break mid-afternoon and dropped off three bags of clothes at the Goodwill store she'd passed on her errands that morning. To reward herself, she went into the bakery next door. Glass cases held cupcakes, pumpkin cookies, and elegant fruit tarts. She bought one of those, and a muffin for tomorrow morning. On her way back to the car, she glanced down at the box of pastries and the grinning black jack-o'-lantern rubber-stamped on the pink cardboard.

The last two weeks had been so busy, full of phone calls and flight arrangements, insurance forms, funeral homes, and selecting hymns. She'd completely forgotten about Halloween. She pulled out of the parking space.

Maybe that was the answer.

One of the academic books she'd recently copyedited was a treatise on Celtic rituals and modern society, and there'd been a long section about Samhain and All Soul's Day and Halloween. A liminal time, when the boundaries between this world and the next were more—permeable. In the north of England, around the ninth century, as she recalled, people in mourning had baked "soul cakes" for the occasion. Children went begging from door to door, promising to say a prayer for every cake they received.

"Trick or treat," she said aloud.

Not that she was going to hand out anything homemade at the townhouse door. The neighborhood watch would be on her in a flash. But baking sounded both soothing and appropriately domestic. Tomorrow she would make a soul cake and have a ritual feast, then scatter the ashes into the eternity of the sea.

Yes. She smiled as she pulled into the townhouse carport. It was just the sort of custom Mother would have liked. A dyed-in-the wool Anglophile, she doted on Lord Peter Wimsey and Twining's Tea, Tiptree marmalade with her breakfast toast.

As for the cake itself, Phoebe imagined it should be like the ones that travelers carried with them in fairy tales, wrapped in a bindle with a bit of cheese, sent off with the prodigal in search of fortune. When she had first encountered those tales in kindergarten, she had imagined a sort of medicinal Hostess cupcake—without the white squiggles. Brown and dry and herbal-tasting. Indestructible, but nourishing.

Inside, she ate half the fruit tart and opened her laptop, searching for a soul cake recipe. There were dozens. Irish, gluten-free, even one from the Hallmark Channel. Some were gingerbready, others more like scones or biscuits. They all seemed to call for nutmeg, cinnamon, ginger. Autumnal flavors, the cakes traditionally set out with a glass of wine. That appealed, too.

Mother didn't have a printer, so Phoebe got her notebook and copied out the recipe that seemed the simplest. She finished the fruit tart and nodded to herself. Things were coming together, and it was a real tradition, not one she was making up on the fly. When dealing with the dead, a do-it-yourself ritual seemed a bit risky.

Energized by the clarity of a decision, she got back in the car and drove to the Publix, so she'd have everything on hand in the morning. Butter and vanilla. Eggs and spices. Plus another bottle of wine and a small frozen pizza for dinner tonight.

Now that she had a plan, she felt more relaxed. She opened the wine—a red blend this time—and sat and watched the sunset on the patio while the pizza heated in the oven. After dinner, she put the plate in the sink, topped off her glass, and settled into the beige recliner in the living room. She'd brought a collection of Angela Carter stories to read on the plane and it had been a week since she'd had time to get back to them. After about twenty pages, she was yawning, the effort of all the completed tasks catching up with her, and she gave in about 9:30. Retrieving the red folder, she tucked it under one arm and headed upstairs to bed, turning off the light only after she'd zipped the bronto-saurus into a compartment of her suitcase.

Phoebe woke in the middle of the night. It took her a minute to orient herself to the unfamiliar pattern of light and shadow. She turned over, kneaded the pillow, and was almost asleep again when she thought she heard the soft metallic *snick* of a Zippo lighter opening, somewhere downstairs. A minute later she smelled cigarette smoke.

She sat bolt upright, her heart pounding in her ears with sudden adrenaline, eyes wide open, staring at nothing. Those same acrid menthol fumes had wafted up to her childhood bedroom so many nights when Mother couldn't sleep.

No. Mother's dead, she thought. She almost said that out loud but knew that the word "dead" in the silent darkness would terrify her. She bit a knuckle to stop herself.

Then came a sound that raised every hair on her body.

Whirrr . . . , snap. Whirrr . . . , snap. Whirrr . . . , snap.

A deck of cards being shuffled, and then the unmistakable *slap, slap, slap* of a game of solitaire being laid out on a glass-topped table.

That was impossible.

Yet the sound continued, soft and regular.

Phoebe pulled her knees to her chest, curling up around herself, and tried to slow her breathing. It was only her imagination. She was alone in a strange house after a long, emotional day. Of course she was thinking about Mother. All she needed to do to reassure herself was get up, go downstairs, and turn on the kitchen light.

She couldn't move.

A minute went by. Two. She started to relax, and then:

Whirrr . . . , snap. Whirrr . . . , snap. Whirrr . . . , snap.

A bead of sweat trickled down between her breasts.

Slap, slap, slap.

Phoebe lay motionless, every muscle tensed, willing the sound to stop and trying to hold off the panic that if it did, the next sound she'd hear would be slippered footsteps coming to reclaim her.

Eventually, sheer exhaustion pulled her into a restless sleep. When she finally got out of bed, every muscle aching from being clamped in fight-or-flight tension, morning light streamed through the window. She dressed and padded silently down the thick carpeted stairs, clutching the only weapon at hand, a slender pale-blue Lladró figurine. That was ridiculous, but she felt less vulnerable than if she'd been unarmed.

The kitchen was spotless and empty. Nothing on the table but the FAMILY box and the small pile of objects. No ashtray. No lighter. No cards. A tomato-smeared plate in the sink, the trash empty except for the food cartons.

Phoebe put down the figurine and felt a wave of self-conscious embarrassment. She'd had a whopper of a nightmare. Not surprising, under the circumstances. With the combination of wine, greasy food, and a lifetime of, well—*issues*—of course she hadn't slept well. Made perfect sense, now that it was daytime.

Cards had been one of their few shared customs, a bloodsport that Phoebe had been taught as soon as her hands were big enough to hold a deck. How wonderful it had once felt to get Mother's undivided attention—until their games had evolved into an arena for inquisition. She'd learned to dread the moment that Mother would stop dealing and say, as if it were a casual thought, "Can't you do something with your hair?" "Have you decided on a major?" "What *are* you planning to do with your life, Phoebe?"

She boiled water, made a rich, milky tea, and wrapped her hands around the steaming mug. The patio door slid quietly on its track. Phoebe walked out to the end of the narrow dock and stood for several minutes, the air cool on her skin, watching the waves break, over and over. Constant and ever-changing.

Sipping her tea, Phoebe planned her day. She'd finish the bedroom, take herself out to lunch and another run to Goodwill, then come back here and bake. Everything would be ready by sunset, and she'd go down to the water and do what she could to banish her ghosts.

Phoebe had never been big on rituals. She had gone to Sunday School by command, and when she was old enough to choose for herself, chose to worship the heretical god of sleeping in. So there was no religion to fall back on, no Episcopal exorcism. The soul cake was a start, though, a focus. She needed *some* structure, couldn't just walk to the end of the dock and fling Mother out willy-nilly, watching the seagulls dive down to nibble at the larger bits before they sank below the surface.

The sun rose fully above the line of palm trees, their fronds rustling in a gentle breeze, and the air began to warm. Phoebe put the mug down and walked along the sand, her hands in her pockets, inviting grief and finding it elusive.

When Mother first got sick, Phoebe had supposed that grief, when it finally came, would be a huge hole ripped out of her life. Instead it was as if some delicate, many-tentacled creature had been attached to a fine mesh, then flown away, leaving a thousand tiny holes. Particles of memory drifted in with no pattern or predictability.

Emotions swirled, chaotic and contradictory. She felt sympathy for the hollow-eyed invalid, felt relief that Vibby Morris's suffering had ended, but did not miss the cool and critical woman who had raised her. And part of her would always long for a loving mother who might have come to her in the dark when she was small and scared and alone. Who might have rocked her, sung her lullabies, and now never would.

It was almost noon when she finally returned to the townhouse. Instead of going out again, she ate the bakery muffin and heated a can of tomato soup, drinking a mug of it standing up. She spent the afternoon browsing again, gathering her offerings from each room in the house: a little figurine; a deck of cards; a selection of photographs.

One in the nursery, baby Phoebe in her mother's arms, swaddled and bottle-fed. One from high school, Phoebe wooden, Mother with a little half-smile, her arm around her daughter, her eyes on someone off camera. And one of Mother after the first operation, flanked by Phoebe and two of the "girls" from her bridge group. She had lost most of her hair, so her head was done up in a turban, but she had put on lipstick, and her pearls, of course. *Those* eyes looked frightened, wary, like an animal caught in an unexpected trap.

Phoebe went up to the guest room and retrieved the bundle of letters from her suitcase. Missives written when she was at summer camp, at college, in Chicago for her first job. All on that same cream-and-blue stationery, the handwriting so familiar, so distinctively *her*.

Returning to the table, she added them to the photos and put everything into a wicker basket. She tore the recipe out of her notebook and read it through once, then turned the page over and did the math to cut it down from a batch to one single, slightly oversized soul cake. She scribbled numbers, crossed them out, recalculating and fudging a bit to eliminate inconvenient measures like 3/32nds of a tablespoon.

Then she laid out each of the ingredients she'd purchased: vanilla, eggs, milk. Cinnamon, ginger, butter. Baking soda. The recipe called for currants, but the Publix had only stocked raisins. Those seemed too frivolous, so she didn't buy any. A soul cake ought to be a pastry without indulgence. A final course, but not a dessert.

She opened the first canister, scooped out a cup and replaced the plastic lid, sifting the flour and baking soda into the mixing bowl. She looked down at her altered recipe. One third cup of sugar. She rummaged in a drawer for a smaller measuring cup, and found a yellow plastic one behind a package of cupcake liners and some corn skewers, one of which jabbed her in the hand as she pulled the cup out.

Ow. Shit. A thin line of blood smeared her thumb. She put it in her mouth, then stopped in mid-suck at a sound from the downstairs bedroom.

Whirrr . . . , snap. Whirrr . . . , snap.

Phoebe dropped the measuring cup as if she'd been stung. She picked up the Lladró, holding it like a club, and walked into the hall. Three steps from the kitchen she heard the soft *slap, slap, slap* of a hand of cards being dealt behind the closed bedroom door.

"*No!*" she shouted in a burst of bravado. She hurled the figurine as hard as she could. It smashed into the wall beside the door with a crack and shattered, pale blue shards littering the carpet.

The sound stopped.

Phoebe waited, her breath ragged in her chest. Silence. After five minutes, she returned to the kitchen, her thumb throbbing, her attention still on the empty hallway, listening, dreading. Picking up the yellow measuring cup, she glanced distractedly at the recipe—right, a third of a cup of sugar—and opened the nearest canister. She filled the little cup, dumped its contents into the flour mixture, then tossed it back inside and closed the lid, pushing the gold-tone can back against the backsplash with the others.

She added the spices—a teaspoon of this, half a tablespoon of that—and began to stir. The smooth white flour became darker and rougher, and when it was all a homogenous pale brown, she cut in the butter and an egg, added the vanilla, and used a fork for a vigorous final mixing.

Sprinkling a little flour on the cutting board, she settled the beige lump and rolled it out until it looked like biscuit dough. The biscuits of the dead.

The hallway remained silent.

She turned the oven to 350° and cut out an irregular circle about four inches across. Noting the time on the wall clock, she slid the greased cookie sheet into the oven.

When she checked ten minutes later, the cake was still pale and felt pliant under the pressure of her finger. Ten minutes more and its edges were beginning to tan, and after another ten it was an even, golden brown. She thumped it with a knuckle, feeling a bit like a contestant in *The Great British Bake Off*, then grabbed a potholder and pulled the soul cake out of the oven. It smelled delicious. She was tempted to taste it, just a crumb or two. No. No such thing as a ritual nibble. She left it on the counter to cool.

As the light outside began to fade, Phoebe dressed in her favorite black sweater and jeans. She put the soul cake in the center of one of Mother's scarves, tying the corners together at the top. She added that to the basket, along with the funereal gold can, four votive candles, and a box of kitchen matches. She poured red wine into a glass, filling it nearly to the brim, then clicked off the kitchen light. She slid the patio door open with her foot, stepping out into the crisp, salt-scented air of twilight.

The sun was a Fiesta-red ball just above the horizon, flattening slightly as it descended, its surface veiled by a few wispy clouds. Phoebe watched it sink into the pewter sea, then took a deep breath, shifted her basket, and headed toward the dock.

She sat, six feet above the water. Small waves broke in front of her, scattering the surface with undulating lines of orange from the neon-sunset clouds. The basket beside her, she watched the surrounding colors fade. Water lapped softly at the pilings and she heard steady creakings from a few boats moored farther down the shore. Lights came on in houses on either side, reflecting like tiny amoebas in the dark water.

Phoebe set the scarf down on the white-washed planks and untied it, laying it flat. Votives anchored each corner. The night was still and when she lit the squat round candles, the wicks barely flickered. The light illuminated the rich colors of the scarf—butter yellow with emerald piping. The glass of wine cast rich ruby shadows.

She encircled the cake with Mother's pearls.

Around the periphery she set the icons of her mother's life: an unopened pack of Salems; a silver dollar from 1943, Mother's birth year; the porcelain shepherdess; a deck of bridge cards with the queen of clubs face up; the small stack of photos. Above the scarf, the bundle of letters. Below it, the glass of wine.

She had just finished arranging everything when the full moon rose above the row of palm trees behind her, a line of white light dancing along the dark water like a path leading to the now-invisible horizon. Phoebe Morris dangled her legs over the gulf and tried to say goodbye.

Taking a drink of wine, she picked up the silver dollar and turned it over and over in her hand. What should she say? "Safe travels, Mother." She threw it far out into the gulf. It sank soundlessly and felt like an empty gesture.

Emptiness. She was at a loss for words. She touched a finger to the soul cake. Prayers. That was the tradition. Beggars said prayers for the souls represented by each cake. She hadn't prayed in years, wasn't sure who or what she was praying to, but—She picked up the cake and took a bite. Bitter. Not sweet at all. Well, that was fitting. The spiced cake dissolved in her mouth, crumbly and a little gritty. She washed it down with a sip of wine.

"Our Father—" she began. No, wrong prayer. This was for Mother. Phoebe sighed and started again. "The Lord is my shepherd, I shall not want." It was a psalm, not a prayer, but she knew it by heart. She closed her eyes and recited it slowly.

Pulling another piece off the cake, she ate it and, after a moment of hesitation, picked up the letters. She read few lines from each of them and thought of all the replies she'd wanted to send back, but had never written. A lifetime of unspoken bravery. "Mother, you never—" she started to say. "Mother, I want—" Her words trickled away into the night air. Even now, the idea of talking back made her stomach tighten. After last night, she half expected Mother to appear, glaring, walking on water.

Another bite of cake, a sip of wine. Then, hands unsteady, Phoebe struck a red-tipped match against the wood of the dock, smelling a wisp of sulphur, and burned the first letter, holding the monogrammed page by its corner until the flames neared her fingers. The ember-rimmed fragments drifted over the side, hissing when they hit the water. They floated for a few minutes, pale against the darkness, then grew soggy and sank below the surface. She burned the others, one by one.

She slid the queen of clubs under the edge of the pearls and picked up the deck of cards. It had taken her a while to decide which queen was most evocative. Spades seemed overly wicked, diamonds too Gábor, and hearts just inappropriate. But clubs? Mother *was* the queen of clubs. Golf club, bridge club, luncheon club, Wellesley Club. A member instead of a mother.

It was unthinkable to think of her spending eternity without a deck of cards. Like warriors taking their shields to Valhalla. She took another bite of cake, half gone now, and held the deck in both hands.

Muscle memory kicked in. Without thinking, she divided the cards and began to shuffle. *Whirr . . . , snap. Whirr . . . , snap.* Her hands jerked at the sound, scattering the cards across the dock. They fluttered and sailed off into the water. Phoebe watched them disappear and picked up the queen of clubs, still lying on the silk scarf. "The queen is dead," she whispered. She ate a bit of cake and tore the card in half, sweeping the pieces into the sea.

"I loved you once," she said. "It hurt. I wanted to be just like you, but I wasn't good enough." A long silence until she spoke again.

"Then, you know what—I left." Her voice grew stronger. "I survived. I made friends. And somewhere along the way, I realized that being like you was the *last* thing on earth I wanted." She drained the wineglass, washing down the final morsel of cake.

A ragged sob surprised her, doubling her over. For several minutes after, she sat with her arms wrapped around herself, tears running down her cheeks, the wind now cold on her face. Time to go in. She felt a bone-deep weariness and a need for this to be *over*.

Without further ceremony, she pried off the plastic lid and tilted the gold canister toward the water. "Goodbye, *Vibby*," she said. A small vortex of gray dust swirled away. Phoebe angled the can down and poured out the rest of the ashes, watching in stunned surprise as the small yellow measuring cup tumbled out and bobbed on the waves.

"Oh, no." A gingery bile rose in her throat. "No, no, no."

The cup disappeared from view. She looked down at the canister in her hands as the significance of what she'd done began to sink in.

"I've eaten Mother," she said.

Not even in a metaphysical way, like the body of Christ that was actually a cracker. She had actually consumed bits of her mother.

Phoebe didn't scream. She sat for a very long time, oddly calm. Shouldn't she be horrified, disgusted? She tried to summon those feelings and found them missing. Maybe she was in shock? Likely. Shock was rather pleasant. She finally felt the kind of tranquil acceptance she'd hoped this ritual would bring her. Closing her eyes, she lay on her side, her cheek against the rough wood of the dock, her mind drifting farther and farther with each rhythmic swell of the waves.

When she woke again, the full moon was high in the starlit sky and the candles had all gone out. Phoebe sat up slowly, light-headed, her body leaden. She tried to stand, legs all pins and needles. Minutes passed. Soon she would gather up the objects that remained, damp from the sea and the night air, and return them to the basket. She smoothed a hand over the silky scarf and picked up her pearls.

With a little half-smile, she reached behind her neck and fastened the clasp with a practiced click.

"Mine," she said.

ELLEN KLAGES is the author of three acclaimed historical novels: *The Green Glass Sea*, which won the Scott O'Dell Award and the New Mexico Book Award; *White Sands, Red Menace*, which won the California and New Mexico Book Awards; and *Out of Left Field*, which won the Children's History Book Prize. Her short fiction has been translated into a dozen languages and been nominated or won multiple Hugo, Nebula, Locus, British Fantasy, and World Fantasy Awards. Klages lives in San Francisco, in a small house full of strange and wondrous things.

GLASS EYES IN
PORCELAIN FACES

JACK WESTLAKE

Imagine waking up each morning and wondering who will have changed. Imagine that being the first thing you think of as you wake. As you get out of bed. As you shower, dress, eat breakfast. As you walk out the door and head to work. Imagine what it's like to get on the tube, scanning the packed carriage for a too-perfect face, for a pair of eyes more vacant than all the others. Imagine seeing such a face on the head of someone whose name you don't know, but who you recognize from your commute at the start of each day. Someone you always nod to, and who always nods back as you both sway and jolt with the movement of the carriage, acknowledgment that never develops into conversation. Imagine seeing them one morning—*this* morning—like usual. Now imagine that their face has changed, apparently overnight. It's a doll's face. Near-white porcelain, with wide blue eyes made of glass. Imagine how it feels, knowing that only you can see this. Imagine they look at you. Imagine how it feels when, despite the change, despite them not being them anymore, they nod at you like usual.

This is what my life has become.

At the office building I do my best to avoid the concierge, but it's no good—you have to pass the main reception desk to get to the lifts. I keep my head down and try to dissolve amongst the other gray-or-black-suited staff passing through the foyer. I feel the concierge's eyes on me. He was one of the first to change.

Once I'm at the lifts I glance in his direction, but he's facing forward, talking to a woman who's standing at the desk. From this angle you can see the neat line where his porcelain face meets his actual flesh, just in front of the ear. The porcelain gleams beneath the overhead lights. I think about that seam where cold white meets living skin, and I wonder if the skin dips beneath the porcelain or if it's the other way around— what's on top and what's lurking underneath. Maybe it's neither. Maybe the two simply meet and fuse together, somehow. I've never got close enough to any of them to really see.

The lift's doors open and I go in with the others. We pack ourselves in like tinned meat. As the doors begin to roll shut, the woman appears, putting her hand out to stop them. Her face has changed now, it's porcelain, and her eyes are hard and dark like polished stones.

That's how quickly it can happen.

She squeezes in, apologizing as she does so, maneuvering awkwardly until she's standing right beside me. Her voice is normal, just sounds like it's coming from behind a mask. But it's not a mask. It's her face, now.

I ring Abigail at lunchtime and ask her what's she's doing. She's still at the flat—I didn't wake her when I left—and she's getting to work on her latest article, the deadline for which is Friday. I ask her if she thinks she can get it done in time and she says absolutely. I envy the confidence, the certainty she holds inside herself. Being around her is like standing in a warm light. She talks about the article, and I let her words tumble into my ear and take up space in my head, temporarily submerging all my thoughts and worries about the doll-faced people.

I haven't told Abigail about them.

What I fear most is that one morning, I will wake up and Abigail's face will be cold and hard, and her eyes will no longer be real.

The commute home takes longer than usual because after my first stop, where I need to switch to a different train, the service has been interrupted. The sign says there's a bus replacement, but from experience I know it'll be quicker just to walk.

I emerge from the underground into the black evening. Everything is dark versus light. Chiaroscuro. Cars, buses, streetlights, shop fronts— swells of light and color like oil slicks on dark water.

In fifteen minutes I'm at the edge of the city center, heading toward the part of town where our apartment is. The road is all takeaways and small shops, a hair salon, a butcher's. Most are closed already, while several are vacant altogether. Battered FOR SALE signs jut out above doorways, flexing in the wind.

A homeless man sits huddled in the entrance of an abandoned kebab house. He's got a sleeping bag clutched around himself, and there's cardboard laid out under him like a carpet, a tattered rucksack by his side. I see all of this on my approach along the pavement, and as I get closer I make a point of looking straight ahead. He sees me coming and with a croak he asks if I've got any change. I keep walking, keep looking forward.

But something catches my eye as I pass. Something makes me look. A glimpse in my periphery.

I stop and go back to him. He holds out his hand, but what I'm looking at is his face—the smooth swells and curves of the porcelain, at how the wide glass eyes seem a little bloodshot, like someone's painted tiny red flecks on to them with a fine brush.

"What you lookin' at?" he says.

I stare. "When did this happen to you?"

"Homeless since I was fifteen," he mumbles.

He continues to talk, but I'm not listening. I'm reaching out and touching the porcelain with my fingertips. It's cold like I imagined. There are hairline cracks all over it like you might see on very old china.

"The fuck you doin'?"

He clutches my wrist and his other hand comes up as if to hit me, but I grab it. Something feels odd about that hand, the way it feels against my palm. As I wrench my wrist from his grip and stagger back, I see it. The hand I'd been holding is made of plastic. I'd always assumed it was just their faces. I'd never noticed their hands.

The homeless man sees my expression and starts to laugh. The porcelain doesn't move. Then he pulls the plastic hand from the wrist and waves it at me.

"False hand, mate," he's saying, cackling. He throws it at me and I stumble away up the road.

"Yeah that's right," he shouts after me. "Keep going, fuckin' weirdo, before I cut your hand off and all."

But then I turn back. The street is empty apart from us and an idea has formed in my head. Beneath his sleeping bag he moves as if about to get to his feet, but I stride up too quickly and clasp his head between my hands. He cries out, swatting my left arm weakly with his remaining hand. With my fingertips I feel for the place where the porcelain ends and the skin starts, just in front of his ears. I find it and run my fingertips along the seam. I try to look but he's squirming too much. He's shouting now, bellowing.

"Take it off," I hiss. "I'm sick of this, just fucking take it off—"

I try to prize the porcelain away, try to get some purchase with my fingernails along the fault line. He jerks forward and headbutts me in the abdomen and, winded, I stagger backward, my fingertips bloody. He's getting to his feet, and somehow his blank white face has morphed into a grimace. The eyes are angry. He takes a step toward me and I run.

In the entrance hall of my apartment building, I use the light to inspect my fingers. I'm uninjured. The dried blood is his, from when I tried to work my fingertips between the seam where porcelain met flesh. I wonder about infections. I wonder if that's how the change happens. If it gets into you through a cut or ingestion or in the air you breathe. But I catch myself, make myself stop. This is how you lose it, I tell myself. This is how you end up wearing gloves and a face mask to work, how you end up washing your hands every five minutes, how you end up locking yourself in the flat and taping up the windows and doors and never going out. This is how you lose your mind.

Abigail knows something is wrong. She's made spaghetti Bolognese, and we're eating at the table when she takes a sip from her wineglass and asks me about it. I pretend to chew although there's nothing in my mouth. I am weighing up whether I should tell her or not.

"Have you noticed how people are different these days?" I say eventually in my best calm, conversational voice.

"How do you mean?" she says.

I make a point of gazing into the middle-distance over her shoulder. Beyond the balcony window, the city's all points of light. The red dots of an airplane blink on and off as it makes its way across the darkness.

"Just different," I say. "Have you?"

"Can't say I have," she replies. Another sip of wine. It's starting to stain her lips. "You need to relax. You work yourself up so much. I don't want you spiraling again."

Abigail goes for a shower after dinner while I do the washing up. I submerge the white plates into the warm water, and as they disappear under the suds they suddenly don't feel like plates any more. I imagine they are the faces of the changed, and I am drowning them. I would like very much to drown them all. Maybe then it would stop.

I hear Abigail come out of the bathroom and make her way into the kitchen. Behind me, she opens a cupboard to get another wineglass. She's drinking more lately, and I wonder if it's me who is causing it.

When I turn around to get the tea towel, I cry out. Abigail's face is off-white, nearly featureless, all her freckles gone. Her cheeks shine bright white beneath the kitchen's spotlights. No, I'm saying, over and over, no no no—

Abigail's gripping my upper arms, looking into my eyes. "Darren," she's saying, "it's just a face mask. Darren. Darren, calm down."

Later, in bed, I tell Abigail that I am sorry. I have drunk the rest of the wine with her, and we've started another bottle. We are both a little drunk. I apologize again, and she tells me not to. I roll toward her and bury my face into the curve where her neck meets her shoulder, and I tell her how scared I am that one day I'll wake up and she'll be different. Abigail whispers that she won't be different. She says about going to see a doctor. Maybe I need medication again. And that's fine, there's nothing wrong with that. I tell her it's different this time. I tell her I'm scared. She strokes the back of my head and says, "Shh, shh."

The tube is a sea of porcelain the next morning. I am surrounded by a hundred pale faces. I am trapped in a carriage filled with dolls.

Even the posters and billboards in the city center have changed. It's like someone came and replaced the real ones during the night. Huge white faces peer blankly down, empty eyes the size of hubcaps.

I worry if Abigail is safe, although they've never been violent. No more violent than people usually are, anyway.

I'm the only normal person left at work. In the restroom I splash cold water on to my face. Every time I look up at the mirror I expect to see one of them behind me, maybe with a carving knife raised high, ready to bring it down between my shoulder blades. Of course, this doesn't happen. One of them comes in and uses the urinal, washes his hands and asks me how's it going. Then he leaves, whistling. It might have been Richie. It's hard to tell when they all look so similar.

Back in the office I stare at the side of Emma's head. I know it's Emma because her desk is the next one over from mine, and it's her mug on the desk by the mouse. Emma has a small birthmark on her cheek, normally. It's in the rough shape of a triangle, no bigger than a penny. I am trying to see if her new face has it, too. After a while, Emma sighs and spins her chair so she's facing me.

"Why are you staring?" she says.

"Sorry."

"You've been doing it for ages. It's weird."

"Sorry."

"It's all right," she says. "Just stop. Okay?"

"Sure."

No birthmark.

I stare at my screen, which is dark from having gone into sleep mode. My reflection is the only normal face I have seen today since leaving the apartment.

* * *

There's no train delay tonight but I walk home anyway, take the same route as yesterday, hoping to see the homeless man again. I tell myself it's because I want to apologize to him, but it's not the truth.

He's in the same doorway. His prosthetic hand is attached to him again, poking stiffly out from the sleeve of his coat. For a moment it's as if there's the suggestion of worry in his face as he watches me approach, but of course it's hard to tell.

"Leave me alone," he says as I get near.

I hold my hands up. "I just want to talk."

His doll-eyes watch me. I've never seen any of them blink. I wonder if they even close. If when they lie down, the eyes roll downwards to reveal fake eyelids.

"Does it hurt?" I ask.

"The hand? No."

"I mean your face."

He doesn't answer straight away. Instead he watches me. The eyes blink once, as if answering my earlier unspoken question.

"Why doesn't anyone notice it?" I ask. "Why was it only me who saw it happening, only me who notices people's faces?"

He cocks his head to one side. He looks left along the street, then right, as if checking that we're alone. Then he leans forward like he's going to tell me a secret. The streetlights leave little arcs of orange light on the surface of his eyes.

"All *we're* noticing is *you*," he says.

He starts to laugh. It grows, echoing off the shoddy buildings lining the street. I get up. The eyes are blinking now, madly, rolling up and down and up and down, spinning like reels in a slot machine, and the laughter's growing, he's roaring, it's all there is, laughter and rolling glass eyes in a leering porcelain face, and I run.

I search the internet. All the faces on there, in the adverts and on the websites, are porcelain. Lifeless eyes stare back from the screen. I wonder if Abigail and I are the last normal people left in the world.

Abigail is at the table, sipping from a wineglass. She watches me. I know she's worried. I want to explain. I want to tell her everything, but I know it won't work, might only make things worse. I have it in my mind that telling her might be the thing that changes her. Like a jinx.

I am going to protect us.

I find what I'm looking for and choose next-day delivery. It feels better when you're finally doing something about a problem. Action always feels better than inaction.

I call in sick the next morning. I can't face the hard-faced crowds again. Abigail's deadline is tomorrow, and she says she needs to be left alone. I won't get in the way, I tell her. She'll barely notice I'm there. I describe it as a self-care day, tell her I need to just recharge, get myself back on track. She warms to the idea.

The package arrives a little after ten. I try not to look at the delivery man's face as I sign for the parcel. It's surprisingly heavy. Abigail doesn't even notice there's someone at the door—she's absorbed in her writing, papers and books and laptop spread out all over the dining table.

In the bedroom, I sit on the end of the bed and open the package.

They're perfect.

I show them to Abigail before bed, removing the lid and presenting her with the open box. The masks are nestled in plum-colored tissue. They have thick black elastic straps so you can wear them—the straps have to be thick because of the weight of the porcelain. They're identical, although I've colored the lips of one of them with Abigail's favorite lipstick.

"It'll be good for us," I tell her. "Maybe we can be like everyone else."

She lifts hers out of the box, feeling the heft of it in her hand. Turns it over and looks at the inside, the face embossed now, like a photo negative.

"I don't think everyone else is into this," she says after a while.

"Into?" I ask.

She looks at me. "Oh." She gestures vaguely at the bed. "I thought—"

"No," I say. "No, it's not that. It's for us to just wear around the place. Maybe wear outside."

She's watching me.

"So we can be like everyone else."

Abigail puts the mask down on the bed and stands up to leave. I grab her hand.

"Please," I say.

She studies me for a long moment before sitting back down. She exhales. None of this is easy for her, I know that. It's difficult for me, too. I tell her this.

Abigail takes my hand. "Fine," she says. "We'll try it, just tonight. But tomorrow we're ringing the doctor."

"Of course," I say. "Of course."

We put our masks on and lie down on the bed in our clothes. I switch off the bedside lamp. The mask feels like an embrace. It feels like a shield. The porcelain gradually warms. I feel contained, and it is good.

I wake up late, still wearing the mask. The bed is empty—Abigail's already gone to her office to go over the final article with her editor. Her mask is on her bedside table, and panic washes through me. They'll be noticing her. She'll stand out. I picture them gathering around her, staring, pointing, and what then?

I go out into the lounge and call her mobile. She answers and tells me to be quick, she's about to go in with the editor.

"Are you okay?" I ask.

"Yes," she says. Pause. "Are you?"

Sigh of relief. My breath lingers warm and moist inside the porcelain. "Yes," I reply. "Although I'm late for work. I can still make it, though."

"Okay," she says. "I'll see you later. Don't wear the mask out. Promise me. And ring the doctor."

"Okay," I reply. "Promise."

She says she has to go, and hangs up.

I shower, leaving the mask on. It feels important to keep everything normal, to act as if there is no mask, to act as though I'm just like everyone else, which is something I am used to doing. I dress and head out.

* * *

The commute to the office is the best I've had in a long time. The faces on the tube don't bother me as much. Things almost feel normal again. There are the usual nods in my direction, which I return. One or two of them stare, but it's a good kind of staring. It's because they are used to seeing me with my old face. Inside my new sleek, pale visage, I smile.

Things start feeling wrong when I get to the office. My co-workers stare as I walk to my desk. At first I try to ignore it, but then the doubts come avalanching in. It's like when you were at school and the square kid came in one day wearing trendy clothes—it only made things worse for them. Know your place, the staring says. You aren't like us. It's a mask, it's not real.

Through the glass wall of his office, my supervisor watches me while he talks on the phone.

Inside the mask, my face burns with shame. But I can't take it off. Not now. I've committed. Ride it out, I tell myself. They'll come around. They'll see you're just like them. Maybe they'll recognize the effort. Maybe they'll see that I'm really trying.

Within an hour Abigail comes rushing in. She looks flustered, red-faced, there's a sheen of sweat on her brow. She sees me and her face takes a moment to almost ripple, shiver, before settling on an expression of dismay.

"Abigail," I say, confused. "What're you doing here? Why didn't you wear your mask?"

"Your boss called me," she says.

My supervisor is there then, between us, and with a smile he directs her to his office. Then he looks my way, the smile gone now, and says, "Come on."

Inside his office, he flicks a switch and the glass turns opaque. I've never been on this side of the glass when it goes like that. Beyond, the main office is deathly silent. Abigail and I sit down in the chairs in front of his desk, while he walks around to his side and sinks down into his leather seat.

"Take that thing *off*," Abigail hisses at me.

My supervisor starts talking. He keeps his tone gentle, soft. He smiles sometimes. They must teach this stuff in supervisor's school. But I'm not really listening. His words become blurry, faint. I am looking at his face. It's not porcelain. It's flesh. He's got human eyes and a bulbous nose and ruddy drinker's cheeks, and when he talks or smiles you can see little flashes of his yellow teeth. I look at Abigail, but of course her face is as it's always been—we were the only ones left. I realize I'm talking over my supervisor. I'm telling him how great it is to finally see his old face, it's been so long.

I'm getting up, knocking my chair over by accident, and I'm pulling open his office door to gaze out at the dozen or so faces of my co-workers. I'm going to tell them to their smug flawless porcelain faces that it's not just me, our boss is the same, but the faces looking back at me are all made of soft skin, all different hues and shades and complexions. Someone behind me tries to grab my shoulder, but I wheel away, staggering into the main office. Some of the guys come toward me and grip my arms, and I am sinking, sinking to the carpeted floor amongst pressed trouser legs and polished shoes. Abigail's face floats above me, surrounded by all the others. Hands reach down, they're Abigail's, and I feel her delicate fingertips running up and down either side of my head. Everyone's pushing down, I can't rise, I just want to sit up, but all these strange fleshy faces crowd in instead, they're nothing like mine. Where are your faces, I'm screaming, where have your other faces gone, and the only reply is Abigail, crying now as she pulls at the porcelain and tries to dig her fingers in.

"I told you not to wear it out," she says. "What's *wrong* with you? What's wrong with your eyes? Take it off. Take it off. Why won't it come *off*?"

JACK WESTLAKE lives in the UK. He writes dark fiction which has appeared *Black Static*, *BFS Horizons*, *The Dark*, *PseudoPod*, *Ambit*, and elsewhere. He is currently working on a novel.

PHANTOMS OF THE MIDWAY

SEANAN MCGUIRE

T he sky over Indiana was Dorothy Gale blue, that shade of sun-
bleached denim that spoke of faded dreams and dying youth and
all the wasted days of summer. Aracely squinted up at the sky and wondered what they'd called that color before Baum came along with his
silver slippers and his golden roads and his green, green fantasies of a
better world. Probably nothing. Some things were so much a part of the
way the world was that they never stood out until someone pointed out
that it wasn't always, hadn't always, couldn't always be that way.

People in Indiana lived and died under this sky, and they thought it
was exactly right, and she thought that was exactly wrong. She lowered
her eyes and walked on, cutting a path across the boneyard as around
her, the carnival bloomed like some incredible flower. Tents for petals,
people for pollen, and the straight metal spine of the Ferris wheel for
a stem, rising from the dry-baked ground one piece at a time. It was a
miracle of modern engineering, the way the whole thing broke down
and came back together, and she didn't understand it and would only
be in the way if she tried to help, so she kept walking, waving to people
who weren't too busy to wave back, smiling at the rest, so they wouldn't
have to worry she'd feel slighted when they didn't drop everything to say
hello to the boss's daughter.

The carousel sang as it was tested, calliope music drifting sweet as a dream over the field. A speaker buzzed with static louder than a beehive, sweeter than any honey. The garden Aracely had been cultivated for took shape, light and color and glorious, controlled chaos, and she breathed it in with a grateful heart, filling her lungs from tip to top with home, home, *home*. She did all right in motel rooms and trailers, but there was nothing like the honest, open air of the carnival.

Her mama's tent was already up, walls fluttering gently in the breeze, neon sign above the door flickering to draw the midway moths inside. The buzz of the needle cut through the tarp, and Aracely relaxed that tiny bit more. Everything was normal.

She swept the hanging door aside with one hand and stepped through, into the surprising brightness of the tent. Her mother's lighting array had been refined over more seasons than Aracely had been alive, until it would have taken a grand search to find a place—any place— with better visibility. The racks of inks and books of flash were in their places, and her mother sat, regal, next to Charlie, who drove the main wagon, his face pressed into the table, her needle pressed against his skin. A river unspooled behind it, waters dark and deep and beautiful, filled with mystery.

"Hi, Mama," said Aracely.

"Hello, sweetheart. You have a good nap?" Her mother didn't look away from her work, and that, too, was normal; that was the way things were supposed to go.

Aracely, who had been sleeping when the carnival pulled into this new resting place, nodded. "I did," she said. More shyly, she added, "I like to be asleep when we arrive."

Being asleep when the engines stilled and the unloading began meant waking to a garden already coming into bloom, a busy hive of chaos and choices. She hated to see the fields empty, knowing they would only be full—only be fully alive—for such a little time before the carnival moved on again, and the silences returned.

"I know, baby." Her mother reached for a cloth, wiped the tattoo, and went back to work. The carnie stretched out on her table didn't make a sound. "Run along, now. I have a list to get through before we open."

Technically, tattoos could be done anywhere with light and power, and Daisy had done her share of work in roadside motels or while parked at rest stops. But there was something about the carnival air that the carnies swore sped their healing, and there was no advertisement like someone walking around with a smug smile and a bandage on back or bicep. Daisy only tattooed her employees on arrival day: after that, it would be townies until they rolled out again, and that made time on her table rare and precious.

Aracely nodded. "All right, Mama. I love you."

"Love you, too, flower," said Daisy, and then her tall, dream-dazed daughter was gone, leaving her alone with the buzz of the needle and the man on her table, who might as well have been a corpse for all the word he offered.

"You dead there, Charlie? Because I'm not wasting any more of this ink on a dead man."

"Just thinking, Daisy."

"Thinking about what?"

"Aracely."

Most men with the show, they'd said that, they would have had concern for their anatomy immediately after. Aracely was seventeen, sweet and kind and lovely as a summer morning, and her mother protected her like she was the last rose in the world. Daisy had her reasons. No one questioned that. She looked down at Charlie, thoughtful, needle in her hand shaking and ready to sting.

"What about her, Charlie?"

"She doesn't know much outside the show, does she?"

Daisy shook her head, aware he couldn't see her, unable to put her answer, vast and awkward as it was, into words. Born in the back of the boneyard, that was Aracely, her first breath full of popcorn and sawdust and the tinkling song of the calliope. Raised where walls were either tin or canvas, where everything could change in an afternoon—that was Aracely too, daughter of the midway, anchored to the open road. Her life was an eternal summer, bracketed by deep-dreaming winters that passed without comment, leaving her exactly as she'd been before the snow fell.

"Her daddy's people were town," she said finally. "We don't go there anymore. No point to it. He didn't want to know her when she was just getting started, he doesn't get to know her now."

"How's she going to take it when she has to leave?"

Daisy sucked in a sharp breath, putting the needle down before she could do something they'd both regret. Her art was more important than her anger. A flare of temper could last a moment, but a line mal-formed by a hand that pressed down a bit too hard, a needle wielded in anger . . .

Those were things that would last, and they would shame her. More than anything else, Daisy was a woman who hated to be shamed.

"She never has to leave, Charlie, so you set that thought out of your head," said Daisy, picking her needle up again. "There's nothing in the world outside that she can't find right here."

Charlie, if he thought otherwise, was clever enough to keep his own counsel. The needle flashed and buzzed, and nothing more was said, and too much went unspoken.

Aracely walked the midway as it came alive, a smile on her lips and a song trapped against her tongue, filling her with the heat of its hum. She walked the whole shape of the show, learning every inch of the land, every step of what was going to become her home, transformed by the sweet alchemy of light and sound and intention into something bright, and beautiful, and temporary.

Always temporary.

She stopped at the edge of the space portioned off for their use, melancholy washing over her like a wave, so that she had to press a hand against her chest to keep her heart from beating itself free and flying away. It wasn't fair. Everyone else had a home that was allowed to endure more than the span of a season, but *her* home, *her* place had to disappear every time the wind changed.

Was it so wrong to wish for something that could *last*?

A piece of unsecured rope fluttered in the breeze. She glanced toward it and went still, gazing at the distant shape of a farmhouse. No: it wasn't a farmhouse. She'd seen plenty of those, scattered across

America's heart-land like a gambler's dice across a felted table. They possessed a certain similarity of form and function, all drawn from the same blueprints, all with their own detail and design. Farmhouses were like people. You knew them when you saw them, and every one of them was different, and every one of them was the same.

This was a mansion. This was the kind of house where movie stars lived, the kind of house that got written up in the magazines that Adam who ran the hoochie-koo show liked to read, the ones he always hid when he saw her coming. Aracely didn't understand why: there was nothing shameful in pictures of nice houses, or interviews with the nice people who lived in them. But Adam acted like he couldn't think of anything worse, like she had no idea there was a world outside the carnival, and so Aracely went along with it. She didn't want to make him uncomfortable.

She went along with a lot of things for the sake of not making anyone else uncomfortable. She thought, sometimes, that *she* was uncomfortable, and then realized if she started dwelling on *that*, she would never do anything ever again, because the impossibility of living her life without doing harm would be too much for her narrow shoulders to carry.

This house didn't look like it worried about doing harm. This house didn't look like it worried about much of anything. It was tall, and every line it had was perfectly straight, except where the architect's hand had decided it should be bent, had coaxed an angle into an arch or a corner into a curve. It was white as bone, and it was beautiful, and Aracely couldn't imagine anything more wonderful than seeing it up close.

She started to step across the line the roustabouts had chalked on the ground and stopped, overcome with indecision. She wasn't allowed to leave the carnival. That was her mother's first and strictest rule. She could murder a man out of boredom, she could lie and cheat and steal and howl down the heavens if that was what she needed to do, but she couldn't leave the show. She had *never* left the show, not really; had been packed away with all its other pieces ever since she could remember, always traveling within the tenuous shell of "carnival." She'd talked to townie kids who said they envied her freedom to travel the country and see the world, not confined in classrooms and expectations, but she thought maybe freedom was one of those things that looked different depending on which side of the cage door you were standing on.

Almost without thinking about it, she lifted a foot, set it down, and was standing suddenly outside the chalk, outside the carnival, outside the shell of everything she'd ever known. Aracely gasped. The wind took the sound and made it disappear.

She took another step. Then she took another step, and another after that, and she was suddenly running across the open field, that thieving wind blowing through her hair, urging her onward. The delicate spring grass bent and broke under her feet, filling the air with the smell of green, growing things, of life beginning and ending in the same careless, carefree step. She didn't stop. She didn't slow. She was running—for the first time in her life she was running—through a world that didn't know her mother's name, that didn't know she was the flower of the midway, too precious to pluck, too delicate to—

The stone that turned under her foot knew nothing of malice, nor of carnivals, nor of runaway midway princesses fleeing gilded cages. It was an accident, nothing more, but it was enough to send Aracely tumbling head over heels down the slope, over and over again, until a strong hand caught her ankle and jerked her to a sudden, bone-jarring halt.

Aracely lay facedown, panting, trying to reconcile the end of her flight with the way the world had turned itself upside-down and wrong-side-up all at the same time. Her chest was tight. Her knees burned, and she knew when she looked at herself, she'd find grass stains and mud and a hundred other proofs of her transgressions.

"My mother's going to *kill* me," she moaned.

A voice—a *new* voice, a *strange* voice, unfamiliar as a motel room in the light of morning—laughed, and the hand holding her ankle let go. "Maybe I should have let you keep rolling, then. A broken neck isn't pleasant, but nobody's mother ever killed them after they were already dead."

Aracely stiffened. New voices meant townies, and townies meant danger. She'd listened to the older ladies talking when they didn't think she was close enough to hear, cigarettes cupped in their hands and secrets hidden in every honeyed syllable. They were her oracles, the grand dames of the carnival, and when she was old enough and wise enough to know everything they knew, she would be allowed to go wherever she wanted. That was how it was, for flowers. They were delicate when they were fresh, but once they'd had time to dry and wither, they were strong. They could perfume the world.

"It's all right. I'm not mad at you or nothing. Lots of people fall down in this field." The voice paused. "Well, I suppose not *lots*. That would take having lots of people hanging around, and that doesn't so much happen anymore."

Aracely hesitated. Whoever it was didn't talk like any townie she'd ever met. Carefully, she pushed herself up onto her hands and twisted around to look over her shoulder.

The girl—woman—girl behind her offered a lopsided smile of greeting, raising one hand in the smallest possible iteration of a wave. "Hi."

She was striking. Not beautiful: there wasn't enough softness to her for beauty. There were girls at the carnival that everyone agreed were beautiful, who could stop traffic when they walked the midway, who could talk townies into anything they wanted. This girl wasn't one of them. She wasn't quite a woman yet, either; she had the same softness and smokiness that Aracely had, like she could still decide to go in any number of directions, rather than growing up to be one singular thing.

Sometimes girls who weren't beautiful could be handsome, but that wasn't this girl, with her hair like coal and her eyes like cinders, with the scars of a bad burn pulling the skin of one cheek upward in a permanent, secretive smile. There were men at the carnival who would say that scar had ruined her, and even without hearing them speak aloud, Aracely felt a wave of hot, terrible hatred for them and their judging eyes. They didn't have the right to judge. They never could.

"Something wrong?" asked the girl, smile fading.

Aracely's hate turned into horror in her belly. She thought—the stranger thought—she thought Aracely was staring at her scars. It was plain as anything.

It was awful.

"No," said Aracely. "I just took a worse tumble than I thought, I guess. I'm sorry. I'm . . ." *I'm away from the carnival for the first time in my life, I'm scared, I'm not supposed to be here, I'm never leaving again.* ". . . I'm Aracely."

"Pretty name," said the stranger, and offered her hand. The only one she could offer, Aracely realized: her other hand was as burnt as her face, and hung, stiff as an old tree branch, at the end of a motionless arm.

I want to kiss her scars, Aracely thought, and her ears burned as she took the offered hand and let herself be tugged to her feet.

"I didn't choose it; my mama gave it to me," she said.

"Still, it suits you," said the stranger. "I'm Joanna."

"That suits you, too." Aracely realized she was still holding Joanna's hand and dropped it, cheeks flaring red. It felt as if there wasn't any blood left for the rest of her body, with the way it was rushing to her face. "I—I mean, you—I mean, do you live around here?"

"In a manner of speaking." Joanna jerked her chin, indicating something beyond Aracely. Aracely turned, and there was the house—the big, white, impossible house that had lured her away from the carnival. The mansion in the middle of nowhere, the house that shouldn't have existed.

"I came back after the fire," said Joanna. "I couldn't think of any-place I wanted to go. This was home. Didn't matter if it had gotten a little singed-up and smoky. Same thing happened to me. It didn't seem right to leave without fixing what we'd lost."

There was a story in every sentence, and Aracely knew if she peeled them back, if she looked them straight in the eye, she'd find things she didn't want to see. Instead, she smoothed the wrinkles from her skirt and sighed.

"I'm with the carnival that's setting up over the ridge," she said. "I'm sorry to have disturbed you."

Joanna raised an eyebrow. "Carnival?" she asked. "I own the land for a mile around here, and this is the first I'm hearing of a carnival."

The blood that had been rushing to Aracely's face drained away, leaving her pale as paper. "I . . . Our frontman was supposed to make sure everything was in order," she said. "He has the papers." Or did he? She never left the carnival boundary, not under normal circumstances. How would she know if everything was being done correctly?

There was never enough money. She knew *that*. There was never enough money, and the Ferris wheel needed repairing, and half the games were privately owned, they came and went like flowers in the fall, undependable, nothing you could pin a midway on. Her mother had been making concessions on their rent for years, letting them have their spaces for less than she should have, just to be sure of having steady attractions to sell towns on allowing the carnival to stop there. A big, empty field, near a house that had almost burned down . . . it would have seemed like a good place to set up without paying.

News of disasters travels fast. They could have been states away when the fire happened and still have heard about it, her mother filing the information for a dry spell, a time when an unguarded field would be a necessary thing. News that it had been rebuilt, that someone was living there, well. That wasn't as interesting. It wouldn't have traveled nearly as fast.

"I have to go," said Aracely.

"I suppose you do," said Joanna—and was it Aracely's imagination, or did the other girl's face fall, just a little, the expression dampened by her scars? "No one lingers here for long."

Aracely wanted to tell her no, no, she wasn't running *away* from Joanna; she was running *toward* the carnival, toward her mother, toward the answers to the uncomfortable questions she was asking herself. She wanted to stay where Joanna was more than almost anything she could think of, wanted to keep looking at this beautiful girl with her tousled hair and her suspicious eyes, wanted to daydream about what it would feel like to run her fingers down both sides of her face at once, to read the secret stories tangled in her scars. Her throat was dry; her tongue was strangled. All she could do was shake her head, and turn, and flee.

When she reached the ridge, she looked back.

Joanna was gone.

So was the house.

* * *

The carnival had continued to unfold while Aracely was running, was tumbling, was falling, although she did not know it yet, into the fringes of a thing that looked very much like love. As she walked along the familiar, ever-changing aisles, lights twinkling on every side, the Ferris wheel turning gently in the distance, she worried.

To any other girl, it might have seemed strange for a house to be there one moment and gone the next: houses were meant, after all, to be rooted, stationary things. But Aracely had grown up with the carnival. It moved. If it stopped moving, it would die. She hadn't heard of houses that did the same: that didn't mean they weren't out there. Maybe the house had simply wandered off for a little while, and would be back when it felt like it.

The entrance to her mother's tent was closed, but the buzzing of the needle had stopped. Aracely tugged it aside and peeked through. "Mama?"

Daisy looked up from cleaning her needles and smiled. "There's my girl," she said. "Everything coming together out there?"

"Not from anything I've done," said Aracely, stepping inside. "Mama, did we pay to set up here? Do we have permits?"

"Aracely, what . . ." Daisy stopped mid-sentence, eyes narrowing. "What have you done to your dress?"

"It's not nice to answer a question with a question," said Aracely. "You taught me that."

"I also taught you to respect your mother, and not to go getting grass and mud all over your clothes. Where have you *been*?"

Aracely lifted her chin, trying to look brave. She wasn't sure what brave looked like, but she thought she could do it, if she didn't flinch. "I went running in the grass. It's beautiful out there, Mama, you wouldn't believe how—"

But her mother was on her feet, eyes wide and horrified, cleaning rag and tattoo gun forgotten in her haste to cross the tent and grasp Aracely's shoulders, fingers digging in until they left paths of pain behind them. "You went outside the carnival?" she asked, and her voice was as shrill as the screams from the roller coaster, the ones that hung in the air like a promise of bigger fears to come. "You left the boundary?"

"I wasn't hurt! I met the girl who owns this land, Mama, and she's beautiful too, she's not like a townie at all. She lives in the house past the ridge." The house that wasn't there. But that was all right, because it would come back. Right? That was probably the real difference between a carnival and a house. Houses had to stay on the same land all the time, planted like roses, while carnivals went wherever they wanted to go, like wildflowers.

"Did she touch you?" Daisy's hands grasped tighter, tighter, until Aracely gasped and pulled away, shoulders throbbing.

"Mama, *stop*! You're scaring me!"

"Answer the question!"

Aracely took another step back, and did the unthinkable.

She lied.

"No, Mama. She didn't want to get her hands dirty."

Lies are meant to be false things that seem believable, but this lie didn't seem believable to Aracely. She couldn't imagine Joanna—beautiful Joanna, with her house that is and isn't there—being afraid of a little mud, especially not when that mud came from land that she already owned.

Daisy relaxed, and Aracely did the same, knowing her deception had been successful. A pang of pain shot through her heart. She was a bad girl now. She was a girl who could deceive her mother, and not even feel a little bit sorry for it.

"Good," said Daisy. "I don't know what possessed you to leave the carnival, but you must never, never do that again, and even more, you must never, never let an outsider touch you. You're delicate. People like that, in places like this, they don't understand how to be kind to delicate things. I won't have you risking yourself like that. All right?"

Aracely didn't answer. Daisy grabbed her again and shook her by the shoulders, seeming to have forgotten her own warning.

"*All right*?" she repeated.

"All right, Mama," said Aracely.

This time Daisy let go of her own accord. "Good girl," she said, voice barely above a whisper. "Good, good girl."

Aracely turned and fled the tent, and Daisy did not pursue her.

* * *

The sun dipped lower in the sky. Not quite sunset, when the midway would light up like a summer morning and the townies would start rolling in, drawn by the lights and the sound and the promise of something better than their quiet, ordinary homes, but getting closer. The sun dipped lower in the sky. Not quite sunset, when the midway would light up like a summer morning and the townies would start rolling in, drawn by the lights and the sound and the promise of something better than their quiet, ordinary homes, but getting closer. Dawn was a distant memory, the moment closer to tomorrow than yesterday.

Aracely stumbled between the familiar attractions, clutching the front of her gown and trying to swallow the fear that had grown in her breast with every panicked word that dropped from her mother's lips. Daisy wasn't supposed to lose her temper. Not with *her*. Daisy was her mother, her sole protector in a world full of dangerous things, and if Daisy was a danger, too, well . . .

Aracely didn't know what she'd do if her mother had somehow become another danger in a world she'd always known was out to do her harm. She was innocent, yes, and she was delicate, but she was both those things because it had been safer than the alternative. If she allowed herself to be innocent and delicate and naïve, her mother would take care of everything, and the dangers of the wider world would never be able to consume her.

"You look lost."

Aracely froze. Charlie emerged from the shadows between two tents, a bandage on his arm and a rolled cigarette in his hand, sweet smoke drifting up to tint the air. He looked at her frankly, assessing her fear. Aracely clutched her gown tighter, the fabric bunching under her fingers.

"What happened, Aracely?" he asked, and his voice was kind— kinder than her mother's had been, kinder than she would ever have expected it to be. "Somebody hurt you?"

Silent, she nodded, unable to make her traitor tongue admit who had done the hurting.

Charlie sighed, taking a long drag on his cigarette as he considered the mud on her hem and the grass stains on her skirt. When he spoke again, it was to ask, "You go off the grounds?"

This time, her nod had a sliver of defiance in it. She glared at him, her fingers unclenching from her gown as she silently dared him to say something, anything, against her going wherever she liked.

Instead, he smiled. "Good girl. You're almost grown. You have the right to leave if you want to. It's not right to keep you cooped up. You're not the first person born to the midway, and I daresay you won't be the last—the world may be shutting shows like ours down as fast as it can manage, but people keep making babies, and we've got a little time yet. That doesn't mean you have to stay here. You can't choose the carnival if you've never once been outside it."

"Mama says I do," said Aracely.

"Your mother . . ." Charlie paused, choosing his words as carefully as he could. "Your mother worries about you. That's all. Mothers always worry about daughters. Yours maybe more than most. But she has her reasons."

"What are they?" Aracely narrowed her eyes. "Everyone says she has her reasons, everyone says she's doing the best she can, but everyone also acts like it's normal for me to always be in the carnival, even when they come and go as they please. I've never even been inside the Walmart!"

Her last complaint was delivered with such an indignant wail that it was all Charlie could do not to laugh. He sobered quickly enough, regarding her with steady eyes.

"You know it wasn't easy, birthing you," he said. "Your mother thought she'd lost you, a whole bunch of times, both before and after you were outside her belly and looking at the world. If she's a little protective, you can blame it partially on that."

"But I didn't *do* that," said Aracely. "It's not my fault if I was sickly when I was born. I didn't decide any of that, and it's not fair to keep holding it against me. I've never done anything wrong, not on purpose. I just wanted to see the house."

Charlie stilled. Finally, in a soft voice, he asked, "The house?"

"On the other side of the field. I met the girl who lives there. She didn't know we were coming. Charlie, did we not pay our rental fees? Are we here when we're not supposed to be?" Aracely looked at him anxiously. "I don't want to have to move along when we've just gotten everything set up, but if we don't have permission, I guess that could be what we have to do."

"There's no house there," said Charlie, voice still soft, like he was afraid that to raise it would be to shatter some thin and impossible peace. "This field . . . the people who owned it all died. The bank owns all the land for almost a mile, and we did all our rental paperwork through them, exactly as we're meant to do. I don't know who you met, girl, but there's no way she lived in a house that doesn't exist, and there's no way she gets to say whether or not we're allowed to linger here."

Aracely stared at him, eyes gone wide and heart gone narrow until it felt like it was barely beating at all, like she was on the verge of toppling over. Then she turned and fled, not deeper into the midway, but out, toward the boundary line, toward the vast and formless freedom of the fields behind. Charlie swore and ran in the opposite direction, fleeing toward Daisy's tent.

Two figures running, both as fleet as fear can make them, one heading for a secret, the other for a story. See how they run, these children of the carnival sky! The man, with his fresh tattoo still aching on his skin, who remembers rumors, yes, stories that will linger after he is gone, who knows that everything is about to change. The girl, as guarded and sheltered as any hothouse flower, perfectly adapted to the climate of the carnival, where walk things that are neither here nor there, now nor then . . . living nor dead.

She ran not because she knew the shape of the story she was becoming, but because she didn't know it; because she was afraid, as all sheltered things are, of the aching unknown.

He ran because he understood.

Aracely was younger, more frightened, and less aware of her own limitations; when she ran, it was with the wholehearted abandon of a young thing, and this time, when she crested the ridge and saw the house set out before her like the shadow of a dream, she did not lose her footing. She ran, and ran, and ran, until her feet were pounding up the front steps of a house that shouldn't exist, until her hands were hammering on the door. Was this how people knocked? She had seen it in movies and on television, but she had never really had the chance to try it for herself. Doors in the carnival worked a little differently. Knocking on a tent could knock it over; knocking on a tin-walled trailer was loud and hollow at the same time, taking so little effort that a child could do it.

Knocking on wood was different. The house felt solid, like she was beating her fists on bone, and when she pulled back for another volley, the skin on the sides of her hands was red and hot.

The door swung open. Joanna stood framed in the entryway, only blackness behind her, a quizzical expression on her beautiful, scarred face. "Aracely?" she asked. "What are you doing here?"

"Are you real?" Aracely blurted.

Joanna's confusion melted into sad resignation—and yes, acceptance. "Ah," she said. "Someone told you. I guess that was going to happen, once you went back to your carnival and told people you'd seen me."

Aracely said nothing.

"I'm real. I was real, anyway, before the fire. I don't know if you'd consider me real now. Are ghosts real?" Joanna looked at her, sidelong and thoughtful. "Are *you* real? The living can't see the dead, usually. They sure can't touch us. You didn't have any trouble touching me."

"Dead?" whispered Aracely.

"In the fire," said Joanna. "We all died. I woke up alone in the ashes. I think . . . I think I stayed for my horses." She waved a hand, indicating the rear of the house, the fields that rolled on behind it. "They died so quickly that they didn't realize it had happened. They're all still here, with me. I guess they will be until someone comes along and paves these hills to build condos or shopping malls or something. Even ghost horses don't want to stick around to argue with bulldozers."

"What happened?"

"Bad wiring in the walls. It was over a century old, and I guess every generation had decided it could be somebody else's problem, until the place went up in the middle of the night, and no one made it outside to watch the burning." Joanna reached up and touched the scar on the side of her face. "I could wish these away if I wanted to, be the girl who'd never known what it was to burn, but it feels like that would be cheating, somehow. If I get to stay here, I should stay here as the aftermath, not the anticipation. How is it that you don't know this?"

"Why should I know it?" asked Aracely. "I've never been outside the carnival before."

Joanna hesitated. Then, without stepping out of the entryway, she extended her hand toward Aracely. When the other girl took it, she sighed, the sound as soft and sad as wind rustling through the boughs of an old oak.

"I thought you knew," she said. "Aracely . . . did none of them ever tell you that you were dead?"

Charlie burst into Daisy's tent to find her sitting with an open bottle of wine and a book of baby pictures, drinking from the one as she wept over the second. Her head was bowed, her shoulders slumped; she looked years older than she had when they'd rolled into town, a comfortable caravan that carried its secrets inside closed boxes, where no one would ever have to see.

"She gone?" Daisy asked, not looking up.

Charlie stopped. "Daisy," he said. "What did you do?"

"You were with us," said Daisy. She turned another page. When was the last time he'd seen that book? When was the last time he'd seen a camera pointed at Aracely, for that matter? "She was such a beautiful child. Remember? Always running around like she thought she was going to get her feet nailed to the ground. So busy. I used to watch her go and wonder what it would take to make her stop. Seemed like it would need a miracle."

Charlie frowned. "Daisy . . ."

"Didn't take a miracle. Not unless you think 'miracle' is another way of saying 'truck.' Only mercy was that she didn't see it coming. She ran out into the road so fast, and the brakes were old, and there wasn't time for her to suffer." Daisy looked up, a tear running down her cheek. "Guess there wasn't time for her to notice, either, because she came running straight over to me, little pigtails bobbing in a breeze that blew right through her, and she didn't seem to realize her body was lying in the dust, like a ticket stub at the end of the night. She asked me to play with her."

Charlie was silent.

"It took everything I had and then some to not start screaming, but I kept my wits about me, and by the time the sun went down, I had a ghost trap drawn all the way along the midway. By the time we rolled out, every truck and every trailer we owned was safe for a haunting. As long as she stays in bounds—and I've pushed them further every year, so she could have truck stops and motel rooms and convenience stores along with all the rest—she's solid, she's real, she's growing like any other girl would grow."

"But she's dead," said Charlie softly.

"She's *mine*." Daisy bared her teeth in a snarl. "*My* daughter, *my* flower, *my* responsibility. She's always been able to be happy here, despite her circumstances. She's always known that she was loved, and how many townie children dream of growing up to run away with the carnival? I gave her the life she would have wanted, if she'd been in a place to choose."

"You didn't give her any life at all," Charlie countered. "She's a shade. That poor child. Does she have any idea?"

"How could she?" For a moment, Daisy's expression was pure smug-ness. "She's grown up within the confines of the carnival. She's changed with every passing year, exactly as a living girl would. There's nothing stopping her from being happy, from doing everything she could ever want to do, as long as everything she ever wants is within reach of the midway lights." The smugness faded, replaced by sudden sorrow. "Or she would have been happy, if she'd only been content. Is she gone?"

Charlie nodded slowly. "I think so. She ran from me when I told her there was no house."

"Then I'll have to go and get her back." Daisy set the book aside and stood. Her skirt was hiked high enough to show the garlands of wheat and roses tattooed around her calves, climbing ever higher toward the secret mysteries she had shared with no one since Aracely's birth. Charlie felt his cheeks redden, but didn't look away.

Daisy stepped toward him, spreading her empty hands in supplication. "Will you help me?" she asked.

He didn't want to. Dead was dead and living was living, and the two were meant to exist side by side, not share a single space. But Aracely . . . she'd been dead for so long, and he'd never known. She'd been *happy*, despite her circumstances. Did he really have the right to refuse her mother?

"I will," he said, and Daisy smiled.

They walked toward each other, all unknowing of their unison, drawn by forces greater than the moment, forces that had been building for years. Since a fire; since an accident; since a mother's stubborn love had refused to let go what should have been gone and buried. Four people on the green hills between carnival and crypt, between midway and mansion.

Daisy walked with her head high and her skirts bundled above her knees, a jar of salt in one hand and a jar of grave dirt in the other. Her witchery was not complicated, old and slow and comfortable in its working, pouring like molasses into the world, stirred and spelled and carefully tended. She worked the way her mother had taught her, the way she would have taught her own daughter, had it not been so dangerous to teach those workings to the dead.

Charlie walked beside her in silence, his own hands empty and his own heart pounding. He was a simple man. He ferried the carnival from one location to the next, and all he asked in exchange was a paycheck and a clear map of his next destination. This was a bit beyond him. Had he been asked, he would have said he didn't understand why he remained, why he didn't turn and run back to the comforting, ordinary shadows of the midway, which lit up the sky behind them like a beacon. The crowds would be coming soon. The night was on the cusp of beginning.

From the other direction came Aracely and Joanna, hand in hand, which granted them both more power than they yet understood, for to hold a ghost's substance is to hold their strength, and they were powerful as specters go, both of them able to pass among the living, if only for a little while, both of them prepared to fight instead of fleeing. They were what their circumstances had made of them, the flower and the fallen, and they walked with the smooth, easy steps of teenagers who had never been quite allowed to cross the line into adulthood.

Aracely's childhood had been a dream given to her by her mother, but it was hers all the same, and the length of her limbs and the clearness of her eyes belonged to her entirely. Some gifts, once given, can't be taken back. She walked with her fingers tangled in her new companion's, like bones buried in the same earth, and she felt the wind blow through her, and she was not afraid. Part of her, she thought, had always known; had simply been waiting for permission to remember. Part of her was less afraid of letting go than it was of holding on.

They were not lovers, both of them scarce seventeen and dead besides, both of them trying to decide what they wanted to become, as the long years of their existence stretched out in front of them, an endless line of tickets to spend at any midway they chose. But they might be. Aracely flushed when she tried to look too long at Joanna, who she thought still burned, somewhere deep inside, a body built around a cinder in the shape of a heart. And as for Joanna, she couldn't look Aracely in the eye without tasting honey on her tongue, without feeling her skin grow tight and hot in a way that had nothing at all to do with flames. So they were not lovers, no, but one day . . .

Time was on their side. It had been since the moment that they died.

They met at the center of the field, and the carnival shone on the hill behind Daisy and Charlie, and the house that was and was not there flickered ivory and ash behind Joanna and Aracely. Daisy looked at their joined hands and felt her heart break, just a little, just enough to let the light pour in. Aracely looked at the anguish in her mother's eyes and forgave her, just a little, just enough to let the love inside again.

"You should have told me," said Aracely.

"Ghost children don't always grow up," said Daisy. "Living children do. If I lied, it was so you'd be able to stand here like this, and not be trapped forever where you were."

"Were you ever going to tell me?"

Daisy rolled her shoulders in a shrug, and said nothing.

"Are you coming home?" asked Charlie. It was a blunt question, and it fell into the delicate web of things unspoken like a stone. Aracely looked at him.

"Should I?" she asked.

"Yes," said Daisy.

"No," said Joanna.

"Only if you want to," said Charlie.

Aracely was silent for a long beat before slowly, finally, she let go of Joanna's hand. The other girl flickered for a moment, like a sheet whipping in the wind. Only for a moment, though, and moments pass.

"Mama," said Aracely. "Why could I grow up inside the carnival?"

"It's a ghost trap," said Daisy. "I designed it that way. To protect you."

Aracely nodded. "Then this is my answer. When you drive away, I won't come with you."

Daisy made a small, pained sound of wordless longing.

"Winter where you like: I won't be there," said Aracely. "But when you come back in the spring, you can collect us both."

Joanna shot her a surprised look.

"I need some time to think, and then I need to see what else is out there in the world," said Aracely.

"Baby . . ." said Daisy.

"No, Mama. You owe me this."

Daisy looked at her. Then, slowly, she nodded.

"All right, baby," she said. "I'll see you in the spring."

There is a carnival that tours the Midwestern United States on a shifting schedule, like all touring shows of its kind. It is among the last of a dying breed, but still it moves, and still it unfurls like a flower whenever it lands, the petals of the midway spreading wide. People who've seen it say there's something special there; something that may endure when the other traveling shows have closed.

"It's like a haunted house," one said, when interviewed by a local paper. "It's a little shivery, but you want to be there anyway. You want to know what happens next."

What she didn't say—what none of them ever say—was that as she was leaving on the first night the show was in town, she had looked back over her shoulder and seen two girls, barely blurring into women, appear at the top of the Ferris wheel. Their hands had been locked together, tight as chains, and their eyes had been on the moon, and even with all that distance between herself and them, she would have sworn that they were smiling.

SEANAN MCGUIRE—best known for her October Daye urban fantasy series, the InCryptid series, and the Wayward Children series—is a native Californian. This resulted in her being exceedingly laid-back about venomous wildlife and terrified of weather. Since her debut as an author in 2009, she has published more than forty novels and is the recipient of the Campbell, Alex, Hugo, and Nebula Awards. She's also won the Pegasus Award for her work as a filksinger. She now lives in Seattle with her cats, a vast collection of creepy dolls and horror movies, and sufficient books to qualify her as a fire hazard.

HUNTING BY THE RIVER

DANIEL CARPENTER

It was her eighteenth birthday and since she was his sister, he thought he'd head home and surprise her. He grabbed a bunch of flowers from a store in Manchester Piccadilly station, and walked across the city. It was early still, and he shared the streets with bleary-eyed tourists, dawn commuters, and the sleeping homeless. He'd forgotten how the air felt in the city he grew up in: gray and wet, even on the sunniest of days. He'd missed that.

So much of the city had changed since his last visit. It felt alien to him, and the pockets that remained were small safe havens of relief. His mum had always called it a city under construction, and it was as true now as it ever had been; looking up he spotted cranes on the horizon. When he was old enough to come into the center on his own, it had been the Arndale they were rebuilding after the bomb, now though, it was housing. Glass blocks of flats squeezed into every space. The skyline changed so often he could barely remember what it looked like.

He crossed Deansgate and turned down the road toward Salford.

The key he'd had since he was twelve still worked, and even before he opened the door he could smell home, something so comforting and so impossible to describe in any other terms.

In the living room, his mum sat watching daytime TV, sunk into an armchair. When she saw him, she smiled briefly before bursting into tears.

"Jesus mum, it's just me." He dropped the flowers, ran over and hugged her.

Between tears she said, "She's gone again."

Kirsty left in the night. She'd done it before. The last time, he remembered, was when she was thirteen. They'd found her a few days later in a squat out in Oldham, sigils etched into her skin with her school compass. There had been more since he'd left.

"The last time was a week ago," his mum said, sipping a cup of tea he'd made her. "I tried the police, but they know us. We're a faff to deal with and they know she comes back."

"She will come back then?"

"Something feels different Lee, don't know what, but this isn't like the other times."

"I'll find her. It'll be like before."

His mum nodded, staring down at her mug. He'd never seen her this bad before, her face pink and pained, eyes squeezed small. As though she was trying to keep the world out of her head. He leant over and put his hand on hers.

"We'll get her back. We always do."

He didn't know the city as well as he used to. It was ebbing from him, everything that tied him to this place was vanishing piece by piece.

"Who's she hang out with these days?"

Lee finds the shop, nestled out beyond the university, near Rusholme. Places up that way feel hidden and this is no different. He almost walks right past it. It's a newsagents, though he knows it isn't really. Terry, the bloke who runs it, had a nice line in coke back when Lee went clubbing. The shop has moved a few times since then, used to be up near the library till some private landowner came and bought up the ground beneath them. Now he's here, sandwiched between restaurants on Curry Mile.

Terry doesn't remember much, or at least he says he doesn't. She bought from him for a while, a bit of weed here and there, once or twice some pills. Nothing too drastic.

"Can't say I thought much of the lad she was with. Too old for a lass like her."

His name is Nathan. Lee doesn't get a surname from Terry, but he gets an address. An estate over in Wythenshawe. No one knows for sure how long Kirsty's been with him. Terry delivered stuff to him once or twice.

It's a cul-de-sac, ringed with houses. Practically every one of them the same. In the middle of the day it's quiet. Most people at work, kids at school. Driveways lie empty. Scaffolding is stacked against one property that he passes, builders chatting with drinks. They take no notice of him.

What is he planning on doing? He isn't sure. Knock on the door? Break a window? Try and find a spare key under a mat somewhere? He'd bet a tenner that none of those would work.

Lee finds number three. It stands out amongst the others. The front window is boarded up, though the glass appears to be intact. The grass in the front garden is overgrown, and a horrible smell is coming from the piled-up beanbags lying against the hedge in front of the property. He glances at the upstairs window. The curtains are drawn and the lights are off.

Fuck it. He knocks on the door and waits.

There's no sound from the house. If she knew he was coming, she'd have found somewhere else to stay.

In the corner of his eye he spots a gap in the boards on the window. Inside he can just about make out the living room. It's dark, and it takes a moment for his eyes to register everything. A small coffee table sits in the center of the room, wax melted into it from candles that have been placed all around it. They've been burned down so much that they're barely there anymore. On the table, spread out and stuck by the wax, is a map of Manchester. Thick black lines etched into it with charcoal. He recognizes some of the places that he can make out from here: the town hall, the old cinema on Oxford Road, the Arndale.

There's writing on the walls, illegible scrawls. Lee remembers finding Kirsty that day years ago. Bloodied arms with symbols scarred into them.

What is she planning?

The next day he heads to Koffee Pot for breakfast. He has an urge to immerse himself in the city, in the places he used to go. The Koffee Pot has moved. It's somewhere up a road in the Northern Quarter now. No longer resident on Stevenson Square. Doesn't matter, it still feels the same inside. He takes a seat by the window.

After a few sips of coffee, he notices someone sitting opposite him. A young lad, no more than about thirteen. He's skinny as fuck, baseball cap pulled down over his eyes and he doesn't look up at Lee.

"Alright Lee?" he says in Kirsty's voice.

"Who's this you've come to me as?"

"Does it really matter?" The boy fiddles with a napkin, doesn't look up. "I know you're looking for me, and I'd like you to stop. I'm okay."

"You're so okay that you've come to chat in someone else's body. Is that okay?"

The boy looks up at Lee, and he can almost see her eyes, witchy and hazel, somewhere behind the boy's own.

"Mum's worried sick."

He jumps at someone banging on the window. The boy doesn't react at all, he turns to spot a stag do barreling past down the street. When he turns back, the boy has his head down again.

"Thanks for giving a shit, but I don't need rescuing. Not this time."

"I went to Nathan's. I saw the map."

What have you got planned? He doesn't ask.

"Yeah, I guessed that was you. Bloody Terry, right? I told Nate not to trust him. Doesn't matter. We're long gone now."

Lee reaches out to the boy, feeling as though he can reach through and find his sister and pull her out of the body and back into reality. The boy shuffles back.

"Please don't. Might wake him up, then we can't chat. I've missed you Lee. You've not called in a bit."

"Been busy."

"London's changed you, you Southern cunt." He can hear her laugh, though the boy's mouth doesn't change expression.

"I noticed this place has moved."

"About a year ago I think. Cocktail place moved in. The city's different. Don't you feel it? Doesn't it make you sick?"

The boy looks around at the people sitting near them, suspicious. Lee looks around too, copying him, but not understanding why. A waitress comes over to take his mug but he clutches hold of it even though it's empty. The boy with Kirsty's voice hasn't ordered anything.

"I don't know what I feel Kirst, I've not been here for years, it doesn't feel like home anymore."

"Exactly. Exactly. No more mithering about. Things have got to change Lee. They have to. It's got to go back to how it all was."

"But that's not the city. It's just me. Places change, people change, sometimes at the same time. Doesn't mean anything bad. Doesn't mean anything. Just means stuff evolves."

"You're wrong Lee."

The boy grabs hold of his wrist and his eyes roll into his head, the whites stare back for just a moment, then the color returns and he stares back at Lee.

"The fuck's going on?"

He goes back to his mum's empty handed and she cries on his shoulder for a little while, before he makes her a brew, and they sit with the TV on in the background, talking about Kirsty.

When Lee went to look for her all those years ago, the first time she disappeared, he remembered the stories, little snatches from her friends, sometimes from strangers. The names they called her. Nicknames whose origins he could never pin down. He saw those same nicknames on the bus months later, etched into the metal headrests, scored into the glass on the window, and he winced when he saw them. Lies, tales, and rumors had lead him to the squat out in Oldham. How she'd fallen in with the scally fuckers who lived in that moldy, broken home, he'd never known, but he'd dragged her out by her arm. She'd called him all sorts but he was keeping her safe, he was doing the right thing. None of the others in that place had tried to stop him.

His mum had been so relieved. They sat vigilant all night in case she tried to leave again.

Tonight, they sit together the way they did all of those years ago, hopeful that she will walk down the stairs as though nothing has happened.

The sightings came in few and far between. Texts saying she'd been seen walking through The Printworks in tattered clothes, bleeding. No, make that lying prone in the middle of Deansgate, speaking in tongues. Another one said she'd been lying low in Heaton Park, sleeping rough in a tent she'd stolen from the Trafford Centre. But none of the leads came to anything, and all of them contradicted one another. Kirsty, for a few days, existed across the whole city all at once.

Then there was a sighting of her in-between the cities. A patch of wasteland just beyond the Irwell. She'd been standing there in the rain, arms aloft, soaked to her skin. Another boy there too, probably Nate. She was screaming at the sky. He was reading from a book. That had been three days earlier, according to the friend who rang him. Lee felt frustrated, how slow it was for news to come his way, but at least it was news. That was something.

He walked there one morning, it was just ten minutes from his mum's place, just ten minutes from where Kirsty had lived. There had been something here, years ago. He remembered something vague: a hotel, an estate? Something he'd never dared enter. Now whatever had been there was demolished, and a mound of dirt had been stacked at the verge, next to the road. There was no building equipment, no sign of any presence there anymore. Just an empty patch of land that belonged to no one. Except that wasn't true. He trod through dewy grass toward the center, stumbling over rocks and holes where foundations and pipes were supposed to be laid, and looked up at the sky. Gray clouds shifted across Manchester, a light rain fell, and he dreamt of his sister, standing there, scarred and screaming. Up ahead of him, rising up fast and different was the city. The towering hotels and old warehouses dulled and washed out in the rain. This is what she had seen, he thinks shaking himself out of the past, focusing on the here and now.

This is why she had been so angry. So scared.

A woman leaves the block of flats next to the wasteland and stares at him. For a moment he's convinced its Kirsty. Another one of her tricks. But the woman turns and walks away quick, lifting her coat above her head to protect it from the rain.

He knows then that he will see her everywhere.

Nate's body washes up at the Deansgate locks two days later. The smokers outside of Revolution spot him. There's no sign of injury and he's reported in the papers as a "reveler" who fell. It takes a call from Terry to tell Lee that this is the bloke.

"You should quit," he tells Lee. "She doesn't want to be found."

But there's something about Terry's voice that doesn't sound right.

He doesn't go back down south, not right away. There will come a time when he'll have to, when his life down there will catch back up with him, but Manchester has a way of stalling time, keeping things still for longer than they should. He feels as though he's exhausting his moment of stillness, draining the goodwill of the city. There are days when he feels a haze fall over him, a thick mist coating him, and when it leaves he finds himself in a part of the city he doesn't recognize right away. He wakes up in the industrial estates of Trafford, under the pagoda in Chinatown, and halfway down Princess Parkway, passing cars honking at him. Then there are worse days, days when he feels he's in control of himself, days when he goes out looking for her still. Wandering the streets of the Northern Quarter he feels someone brush past him and a whisper in his ear,

"What are you still doing here Lee?"

And he knows who it is, but when he turns around, the stranger who spoke to him is already walking away. He can't touch them. He knows what will happen and so there's no point. Some days, in cafes and shops, he'll see someone watching him and he'll know it's her, and he'll approach them, and say, "Please Kirst, come home. Mum misses you."

It's all he has left.

But their blank expressions tell him everything he needs to know, and he apologizes, and pays for his coffee.

Lee sleeps at his mum's place, in Kirsty's room. It's that or the settee. At night, when he can't sleep, he walks from the house, away from Salford, toward Manchester. In Manchester, they call Salford *the other city,* but to him, it's the other way around. Manchester, a strange, enlarged reflection of the place he grew up. He skirts around the edges of it, as though he's looking for a door, and he crosses Bridge Street over the Irwell.

Dawn is coming up, an eggy cream blasting the sky beyond the clouds. It should be cold but he doesn't feel it. The walk has kept him warm enough. He follows the river as it runs parallel to Deansgate, bordering Manchester like a moat, keeping on it for as long as he can until it shifts direction and runs away, twisting around and flowing toward Bolton and Pendle. Witch country.

He recalls the lines on the map in the house, and he looks at the way the river flows. Has it always flowed this way?

And he notices things within it, bobbing on the river, being carried away from the city. At first it's just bricks, shopping carts, bottles. But then, the detritus grows, and he sees everything there: bicycles, entire streets and houses, crumbled and broken, and being flushed out. Jagged blocks of tarmac rolling in the current, knocking into road signs, and bulldozing over hi-viz jackets which float of the surface of the water. Some building equipment floats past, and Lee notices the hook of a crane sinking slowly into the depths.

He sees the first person. They are dead, bobbing on the surface the way Nate probably did. *Just another reveler,* he thinks briefly. More people come next, so many people. Some are dead, drowned and gray and bloated, but some are alive, desperately looking up at him to save them, clawing at the edges of the river, their bloodied fingernails breaking on the brick.

He watches as they are carried out of Manchester toward witch country. Then he turns, and starts walking into the current, back toward the city, toward her city.

DANIEL CARPENTER's fiction has been published by *Black Static*, *Unsung Stories*, *Unthology*, *The Lonely Crowd*, and more. He is the host of *The Paperchain Podcast* (currently on hiatus), a monthly podcast asking writers and artists to respond to prompts set by previous guests. He lives in London with his family.

BOILED BONES
AND BLACK EGGS

NGHI VO

The sign that sits over the lintel of the Drunken Rooster reads "we have served tea to all the world," and it is only a slight exaggeration. The inn sits just south of Tsang and just north of Wu. The Sai River, which starts in Pa'i and doesn't end until it has reached the land of the Engs, flows right by the front door. It is a borderland, on the margin of every country's map. It is a place where the dead get of hand if they aren't placated, honored, and fed.

I own the Drunken Rooster now, but before me came Shang Hua, my aunt by marriage. My father owed her a debt for some very fast talking and two bottles of fermented millet, difficult to come by in that part of the world. When it came to pass that I could see over the edge of the table and somewhat handle a knife without hurting myself, I traveled a full month overland to live with my aunt.

She let me cry myself out that first night before lifting me up on a sturdy stool and showing me how to cut pork against the grain, with a cap of fat and skin left on top to caramelize in her enormous pot. She lined the pot with onions, letting them cook in a fragrant broth of sugar and fish sauce, and then she directed me to tip in the pork and to splash it over with water.

"Now what?" I asked, scrubbing at my eyes with the back of my hand. I was still heartbroken at being so far from home, but I was hungry, too.

She shrugged her round shoulders, the short embroidered cape she wore making them even rounder. She didn't look like the women I had grown up with. Her face reddened fast in the steam, and the kitchen was always filled with steam. Her eyes were small and often narrowed with distrust. She hadn't once told me to stand up straight or directed me to practice my handwriting, though, so I was cautiously hopeful that perhaps things would not be so bad.

"Now it's just waiting, niece," Hua said. "Then after we wait, there will be something good to eat."

It was quiet at the Drunken Rooster that night, one of those evenings where the world seemed to pause for breath. I could hear the murmur of the Sai in its banks, and the wind whistled a little, coming down from the mountain to say hello.

In an hour, a little more, Hua whipped the lid off the pot, and the most delicious smell spilled out. Caramelized pork and onions, brown and salty, sweet and glistening with fat. Eaten hot over pure white rice, I thought it was food fit for a princess, but before I reached for the blue bowl that I had brought with me all the way from Chu-hsien, I hesitated.

"What about Uncle?" I asked timidly.

He was my father's youngest brother. The only thing that I knew about him was that he had run off with a wild woman four years ago who had come through town carrying a pan big enough to fry a small child.

In response, my aunt scooped out a generous portion of rice, dressed it with some pork and onions, and stuck a pair of chopsticks straight up and down in the bowl.

"He died two days ago," she said calmly, setting it on the table.

I didn't know what to make of that, wondering if I should be sad for the death of a man who I had never met, but then there was a scraping at the rear of the inn, a noise that echoed through the darkness. I hunched my shoulders in fear, but my aunt only nodded.

"Ah," she said, "that should be him now."

When the dead come to the back door, their bellies empty and their eyes gazing jealously on the lives that used to be theirs, the food you give them must be the very best. In Tsang, especially in the capital, they don't consider it a meal unless it's spicy enough to make your tongue go numb. In Wu, the food is plainer, and Hua said they made it into a virtue, relishing the purest white rice dusted over with a sprinkle of black salt. The people from Pa'i, seafarers, firebreathers, and storytellers come to rest on their shoal of small islands, like their food fatty and plentiful, sweet with plenty of rice wine.

We couldn't serve all of them as well as they would have liked, but we did our best. After all, my aunt would say, most people won't say no to something that starts with a chopped leek and a dead chicken. Living right on the Sai gave us an advantage, both in terms of the food that we could get from the traders and the custom that came in the door. A fair day might see a Pa'i mercenary in for a breakfast of rice porridge, a prosperous Tsang merchant and his family for a lunch of lacquered duck, and a pair of nuns in saffron for a large shared dinner of last winter's salted pork cooked in apples.

"I didn't think that nuns ate meat," I said, fortunately not so loudly they could hear me. My aunt grabbed me by the arm and dragged me back to the kitchen where she glared at me, her eyes small with anger.

"Don't ever let me hear you talking about what people order," she said, so sternly that it made tears well up in my eyes. "If they ask, and we have it, all I ever want you to say is 'please enjoy the food,' understand?"

I nodded, and then she sighed at the tears that were running down my face. I was a sensitive child, and she had never had to deal with children at all before my father sent me west.

"Those ladies aren't nuns," she said gently, "but it's not polite to point it out, right?"

I understood 'not polite' at least, and I learned to set down the platters of slivered duck and bowls of rice or millet with a cheerful 'please enjoy the food!', just as Hua directed. After a few months, I stopped batting an eye, taking after my aunt's philosophy that everyone needed to eat, no matter how good, bad, or strange.

Good, bad, or strange described our clientele at the Drunken Rooster very handily. The year I turned seventeen was especially busy because Tsang was warring again. There were plenty of people on all sides of the conflict who had no interest in being ground up, whether it was under the hand of the Boar Emperor or the various warlords who had decided they wanted their try at being the Great King Under Heaven.

We fed the people coming through, and we fed their dead as well. There was a small graveyard behind the inn that grew larger that year. The ferry workers brought accidental deaths to us, people who drowned in the river or fell from the barges to be dragged under the steep hulls. Once in a while, some old pilgrim would slip on their sandals and keep walking, leaving their barefoot body behind.

The locals paid my aunt a twice-yearly fee to make sure that she kept the dead fed and happy. The dead like to eat as they did in life, and so we were always very busy. Between the fee and the living customers that came through, we made a nice living.

My aunt handled the dead and the living alike with a shrug and the understanding that people should be fed what they liked, if we could do it. Early that summer, there was a slender little miss who had committed love suicide with her man. She refused to move on until we could find lotus nuts for her, and that took almost four weeks. It wasn't so bad, even if she sat next to the stove and asked me what I was making every few minutes, and when she moved on, she gave me a cool little kiss on my cheek that made my aunt giggle for what I imagine must have been the first time in her life.

The evening that Lord Ning appeared, there was a storm waiting to fall on us from the north. The air prickled with uneasy heat, and the only guests were a group of monks who ate their rice and vinegar pickles in the courtyard, even though my aunt said they might as well come in since custom was so bad.

I was scrubbing out the giant pot with sand when there was a sound like a thunder clap, so close that my ears popped. I thought that lightning had finally hit the dead tree on the bank, and I rushed out to make sure that no one was hurt.

In life Lord Ning was a big man, and when he appeared at the inn's wooden gates, mounted on an enormous chestnut mare, he looked even larger. He was dressed in a suit of armor made from linked and laminated leather plates, all painted a glittering green that must have cost a fortune. He had a sword with him that he named the Lightning of Wei Lu Xin, and he rode straight into the courtyard, scattering the monks like saffron rice.

"I was told I could get a meal here, woman," he said, peering down at my aunt from behind his bristling mustache. She had a bag of greens in one hand and a chicken clucking madly in the other. Her face was stone, and she scowled.

"Of course you can, sir," she began, but then he spurred his horse forward, its thick hooves lashing out dangerously, missing my aunt by a handspan. Hua fell back with a curse, glaring up at the warlord who was glaring down at her.

"It is *lord* when a Tsang woman speaks to me," he said, his voice full of cannon fire and gravel. "You will lay out your best food at once for me, for I am Lord Ning of the Eight Valleys, martyr of the Battle of West Ridge, and favored son of the Great Emperor of the Heavens. I conquered the Red Court of Shao Fan, and I will have my due."

"Of course, my lord. At once, my lord," my aunt said, her voice flat.

Lord Ning peered after her as if he was uncertain about her tone, but he still dismounted, throwing the reins of his horse to one of the monks who were just beginning to recover from the start. It turned out to be a bad idea, as that teenage monk lit out for Wu that very night, riding Lord Ning's mare. The old abbot said he had never had much of a head for the monkhood, but a life as a southern pirate, as I heard later, suited him quite well.

As for Lord Ning, he never noticed the loss of his horse because once he took his seat at the head of our largest table, he settled in and seemed to have no intention of leaving.

My aunt went about her business; just another day, after all. She roasted the chicken she had had tucked under her arm and dressed it with soy sauce and stuffed with ginger and bright red sausage. She prepared a thin water spinach broth and set out a small bowl of white rice next to it.

She brought it to the table and laid it out in front of Lord Ning. It was an excellent supper, and I had helped her with the roasting. I knew that it was good, and at first, from the way Lord Ning started to wolf it down, tearing the chicken with both hands, I thought we would soon be rid of him.

But when the dinner was nearly scraps, the broth drained, and the rice bowl empty except for a few stray grains at the bottom, he glared around and bellowed for my aunt again.

"This food is not fit for a man who has straddled the Earth like a giant," he thundered. Honestly, that lost its effect after the fourth or fifth time he did it. I covered my ears against it, but my aunt stalked into the dining room, glaring at him.

"I am sorry that the food is not to your taste," my aunt said, her courtesy stiff and rusty. "But it is all we have tonight."

And of course you can certainly try to do better elsewhere, was the unspoken ending.

"Fine, fine," Lord Ning said, waving his broad hand "Tomorrow you will do better."

The next day, we prepared braised fish drenched in wilted green onions and fresh red radish pickles, a particular favorite of mine. I cooked the whole thing while my stomach was growling, but all the dead are selfish, and I couldn't take one bite before bringing it to the table.

The dead lord smacked his lips heartily at the sight of the meal, but again, he ate it down to the last bite, leaving that contemptuously on the plate.

"Country bumpkins, when will you serve me what is my due? I am Ning who killed Lord Hsieng at the fords of the Sai River!"

One armored fist sent the plate shattering to the floor, and I backed away, teeth gritted.

It went on like this with no sign of stopping, and this was no wispy girl sitting next to the stove. He hovered like a storm cloud in the dining room, and when the living saw him glowering in the corner, they backed out of the inn quickly. Some of them could be convinced to eat in the courtyard, but most hurried on.

"We're running short on cooking oil," I told my aunt, and she snorted.

"We're running short on everything. It all goes into the belly of that cross-eyed frog-eater."

We had actually tried frogs, delicately skinned and then fricasseed. He ate all but half of one, and it was the same story all over again.

"What are we going to do?" I asked, sitting on an overturned wooden bucket by the back door. "We're going to go broke at this rate."

"And be two women living in a ghost-haunted county, on top of it."

The dead lord's lowering presence put off the dead as well as the living, especially since our dead were most of the humble variety. Farmers, fishers, pilgrims, none of them wanted to eat next to Lord Ning, and they cleared out too. It might be as much as a year before an exorcist came around our way again, and a year of Lord Ning's boasts was too terrible to consider.

My aunt cooked when she was frustrated or angry (when she was happy and content, as well, but that hadn't happened since Lord Ning showed up). She bound up her hair with a black cloth and worked herself to exhaustion over ox shanks, duck livers, stuffed fish, and even vegetarian holy dishes. She boiled bones to extract the rich stock from the marrow, and she used it the next day to infuse the meat. She was a frenzy of activity until one night, I found her flat on her back in the courtyard, staring up at the starlit sky. In the inn, Lord Ning was bellowing to an empty house about his killing of the three sons of Minister Shen.

"I have been going about this all wrong," my aunt said presently. "This whole time, I thought I could get rid of him by giving him what he wants."

"That's good advice for ghosts, you always said."

"But not good advice for bad customers. That ass-faced whale-purge doesn't want to move on. He wants to sit and talk about his conquests, while having us run to bring him plates of goat and duck."

"It's not like we can get the local magistrate after him, though," I said. "The magistrate hasn't been by once since Lord Ning took up residence."

"No, I think I know what to do," my aunt said, sitting up. "I need you to watch the inn for a little while."

A little while turned out to be close to a month. She took up the walking stick by the door, put on her embroidered cape, and left me with dwindling supplies and an insatiable dead man to feed.

I was mostly equal to the challenge, what there was of it. At this point, it was achingly clear that my aunt was right. A monk might have said something about the man being a glutton for wealth, fame, and power in life, or perhaps that earthly desires held him to this world, but I'd been waiting tables since I was ten. He was a man who wanted everything he could get for the least amount he had to spend.

I kept the dishes simple, dodged the scraps he threw at me in retaliation, tried to entice real customers dead and living to come in, and gritted my teeth through his stories, which were by this point beginning to repeat themselves. I heard about the three sons of Minister Shen, Lord Hseing, Lady Autumn, and the rest so often that I thought I could imagine them, Lady Autumn's whirling steel fans, Lord Hsieng's stern face, the three identical boys who Lord Ning let slip had been no older than I was.

I slept with my pillow over my head, and by the end of the month, I thought that I might be living in my own personal hell.

My aunt was simply back in the kitchen early one morning, taking stock of the pantry as if she had never left.

"You've let things get a low," she said, "but it could be worse."

"Where have you been?" I demanded. "Did you find anything that will help with . . ."

She spared me a quick glance, but there was a sly glint in her smile.

"Come on, we have work to do," she said. "Take some coins from the jar, and have Lu bring by a goat, a fat one, not one of those bags of bones. On your way back, pick up a big bundle of water spinach, and some sweet potato candy as well."

She was never one for explaining things, so with a sigh, I fell in beside her. She pulled out cup after cup of rice, not the plain white that we mostly used, but her special store of gleaming black rice, brought from Pa'i. I held down the goat while she cut its throat, and then together we butchered it neatly, hanging the meat up to drain until we could get it into the cookpot. I walked out to the tall linden trees, and after some digging pulled up two full jars of preserved duck eggs. They were only six months old, not as good as they would be at a year or two, but when I cleared off the ash and the clay and peeled off the shells, the whites had turned to translucent black jelly and the yolk to a gray salty paste. My aunt nodded with approval.

"Good, they'll do well enough. Now wash up the water spinach, and get out the good dishes."

I wondered if my aunt planned to stuff Lord Ning so full of food that we could simply roll him out to the river and sink him. It was an idea I had entertained in the long month she was gone.

Lord Ning watched with hungry hollow eyes as we set the plates on the long wooden table. Our best china was still only glazed earthenware, but the food that I and my aunt had made gleamed like jewels in the lamplight. At the center of the table was the roast goat, of course, braised and sitting in a salty broth. Arrayed around it were dishes of fried vegetables, cold pickles, fried fish, and braised chicken resting on a bed of shredded orange carrots and white cabbage.

It was like the meals we would cook for the new year, and the table fairly groaned under the weight. My aunt fussed with the placement of the fish, and then as Lord Ning watched, she placed a bowl of the black rice by every seat at the table.

"Stupid woman, what are you doing? I am Lord Ning, who—"

"I know who you are," my aunt said briskly. She began to ladle delicate broth into each of the smaller bowls by each plate. "Our guests tonight know who you are as well."

"Guests? What is the meaning of—"

Four knocks sounded at the door. It would have been tremendously unlucky for any living person to announce themselves in that fashion, but for the dead, it was just right.

"Come in and be welcome," my aunt called, and the door swung open.

The three sons of Minister Han were tall and thin, but their bodies had swollen up from the lake where they had been thrown. They came in on a tide of boisterous shouting and laughter, carrying their leather helmets under their arms and handing me their swords with the usual jokes. They were identical in life, but death had marked them differently, one with a deep dry cut over his throat, one with a hole clean through his heart, and the third with a missing arm.

They came in and sat to the left of Lord Ning, praising my aunt's cooking all the while, flirting with her and saying they hadn't seen better since they left the capitol.

My aunt laughed at their outrageous compliments, mock-scolding them affectionately, but it looked like she was waiting for something. Lord Ning scowled at the three newcomers, one finger tapping hard on the table, but just when it looked as if he had summoned up the liver to say something, the door knocked again, four times.

At my aunt's call, the door opened and Lord Hsieng, short and round as a cauldron, clad in his famous red lacquered armor, strode in. People always said that he was a big man, but that wasn't quite right. He would have come up to my nose if we were standing face to face, but he entered the room like a boom of lighting, and no one would ever have found him small.

He greeted my aunt with a fond bow of his head, and he took his place at Lord Ning's right, laughing with the sons of Minister Shen. They had known each other once upon a time, and of course he had embarrassing stories about all three.

By this point, Lord Ning looked downright green. He must have thought he was being discreet when he rose, but Lord Hsieng took him by the arm, keeping him where he was.

"There's still more coming, warlord," Lord Hsieng said with a deadly joviality. "This is your feast. This is your honor."

If a corpse could pale, Lord Ning did. If he had been alive, sweat would have popped from his brow like drops of grease from the skin of a roasting pig. He sat still, however, and four knocks came again.

Lady Autumn was as tall as Lord Hsieng was short, and her face was as brown as cinnamon bark, death taking none of its color. She moved as if she had no feet at all, floating as smoothly over our floor as she had over the stage, and she declined to surrender her war fans. She gave me and my aunt a regal nod and seated herself at the other end of the table from Lord Ning. She did not joke or laugh.

The silence was thick enough to mire a water buffalo. Still we waited, and I knew that somehow, there were yet more coming. My aunt looked calm, but there was a rustling energy about her.

This time, there was no knock on the door, only a humble scrabbling, and when my aunt called for them to enter, they came in one at a time.

These dead were nameless. They had not always been, I knew that. Somewhere, there was a parent, a spouse, a child or a friend mourning the loss of someone who could never be replaced. However, the mass graves that littered the frontier afforded no fame or recognition, and there were far more of these soldiers than there were minister's sons or courtesans turned general.

They filed in, their grave-muddied feet leaving no trace on the floor, and they were a tide of angry mutters, tired whispers and low growls. They filled the room until I hopped up on the tall barrel of spiced brine to get out of their way. There was no space left at the table, but the soldiers thronged close, close enough to make even a man as big as Lord Ning shrink into himself.

I had served the dead for almost ten years at that point. They didn't frighten me anymore, but now, their anger did. The fact that it was not focused on me was the only thing that kept me breathing. There was death in the air, and it didn't matter at all that some of those deaths were years old or had happened over the mountains or across the sea.

"Well, what are you waiting for?" my aunt said as if it were a normal night. "Eat, eat."

Her words broke the storm, and there was a rush—toward the table, I thought at first. The food we had spent all day preparing was torn apart and devoured greedily. It disappeared down to the bones, down to the broth. Then they started on Lord Ning.

They tore into him as if he were steamed dough, harsh fingers digging at the plates of his armor. The three brothers circled him while Lord Hsieng tore at his belly, the armor offering no more protection than the crust of good bread. Lady Autumn's fan lashed out, sending a scatter of fingers to the waiting horde. I am sure he cried out, but it was lost under the sound of smacking lips and groans of satisfaction.

Somehow, he freed himself from the crowd, shoving his way across the inn. For one terrible crystal clear moment, I saw him, the fat and flesh and muscle ripped from his bulk, the armor hanging in tatters, and most of his mustache pulled off.

He bludgeoned and barreled his way to the door, opened it, and then he was gone, the hungry people he had slain in his life swarming after him.

The air in the inn lightened immensely. I felt as if I could truly take a breath for the first time in months. The dining room was empty, but soon it would be full again, with living and dead who only wanted a bit of something to eat before they passed through.

My aunt made a brief noise of satisfaction, a tick of her tongue behind her teeth, and started to gather up the dishes.

"Well, come on," she said lightly. "There's dishes to do."

NGHI VO lives on the shores of Lake Michigan and her fiction has appeared in *Strange Horizons*, *Uncanny*, *PodCastle*, and *Lightspeed*. Her short story "Neither Witch nor Fairy" appears on the 2014 Tiptree Award Honor List. She believes in the ritual of lipstick, the power of stories, and the right to change your mind.

HIS HEART IS THE HAUNTED HOUSE

AIMEE OGDEN

The monster hunter has lived too long.

Karyn sits silently in the passenger seat of his old GMC truck while he pops two Vicodin and downs them with a swig of PBR. He grunts in frustration when the lever on the side of his seat refuses to give, and the busted-up mechanism grinds out a reply in kind before shifting to recline. Karyn wonders sometimes which will give out first: the man, or his truck? She hopes it's the man, but if the truck goes that shock might be enough to do him in. And then she can go, too.

Karyn has been dead for too long.

The hunter pulls his cap down over his eyes and coughs, settling into what he seems to think is a restful position. The second his breathing slows, Tish mists head-and-shoulders up out of the dashboard. She squints at Karyn, who shrugs. It's Tish's turn tonight; she's not going to butt in line.

Satisfied, Tish sinks into the hunter's chest. He winces but doesn't stir. In dreams, he can almost hear them. In dreams, they're almost real. The reverberations of Tish's rage roll off the hunter's shoulders, rocking Karyn all the way over on the passenger side. He took Tish away from her home—took Tish and won't let her go. Won't let any of them go. They remind him, night by night, what he's done, what he's stolen. Karyn's not sure if he hears, but hammering at the inside of his skull is better than giving up and letting him tow her around like a kite.

Sometimes Karyn likes to linger and absorb the others' rage—that can be enough to rekindle her own when it gutters. But tonight she slides away, putting space between herself and the blunted knife of someone else's pain.

There's a fist-sized rock on the ground beside the front tire. It would fit perfectly into the GMC's tailpipe. Karyn and her sister Rena once crammed a potato into the muffler of Rena's douchebag ex's Grand Am with satisfying results; a rock won't fit quite as snugly but it would at least fit. *Would.* Karyn stoops, swipes at it a few times. The rock doesn't budge; her fingers pass clean through. A few wisps of silvery mist swirl off and unravel into nothingness.

There are two kinds of ghosts: their own, and someone else's. The ghosts who choose to stay behind, those are the ones who get to break the windows and slam the doors and push the unsuspecting hunters down flights of stairs.

And then there are the ones who get towed helplessly in the wake of someone else who won't let them go. The ones who don't get to do, who only get to be carried around. The ones used to abrade the old scars of someone else's guilt and shame.

Karyn is the wrong kind of ghost.

The others are close by. Tish still stalks the hallways of sleep in the hunter's head, looking for his face in the mirrors, trying to make him see hers.

María-Belén sits on top of the truck, picking at non-existent cuticles. "Nice night," she says and Karyn scoffs.

Meanwhile, Easterday is a pale white smear against the darkness, tugging at the short tether of her afterlife. Easterday is new, scarcely more than a kid. It's not fair, and Easterday knows it. She still strains at the boundaries death has imposed on her. Karyn doesn't try to leave the hunter anymore; she's his now, for whatever time they have left together.

She grabs once more for the rock. It stays where it is, and so does she.

* * *

They've been on the road for two days straight, making aimless circles across the American Midwest. Aimless *squares*, really, interlocking and of all different sizes, around tall waving cornfields and short squatty grids of soybeans. In the mornings, the hunter sits in one of a thousand identical diners and peruses the newspapers. Karyn strokes the toothed edge of an ancient butter knife while he nurses a cup of gritty coffee. The butter cools into hard clots on his toast.

Over by the windows, Dawb perches on a high stool with her knees drawn up. Mrs. Thelma Owens drifts back and forth behind the grill, occasionally criticizing the line cook's technique with the eggs. "Sloppy," she mutters, as he breaks another yolk, and her deep-south accent wrings several extra syllables out of the word.

Jaspreet reads over the hunter's shoulder and groans each time he turns the page too soon. She slides into him, tries to force her hand into his and hold the newsprint flat. No luck. He shakes his hand out, once, but keeps browsing without lingering.

Out in the parking lot, by daylight, Easterday is a mere trick of the eyes, an illusion. Blink, and she's gone.

There's a lead in Kansas: *could be werewolves*; the hunter circles one tidbit in the paper's police blotter. The ghosts sigh. None of them died anywhere near there; little hope of a chance encounter with a lost teacher, classmate, loved one, friend.

They drive hard all day. Karyn and María-Belén swap barbs on whether this is the time the hunter bites it. "Werewolf" is Karyn's pick for the dead pool. Not that anyone will be around to collect if one of them has called it right; hopefully, they'll be swept along into the trash bin of memory once the hunter breathes his last. But there's a certain sick satisfaction in the betting.

María-Belén has put her stock in a heart attack. When the purported werewolf turns out to be nothing more than a feral half-coyote, it looks for a minute as if she and the hunter are both about to cash in. But he leans on the GMC until the scarlet drains from his face and his angry ragged breathing has faded to his usual soft ragged breathing. He slams the car door shut behind him and peels out. The women follow along, unasked and unwilling.

The coyote carcass stays behind to feed the hungry night. The black-flies are already drawing in when Karyn takes a last look back.

The hunter drives south the next day, toward a little town some hundred miles south of Wichita; an off-the-beaten-path destination, but a frequent one for him. When he makes his way up the long winding driveway past acres of wheat, his friend is sitting on his ramshackle porch, cleaning the rifle laid out across his lap. He looks up at the GMC's rattling roar and lifts a hand in greeting. He doesn't get up. He lost his left leg below the knee to the same poltergeist-addled house that took Easterday.

The hunter joins him on the porch, sitting on a crate of bottled water, resting his feet on an ancient sun-bleached cooler. Both nurse tin cups of coffee and swap the same catalog of stories: favorite victories, favorite scars. A favorite waitress in a little taqueria off Route 66. The barbacoa tacos in the same joint. Talk winds down around the well-worn spool of the ones we lost. Easterday has the honor of being referred to by name, though the hunter's friend calls her Angie, like her mother did. Mrs. Thelma Owens is *that old black lady, the one we found out behind the church*. Dawb gets called out by name too, though the hunter mispronounces it as Dob because he's only seen it printed in the obituary, never pronounced out loud.

He carries obituaries around the same way he does the women. They're stashed in the dashbox, newsprint smeared and bleeding where wet splatters of beer or booze have dried.

Beans and toast for a late breakfast and the hunters are still savoring every scrap of guilt they can wring out of themselves. Karyn wants to slap the tin cup into the window hard enough to break it. She wants to upend the cooler of fish guts over his head.

She stares off into wheat rows so straight they might have been combed out by the hand of God. When the hunter gets to her death, he calls her *that cute redhead*. He and his friend roll descriptions of her dogman-gnawed corpse alongside mouthfuls of masticated bread. The splintered bones. The sewer smell of her ruined guts.

Easterday is out there in the wheat, trying to lose herself in the vast terrible sameness. It won't work. It never has.

The hunter's friend has a tip, a phone call he got yesterday morning but isn't up for handling himself. West side of Michigan, he says, and electric potential runs up and down the place where Karyn's spine used to be.

The hunter leaves the dishes next to a pile of others on the counter. There are ants. He leans over the cooler to shake his friend's hand before he goes, like he needs distance from something as truly deadly as giving the old man a hug. Karyn is waiting at the truck by the time he swings into the driver's seat, keys jangling.

There aren't any men in the stories the hunters tell. It's not that they don't die just as much as anyone else. Karyn's seen plenty of men die in the hunter's orbit. Max and José and Kev, other hunters who went down in the line of duty; Clayton and Tim, the two well-meaning young idiots who thought they could learn how to smoke out a demon possession after reading a few articles online; Ángel and Aarón, who died protecting their farm. The hunter doesn't keep them, doesn't treasure them to hone the sharp edges of his regrets. He brings them up now and again. But he doesn't need them.

Karyn doesn't want to be the unanswerable void to someone else's cry of *but what else could I have done?* She has her own questions she wants answered.

The hunter yanks the atlas from the floor in the back and tosses it open on the passenger's seat. He thumbs through to Michigan, gives it a quick onceover. The car turns over on the second try and he cranes his head to back up all the way down the long drive. Karyn perches on the center console and runs her finger over the blue-veined map until she imagines she can feel the familiar names of tiny towns where they're inked onto the paper.

They spend the rest of the day on the unlovable stretches of country highways that network Kansas and Missouri and Illinois. The GMC sets to knocking if the hunter spends too long on the freeway. Somewhere past Peoria, he pulls into a rest stop and sets up for the night.

His dinner comes from the vending machine: two bags of Fritos, a soda, and an Almond Joy for dessert. He adds a little Jack to dilute the last few drops of Coca-Cola, when that's gone he adds a little more. On unsteady feet, he lurches out of the truck to throw away the empty wrappers and relieve himself one last time. When he comes back, he takes a big canister of Morton's Iodized Salt from the back seat and pours it in a lopsided circle. He steps over it, climbs back in, and retrieves a sprig of sage from the back seat. This he sets aflame with a lighter from his pocket and tosses it on top of the dashboard to spark and smolder. The car fills with smoke fast and finally he cracks the windows open to cough foul air into fresh. Only when it's aired out a bit does he crank the chair back into its reclined position and close his eyes.

Salt and sage won't keep the dead women out. Neither have antihistamines, sleep aids, or a host of hard liquor. The circle he's drawn is in the wrong place. His heart is the haunted house, and the ghosts won't go until it quits beating.

It isn't Karyn's turn tonight but she rises into his head like swamp gas anyway. The other ghosts fall away in the face of her hungry need. They know their destination too. They know how close she is to coming home.

He knows something is wrong. He must expect it by now, that dark ripple on the surface of his dreams that soon gives way to wounded, weeping women. In here, she's more real than he is, and she slices through him like an ax through spiderwebs.

"Listen to me," she demands, chasing the unraveling thread of his subconscious as it careens between memories of family reunions and football games, cowers behind an old aftershave jingle. "Listen to me!"

His body rolls up onto one shoulder and the shape of the dream shifts with him. "Why didn't you save me?" Karyn's voice echoes from somewhere outside herself. No. That's not her. The word *you* is the furthest thing from her mind. She wants her scholarship back, a chance to finish school and come back home and grow the best grapes Greenhill has ever seen and put the town on the tourist map for real and bring the tourist money along with it. She wants to know if her sister ever settled down with either of those two shitheads who'd been stringing her along, if she has kids or a dog or a cute little house north of town that she can walk to the beach from.

"You could have done more," Karyn's voice says, without her mind behind the words, "you could have—"

No. Karyn wrests control, crumbling the false words into ash. "Listen!" she screams, spreading out into him, forcing herself into every corner.

For a moment, his fists clench. He lurches, as if to sit up. Karyn startles, and his waking mind crushes her into a corner of itself. She ebbs free as he gags, curses, presses his sleeve to his face. His nose is bleeding. There's no more sleep for the hunter after that. Karyn sits on the passenger seat the whole night, watching him blink dryly at the scratched ceiling.

He gets a late start the next day, long after dawn rakes its coals across the sky. But he doesn't hit the road north. Instead he pulls over at an urgent care clinic. At the reception desk, he reluctantly peels a few bills out of his wallet and goes to sit beside an aquarium with nothing but a ragged-looking pleco to occupy it. It's an hour of waiting alongside sniffly kids and a teenager with his arm wrapped in a bloody towel. Karyn reads the headlines of every year-old magazine in the racks before a nurse calls for the hunter. After a brusque exchange of health history and a blood pressure reading, the nurse disappears.

While he waits, the hunter doesn't leaf through *National Geographic* or read flu shot factoids from the wall poster. He stares into space, eyes glazed. Karyn counts the wrinkles on his forehead until, for a moment, she thinks his half-lidded gaze has sharpened on her. Then the door opens and a doctor with the faint divots of acne scars on his forehead pops inside.

He checks the hunter over, then hovers on the border between kindness and condescension as he reassures the hunter that the occasional nosebleed is nothing to worry about, and has he ever considered modifying his diet or implementing an exercise routine? The hunter takes the pamphlets the kid hands him without a word, and shreds them in the parking lot. The confetti swirls in the stiff midday breeze; some of it flies up past Easterday, who is perched atop the two-story clinic as if she's thinking of jumping. As if she's thinking that jumping would do anything, change anything, mean anything.

He gases up at a Kwik Trip and buys a plastic mug of plastic-flavored coffee. Karyn follows him inside and runs her fingers over—through—rows of orange Reese's cups and golden Twix. They didn't have peanut butter M&M's when she was alive. She wonders how they taste, if the candy-peanut butter ratio is more generous than Reese's Pieces in their stingy little shells. For a moment, as he peruses snacks, she slips back inside the hunter and tries to convince him to buy a pack. She imagines the sugar shell cracking between his teeth, the smooth change of texture inside. He grabs a packet of Twinkies. Disappointed, she cuts free of him and drifts outside.

María-Belén is watching a wasp crawl in and out of the inch gap of the open window. "Maybe it will sting him while he drives," she says lovingly.

"You bet on a heart attack, not a car crash." Mrs. Thelma Owens is the one with the line on vehicle-related mortality.

María-Belén shrugs. "A falta de pan, buenas son tortas."

The door jingles, and the hunter emerges. He doesn't head for the GMC but skulks around the side of the building. Karyn follows him to what must be the last payphone in the state. He punches a familiar string of digits: his friend's phone number. His finger hangs over the 7, the last digit, for the space of a long ragged breath, a cough, and a curse. Then he jerks his hand up and drops the phone into its cradle. Quarters clatter in the coin return and he turns his back on them.

Karyn can smell the cold damp of Lake Michigan drawing close, like its own kind of ghost. She recognizes the bump-bump-bump of I-94. The exits before Greenhill fall away one after another.

"Please," Karyn whispers, with the rhythm of the road. In the passenger seat, she clenches her fists on her lap and releases them again. "Come on. You remember the place. Pull over."

María-Belén leans on—through—the seatback. "It's too far off the highway, Karyn. He'll never stop over there. I'm sorry."

When she sees the overpass that will carry them past Greenhill, Karyn winces. "Pull over," she chants. "Pull over. Pull over."

The exit lane opens up to the GMC's right but the tires stay pointed straight ahead. If Karyn's post-corporeal body could weep, it would. But it does still know how to scream.

"Pull over!" she cries, and shoves herself sideways into the hunter to yank the steering wheel.

The truck wobbles. The hunter swears and puts one hand to his chest even as he adjusts course with the other. The hollow hole of Karyn's chest thunders with his heartbeat. She tries again to jerk the wheel, to force his foot toward the brake pedal. Nothing gives. Maybe it was just a heart palpitation in the first place.

She drifts to the back of the truck, past Tish and Dawb and Mrs. Thelma Owens and Anamaria and Lucy and Jaspreet and Janine who ride silently in the flatbed. Easterday hangs behind and overhead, refusing the proximity of the truck but unable to stop herself from being towed along in its wake. Tish says something that's lost to the roar of the road. Karyn shakes her head and looks backward. Greenhill's too deep into rolling land to see from here but she watches the county road shrink into a dull point and then silent nothingness.

The moon is full, not that it matters this deep into the woods. The GMC's high beams blast out from its parking place, and the bright light casts long shadows. The hunter kills the ignition and the meager light dies with it.

When he leaves the car, he makes his way through the forest by feel. Vines of Asiatic bittersweet snag at his ankles, though hardly a stick cracks beneath his feet. Where sight is gone, sound and feel remain. As a ghost Karyn might have hoped to be blessed with some kind of night vision, but she moves through the forest as sightlessly as the hunter.

The other women are brief faded spots on the retina, soon eclipsed by other trees. They wait. They listen. Somewhere far away, Easterday is crying, or laughing hysterically, the sound muffled by greenery and ghostly hands.

Karyn hears the beast before the hunter does. She can't help the cry of warning that rips out of her, but it rolls past him unheard. He spins, perhaps too late, at the wet protest of claw-torn vines. By the creature's slavering snarl, by its sheer size, Karyn recognizes it for a werewolf, and now she doesn't know whether she's crying or laughing either. Of course it would be a werewolf.

The hunter's favorite knife, his well-honed Woodman's Pal, is already in his hand. He brings it to bear but the creature has the advantage of him and blood splashes through where Karyn stands. The hunter cries out but it's not his knife arm that's taken the wound, and he stabs out in kind. Hot breath, gnashing teeth. Karyn can barely tell where man ends and wolf begins as they grapple and slash and bleed.

A misstep, then, or the gravity of exhaustion. The hunter tumbles backward and the wolf is on top of him. A glint of ghost-light glitters on the knife blade, between them now. The hunter's hand is still on the hilt but the werewolf's wiry arms have turned the blade inward. The hunter strains, fighting it back, losing ground. The wolf snaps at his face—inches away, but its saliva flecks his bloodied face.

Karyn holds as still as death and watches the hunter's arms start to give way. He chokes out a curse as the knife's point taps a button on his shirt. He's going to die now, and then Karyn will be dead too. In death, no one can lay a claim on her. She will be her own.

In death, true death, she'll never go home again. The monster hunter has lived too long, and now he's going to go before he's had a chance to make amends.

She's already moving before she realizes she's made the decision. She drops through the werewolf and into the hunter. She lends what strength she has to him.

It's not very much. His arm trembles, and the knife stays on the button. It starts to press inward. A garbled prayer leaves the hunter's lips and Karyn wonders if she'll feel what he feels, if she stays in here, if she'll know a death by blood and torn bone one more time.

The hunter's frame shudders again and Mrs. Thelma Owens is in here too. "Well, don't just gawk," she says, schoolteacher-stern. "*Push*, honey."

Karyn pushes.

María-Belén squeezes in, Janine too. The knife's momentum slows, then stills. Dawb and Anamaria. Lucy and Jaspreet. Others, shoving in, one by one. Making room where there is none. The hunter stops shivering with each new addition and the knife turns upward.

Before the knife can pierce its hide, the werewolf bellows its confusion and leaps back. It huffs and circles cautiously. The hunter doesn't rise in answer, he stays on his back, knife hand up and the other to brace it.

Karyn understands. "Up," she begs, and together the women bend joints, contract muscles. He moves like an ill-used marionette. But he moves. The knife hand comes up again and he lumbers toward the werewolf.

The beast retreats a few paces to snort and study the hunter again at a distance. It takes in the uneven gait, the jerky twitches of the arms. It's calculating its odds, and it seems to like what it sees. It lunges.

Easterday slams into the hunter with a scream, and the hunter screams too. He launches himself at the werewolf faster than he's moved in years and he opens its belly from intestines to sternum. The women jerk his arm to pull the knife free and they stoop down to take the head—the head, you have to get the head. They've all seen this show before, though not from a front seat vantage. In his hand, their hands, the knife grates across the beast's throat and gristle and sinew tear and blood soaks into the ground beneath the hunter's boots.

After, they clean the knife as best they can and walk on unsteady legs back to the car. He falls, twice, along the way; they pick him up and keep him moving. Through unspoken agreement they wash his face and hands and chest with water from a canteen and change him into a more presentable shirt. When they turn the rearview mirror toward his face, Karyn can almost see herself peering out from his eyes. His shoulders rise as she pulls with need and purpose and the others echo the same back to her.

Their turns are coming, too.

* * *

Driving is an exercise in teamwork. The GMC takes a ding from a highway railing, but the trip is otherwise uneventful.

The Greenhill Family Diner still stands, with the same yellow-lit sign flickering over the front entrance. It's had a fresh coat of paint in the past twenty years, though. Maybe more than one. The bell on the door is new, too, higher-pitched than Karyn remembers. The hunter slides into a seat at the counter and she moves his head to look around at patrons and waitstaff, scrying for familiarity. The other ghosts move the hunter's hands, playing with the salt and pepper shakers. Fiddling. Fine-tuning.

It turns out that there are three kinds of ghosts, and the kind that's still alive comes out from behind the grill and heads straight toward the hunter.

"What can I get you?" says Rena, taking a pencil stub out of her steel-gray bun and a pad of paper from a stained apron pocket. At the sound of Karyn's sister's voice, the hunter's hand jerks and crystal grains of salt bounce across the Formica counter. Rena doesn't notice, scribbling out some prior entry on her order tablet. "The biscuits are good today. The biscuits are always good."

"Your dad used to run this place." The hunter's voice comes out scratchy; anyone listening closely might hear the echoes underneath the words. A creak of tone at the end almost, but not quite, turns the statement into a question.

Rena looks up from her pad, nods slowly. "You knew him?"

Knew. Karyn throbs with sorrow. She keeps grinding words out of the hunter's mouth. "I was—a friend of your sister's. At school. Ag department." A believable lie. The hunter's tongue sticks to his teeth. Karyn wants to reach across the counter and pull Rena into an embrace, but she can't. Not while she wears the hunter's face in place of her own. There are a thousand things she wants to ask, to say; she ekes out one. "She talked about the diner a lot. She'd be proud of how it looks. Proud of you."

Rena rocks back on her heels. "Thanks," she says, and her voice is husky. Karyn's sister has never been a crier, except the year she didn't make the varsity swim team. "I still think about her every day, you know?"

"Yeah." The hunter's head turns toward the menu board. His throat jerks in rhythm with Karyn's. "The biscuits sound good. With honey? And a coffee too, please."

"You bet." Rena smiles and slides off. As she goes, she dabs the corner of her eye with her apron. The hunter's neck cranes, trying to peep at the pictures jammed on the inside of the counter. Karyn spies one with Rena and another woman, two skinny kids squeezed between them.

Later, on a cigarette-scented hotel bed, they page through the atlas, planning routes. Easterday seizes the hunter's hand and heavily taps an intersection just south of Dayton, Ohio. Karyn remembers it well, the copper sting of blood in the air, the electric hum of a new ghost screaming through the darkness toward her captor. The ghosts agree on their next destination, and set the atlas aside.

The room phone is an old beige plastic model. The ghosts lift the receiver and key in the old ten-digit string, stabbing the 7 last of all. When it starts to ring they all flicker out of the hunter at once, leaving him to panic and gasp until his friend picks up on the other end.

"It's me," he gasps, "it's me." The fingers of his free hand dig deep into his shirt, five sharp disruptions in the plaid flannel pattern. "I— Jesus."

Karyn, perched on the windowsill, half stands now. Maybe he's forgotten how to breathe, how to keep his heart beating, with all that time out of the driver's seat.

But then a great sob rattles the cage of his chest, and she freezes where she is. The only thing he's forgotten is how to express a genuine emotion. How to feel one at all.

"Something weird's happening to me, man. Things I say without knowing why—stuff I do without meaning to do it. It's like I'm losing control and—and somehow it feels like the right thing to do. Am I going nuts?"

From the sill, Karyn can't hear the voice on the other end of the phone. That's all right. The phone call is for him and him alone. The hunter will give up enough of his privacy in the coming weeks; has given up quite a lot already. When he hangs up, he weeps again, small shuddering sobs that wear him down into a deep dreamless sleep.

No one slides into his head tonight. He'll need his rest. Karyn runs her fingers over and through the tattered edges of the atlas. She closes her eyes and remembers the feel of the paper, the way the pages riffle at the touch.

AIMEE OGDEN is a former science teacher and software tester; now she writes about sad astronauts, angry princesses, and dead gods. Her work appears in *Analog, Shimmer, Beneath Ceaseless Skies*, and more. She also co-edits *Translunar Travelers Lounge*, a new zine for fun and optimistic speculative fiction. Ogden lives in Madison, Wisconsin, where the beer is always fresh and the curds are always fried.

IN THAT PLACE
SHE GROWS A GARDEN

DEL SANDEEN

All the students at Queen Mary Catholic High School knew about Principal Vargas's death before the first bell.

To Rayven James, it was welcome news.

The entire student body swarmed through the hallways like a many-headed ocean with straight brown, blond, and black hair coloring the seas. An occasional pop of red floated past like flotsam. But one thing as rare as finding a perfectly formed pearl within the tight clasp of an oyster's shell was any hair that didn't flow in silky sheets, that didn't bounce like those no-rhythm-having girls trying to twerk in the restroom, that didn't accept a fine-toothed comb as readily as a mother's hand opening for her child's.

Rayven was that rare pearl.

Her locs, four years in the making, trailed down her back that Tuesday morning, the tips grazing her waistband. A shortage of time had prevented the usual adornment, a green-and-white ribbon to match the green-and-white plaid skirt. No, that morning had been a blur of three snooze alarms, a two-minute shower and a single slice of dry toast snatched out of the toaster as Mama's horn blatted with impatience from outside.

"Rayven!" had come the call, for the fourth time, right before the high-school junior had bolted out the front door, sure that the neighbors were cursing the early-morning chaos that routinely got them up and moving. Barely had her butt touched the seat before Mama zoomed the car into reverse, shaking her head and flicking a cigarette at the same time, her hold on the steering wheel not extending past two fingers of her left hand.

So there was no time for ribbons that morning.

Rayven tossed her head, the sheet of her locs shifting like a curtain with a curious neighbor behind it before twitching back into place.

"Did you hear about Vargas?"

Rayven glanced to her right, where her friend Sonia Williams matched her step for step, like they were the Rockettes of Radio City Music Hall or something. They might not be high-kicking chorus girls, but according to the majority population of Queen Mary, it was hard telling them apart anyway. Although Sonia was several shades lighter than Rayven, wore a completely different hairstyle—short relaxed bob—and stood two inches taller. And yet, to the white kids they attended school with, these two black girls had practically shared a womb.

"I heard something," Rayven said, twirling around the dial on her locker. "Is he really dead?"

"Yep." Sonia leaned in closer, though any fear of being overhead was unwarranted, considering the loud chatter going on around them. "I heard he shot himself."

Rayven shrugged. "So?"

"So that's a *grave mortal sin*. He can't go to heaven." The white around Sonia's liquid brown pupils seemed to pulse. "You know that, right?"

Rayven nodded, mainly to stem the tide of any religious teachings outside of Theology class. Sonia, like almost every other student there, was Catholic, so she knew all the ins and outs. Sonia also wasn't on scholarship like Rayven. Although her friend didn't live in a three-story mansion like some of their classmates, Sonia's upper-middle-class back-ground was still quite an upgrade from Rayven's lot.

"Why would he kill himself, though?" Rayven asked as they walked to first period, hers being English Comp and Sonia's being World History, across the hall from each other.

"I heard he was having family problems."

Throughout the rest of the day, rumors and gossip flew through the air like invisible bullets, propelled by little more than breath and boredom. By the time Rayven made it to lunch, the late principal's death had been attributed to everything from poison, hanging, gunshot and carbon monoxide in the garage to his mistress's fury that he wasn't actually going to leave his wife. To Rayven, that was definitely the best one.

"You can't stay mad forever."

Mama's words danced in Rayven's head, one of Cathy James's *mamaisms,* as she thought of them.

How did she know what Rayven could do?

But Mama had issued that *mamaism* after Rayven's father had left to live with his baby's mama six years ago, after she had grounded Rayven for a week for wearing lipstick when she wasn't supposed to five years ago, and after Principal Vargas had suspended her for skipping class and therefore preventing her from playing in the girls' varsity basketball quarterfinals last month.

Queen Mary had lost without Rayven's handles on the court.

Unknown to Mama, Rayven *could* stay mad and she'd certainly hold onto that rage forever if she could.

Trouble was, her rage was soon to have a brand-new target.

Mrs. McGee replaced the dead Richard Vargas as principal at Queen Mary. The student body reserved opinions publicly, although privately, text messages and DMs had already sized the woman up.

Rayven had no opinion, one way or the other, until one week after McGee's appearance.

"Mr. Holloway?" the mechanical voice filled the Chemistry classroom. "Can you send Rayven James down to the principal's office?"

Silence, heavier than noise, pressed on her skin as she made her way to the door. She imagined everyone's eyes shining in her direction. Once the door clicked behind her, a rush of voices would break out from every corner of the room. Walking down the steps, Rayven wondered what this was about. When she made it to the main office, the principal's secretary ushered her inside Mrs. McGee's room.

"Good morning, Rayven."

"Good morning, Mrs. McGee."

Thus far, Rayven had only heard the woman speak at the morning assembly where she introduced herself and went into a rambling monologue about her experience, her past positions and what she hoped to bring to Queen Mary. The leather seat sank miserably under Rayven and she glanced at the woman on the other side of the big oak desk—a picture of unflattering bangs and milky blue eyes that just missed the boat of prettiness—before settling her gaze on the potted plant in front of her.

The only other time Rayven had been in this office was before Mr. Vargas had either killed himself or been in a grisly car accident driving home drunk from a late-night poker game, according to the latest rumor passing from mouth to ear.

"I hope your classes are going well. Although, I am aggrieved to come in and replace Mr. Vargas under the circumstances."

Aggrieved? Rayven's mind stumbled around in the dark, looking for a light switch. That had been a vocabulary word a few weeks ago, but she'd never heard anyone use it in regular conversation. She nodded, unsure what to say.

"Well, as your new principal, I have reviewed some of the school's policies." A clearing of the throat which sounded completely unnecessary. "And one of those policies regarding dress code had been rather lax under your former principal." Another *cough-cough* coming through a clear passageway. "It's about your hair."

Rayven's attention, which had been teetering on exiting stage left, made a quick about-face.

"What about my hair?"

Here, Mrs. McGee consulted a paper on her desk. Gone were the uncalled for *ahem-ahems* as the woman settled into more comfortable territory.

"I'm now enforcing the policy of Queen Mary School that no student sports any extreme or distracting hairstyles, which includes unnatural colors, shaved images or words, or dreadlocks." Brown eyes locked onto blue ones as the bobbed head gave a brief nod. "You'll have to cut your hair, I'm afraid. You have until Monday."

Later that night, when Rayven was finally able to think about the day without an excruciating buzz drowning out everything else, she tried to replay the rest of her conversation with the principal. All she recalled were perfunctory words and phrases: if you don't cut your hair . . . expulsion . . . school policy . . . changes.

"We're gonna fight this, baby," Mama had said as soon as Rayven told her. "I'll call the news station."

Even as the words left her mother's mouth, Rayven felt no conviction there. Because if Rayven left Queen Mary, what were their options?

Mama worked two jobs—one as a teacher's aide in a preschool and the other as an after-hours office maid—to make up the difference that Rayven's scholarship didn't cover. It was either that or their neighborhood high school, R. G. Franklin. The "R. G." stood for Rupert Godfrey, but these days, everyone called it "Riots and Guns Franklin."

Rayven's tears stopped long enough for her to speak clearly.

"Mama, I'm almost done with my junior year. I don't want to go somewhere for just my senior year."

The truth was, Rayven had no other school to attend. And they both knew it.

It's just hair. It will grow back. You might like a short 'do.

Rationalizations tiptoed in before Rayven blasted each of them aside. She spent the entire weekend riding one emotion after another, sometimes one coming so quickly on the heels of the last that processing anything was impossible. Tears—sad ones, angry ones, frustrated ones—each took their turn. With her mother's emotions mixed in, Rayven wondered how they'd survived.

By the time Sunday night arrived—insistent, swift—Rayven felt like an abandoned water bottle lying on a beach somewhere. Flattened and empty.

"You want me to help you?" Cathy's voice, thin and young all of a sudden.

"No. I'll do it."

"I can help you shape it up, a little, if you want."

"Mama, I'll be fine, just let me do it."

The bathroom door clicked, a barrier of wood between them.

Rayven picked up the black-handled scissors and faced herself in the mirror, squaring her shoulders.

On Monday morning, heaviness pressed on Rayven's eyelids, the weight of unending tears. Mama asked her if she wanted to stay home from school that day, and while the idea had tantalized her, Rayven decided to go.

What was putting it off for another day going to do? She already felt ugly, she may as well share it with everyone.

Quiet hummed in the car ride, tardiness nonexistent.

Mother and daughter stared through the windshield, eyes haunted and hollow.

The whispers were worse than outright insults. She couldn't tell what they held, the words swirling on the edge of her hearing before breaking into pieces of silence. The not-quiet hung in the hallways, parting for her as she passed.

"Shhh."

"W.T.F."

" . . . glow down for sure."

Even Sonia's eyes couldn't hide the shock and despair, though her friend made a valiant effort. Rayven imagined she could see the lump working its way up Sonia's throat.

"I hate it," Rayven hissed as soon as they made their way into the restroom.

"Ray, it's not that bad. Really."

Sonia's hand crept up before falling under the shame. Even she wouldn't touch it.

Rayven's reflection scowled back at her.

"It is that bad. And it's all McGee's fault. I hate *that* bitch."

* * *

Anguish had prevented her from doing anything with her locs the night before except place them in a bag. Rayven had no idea what to do with them. She wanted to keep them, memorialize them in some way, but grief had to wane before she could think clearly.

When Rayven entered her bedroom that afternoon, ready to flop onto her bed while her mother made a quick dinner and changed before her night job, her eyes traveled straight to her small desk, where she'd left the bag.

It wasn't there.

What the—?

Under the desk, around the desk, on and under her neatly made bed, in her closet and then a search of the entire three-bedroom house. All twelve-hundred feet of it. Outside to the carport.

No bag. No locs.

"Mama, did you throw that bag away, the one with my locs in it?"

Mama was tying her maid apron behind her and reaching for her car keys.

"What, Ray?"

"Did you throw my locs away?" The shrillness in her voice threatened to crack and break.

"No. Why would I do that? Where'd you leave them?"

"In a bag in my room. They were on the desk when I went to school this morning."

"Girl, I'm gonna be late if I don't leave right now. Dinner's on the stove, so you eat. You'll find them, you just forgot where you left them."

"I didn't!"

In the silence that followed, Rayven could almost feel the charge in the air. Mama's gaze was level and unflinching, driving Rayven's down to her shoes. Clearly, her mother sensed her distress and was giving her a break, letting that one white-girl-drama moment fly. But she knew Mama wasn't going to allow another.

"I'm sorry, Mama."

"Mm hmm. We'll talk later, I have to go."

A moment later, the car's engine roared before fading away.

* * *

On the closet floor, pushed behind a spare quilt, sat the bag. Rayven didn't remember tossing it there, but she must have. In all of the heartache of the night before, she had no memory of most of it.

Except each *snip*.

That small sound had echoed in the tiny bathroom. After the first one, she couldn't look any longer—she continued cutting by feel. In the end, a two-inch Afro remained. Shorn and weary. Had she shampooed her hair next? She must have. She must also have rubbed coconut oil throughout it and twirled what small pieces she could in an effort to make it look . . . different. At some point, Rayven assumed she'd given up on all of that and just gone to bed, where sleep welcomed her into its embrace of forgetfulness.

The bag's mouth gaped, a stray loc poking out as if to test the air. Rayven pulled it out, then the next, and all the rest. *They were so long*, she thought. Four years of life resting on her lap.

Gone.

Gathering them into a bouquet, she tied a thick white ribbon around one end to keep them together and snagged a white carnation from the short vase on Mama's nightstand. The flower peeked out from the ropes, nestled within them. Rayven carried the arrangement the same way a parent might carry a dead child pulled out of a river and placed it on her bedroom windowsill.

During the day, the sun would shine on them and at night, the moon would tell them secrets.

One week later, the student body chatter had moved on to a new target, to Rayven's relief. She'd resigned herself to her short haircut but not actually accepted it. Thin headbands that matched her school uniform did nothing to assuage her ongoing sorrow.

Kids milled around her, some grabbing books out of their lockers, others walking to class. She peeked at her reflection in the small mirror stuck inside her locker door, wondering why she continued to look for something hopeful.

A pop of yellow caught her eye.

Rayven reached up, expecting the worst because it wouldn't be the first time one of Queen Mary's finest had snuck an object into her hair—the end of a broken pencil once, a hermit crab shell another time.

"Ow," she breathed. When she'd pulled on the yellow thing, whatever it was, it stung, as if she had pulled her own hair.

Rayven rifled through her bookbag until she found the compact. She held its mirror behind her as she gazed into her locker door reflection.

A yellow flower poked from her 'fro.

Even the shrill bell went unheard.

She tugged at it and again, felt that sting. Her fingers burrowed deeper, straight to the roots. And indeed, the base of the flower felt like roots. Plant roots. Growing from her head.

"Miss James," a sharp voice clapped from behind her.

The locker door slammed.

"You're going to be late, you better get going to class," Mr. Baxter said.

Rayven looked around and indeed, the hallways were mostly clear, except for one boy racing to get somewhere.

"Yes, sir," she managed to say. Rayven completed the walk to Chemistry by memory alone because the odd yellow flower consumed her entire mind.

She pulled Sonia into the restroom at lunch.

"Do you see it?"

"Yeah," Sonia said.

"It's growing out of my head."

Sonia looked at her.

"I'm serious. Dig down in there, you'll see."

Sonia's fingers gently obeyed and after a moment, a small gasp escaped her lips.

"What is that, Ray?"

"Don't pull it!" Rayven hissed, but it was too late. Sonia jumped back, her hands in the air. "I don't know what it is."

"It's growing there just like it would grow out of the ground. Hang on, I'll take a picture." As Sonia dug around in her bookbag, she described the petals and the small green stem emerging from Rayven's scalp like the hair around it.

Rayven heard a series of quick shutter clicks.

"Here," Sonia said, handing over her phone.

In the photo, the small yellow carnation contrasted with Rayven's dark hair. She zoomed in on it to get a better look. Nothing seemed extraordinary about its curled petals and circular shape, except, of course, where it grew.

The girls looked at one another in the mirror over the sink, wearing matching masks of confusion.

The next day, two more flowers had sprouted in Rayven's hair. White and pink, their soft petals just poking out against the black coils. She showed them to her mother, who shared her silent puzzlement.

"I'll take you to the doctor," Mama finally said.

"But I'm not sick."

Mama's mouth worked. "Well, what else are we supposed to do? This ain't normal, Ray, to have flowers growing out your head."

"What's the doctor going to do?" For some reason, she feared him snipping the flowers away. She wouldn't let him. Her fingers bailed over the petals. They weren't hurting anything, the flowers. They were just . . . growing somewhere they weren't supposed to grow.

Plus, someone at school was sure to say something.

And they did.

"Miss Clarke, can you send Rayven James down to the office?"

Again, those milky blue eyes that Rayven imagined spitting into. The *cough-cough* through a clear throat.

Just get to the damn point.

"Rayven, I can't help but notice your new hairstyle."

"Why, thank you."

The pink lips downturned at the smooth sarcasm, wrinkles standing out against the lipstick, just outside of the lines.

"While hair bows, ribbons and headbands are acceptable for girls, flowers are not."

"I'm aware, but I don't exactly have a choice here."

"Pardon?"

Rayven exhaled. The cat was out now, she may as well send it running down the street. "The flowers are growing out of my head, Mrs. McGee." After a beat, she continued. "I tried pulling on them and it was just like pulling on my hair. It hurts. So I can't take them out."

Disbelief shone in the principal's eyes. Of course. Why would she believe something so fantastical?

"Let me see."

Rayven shrugged, standing. What was the old bat going to do? She wouldn't let her touch her or put her fingers on the flowers. Mrs. McGee came from around the desk and stood beside Rayven, her eyes fixated on the petals. Her hand began to raise.

"Don't touch my hair," Rayven warned.

"Now, young lady, I've already told you—"

"And I told you that they're growing out of my head! You can't just pull them out."

"Okay." A change in tone, like a thick coat of honey poured over a slice of bitter lemon. Rayven didn't trust it. "We'll have the nurse take a look at you, will that be all right?"

"That's fine. My mother's taking me to the doctor to get looked at anyway, but I'll go to the nurse. You'll see."

"Perfect."

They entered Nurse Bennett's office a few minutes later. Rayven stood silently as Mrs. McGee went into an explanation that dripped with derision. *She may as well call me a liar,* Rayven thought. The nurse didn't ask any questions, as if she saw students every day with odd things growing from their scalps.

"Do you mind if I take a look, Rayven?" she asked.

"No, ma'am."

Rayven sat in the chair and the nurse slipped into plastic gloves. She felt a gentle prodding across her head.

"Ouch!" she hissed.

"I'm so sorry," the nurse said, her hand over her mouth. She'd tried to pull one of the flowers away. She turned to the principal and stammered for a moment before getting the words out. "Mrs. McGee, they're really growing out of her head!"

Each morning, more flowers bloomed in random places. Once, three small morning glories curled behind Rayven's ear, but otherwise, they showed up in singles: a red snapdragon at the crown, an orange poppy at the nape. Within a few weeks, only half of her hair was visible. The rest of it was a garden of colors. Purple violets, pink meadowsweets, and white doll's eyes nestled next to blue forget-me-nots. On occasion, a single petal or bud fell off on its own, to be found later on a couch back or pillow, its replacement already filling in the gap it left behind.

Her mother had taken her to a doctor, who'd been just as puzzled. He'd wanted to cut one flower away to study it, but Rayven had refused to let him.

What if it was like cutting a piece of *her*? Would she bleed, feel real pain? She didn't want to find out.

The doctor suggested a specialist, but for what? What were they going to do? The flowers weren't harming her, they were just . . . growing. So that's what he wrote on a note that she took back to school. Not that it did anything to calm Mrs. McGee down.

The threats started. Expulsion was tossed out. Rayven eavesdropped on the conversation between her mother and the principal one afternoon as Mama dared the woman to expel Rayven.

"It's a *medical condition*," Mama snarled into the phone.

"It's also a distraction, Mrs. James," came the voice from the speaker. "Students aren't getting their work done because everyone is so busy talking about Rayven's hair and the flowers. We simply can't allow it."

"Then maybe you need to teach your students how to focus! You expel my child, you better expect to get sued."

If Rayven thought her mother's counterthreats would get her off the hook, they didn't. The principal seemed to take the entire weird situation as a personal affront, as if Rayven grew the flowers herself.

She didn't know how she felt about them. On one hand, they drove Mrs. McGee crazy, which was incredibly rewarding. But they also made

Rayven stand out in a way she didn't want. Girls staring at her as she walked down the hall, conversations stopping when she walked into class, even teachers tearing their eyes away. If she could have her original hair back, she'd gladly take it.

Brody Tatlinger wasn't the brightest student or the nicest or the handsomest, but he was a varsity football player so at Queen Mary—that made him a god.

Prior to Rayven sprouting a flourishing garden from her head, he'd never paid attention to the girl. She was one of the scholarship kids and he didn't want anything to do with her, her people or her world. But now *everyone* at the school knew Rayven. Their feelings ranged from wonder to confusion to jealousy. Mostly, however, they kept their distance.

On that Thursday afternoon, when she passed him on her way to World History, he didn't know why his interest was piqued. He'd seen the flowerhead dozens of times by then. According to school lore, the weirdo really did have plants growing out of her scalp, some kind of strange medical condition.

Rayven passed and without thinking about why he did it, he followed, although his next class lay in the opposite direction.

Rayven stuck to the right side of the halls, though the occasional rulebreaker fought against the flow of traffic and forced the pack to separate briefly before blending back together.

Two things happened almost at the same time: a violent tug at the back of her head and Brody's loud curse ringing through the hallway.

"Oww—*shit*!"

All heads turned toward him, including Rayven's, though her hand went to where the pain hummed.

Brody's eyes were fixed on his thumb, from where a small black stinger protruded.

Only Rayven saw the bright yellow flower fall from his palm and the dying bee beside his foot, a coil of black hair wrapped around one of its legs.

* * *

It had hurt, but it seemed that Brody snatching a flower from her head didn't leave any lasting damage. There was no bleeding and the spot didn't feel empty, what with Rayven's thick hair and remaining foliage. The anger simmered for a while, but at the same time, he'd received his just desserts.

Let that be a lesson to all of them, she thought.

But McGee proved herself to be a hard sell.

Rayven kept her head down and laid low as much as she could. She knew the principal was just waiting on her to shp up, to give her any reason to put Rayven out of the school. To prevent that, Rayven made the honor roll during the third quarter, excelled in Debate Club, and participated in class without being obnoxious about it.

So the fourth-period call, "Mr. LaSalle, please send Rayven James to the principal's office" came as a complete surprise.

What now? drummed through her mind as she walked downstairs.

The same unpleasant air hung heavily in the room as the two squared off across the desk.

She can say what she wants, Rayven thought, *she just better not touch me.*

The glint of the scissors caught her eye. Mrs. McGee's fingers tapped next to them before she picked them up.

"You've proven yourself quite formidable, Rayven."

What? Bewilderment held Rayven's tongue in place.

"At every turn, you've fought against me, even had your mother threaten to sue me. All I'm trying to do is run a school and running a school is a big job, young lady. I want everyone to excel and do well here. After all, we're preparing young ladies and gentlemen for the next phase of their lives."

The principal rose out of her seat, scissors hanging from her right hand, the pointed end punctuating the air as she spoke.

"We cannot have major distractions such as you when we're trying to do our jobs. We cannot have one student wreak so much havoc all on her own."

"I'm not doing that, Mrs. McGee, I have no control over—"

"You may not," she cut her off, "but I will."

Rayven rose slowly, her eyes never leaving the scissors, which seemed to float toward her as the principal made her move. A surprising swiftness propelled the woman, more quickness than Rayven had given her credit for. She turned and reached for the doorknob. A hand clamped on her shoulder. The hiss of scissor blades opening rasped in her ear.

No . . .

Rayven turned back, too focused on making a fist to register the tingling on her scalp and the rush of air over her. If this meant getting expelled, she'd gladly accept it.

A thick wall of bees, wasps, hornets, and even hummingbirds hung between her and Mrs. McGee. Their buzzing overwhelmed everything, but Rayven did pick up a weak "Oh my God!" underneath it all. The cluster of creatures hovered for a moment, a riot of swirling color, the beat of many wings flapping noisily in the small room. Rayven was too transfixed to feel any satisfaction at the fright pasted all over the principal's face. The mass of insects and birds—wider than the big desk—rose almost to the ceiling before driving down toward the principal. Mrs. McGee had two options: remain there and be assailed by hundreds of stingers and sharp beaks or flee her own office.

She chose the latter.

The last Rayven saw of the principal was her pumping legs heading away, a huge knot of insects and birds trailing behind.

Queen Mary was cursed.

At least, the principal's position was, according to the latest school lore. For the remainder of the school year, Vice Principal Lozado acted as interim principal, an unwillingness to accept the top job forcing the school system to begin searching for a replacement.

Soon after, Rayven woke to find several flowers pressed into her pillow. When she reached up, she dislodged a few more and they drifted down onto her bedspread.

Oh no, she thought. Just when she'd more or less accepted that she wasn't going to have hair like everyone else. If not for the cloud of insects and birds that had driven McGee out of the school, where would

Rayven be right now? Of course, her old principal had caused all of this to begin with, but Rayven couldn't help the conflicting emotions churning inside her now that the flowers were dying off.

It continued over the next couple of weeks. Each morning, more flowers rested on her pillow, fewer growing from her scalp. Her hair filled in the spaces the flowers left and by the beginning of May, her slightly longer Afro showed no hint of the garden.

Sadness mingled with relief, both tussling for the top position. She wondered what would happen next year, with the new principal. Would that person allow locs?

Rayven decided she'd begin cultivating them over the summer. Without the distraction of the flowers, as long as she did her work and stayed out of trouble, surely they'd leave her alone for her final year.

In the fall, on the first day of her senior year, Rayven sat in the auditorium for a special session. Budding locs sprouted from her head, a green-and-white headband holding them off her face. Absently, she twisted one as the new principal, a Mr. Abbott, introduced himself. Like most other adults Rayven had interacted with at the school, he sat firmly in the camp of The Others, no matter how affable he tried to make himself. She didn't care about his vision, mission, or goals. This was her last year and her sole priority was marching across the graduation stage next summer.

And seeing her locs grow back.

Three days later: "Miss Simmons, can you send Rayven James down to the principal's office?"

The office was the same, although Mr. Abbott's demeanor differed from his predecessor's. He smiled a lot, for one thing, although the mirth didn't exactly reach his green eyes. He attempted some little jokes and posed a few introductory questions, until time for small talk ended and he finally presented the reason for the summons.

"As you know, Miss James, we have a strict dress code policy here . . ."

* * *

Rayven stared out the window of Sonia's three-year-old BMW, a recent birthday gift from her parents. She'd told Sonia about the meeting with Mr. Abbott on the drive to her home.

"Well, you can comb them out, right? Since they're still so new?" Sonia asked, hesitancy dragging out her questions.

"I guess." Rayven sighed, running a hand over her head. Sure, it wasn't a four-year commitment, but it was still *her* hair. One welcome day in her future, no stupid rules and restrictions would dictate how she wore it.

"Thanks for the ride," Rayven said as she exited the car. "See you tomorrow."

Before she shut the door behind her, Sonia's voice pushed out: "Wait, you have something on your shirt."

Rayven looked down and, seeing nothing, turned her head to her left shoulder.

A spot of pink.

DEL SANDEEN is a writer based in Northeast Florida. From 2009 to 2017, she was the Black Hair Expert at About.com. She writes adult magical realism and speculative fiction, as well as young adult books on race issues. She's the author of the Grateful American Book Prize–nominated *Thomas Jefferson and Sally Hemings: Joined by Fate*. Currently, she's working on a novel she hopes Octavia Butler would have loved. Her favorite TV shows include oldies like *The Twilight Zone* and *Star Trek*, mainly because Lt. Uhura's makeup game was always so tight.

THE BLUR IN THE CORNER OF YOUR EYE

SARAH PINSKER

It was a nice enough cabin, if Zanna ignored the dead wasps. Their bodies were in the bedroom, all over the quilt and the floor, so she'd sleep in the living room until they ascertained whether there was a live wasp problem as well as a dead one. If she ignored the wasps, it was lovely.

She'd have to ignore the tiny dead mouse in the ominously large trap in the kitchen, too. If they swept mouse and trap into one of the black trash bags she found under the sink, and ignored the bulk package of rat traps, and ignored the bulk rat poison, and celebrated the wasp spray, everything was good.

The bucket in the main room's corner held a few inches of brackish water. The discolored spot above it was shaped like a long-tailed comet, and probably wouldn't present a problem unless it rained. An astringent lemon-scented cleaner just about covered the delicate undertones of mildew that permeated the walls.

"This place sucks," said Shar.

Shar, her childhood friend, her assistant of who knew how many years, who had always been impervious to magical thinking. Shar, who was right.

"Um, you booked it," Zanna pointed out.

"These aren't usually the things they list under 'amenities.' You said to find someplace cheap and remote, with no Wi-Fi."

True enough. Cheap, because Zanna was between royalty checks. Remote, because she couldn't have any distractions if she was going to finish this book on deadline. No Wi-Fi, ditto. All she needed was power, since her laptop battery no longer held a charge.

She smiled. "It's perfect. I'll push that little table under the window. The view is what counts, anyway."

Shar returned her smile. "Whew. Okay. You get settled, and I'll see what I can do about the wildlife."

That worked. Zanna went out to the car for her bag. It didn't roll well in the dirt, and she let it bang on the three steps to the porch, rather than bothering to lift it. She paused to appreciate the view: below her, the mountainside spread in a dappled blanket of red and gold. There were other houses along the road—they'd stopped at the owner's on the way past to get the keys—but none were visible from here. Perfect.

She parked her bag inside the door. No point in moving it further until she knew which room she'd be sleeping in. The couch was more of a daybed, so she'd be fine with that option. The small writing table—she already thought of it as a writing table—looked solid, old. She felt the years in it. The chair looked a little hard for her taste, but she'd brought a cushion and a lumbar support for that contingency. This wasn't her first rodeo or her first cabin, and these weren't her first wasps or her first mice. If she'd wanted something less rustic, she would have said so, and Shar would have booked Posh Retreat rather than Wasp Hotel. This was what she needed: no distractions, no comforts, just a desk and a chair and a window.

Out and back again for the milkcrate of research books. Shar had found a broom to sweep away the dead wasps; she'd already disappeared the mouse. Zanna didn't know what she'd done to deserve an assistant who disposed of dead things for her.

The fridge smelled okay, a small blessing. There was nothing in it but an open box of baking soda.

"Make me a list and I'll go shopping for you while you write this afternoon." Shar stood in the doorway, tying off a trash bag.

"Is there a microwave?"

"I saw one somewhere. Hang on."

Zanna stood aside and let Shar rummage in the cabinets. She pulled out a drip coffee maker from a drawer, and a pack of filters. "Hmm . . ."

Shar left the kitchen and returned a minute later with a small microwave. "It was in the broom closet."

They both had to stand sideways for Shar to put the microwave on the counter. She smelled like cumin, never Zanna's favorite scent. Zanna rummaged in the drawers until she found a torn envelope. She wrote a list on the back, all the easy meals she could make without taking too much time away from her writing. Microwave dinners, mac 'n' cheese, salad kits, eggs, cereal.

"Back in a few hours," Shar said.

They could have stopped at the grocery store on the way in, but Zanna knew this was Shar's way of giving her a head start on her work.

There was nothing for her to do here but write. Okay, or hike, or read, but those were reward activities. More importantly, there was no cell service, no internet, no television. The rental car spit gravel as it backed onto the road. She was alone.

She turned the milkcrate of books on its side on the table, so the spines faced outward. *Birds of West Virginia*, *Trees of West Virginia*, *West Virginia Wildlife*, *Railroad Towns*, *Coal Country*. She'd done all her research at home in New York, all her character-building, all her outlining, but when Shar suggested that she actually come here to do the drafting, it had felt perfect, like something she should have thought of her herself. She plugged her computer in and sat down to write.

Shar returned with four grocery bags just as Zanna started to get hungry. "You didn't put coffee or tea on the list, but I figured they were both givens."

"Bless you," said Zanna, standing to stretch and help with the bags. The kitchen wasn't big enough for them both to be in there, but if Zanna didn't unpack, she wouldn't know what had been purchased or where to find it. Shar still smelled like cumin, overwhelming in the tight quarters. Inspiration to put everything away quickly.

"How's it going?" Shar knew her well enough to never ask in terms of word count. Instead, a generic "how's it going" that Zanna could answer specifically if she'd written or vaguely if she'd gotten stuck.

"Got through the first chapter," Zanna said. No need to hide behind euphemisms today. Chapter one was always easiest anyway. Reintroduce Jean Diener, reluctant detective. Find an excuse to get her to where she needed to be.

"Nice! Do you want me to make you some dinner before I leave you alone?"

"Nah. I'm going to have a snack now and write a little more. I'll probably just graze tonight." Zanna held up a pre-mixed chef salad in a plastic clamshell. "You can go check in to wherever you're staying. Where are you staying?"

"Motel at the foot of the mountain. It's dirt cheap this late in the fall, and this isn't exactly a tourist town."

"Are you sure you don't want to stay here? You can have the bedroom, I'll take the couch."

"Like you were going to sleep in a bedroom full of wasps. Nah, I'm good. I don't want to disturb you."

"Fine, then. How can I reach you? I don't have a single bar of reception up here."

"I'll check on you first thing in the morning. Or I can check if there's a landline phone hidden here somewhere?"

"Nah. It'll be okay. Maybe not first thing, though? If I get on a roll tonight I'm sleeping late tomorrow."

"Check. How's ten?"

"Perfect."

"Anything else I can do for you? Or should I get out so you and Jean can get reacquainted?"

Zanna grinned in appreciation.

The cabin had a good writing feel. She actually made it halfway through chapter two before stopping to eat the salad. After that, she put her sheets on the couch and pulled a moth-eaten blanket from the bedroom closet, and curled up to read *Railroad Towns*. It was full of useful information, but the combination of long drive and writing had exhausted her, and she fell asleep before ten. She woke once for no reason at all, and then again to a scuttling sound that probably meant the dead mouse had friends.

She woke at six a.m. without an alarm. The electric baseboard heater under the window had kept the couch warm enough, but she could tell that outside her blanket, the mountain morning held a chill. She'd make coffee and breakfast, then get working. She flicked on the lamp.

Her throat felt scratchy, her chest sore like she'd been coughing, and the floorboards shot cold through her socks as she padded into the kitchen. Shar had left the coffee and filters next to the coffee machine, so she didn't have to search for anything before she'd had coffee.

She didn't know what she'd done to deserve Shar. She hadn't even known she'd needed an assistant until her childhood friend had suggested it, and now she couldn't imagine life without her. It wasn't that she was unable to do the stuff Shar did, other than driving, just that having someone else shop and correspond and plan travel freed her to concentrate on her books. Shar had always been there for her, but formalizing the relationship had actually helped it.

She'd written forty-something novels now and they'd all been dreams to write, almost literally. Research was still a present-brain puzzle, outlining a necessary torture, but the books themselves had gotten so much easier over the years. A quiet cabin, a desk in front of a window, no distractions.

She plugged in the coffee maker. While it gurgled, she dumped an instant oatmeal packet into a bowl from the cabinet, added some water, and stuck it in the microwave. When she hit start, there was a pop, and the power went out. The fridge still hummed, but the cabin had otherwise gone dark and quiet. Was the whole place wired on one circuit except the fridge? That meant no power for her computer, either, and no power for the baseboard heater.

Why did this kind of thing always happen before coffee? She checked all the closets and cabinets for a breaker box, but couldn't find one, which meant it was outside. Two shoes and a jacket later, she stood behind the cabin, swearing to herself. Crawlspace. She didn't quite remember what had freaked her out in a crawlspace when she was a kid, but she still hated them. Anything might be in there.

A baseball bat stood propped against the wall beside the tiny door. It had "Snake Stick" written on it in blue Sharpie. Whoever had labeled it had also drawn a crude cartoon demonstrating its utility. Swing them away, don't kill them. No bloodstains on the bat.

She could wait for Shar, but she'd lose hours, and her head was already complaining about the lack of caffeine. Better to do it herself.

The half-sized door creaked when she squeezed the latch and swung it open. She waved the Snake Stick in front of her to clear cobwebs and wake any snakes snoozing inside. When nothing moved, she dug in her jacket pocket and pulled out her phone. It was useless for calls out here, but the flashlight still came in handy. She swept it around the space, which looked mostly empty. No use delaying.

She crouched and stepped in. The ceiling was a little higher than she expected, the floor a little lower; she could stand if she stooped. Something crunched like paper under her foot, and she swung the light down to find a snakeskin, at least three feet long. She shuddered.

The electrical box was beside the door, but it turned out to use fuses, not breakers. Another pan of the space showed a pile of two-by-fours, but nothing else useful. Mystery writer brain declared it a good enough place to hide bodies, but a little obvious. You'd want to dig up the dirt floor and bury them, or the odor would rise through the floorboards. Pile the lumber back over the spot you'd disturbed.

Back to the cabin, wishing she'd worn a hat, dusting cobwebs from her hair. She went through all the drawers and closets, this time looking for a fuse. A hammer and a box of nails, more rat traps, mouse poison cubes, wasp spray, garbage bags, dish soap, sponges. No fuses. Also no matches or candles, which would also have been useful. In the top kitchen drawer, a yellowed paper brochure for "RusticMountain Cabins.biz," complete with grainy picture and phone number. Not that the phone number did any good here.

How far had the owner's house been? Maybe a mile or two. She could hike down and knock on his door. It would still be early, but not unreasonable, given the inconvenience of no power. There should have been a warning not to use multiple appliances at once. Or maybe that explained the microwave stashed in the broom closet. Shit.

She stuffed her hair under a hat, wrote a note explaining where she'd gone in case Shar arrived before Zanna got back, put her computer in her backpack since she didn't trust the flimsy lock on the door, and headed down the mountain. Down was steep, made trickier by the loose gravel, which skittered out from under her feet. She fell once, wind-milling all her limbs to prevent the inevitable, twisting to keep from landing on her computer or her tailbone. She wound up on her left hip and elbow. The elbow got the worst of it, skinned and begraveled.

After that, she took it even slower, picking pebbles from her arm as she went. If she walked with small steps, the slope from one foot to the other was negligible. If she put her full weight on each foot, penguin-style, she exerted sideways motion instead of downward. Jean Diener would appreciate it; the character was a retired physics pro-fessor, living in an RV which she parked in any given town just long enough to help solve whatever murder transpired, through physics and common sense.

When Zanna reached the first driveway, she realized she didn't know the house number. What had she noticed about the house, waiting for Shar to collect the keys? She closed her eyes. The owner's house was larger than her cabin, larger than this one. A steep driveway featuring a rock Shar had been afraid to drive over with a rental car. Navy blue SUV with West Virginia plates and one of those WV stickers that looked like the Wonder Woman logo. A windchime with wooden—what did you call them? Wooden knocker things. She'd have to look up the word.

Not this driveway, nor the next, but the third one had the right look. Blue SUV, windchime. Less rental-cabin-like, more home-like. Where did the difference lie? Something to do with the decor. Baskets of orange mums hanging from hooks on either side of the porch steps. The porch ran the entire front of the house, with dormant rose beds below it, trimmed low for winter. The soil was weeded and neat except for some animal tracks.

She glanced at her phone for the time: 7:33. Probably still too early to knock on a door under normal circumstances, but she wouldn't have thought twice about phoning a rental office to make this complaint. No coffee, no heat, no electricity. Possibly no shower, depending on the type of water heater. A landlord should expect tenants to come knocking under those conditions.

The front door stood open, as did the screen, which hopefully meant the owner was awake. Zanna stepped onto the porch and knocked on the doorframe. The mat was turquoise with a picture of a llama on it.

"Hello?" She realized she didn't know the owner's name.

"Hello!" she called again when nobody answered.

She stuck her head in the door. There was a grid of keyrings on hooks to the right, all neatly labeled with the cabin addresses, which mystery-writer brain pointed out was an invitation to robbery. Below the grid, a mat with two muddy boots. Beside it, four coat hooks, all holding jackets in hunter's camo; the owner had been wearing one of those when Shar had knocked the day before. That was the only glimpse of him she'd had from the car.

She yelled one more time, then turned to look where someone might have wandered to with their door open. This was far enough off the beaten path that people might leave their doors unlocked, but for someone with such a fastidious entrance to leave the screen open too struck her as odd.

It was only when she walked a few steps left along the porch that she saw the foot. A bare foot, toes up, just visible on the SUV's far side.

"Hello?" she said again, walking around the vehicle's massive front grille.

He wasn't going to hello back. A middle-aged white guy lay face up, one knee crooked, like he had tripped backing away from someone or something. His head rested on a rock, though rested was an odd word; the rock was drenched in blood. His expression was the worst part: he looked terrified. Eyes and mouth open, corners of his mouth cracked.

She stooped to press two fingers to his wrist. No pulse. His skin was cooler than hers. There was gravel on his right hand, but no blood; he'd never even touched the back of his head, so he must have died instantly.

He wore sweatpants with a bloody tear at the crooked knee and another smaller hole in the seam by the crotch. No shirt, no socks, no shoes. The tattoo above his right nipple said "BREATHE" in reverse, mirror-script; a tattoo for his benefit, not others'. The knee exposed by the rip was pitted with driveway gravel, as were the soles of his feet; they were soft-looking feet for what she imagined was an outdoorsy guy. That detail made her own elbow sting, which reminded her this was real. Not a book.

A body. A real body, until recently a real person. A real person wearing pants nobody would want to die in. What did you do when you found a real body? What did Jean Diener and the people around her do when murder came calling?

She dug her phone from her pocket and was relieved to see one bar of reception. It disappeared when she lifted phone to ear, then reappeared when she peeked to see why the call wasn't going through. She walked a few feet onto the driveway rock and was rewarded with a more stable signal.

The woman who answered had clearly been sleeping; a yawn came through before her "Nine-one-one—is this a medical, fire, or police emergency?"

"I found a dead body."

The woman swore and the line faded. Zanna shifted to the left, and the voice came back. "—Sorry, that was unprofessional. Are you sure they're dead?"

"Yes. No pulse. I checked."

"And are you safe yourself?"

"I think so? I have no idea, actually." She looked around. What could have scared him badly enough to send him running from his house without putting on shoes? She hadn't even considered that she might be in danger. She felt oddly calm.

"He looks like he hit his head."

The woman on the line said something unintelligible, and Zanna moved closer to the SUV trying to find the signal. There were animal tracks across the hood. She stared at them as she triangulated reception.

The operator returned. "Ma'am, I asked what your name is?"

"Susan Ke—ah, Suzanna Gregory." Calm, but flustered enough to have almost given her pen name.

"And where are you?"

That one was tricky, too. "Ah, I hate to say it, but I have no idea what road this is, and there's no house number. I'm staying at a cabin, and I just arrived yesterday, and my assistant drove and made the arrangements . . . can you use my cell phone location if I turn it on?"

"That'll take a few minutes, and it'll only tell me which cell tower your call is routed through. Is the body at your cabin?"

"No, I took a walk. I think it's the guy who rents the cabins, if that helps. Outside his house."

"RusticMountainCabins.biz, by any chance?"

"Yes!"

"Does the deceased have gray-brown hair, wavy, longish?"

She leaned over to look at him again. "Yeah."

"Gary Carpenter. You're on McKearney Road. Do you feel safe staying there until I send someone?"

"Yeah."

"Great. Don't touch anything and somebody'll be up there in thirty or forty minutes. Can I get your phone number?"

Zanna recited her number and promised to call back if the situation changed. While she still had one bar, she rang Shar. Unlike the 911 lady, Shar was instantly awake.

"I thought you didn't have reception!"

"I didn't. Or power. The whole cabin shorted out this morning when I tried to make coffee, so I tried flipping the breaker, only it was a blown fuse, and there were no spares, so I walked down the mountain."

"You didn't."

"I did. I can be resourceful, you know. I didn't always have you in my life. But listen, that's not why I'm calling. I'm calling because I got to the guy's house where you got the keys, and he's, uh, here, but he's dead. I didn't want you to get nervous if you got to the cabin and I wasn't there. I left a note, but . . ."

"Dead?"

Zanna probably should have stopped at 'dead' longer. "Yeah."

"Dead how?"

"It looks like he hit his head. There's a lot of blood."

"An accident?"

"It looks like."

"Good. Well, not good, but you know what I mean. Better than some of the other options. Listen, I'm going to come get you."

"Nine-one-one lady said for me to wait here."

"That's fine. I'll come wait with you. No need for you to walk all the way back up."

She really was a great assistant. Zanna thanked her and disconnected.

In her books, Jean Diener would start investigating further. Walk into the foyer, poke around the house now, while emergency services were still far away. In real life, that seemed stupid. She didn't want her footprints added to whatever was in the house. No sense making it harder for the real detectives.

She sat on the porch and leaned her head against the railing. She would have said she'd slept well, but tiredness overtook her. Still too early; no caffeine in her system. She closed her eyes. Opened them again when she heard a vehicle on the road. The rental pulled in far to the left to skirt the driveway rock, and Shar emerged with a paper bag and a coffee.

"Bless you," Zanna said.

"I don't need blessings. Give me your backpack to toss in the car, so they don't start thinking it's evidence. Eat the muffin over the bag so you don't get crumbs on their crime scene. It's blueberry—they didn't have chocolate chip. Also, I need you to stay put when you say you're going to stay put."

"There was no power. Or coffee. You wanted me to sit there for four hours doing nothing?"

Shar sighed. "No . . . I . . . it's just now you're going to get stuck giving a statement, and maybe be considered a suspect, and you don't need things distracting from your deadline."

"A suspect?"

Shar nodded in the direction of the body. "You found him. You write detective books. Isn't the person who found a dead body usually one of the people who has to be ruled out? You had opportunity."

"But no motive. Well, except lack of coffee, but that hardly seems worth killing someone over."

"You're not going to joke about it when they ask you questions, right?"

"Right."

"And you haven't gone poking around by the body? Or inside that open door?"

"I'd never!" Zanna said, like the thought hadn't occurred to her. "Okay, maybe not 'I'd never,' but I swear I didn't. I went to the door, that's all."

Shar raised one eyebrow. "I believe you, just . . . when you watch them do their job, try not to make your interest look too prurient, alright?"

They sat on the porch steps, Zanna sipping a coffee made the way she liked it, two sugars, one cream. A little cool, maybe, from the twenty minute drive up the mountain, but still welcome and drinkable.

A blue-and-gold Taurus with an enormous antenna pulled into the drive, blocking Shar's rental car in. Two cops got out, both white men, young. The tall blond one had stubble dusting his cheeks, and his uniform looked slept in. The dark-haired one's uniform was impeccably pressed, his shave straight-razor close.

"I'm Officer Dixon, and this is Officer Fischer. And you are?"

Zanna gave her name without stumbling over it this time, and let Shar introduce herself.

"And which of you found the body?"

"I did, Officer. Shar just arrived a couple of minutes ago to give me a ride back up the mountain when we're done talking." Zanna pointed in the direction of the vehicle. The two policemen—state, they must be beyond the bounds of the town at the bottom of the mountain—walked over to take a look, taking the long way around the SUV before disappearing behind it, to her annoyance.

She thought about the SUV. It faced the cabin, and he was on the passenger side. She hadn't seen any keys in his hands, and his pants didn't have pockets, so he hadn't been trying to drive away. Maybe to get something from the car? She looked over to see it was unlocked, or the driver's side was, anyway. This might be country enough that people didn't bother to lock, but if that was the case, why not go in through the near side?

She was back to him being frightened of something and trying to put the car between himself and—who or what? An animal? Whatever ran across the hood? A nightmare? Maybe he was a sleepwalker, or a vivid dreamer. Maybe some medication had messed him up. Or a less legal drug, like meth or some hallucinogen.

One of the policemen—Dixon—went back to the car, where she could see him on the radio, but frustratingly couldn't hear the call. Fischer had a camera out and was taking pictures of the body. Zanna sipped her coffee and tried not to look too interested, as ordered. What was the proper amount of interest? Concern with a dash of "when can I get back to my work" seemed about right.

Dixon walked back over to the house. "Okay, obviously you were right that he's dead, so I called it in. We'll have to wait for the examiner to make it official, but I can get your statement and send you on your way. How did you come to find the body?"

Zanna explained about the coffee and the microwave and the fuse, and walking down the mountain.

"That's what, two miles?"

"I think so."

Shar interrupted. "The directions he gave me said one-point-eight miles past his house, if that helps."

"Thank you," said Officer Dixon. "And what time did you arrive here?"

"Seven-thirty-three. I remember looking at my phone and debating if it was too early."

"And then?"

"Then I walked to the door, and it was open, door and screen, and I knocked on the frame and called inside, but nobody answered."

"—And you didn't go inside?"

"No, I didn't." Zanna gave Shar a pointed look.

"Did you touch anything?"

"Only the body, to feel for a pulse."

"Oh, sorry. Let me get this in order again. You knocked and called inside, and nobody answered, and . . . ?"

"And I turned around and then I saw his foot sticking out beside the car."

"And you walked directly over?"

"Yes. Do you need my shoe print?"

He laughed. "I don't think so. That loose gravel isn't going to tell much."

"What about to prove I wasn't in the house?"

"Which you weren't?"

"No."

"Nah. You can tell me your shoe size or something if you want, but I don't think footprints are going to tell us much. He slipped in the dark. Nothing else to tell."

"Other than the one spot, right?" She couldn't resist. Shar glared at her.

"What spot?"

She pointed a few feet in front of the body. "There's a spot where the gravel's dug away, like he was running and slipped, which makes sense with the torn knee, but then the more, uh, chaotic patch is where he fell, like he spun around and his feet slipped out from under him, but he fell backward when he died, not forward. He had to have fallen twice."

"Uh, right. Other than that. I guess you had time to look around a little while you waited for us."

"I guess." She bit her tongue to keep from making any other observations.

"Anything else you noticed, then?"

Shar shifted on the stair, a slight movement that allowed her to dig an elbow into Zanna's arm. "Nothing else, Officer."

"Okay, then. I'll take your phone number and the address where you're staying, and you can be on your way."

"Why don't you take my number instead?" Shar said. "You won't be able to reach her up the road, and I can always go find her."

Dixon took both numbers, then walked them to their car.

"'Other than the one spot, right?'" Shar mimicked as they waited for the officer to move his car out of their way. "You couldn't resist."

"He wasn't doing his job. He thinks the guy slipped and hit his head."

"Firstly, he's highway patrol, not a detective. Secondly, he doesn't need to tell you, random lady who found the body, everything that he's noticed. Thirdly, the guy slipped and hit his head. There are no other footprints. Case closed."

"Case closed? How can the case be closed before somebody looks inside to see whether there's any hint of what scared him?"

Shar started to reverse, then slammed on the brakes. "Shit. I forgot about that giant rock. If I back over it, we'll leave the tailpipe behind."

"Pull forward. You can't turn around here."

"How would you know? You can't drive."

"I'm familiar with the spatial laws of the universe. You're going to have to do a ninety-point turn if you do it here. Just pull into the clearing so you have more space." Zanna licked a drop of coffee off her hand.

". . . spatial laws of the universe . . ." Shar muttered, commencing a ninety-point turn.

". . . And why are you so sure he was scared, anyhow?" she continued as if there hadn't been a pause in the conversation. "Maybe he needed something from his car, but he slipped?"

Zanna considered. "Still kind of weird to need something in such a hurry you don't bother to put shoes on. Or a shirt, on a night that chilly. And to leave the screen swinging open. He looked like a fastidious guy."

"A nightmare, then. Or some personal demon. A guy with a backward 'BREATHE' tattoo has something dark he's getting past."

"Sure. A nightmare. Except . . ." Zanna turned her coffee cup in her hands.

"Except what?"

"I don't think they noticed the other print either."

"What other print?"

"On the hood, the one you elbowed me before I could say. He must've just washed his car, because it was otherwise spotless—which is impressive given these roads—but there were tracks across the hood."

"Tracks? Like footprints?"

"Animal tracks. Something ran through the flower beds and then across the hood of the car."

She dug a marker from her backpack and drew on her coffee cup. "Like two lines of feet with a tail dragging between them. Across the hood, driver's side near the headlight, to the passenger-side mirror."

Shar glanced over. "Okay, so a lizard or a raccoon or something ran over the car. Big deal."

"And trampled grass on his other side."

"Zanna, you didn't know this guy, you are not a real detective, you have a very real deadline, and you've lost hours of your day already. Let the police do their job."

"Hours—Shar, turn around. We still need to get a fucking fuse."

Shar reached into her purse and fished out a plastic bag without looking down. "Voila. Stopped at the hardware store on my way to you."

"How did you know which size to get?"

"I didn't. I got a whole bunch of different ones, and I can return the ones that are wrong."

"Huh."

"'Thank you, Best Assistant Ever. You think of everything. You deserve a bonus.'"

"Thank you, Best Assistant Ever. You think of everything. If I actually finish this book and I get paid, you're totally getting a bonus."

They arrived back at the cabin. Shar, the Best Assistant Ever, unplugged the coffee maker and the microwave, brandished a small flashlight with a price tag still on the base, and headed into the bowels of the cabin to replace the fuse.

Zanna sat at her writing table. She heard the crawlspace door creak, then the shudder of the fridge when the main power cut off. She went to the kitchen and rummaged through the knife drawer until she found one that looked sharper than the others, then returned with it to her workspace, not for any reason she could fully express, even to herself.

She looked out the window, the up-mountain window, with its Prismacolor trees. She pulled *West Virginia Wildlife* from her research crate, its cheesy seventies cover portraying a cougar, a bear, a coyote, a buck, and something that might have been an otter in the same riverside tableaux, and opened to the reptile chapter.

"Aha!" came from under the floorboards. A minute later, the lamp came back on, and the fridge gurgled. "Did that work?"

"Yeah," Zanna called down.

Shar returned a moment later, running a hand through her hair for invisible cobwebs. "Maybe stick to coffee or microwave tomorrow. Do you want me to make you lunch?"

"Nah, I want to get some writing done first. Only . . ."

"Only what?"

"Only there are four skinks and two lizards native to this area, and none of their tracks match the tracks I saw."

Shar looked over at Zanna's reading material. "Maybe they've discovered another since 1975."

"Maybe."

"Any other mysteries I can solve so you can get back to writing yours?"

Zanna hesitated. She wasn't sure if she really wanted the answer to this one. "You—you mentioned the guy's tattoo."

"Uh huh?"

"When did you see it? You got out of the car, came straight over to me with coffee. You couldn't ever have seen more than his foot from where we were."

"The day before, when we stopped for the keys."

"He was wearing a zipped jacket when he opened the door."

Shar crossed the room and settled on the couch. "So, what? You think I'm a suspect? Or your lizard is?"

"I have no idea what to think. These are things I noticed. They don't make sense."

"That's the problem with real life. It's too messy for fiction. Too weird. All those mysteries solved by a single hair found in a drain in fiction, or a single tire track. You'd go out of your mind trying to solve a real mystery. Not that there's a mystery here. Just drop it. Unless there's something else?"

"You never asked," whispered Zanna.

"What did you say?"

"You never asked where the body was. You came and sat next to me. It would have made sense for you to assume the body was inside the house, but you never asked and you nodded in his direction even though he wasn't visible from that side."

"You must've said it on the phone."

"I didn't. I know I didn't. You had to have been there earlier, seen the body or something. What the fuck, Shar?"

They stared at each other. How long had Shar been her assistant now? She couldn't even remember, which was weird in itself, actually. "Maybe I should take a walk down the mountain again. I'll bet those cops are still there. I can tell them what I've found . . ."

"A lizard that doesn't exist?"

"An assistant who is lying to me." Zanna stood. She held the kitchen knife by her side, not knowing what to do with it.

"What if I told you that you really, truly, don't want to know the answers to your questions? That I've taken care of everything you've needed for twenty-two years, and I think I've earned the right to ask you to trust me."

Twenty-two years. Zanna chewed on her lip, thinking. "I'd say I trust you if you flat-out say you didn't murder him, but either way, you know what happened, and you're lying to me. You've earned the right to ask me to trust you, but I don't know if I can when I can see you're not being completely honest."

Shar lay back on the couch and put the pillow over her head. "Just once, in all these years, I'd like you to say 'I trust you completely.'"

"What are you talking about? I've always trusted you. You know my bank accounts, you have my credit card, you . . ."

The pillow lifted. "You say that every time too, but when it comes to it, if I say 'don't poke at the body' you always do. And can we skip the knife thing? You aren't going to use it."

Zanna looked down. The knife looked oddly familiar in her hand, like she had written this scene. She had a thousand questions and didn't even know which one to ask.

She tried to keep the panic out of her voice. "How are 'always' and 'don't poke at the body' in the same sentence? When has this ever happened before?"

Shar propped herself on her elbow. "Tell me about writing your last book."

"*The Mosquitoland Murders*? We flew into Minneapolis and rented an old house in the woods a few hours away."

"The actual writing. Do you remember anything of the time we spent there?"

Zanna considered, then shook her head. "No. I never remember the big drafting binges. It's a shame. We pick these beautiful places, and then it all passes by in a blur."

"Okay. How about your first book? Do you remember your first book?"

"Of course. *Campsite 49*."

"Not the first book you sold—the first book you wrote."

"It was horror, I guess. Dark fantasy, something like that. *The Blur in the Corner of Your Eye*. There was a creature."

"Do you remember anything else?"

"God, I was only a teen. The creature laid eggs in people."

"And why did it get rejected?"

"They said it didn't ring true as fiction. Too messy and weird. Derivative. I never figured out how to fix it, and then I wrote *Campsite 49*, and now I'm a mystery writer instead of a horror writer. What are all these questions?"

"One more: what did you eat for dinner last night?"

"I ate—um . . . I don't know. I guess I was caught up in writing, but I'm pretty sure I ate something."

"Salad. You had a salad. How far did you get on the book yesterday?"

That seemed to Zanna like something she should remember, but she didn't. "Fine. Shar, what's the point of all this?"

"I'm going to tell you something, and you're not going to believe me."

"I thought we did that already at the start of this conversation."

"We did, but this is something else." Shar paused, sighed. "There's this . . . thing. Like in *The Blur in the Corner of Your Eye*, okay?"

"A thing?"

"A creature. Let's say those prints you found belong to something, only it isn't in your book because it isn't native to this area. It hitches a ride."

"Hitches a ride?"

"Yeah. Can you stop repeating me for a sec? You'll get it, I promise. So there's this thing, and like you said, it lays eggs. It does it while the person is asleep, and then the eggs incubate, and the first one that hatches eats the other eggs."

"And then it eats through the person and runs away into the world. I know. I wrote this book, remember?"

"No! You wrote it wrong. It doesn't eat through the person. It hides in their body, dormant, until it has to lay its own eggs."

"How could I write my own book wrong?"

"I don't know. You forgot. You always forget."

"I still don't get what you want me to do with this story. I don't write horror anymore. Why don't you write it?"

"It's not a story, Zanna. That's what I'm trying to tell you. Did you wake up with a sore throat this morning? Your lungs sore, though you don't remember coughing?"

Zanna shrugged. It had only been a few hours, but it felt like ages ago.

"I hate when you make me do this the hard way," Shar muttered. "You always make me do it the hard way."

She reached into her bag and pulled out a baggie of brown powder. "Here, put a pinch of this on your tongue."

Zanna turned her head away.

"Come on, smell it. It's cumin."

"I hate cumin."

"You two have that in common. Come on, I need you to do this. A small pinch."

Zanna didn't see a way out of it, since she was stuck in a room with someone whose reasonable tone belied the deeply weird things she was saying. She swallowed a pinch of cumin, then coughed. A second later, the coughing grew deeper, like the powder had gotten into her lungs. Then something stranger, like claws inside her chest. She gagged, and heaved something up. It helped itself along the way, tearing at her teeth and gums even as she opened her mouth.

The thing that skittered out of her was not a lizard or a skink. It had too many legs, and the middle track hadn't been a tail, it was a long face with a proboscis that touched the ground and it had no eyes and too much skin, slimy, black, loose, and it was so fast, just a blur. It skittered under the couch, and Zanna remembered the sound from the middle of the night. Her mind started to lose both that memory and the memory of what the thing looked like even as it disappeared from her view.

"What. The. Fuck." The words hurt.

"You never believe me until I show you."

She held the knife out to Shar. "Kill it!"

Shar waved her off. "Oh, trust me, we've both tried. Burning, shooting, stabbing, drowning. It has a very strong will to live."

"What was it doing inside me?"

"It lives there. You're its host. I don't think it actually does you any harm."

Zanna ran her tongue around her sore mouth, and Shar amended, "Well, it doesn't normally do you any harm. I think it anesthetizes you when it's not in a hurry. When you don't swallow a mouthful of cumin."

"Anesthetizes?"

"Yeah, so you relax, and you don't remember it leaving or coming back. You never remember these trips at all. When you read your drafts back home you always say 'I must have been in the zone. I don't remember writing any of this.'"

Zanna nodded. She knew she had to ask the hard question, too. "So what's your part in this?"

"I do what I've always done, since we were kids and we got stuck in the crawlspace under my dad's house and it chose you. It got way easier when I convinced you to hire me. Find someplace remote for you to write a couple of times a year when you start showing signs. Powder myself with cumin. Try to make the closest person someone who won't be too missed if something goes wrong, like this time. Try to keep you away from the body, which is sometimes easy and sometimes a disaster, like today."

Zanna again had more questions than she could possibly voice. It was true, she did have lapses, but only when she was writing. Her process had always been weird like that, and two books a year had never felt difficult. She remembered everything in between books, or at least she thought she did. She again fixated on Shar's language instead of the harder questions. "What do you mean by 'if something goes wrong'?"

"That same secretion . . . they're dozy when I get to them. I can usually scrape the eggs out of their mouths, and they never even know anything happened. Only, sometimes, something goes wrong. It gives some of them nightmares, or maybe they see it, I don't know, and they fall down the stairs, or they attack it, or they attack someone else, or like this guy, they run out of the house and hit their head, and I still have to scrape the eggs out so the medical examiner doesn't find anything."

"Why don't you just let them discover the eggs? Or tell someone—a doctor, a biologist?"

Shar looked horrified. "They'd never let you go. They'd have to lock you up to keep it from getting to anyone, and they'd figure out the same thing I have about it surviving everything we try to do to it. You've got contracts. Books to write. Or they'd keep me for having covered it up, and you wouldn't have me to protect you anymore."

That all made a certain amount of sense, even if it was horrible. Shar could be wrong, of course, but she was usually right. "How often does it go wrong?"

"Maybe one in five? They never connect you. Or me."

"But that's why we never go back to the same place twice?"

"Yeah. Somebody would get suspicious sooner or later. But—you believe me now?"

"Yes, I believe you. Are you sure you shouldn't kill me?"

Shar looked horrified. "I wouldn't!"

"But you've let all those other people die. One in five?"

"The eggs have never once survived. The one in you is the only one, as far as I know. Well, and whichever one laid an egg in you to begin with; I guess there must be others. I didn't mean to let anyone die, but it's better than the alternative."

"The alternative?"

"Letting any of the eggs live, or letting you kill yourself. You've suggested that a few times, but what if it survived? How would I find it again to try to keep people safe? You can't do it."

The thought had crossed Zanna's mind. "Then what happens now? I'm not going to let that thing claw its way back down my throat."

"You will. You'll fall asleep tonight and it'll find its way back. It always does. Then you'll wake up in the morning, and you won't remember any of this, and you'll draft your book, and we'll go back to the city, and you'll read your draft and tell me you must've been in the zone, and then when you come up with your next book, the plot'll hinge on a guy who ran out of his house with no shoes, and you'll research it and I'll find someplace remote for you to write it. Rinse and repeat."

They were both silent a moment.

Zanna had a question she didn't want to ask, but asked anyway. "Does it help me somehow? Is this a deal like I can't write without it? That it helps my creativity?"

"Not as far as I know," Shar said. "It might inspire some of your plots—okay, most of them—but I can't see any reason for the rest. Your work ethic and prose are all yours, I'm sure."

"That's something at least," Zanna said. "That would be one ugly muse."

They were silent again. After a minute, Zanna spoke again, the only thing left to say. "Fuck."

"Yeah."

"Shar?"

"Yeah?"

"You really are the best assistant. You deserve a raise."

"You say that every time, too."

"What if I write it down? 'Note to self: give Shar a raise'?"

Shar cocked her head. "Y'know, I don't think you've ever done that before. It's worth a shot, if you mean it."

"I really and sincerely mean it." Zanna opened her computer and created a reminder for herself. A reminder that would chime at her in one month's time, and which she'd open and look at in total surprise and have no memory of writing. Then she'd nod in agreement, even if

339

she couldn't remember what exactly had prompted her to set the alert (or why the second line said "believe her") and she'd make it happen, because she would hate to lose an assistant as good as Shar.

SARAH PINSKER's fiction has won the Nebula and Sturgeon Awards, and she has been a finalist for the Hugo and other awards. Her stories have been translated into Spanish, French, Italian, and Chinese, among other languages. Her first collection, *Sooner or Later Everything Falls Into the Sea* (Small Beer Press) and her first novel, *A Song for a New Day* (Berkley), were both published in 2019. She is also a singer/songwriter with three albums and another forthcoming. She lives in Baltimore with her wife and dog.

THE COVEN
OF DEAD GIRLS

L'ERIN OGLE

The key turns in the lock and you step inside. Until you, we have been adrift in waiting, silence heavy in our bones. Time passes slowly inside these walls, dressed in our plastic coffins. Your sister follows you inside and looks around.

"This isn't a good place," she says.

She's right, but you'll chalk it up to the way Connie's always existed partially in the real world, and part in another place where everything is gauzy and insubstantial. You don't even hear her, but it would have served you better if you had.

Hindsight can be a real bitch sometimes.

You carry in boxes, your entire life divided into cardboard squares, labeled in block letters, marked by a black Sharpie. KITCHEN. LIVING ROOM. WINTER CLOTHES.

There is a box that says PERSONAL.

Everyone's got a box of memories they lug around. We've seen this before. People come and people go. No one stays here very long.

You peel the sticky tape away. The duct tape peels up (of course it's duct tape—we are familiar with that, all of us) and it makes a sick screeching sound that echoes through the spaces between us. We hold our breath and peer over your shoulder. What kind of man are you, anyway?

There are photographs and love letters and even a couple pictures of a naked woman named Jane. Her name is scrawled on the letters, printed on the marriage certificate, and the divorce decree.

You unpack and put your things among us and you don't notice the walls moving when we sigh. Over the years we have cried so many tears that the yellow flowered wallpaper has begun to detach from the drywall. Tears of regret, of rage, of blood. If you were to peel back the faded yellow sheets, our wet copper scent would fill the air. But you don't. You would blame it on faulty wiring anyway.

You are not a person of abstracts. You believe in absolutes.

You brother's realtor found this place dirt cheap. He didn't mention the people from before, the ones who left with dark circles under their eyes, or the man who lived here when we moved in. That man went on to his own future, maybe as bleak as ours. He props himself up on a cane and trawls the urine scented halls of his retirement home. The taste for blood is still blade sharp inside him, but his hands, his body are too soft and weak to sate it.

When Connie visits, she stares at the walls, but we do not move. Our business is not with her. Our business is with you. If you were to ask why, we would not have an answer. We have been here a long time. We don't have anything else to do.

At night you hear things. Creaking, moaning floorboards, a disturbance in the air. You blame it on the house settling, as if houses like this ever really settle. As if they could.

We are here behind squares of drywall, wrapped in plastic, sealed with caulk. Night makes us restless. Night reminds of how dark this place can get, how much it can hurt here.

All sixteen of us wear the maroon scarf we were strangled with. After all this is over, they will uncover us and they will dream about the scarf, a shade too dark to be blood but violent all the same. What's with the scarves? They ask, and we could tell them but no one listens to dead girls. We didn't matter that much when we were alive.

* * *

There was a red scarf in his past. Of course there was.

His mother wore the scarf around her neck until she got all boozed up. She would rub it across her face, smearing her lipstick. She was lonely and sad and she didn't pay him any attention until the drink allowed blackness to fall over her mind. Then, she made him crawl in her bed and drew the scarf over his body, flicking his privates, laughing at his smallness.

She should grieve this but she doesn't. To be fair, she doesn't remember all of it, but there are fragments of her wrongs embedded deep in her soul. She turns and twists restless in her own grave. She knows there is something to atone for but she is too frightened to search for it. This is the nature of alcoholic parents. They cannot face their cruelty. They do not want to see the scars.

Sixteen skeletons, thirty-two femurs. One of Eleven's legs will be crushed by the collapse of a weight bearing wall. She knows it will happen but she doesn't care. I cannot understand that. I am still angry. I am still a whole person, even if I am a skeleton. I turn in my plastic prison, my teeth stripped of gums grinding at the thought of such an insult, being turned into dust.

You put a picture of Jane on the wall. You still love her. Jane is beautiful and her hair is the color of sunshine. We drink in the warmth of it, gulp it like the poison we swallowed to get here.

The poison was different for each of us. Rohypnol, heroin, alcohol, whatever he had, whatever it took. Were there girls that didn't take it? I don't know. Even ghosts cannot travel through all of the places and all of the people.

Sometimes I start thinking about that, if I'd never taken that drink. Regret has teeth. It can cut you up into pieces and leave you gasping at the unfairness of it all. Maybe you know about that, though I find it hard to believe.

* * *

You know me, I whisper in your ear, so like a sea conch. My words turn into waves crashing out into the world. You wake, as your kind tend to do, startled and afraid. We like that, most of us. I like it. I can taste the fear coming off you and it satiates my fury.

I don't know why I am so angry. Times doesn't heal all wounds. My rage did not dull with the years. I fought so hard, but he was so much stronger. I want to hurt someone, so they know exactly what happened to me. I want to be the one doing the hurting, to be so powerful no one ever hurts me again.

He tries to dream of us, that old man with the cane and the scar above his left eyebrow. The one he says happened when a hammer fell off a high shelf in the garage.

That was me. That was the heel of my shoe.

When he tries to dream of us, we feel it plucking at the air around our wall space. We lie still and quiet and we picture the scarf.

He wakes up screaming.

One day he will twist his sheet into a noose. When he drops his weight into it, everything turns red. But not today. We're not ready yet. We have a lot to show him first.

You keep waking up at night. You can hear things moving but no one's there. Sometimes there is the faintest sound of screaming. You start leaving the TV on to drown it out, but we change the channels.

Shadows appear in the hollows beneath your eyes. We have been erased, yet we still leave a mark.

The old woman in her coffin, we visit her too. She made him, and he made us.

I wasn't a bad girl. I didn't deserve what happened to me. I cried my first year here. I asked myself over and over, what did I do wrong?

I took a drink at a party.

I asked God, too, but he never answered me.

There were girls like me that lived here after him. Girls with long hair and straight teeth who laughed. Who slammed their doors and talked about boys and tacked pictures on their dressers. Girls who had futures as bright as Jane's smile beaming from the picture you hung.

Right in front of me, all the time, all the things I could never be.

"Why?"

We asked each other that so many times. We guessed. We thought about it. We went into him to see for ourselves. Eleven and Three and Five, they must have hearts not as withered and shriveled as mine. They could still feel sorry for him. Knowing what happened to him just gave me another person to hate. It never made me feel sorry for him at all.

She lies restless in her coffin and we knock on the lid. We whisper terrible things to her. We haunt her worse than we haunt you. There will be no peace for her, until there is peace for us.

Maybe she had her own horror story. But I cannot find it in my soul to care.

Your ex-wife, the luminous Jane, visits. You have an ex-wife that still cares about you and I am a skeleton wrapped in a tarp. How is that fair? You are a person and I was a person and I died and no one cared and you mope your life away and everyone cares.

Jane tells you Connie is worried about you. You look tired, she says. She wears her concern like a scarf, bright against her skin.

I can't sleep, you tell her. There's something here with me.

Jane asks if you've thought more about seeing someone. About your father. How you love and hate him. I see the marks he left on you. Sure, I get it, he didn't hit you, but he said things to you. He made you feel like nothing and opened wounds that never healed. We all carry scars with us, from this place to the next.

We don't have names anymore. We are the sixteen. I am Twelve. Three thinks you're handsome. Five says we should leave you alone. But the rest of us, you make our teeth set together. We see you, the movies you watch on your laptop, browser set to private. We see what you want to do.

If I could free my fingers, I would gouge your eyes out.

* * *

Time passes funny here.

I have a list of all the things I've never done.

I've never kissed another girl. (I would have liked to.)

I've never made love. (I have had sex. Forcible, awful, soul murdering sex.)

I've never gone to college.

I was never a senior.

I never drove.

I never met my father.

I never fell in love.

I never went to a concert.

I never left the great Sunflower State of Kansas, even.

It's a pretty long list.

We fourteen (minus Three and Five) talk about what we will do when we break free. I want us to ring your bed so you wake up staring up at a circle of dead girls. I want to smell the urine you let loose. I want to lean down and suck your scream out. The things my dead heart wants sets me trembling. It makes my bones chatter against each other and you sit up in bed. I scream as I remain a statue and then—the fury in me becomes a raging hot thing in my chest. It crawls up the scythe ladder of ribs and leaps atop the humerus, slides down the bone slide and into my first finger on my right hand. My finger jerks. It cuts a hole in the plastic. It jabs at the drywall. The heat pulses through it. There is a small, starburst scorch pattern burnt through the wallpaper.

Connie sees the mark two days later.

What's this—she says . . .

She touches her fingers to the small, tiny hole. The wetness of our tears sticks. When she lifts her hand, the wallpaper peels away. We wait and we plead, FIND US.

Oh GOD, what is that smell? She puts her hand over her mouth.

You come to see. It overpowers you both. The stench of decay assaults you, dead girls rotting in plastic coffins. You lean down and peer into the hole. My finger, dirty white porous bone, points at you.

Oh, God, you say. Oh, God.

God has nothing to do with this place.

You get a crowbar. You find the seams in the drywall. You pry a square out.

You know what I am when you see me. My teeth gleam through the plastic.

I think it's a body, you whisper.

The end is coming fast. I knew it, I saw it, but now it is here. Connie is screaming into the phone. You're just standing there, with tears in your eyes, like I matter now. I'm sorry, I think you say, but you are hard to see. You are turning transparent, blurring around the edges. Now time is moving too fast, the last of the sand through the hourglass.

I can feel myself becoming light as air. When I push my ghost fingers against the plastic, they pass right through. People are here, but they are vague shapes and their voices are muted and distorted. Don't, I try to scream, but nothing comes out. Don't do this to me!

I don't want to leave! I'm not ready! I never got to do anything! All I did was die! Don't I get ANYTHING?

L'ERIN OGLE is a mother, nurse, fitness instructor, and author living in Lawrence, Kansas. Her stories have been published by *Syntax & Salt*, *Daily Science Fiction*, *Metaphorosis*, and *PseudoPod*.

BLOOD IS ANOTHER WORD FOR HUNGER

RIVERS SOLOMON

I n a wooden house on a modest farmstead by a dense wood near a roving river to the west of town, miles from the wide road and far away from the peculiar madness that is men at war, lived the Missus, the Missus's grown daughters Adelaide and Catherine, the Missus's sister Bitsy, the Missus's poorly mother Anna, and the Missus's fifteen-year-old slave girl Sully, who had a heart made of teeth—for as soon as she heard word that Albert, the Missus's husband, had been slain in battle, she took up arms against the family who'd raised her, slipping a tincture of valerian root and skullcap into their cups of warmed milk before slitting their throats in the night.

The etherworld, always one eye steady on the realm of humankind, took note. Disturbances in the order of things could be exploited, could cut paths between dominions. The murder of a family by a girl so tender and young ripped a devilishly wide tunnel between the fields of existence, for it was not the way of things, and the etherworld thrived on the impermissible.

Sully's breaths blurred together into a whispery, chafed hum as she stood over the bodies. Blood marked her clothes, hair, and skin. She tasted it in her mouth, where it had shot in a stream from Bitsy's artery. Her tongue, too, was coated, but Sully wouldn't swallow. She couldn't bear to have that hateful woman all up inside her body, slick and salty and merging with her own blood. Saliva gathered in her mouth till she had no choice but to spit on a patch of rug in the second bedroom, where Bitsy and the Missus's daughter slept.

She stumbled downstairs and out to the barn and grabbed the bar of soap from the metal tin that held all her possessions. Determined, she slaked it over her tongue before biting off a morsel and swallowing it, just in case a smidge of Bitsy had made its way into her and needed eradicating.

Sully's whistley, syncopated pants could've been the dying wheezes of a sick coyote or the first breaths of a colt, the battlesong of a screech owl, a storm wind. Sully closed her eyes. In the darkness and quiet of the barn, she could hear every night sound as loud as a woman hollering a field song. The music of it entered her, and she succumbed. When next Sully opened her eyes, she could breathe properly again. A few moments after that, she felt steady enough to return to the house.

Sully gathered the blood-laden sheets from inside and carried them to the property's stream, where the rush of water rinsed away the stains. She knew well how to untangle blood from cotton, having regularly scrubbed clean the Missus's, the Missus's daughter's, and the Missus's sister's menses-soiled undergarments.

When her fingers turned still from the mix of cool water and the brisk night wind, she carried the sheets to the tree and hung them over the naked branches. The beige linens blew back and forth in the wind, possessed. Sully went inside to warm her hands over the woodstove then carried the bodies of her slavers one by one over her shoulder outside. She dug a single grave for hours and hours and hours into the night, into the next day, and into that night, too, never sleeping, and filled the wound she'd made in the earth with Missus, Adelaide, Catherine, Bitsy, and Anna, and covered them with soil.

Her heart should've ached for these women—they'd raised her from age six—but it did not. She was still seething, madder, in fact, than she'd been before the kill because her final act of rebellion had not brought the relief she'd imagined it would. These ladies who'd loomed Goliath in her life, who'd unleashed every ugliness they could think of on Sully, were corn husks now, souls hollowed out. Irrelevant. How could that be? How could folks so immense become nothing in the space of time it took a blade to swipe six inches?

It was Sully's unsoftened anger in the face of what she'd done that cut a path between dominions. The etherworld spat out a teenage girl, full grown, called Ziza into Sully's womb. Ziza had spent the last two hundred years skulking in the land of the dead, but she rode the fury of Sully's murders like a river current back to the world of flesh. Ziza felt it all, wind and sky and the breath of wolves against her skin. She spun through the ages looking for the present, time now foreign to her after being in a world where everything was both eternal and nonexistent.

"Yes, yes, yes!" Ziza called as she descended from the spirit realm down a tunnel made of life. Breathing things, screaming things, hot, sweaty, pulsing, moving, scampering, wild, toothy, bloody, slimy, rich, salty things. Tree branches brushed her skin. Sensation overwhelmed her as she landed with a soft, plump thud into the belly of her new god. Ziza took in the darkness, swum in it. It was nothing like the violent nothingness of her home for the past two centuries. For here she could smell, taste, feel. She could hear the cries of the girl carrying her, loud and unrelenting.

Sully had never been with child before, and she didn't understand the pain that overtook her so sudden as she shoveled the last gallon of dirt over the graves of her masters. Spasms in her abdomen convinced her she was dying.

As she fell backwards to the ground, her belly turned giant and bulbous. She stared up at the crescent moon and spat at it for the way it mocked her with its half-smile. Sully hated that grinning white ghoul, and with all the spite at the fates she could muster, she howled and she howled and she howled at it. She howled until she became part wolf, a lush coat of gray fur spiking from her shoulder blades and spine. It was magic from the dead land that Ziza brought with her, where there was no border separating woman from beast.

Hearing the pained wailing, Ziza made herself as small as possible as she felt herself being birthed, not wishing to damage her host. With her last ounce of etherworld magic, she shrunk herself down to the size of a large baby for the time it would take to come out.

"Help," moaned Sully, but she'd killed anyone who might be able to offer intervention. "Help me!" Sully's womb contracted, and over-whelmed with the urge to push, she squeezed until that baby who was not a baby came out of her.

Sully's mouth hung agape as she watched the birthed-thing crawl from the cradle of her thighs then grow bigger, bigger, and bigger until it was full grown. It was a girl Sully's age, and though she was not quite smiling, she was—Sully struggled to put a name to the stranger's expression—impressed with the situation. "Lordy," said Sully, but she was in too much pain to worry over this oddity. The skin betwixt her legs had suffered from the delivery, now inflamed. Her vulva felt like a broken bone.

She tried to stand but was too weak, and the freshly bornt teen-ager offered a hand. Sully took it but shoved it away once she was up, then limped along to the kitchen where she fixed herself a poultice of mashed bread and soured milk. The smell of it turned her stomach and she vomited on the table before collapsing over a chair. Was this how it would end, in this dank kitchen, on this dank farmstead?

Sully felt a hand on her back. "Ma'am?" the fresh-bornt teenager said. "My name's Ziza. I'm going to take care of you," she said. She had a small, squeaky voice that reminded Sully of a mouse. "Don't you worry," she said.

Ziza pressed the bread-and-milk poultice to Sully's vulva, fastening the mixture to her body with strips of cotton. She mashed herbs into a thick, leafy tea. "Drink this, girl," she said, smiling with a joyful warmth that did not match the bloodiness of these hectic circumstances. "It'll help along with the poultice."

Sully's nose curled up at the scent of it. "You just raised me up from the dead, and now you're telling me you can't swallow a little of my brew?" asked Ziza.

Lulled by Ziza's gentle, chiding way, Sully obeyed—her first time ever to do so not under the threat of violence. "Shhh, now. Sleep," said Ziza. She began to hum, but it wasn't a lullaby sort of song. Too lively.

"I'm not tired," Sully insisted, but she couldn't breathe through the pain between her legs and her words came out as a series of gasps. "Am I dying?"

"You're passing out," said Ziza, stroking Sully's face.

"You an angel or something?" asked Sully.

"Oh, I think you might be the angel. An avenging angel," said Ziza.

Sully hadn't spoken to a soul besides her masters in years. She hated how heavy her eyelids felt, how much of a strain it was to keep them wide open. The limits of her body were robbing her of this moment, this bewildering, strange moment.

"Sleep," said Ziza. And then one more time, "Sleep."

For once it was a blessing for Sully to do as she was told.

Two days later, Sully stirred awake. The pain had gone, and someone had carried her to Missus's bed, which was made up with the linens Sully had washed.

"Ziza," she called out, remembering her savior's name. It slipped prettily off her tongue and teeth. "Ziza? You there?" Distantly she heard singing, but it was so faint she wondered if she was hallucinating it. She swung her legs over to the floor and stood, her bones and muscles creaking stubbornly. "Ziza!"

When no answer came, she went downstairs. The farmhouse had been recently cleaned. A metal pail filled with gray water sat in the corner near a mop and a discarded rag. The layer of dust usually visible on the floors and walls and wood stove had been washed away. Layers of grime that Sully had previously believed permanent had been scrubbed clean. The scent of lavender had done away with the previous odor of musk and sweat. Sully rubbed her eyes, made a shade out of her hand to block out the midday sun.

"Good afternoon, you," said Ziza as she poked her head through the open window. Sully turned around to see the girl she'd birthed wearing a smile, one of Sully's head scarves, and the Master's church shirt, trousers, and suspenders. "Glad to see you're finally up. I was getting lonely with only livestock as company." There was that smile again, so wide and open it hardly fit on her face.

"You've made yourself quite at home," Sully said.

"It got tiresome trying to be the polite house guest. There was too much needed doing," she said. Sully saw that the panes of glass in the door, which had always been a murky brown, had been washed clean. They were clear and bright, sparkling just about. Ziza had turned this ramshackle cottage into something palatable, something the Missus had always hoped Sully would do. "You should come out here if you're feeling up to it," she said.

Sully peered around the main room of the farmhouse, all evidence of her murderous deed erased. Ziza had cleared away the pot of tea she'd brewed with analgesic leaves. The bloody clothes Sully had been wearing on the night in question were cleaned, dried, and ironed. They lay folded on a chair.

She wished she missed them. She wished at the very least she felt sadness or guilt. But all she felt was the same old rage. It burned her up, leaving her numb, nerves charred. She'd done the thing she'd always dreamt of doing, and now what? Perhaps now it was her time to die.

"You coming or not?" called Ziza.

Sully joined Ziza outside, where the sun was too bright. Her legs still weak, she leaned against the rotted wooden frame of the house, chewing her lip, arms crossed over her chest.

Across from her, not far from the chicken coop, Ziza drank in the sky. Her head tilted back at such a sharp angle that the base of her skull was perpendicular to the line of her neck. She touched her skin. Patted it. Poked it. Pinched it. Her whole body gestured joyousness. "Hallelujah, hallelujah," she said.

Sully rolled her eyes at this stranger who'd made a house of her uterus. "What are you so happy about?"

"Haven't you seen the sky today? Isn't that reason enough to be happy?"

Sully slid her hands into the pockets of her apron and focused her eyes hard on Ziza. "No."

"How can you be sure unless you have a look at it? Go on. Do it."

Sully didn't like to do what people said, so she looked out at the expanse of poorly managed land before her instead. The Missus's family hadn't been the most skilled of farmers, their approach to tending the earth one of brute force. They beat the ground with their hoes and rakes and called it tilling. The dirt was hungry. It needed feeding, cajoling, coaxing, singing to. Building up not breaking down. What had the Master and Missus known about growing something? All they knew was how to bleed something for all it was worth. What must it be like to live life when every interaction included the question, *How much value can I extract from this?*

"I can't make you look, but it sure is beautiful," said Ziza, eyes now affixed to Sully. She was small and birdlike, her mannerisms sharp and jittery. Her body was too small for her spirit.

"I don't believe in beauty," replied Sully, saying it because it sounded controversial, not because she particularly meant it. She counted the rows of cotton plants, which looked as scraggily and ugly as anything she ever saw. Ugliness was something she could count on.

"If you don't believe in beauty, then I suppose you must've never seen your own reflection before," said Ziza.

Now Sully didn't have a response for that. "What did you say?" she asked.

Ziza returned her gaze to the sky. Her face was angled away, so Sully couldn't see it properly, but she thought the girl was smiling.

"You're nothing like how I imagined a ghost would be," said Sully.

"Maybe because I'm not a ghost. If I was, could I do all this?" She grabbed a stick off the ground and flung it at Sully.

Sully batted it away then picked up another and tossed it right back. She reached down and grabbed handfuls of dirt and pebbles and threw them at Ziza, too.

"Stop! Stop!" Ziza cried, all the while laughing wildly.

Worn out from Ziza's constant frivolity, Sully huffed a breath. "What are you even doing here? Leave me alone. Go away."

"I promise to stop pestering you if you look at the sky," said Ziza.

"I don't think you could stop pestering if you tried," Sully said and mashed a little dandelion into the ground with her boot.

"Damn, girl, just look."

Sighing, Sully cast her gaze upward. At first all Sully observed was the cloudless, bright blue that she suspected had entranced Ziza so much. She felt disappointed that after all of Ziza's haranguing for her to look, there was no revelation, no moment of transcendence. Sully didn't feel moved at all. The sky was the sky, like it had been yesterday and so many days before. She was about to look away when out the corner of her left eye she saw a fluttering of white. A flock of seagulls approached, so far inland that surely they were confused. "What in creation?" said Sully, mouth and eyes wide. The seagulls dipped low to the ground to give her what looked like a bow.

"Mercy," Ziza cried out, then laughed in astonishment.

The chorus of squawking hurt Sully's ears, so she yelled for the birds to hush. At once, the seagulls became silent. She covered her mouth to stifle the gasp.

Ziza, grinning widely, turned away from the circling birds and the cavernous sky to look at Sully. "You did this, did you know that? You are astonishing."

Assaulted with such strangeness, Sully didn't know whether to be joyful or frightened, to revel in this new inexplicable power or cower in its presence.

Sully removed the artifacts of her past life from the house and burned them in a bonfire outside, thinking these vestiges of the Missus were the reason for the sick feeling she still had even now that the family was dead. What could not be burned, she smashed. What could not be smashed, she buried in the woods past the property line. The Missus had collected all sorts of knickknacks and bric-a-brac over the years. Needless figurines. Stacks of newspapers ceiling high. Old, busted musical instruments that no one played. Bottles of snake oil bought from this and that traveling salesman, promising to cure ailments no one even had.

"With all the accoutrements gone, this place doesn't feel like much of a home at all," said Ziza as she helped set the table for supper. She'd invited herself to stay. "Looks like a tomb in here."

"You'd know all about tombs, wouldn't you, Miss Dead Girl?" Sully said, experimenting with a partial smile so Ziza would know she did not intend her comment anything but facetiously, but she hated the way it felt on her cheeks. She resolved never to do it again.

Ziza snorted as she folded a cloth napkin and placed it on the table, laughing with her tongue against her teeth so the sound of it was a soft hiss. "What's a woman like me know of tombs? I died in a outhouse and was surely buried in an unmarked grave or burned. Tombs are for kings and queens." She grabbed a piece of cornbread from the basket at the center of the table and brought it to her mouth, her manner far from proper. Crumbs stuck to the corner of her lips and she wiped them away with the fabric of her shirt cuff. In the days since she'd been here, she had yet to take off the ivory-colored button-up that used to belong to the Master. His single bit of fancy attire. Clean and barely worn. Though Master Albert had been a small man, the fabric draped like a carnival tent over Ziza's miniscule skeleton.

"I don't mind that you're so very uncouth," said Sully and sat down to join her new guest, her sort-of child, at the table. She'd taken—not quite pleasure, not quite comfort, perhaps reprieve—in the routine she'd fallen into with Ziza, enough that she could try to make pleasant conversation through the numbness.

"Says the girl who slain five womenfolk with no more thought than she'd throw out dirty bath water," Ziza said.

Sully reached with her fingers beneath her head wrap to scratch her sweaty head and sized up Ziza from across the small wooden round table. She didn't look like any girl Sully had seen before with her light brown skin and green eyes, sun-colored nappy hair, a cornucopia of freckles.

"Was you always that color?" Sully asked. She'd heard tales about ghosts possessing women, turning them white with death. "Or was it what happened to you in the Thereafter? I knew a boy who had a patch of white in his black hair from all the worries of his life, though I've always been an aggrieved sort of person, and that never happened to me. They say I'm dark as a raisin."

After a few bites of beans, Ziza had a gulp of lemonade. "I was just born like this," she said. She dipped her cornbread into a bowl of spicy red beans, thick pieces of meat from the ham hock mixed in among the onion. She ate every meal so ravenously, and it occurred to Sully there might not have been food in the Thereafter.

"Isn't there food in the place you came from?" she asked.

Ziza hummed as she played with her spoon, tapping it against her bowl. "It's hard to say," she said. The only times Ziza wasn't actively cheerful was when Sully brought up anything that took place before she'd come to the farm.

"So you don't like to talk about it or what?" asked Sully, aware she sounded coarse but unsure how to fix it.

Ziza squeezed her eyes shut. "It's just, what happens when you die isn't a thing you can talk about. It's not a place that exists where I can just describe the color of the sky and the whoosh of the water and the subtle hue of violet in the flowers in bloom. It's more like being drownt and you seeing everything through icy water."

Sully blew on another spoonful of beans, but she didn't bring it to her mouth. "Does it hurt your lungs like drowning does?" she asked. She leaned across the table toward Ziza, hungry to know the ways of death.

"It's more like the moment of letting go, when the fight is out of you. When you about to pass out so the pain of being denied air is gone."

Sully exhaled slowly, her lips trembling as she whistled out air. "I don't see why you'd ever want to leave a place that feels like that," said Sully. "Like peace."

Ziza stirred what remained of her food, the hand holding the spoon shaking. "Don't say that," she said.

Even when the voice bearing the edict was as gentle as Ziza's, Sully didn't abide commands. "If you're free to blather on and on about what a glorious day it is and hallelujah this and that and such nonsense, I can talk about what I want to talk about."

Ziza sucked in her lips and let her head droop a smidge, eyes averted from Sully. "You're right," said Ziza. "I spoke out of turn. I'm a guest in your home."

Sully didn't expect the girl to capitulate so easily, and she was sorry her hostility had whipped the fight out of her. "It's not my home," said Sully after a moment.

"Isn't it?"

"It's not like I got papers saying it's mine," Sully said, and everybody knew papers were everything.

"Did you not kill the folks who had the papers? Therefore could you not change the papers? Is an owner anything but he who kills for the papers?" asked Ziza. The temporary contriteness that had overtaken Ziza went as quickly as it had come.

"But what would I do with this place?" said Sully, standing, finding Ziza's inquisitive stare suddenly oppressive. She leaned back against the wood burning stove, where her cup of coffee sat keeping warm. She drank what remained, but still did not feel settled. She filled Master Albert's pipe with tobacco and began to smoke it.

"You could live out your days here," said Ziza.

"Why would I want to live out my days here?"

"Why wouldn't you? Do you wish to travel instead?"

Sully inhaled smoke then blew it away from Ziza. It felt good to do this in the house. The Missus had always forbade Albert from doing so. "Travel? For what purpose? I thought travel was for seeing things, and I've already seen all I want to ever see, I think."

"For the pleasure of it. Or you could stay here. Whatever you do, I'll do it, too. You bornt me, girl. Look at this," she said, untucking her shirt from her trousers and lifting it up to reveal her belly button, where there was a large, black stump. The remainder of the umbilical cord that had connected them. "We can go or we can stay. Which do you want to do?"

"I don't want anything in particular," said Sully.

"Then I'll want for the both of us. I've decided. This is your home and my home, now. Our home. And it will be others' home, too."

"The others?" asked Sully.

"They'll surely be riding your murder wave here," said Ziza. "You kilt five, did you not? And I am only one. When we disrupt nature, she likes to reestablish the balance."

"The gods like a defiant streak," said Ziza. She'd taken it upon herself to teach Sully the ways of the world. Her lessons came over many weeks, given as she and Sully roasted corn and hot sausage over the fire together, or scrubbed mud-stained clothes in the stream, or swept, or planted crops of peas, or gathered wood or stone to build dwellings for their impending arrivals.

She learned about tinctures, roots, and bones. Some of it Sully already knew, like how to bring sickness to heel with the right cocktail of plants. The subject of resurrection was what interested Sully most, and she played close mind as Ziza babbled about necromancy, zombi-folk, mojo, herbs, conjurers.

Ziza described a bridge made of dreamscape, said Sully had accessed a way to pull people across it. "Why me?" asked Sully.

Shrugging, Ziza continued her work devising a crop rotation schedule for their land. She insisted that most of the acreage needed to lay fallow for at least a year, perhaps two, up to three, time over which they'd feed it with the manure of chickens, cows, pigs, and goats. "I guess the etherworld saw something in you and rooted up in you," she said.

Sully had always been touched by a flash of darkness. On the plantation where she was born, slave women gossiped about her true nature. Her mother, who'd been sold away when Sully was five, called her *moskti* after the blood-eating fairy in stories of their old home back across the water. They possessed human bodies and kept them alive by feasting on the blood of anyone nearby. As soon as she had teeth, Sully drew blood whenever she fed from her mother's breasts. Four months old.

"When it comes to the divine, it's best not to worry too much over the particulars, or you'll lose the forest for the trees, you understand?" asked Ziza.

"No."

But everything Ziza said and predicted came true. Sully did give birth again, this time to a boy of ten named Miles. Two months after that came a forty-one-year-old woman named Liza Jane and a few days later her twin sister Bethie. Next came a man named Nathaniel with gray hair and skin dark like a fever dream who didn't talk much but to recite lines of poetry. Including Ziza, five revenants in all came to stay, one for each of the lives Sully took.

Sully kept her distance from all but Ziza. She watched from afar as they made a home out of the farm over the weeks and months. They sang songs without her, swam in the stream without her, tilled without her, picked blackberries without her, and laughed without her. They were a family, as exuberant in their togetherness as they were in their resurrections.

Ziza was their shepherd—not just for the revenants, but for Sully, too, coaxing her like a lonesome, lost lamb back into the fold. "Sully," Ziza said one day. "I've been missing you."

Sully wasn't the sort of person people missed, so when Ziza said that, she didn't know what to do with herself but fiddle with a piece of flour-water paste caked to her palms. She peeled off the flakey remnants onto the wooden porch, where she sat rocking in the Missus's old chair.

"Don't you find yourself missing me, too?" asked Ziza, kneeling in front of Sully. She laid her hands on Sully's knees and squeezed, and Sully stood up from the rocking chair so fast it almost toppled.

"You're the one who doesn't want to talk anymore now that you've got your new friends," said Sully. She cast a glance out onto the fields, where the newer revenants, Miles, Liza Jane, Bethie, and Nathaniel, were picking wild flowers—weeds.

"It'd be easier to keep up with you if you didn't sequester yourself away like you do," she said, then shook her head and walked off. When she was almost out of earshot, she turned around and called, "I'd love you forever if you'd just try. Not that I don't already love you forever."

It was foolishness. Ziza was a silly girl, prone to bouts of childish whimsy, yet Sully found herself enticed by the promise. She didn't care about getting closer to the others, but Ziza? She could bask forever in her attentions.

Miles, the little one, was a rascal and then some, always playing tricks on Sully. He'd replaced her jar of talcum powder with ashes once and another time laid a dead mouse inside her boots. But he was also a master of languages. He'd grown up in a boarding house up north where he'd learned German, Czech, Spanish, Russian, and Italian from the boarders. She liked listening to him rattle on in foreign tongues.

Miles taught her to read and how to do math, and called her "Sis." She didn't like him, but she didn't unlike him, either, and she found her hostility toward him and the others melting to indifference and then to a reluctant fondness as the weeks passed by.

* * *

There were enough of them now that they were a proper brood. Food stores had dwindled to dregs. Though the seagulls brought them fish daily, some of which they ate, some of which they smoked for future rations, they wished for more meat and more flour for cakes and biscuits. They needed more clothes, more shoes, more horses. They'd used what they could of what was available at the house, and to get more, they'd have to leave the cocoon of wellbeing that was the farmstead.

Sully, knowing the local territory the best, drew up a plan to help them secure not only more supplies, but permanent safety. It was a plan of blood, for that was the thing she knew best.

Ziza had called this place their home, but what was a home if it could be scooped out from under them at any moment? If someone else could come and take the papers? If whenever any of them needed anything, they had to live in fear of discovery by the townsfolk who wouldn't look well on a former slave and other dark folk occupying a property in a white family's name?

It was no way to live, and if it was Sully's last deed on this earth, she'd make the killing of the Missus and her family worth more than just her own peace of mind—because it hadn't even garnered her that. Sully was a lost cause, but these folks could be happy here if she made it into a proper dwelling for them. Ziza could be happy.

"I'll do this alone," Sully said as she explained her plan to others. She would raise an army, an army of revenants.

Liza Jane shook her head. "Don't talk nonsense." She had a strong island accent that Sully loved. She'd stayed up many nights listening to Liza Jane's tales about how she had escaped her plantation as a teenager and lived most of her remaining years as a pirate on a ship called the *Red Colossus*. "We are brave," she said. "We'll do whatever you say."

Miles nodded his head and so did Bethie. Nathaniel, looking sage with his gray hair and knowing eyes, said, "You will never be alone again, Miss Sully."

So be it.

For several weeks, they raided the nicest wagons that passed by along the main roads, stealing their supplies, bringing the drivers and passengers back to the farmstead for Sully to kill. For each body disposed of in this way, Sully birthed a ghost. She numbed to the agonizing pain of labor and let herself be comforted by Ziza's vast knowledge. She spoke of a goddess named Artemis who watched over young girls, unwed women, wild animals, the wilderness. "You could be like her, don't you think?" said Ziza.

Sully was laid up in bed where she'd spent the last several weeks. The constant birthing had worn her to bone. The killing, too, hurt. "Army or not, I can't do this anymore," said Sully, worried she'd disappoint Ziza, but Ziza only nodded and took Sully's hand in hers, kissing several times so tenderly, like no woman was supposed to do to another. It made Sully shiver.

"I think we've got enough now anyway for your plan to work. There's twenty-six of us in all," Ziza said. She dipped a cloth into a bowl of hot water and pressed it to Sully's head. "I'll fetch Miles and tell him he can go into town to start the next phase."

The plan was for him to tell the sheriff about all the murdered folk at the farmstead, and when the sheriff led his troops here, they'd mount a full-on attack on their home territory. Take them by surprise. They didn't know how great their number was. They didn't know what weapons they'd raided, what traps they'd set. "We'll be able to take over the town and make a fortress of it. We'll be safe, and we'll make a place where others can be safe, too," said Ziza, squeezing Sully's hand tight in reassurance.

Sully wept in Ziza's arms. She didn't know where the tears came from or why they fell. Everything was going her way. Having killed twenty-six and birthed twenty-six, the count was even. She didn't have to fear another tumultuous labor.

"I'll stay here with you as long as you want," said Ziza, that warm smile that was always there shining brightly at Sully.

"You should go help. I want you to go," said Sully. "You been here the longest. You're the one who can lead them."

Ziza's smile began to waver as she worried her bottom lip. "I'll go," she said, "but you stay right up in here, you understand? If you leave, there's a chance you could get caught in the cross fires. You might kill someone by mistake and then have to bring another back. Your body needs rest."

It was dark when Ziza finally went and the sheriff came with his cavalry. Sully let herself drift in and out of consciousness. She awoke to the sound of shots firing. She saw the spark of a blaze.

Their entire property had been booby-trapped, sharpened branches primed to raise up and stab any person or horse who tried to get through. Sully heard their cries of pain.

When the night grew more silent, she stumbled out of bed and into a pair of old boots. She walked down the stairs and out the front door. She saw Miles running toward her, a hand on top his head to keep his floppy sun hat from falling off.

"Miss Sully," he called, out of breath. With only the moon as light, she couldn't see whether he was injured or if his clothes were stained with blood.

"They're all dead," he said then whooped and laughed and ran up to her to give her a hug. She patted his back and told him to go inside and wash his face. It seemed like a big-sisterly thing to tell a boy.

Sully walked to the barn where the weapons for slaughter were kept, where she used to sleep. Inside was the blade she'd used to kill the Missus. She felt nothing as she touched it, neither relief nor rage. Any memories she had associated with the event sat inside her unrecalled. The battle with the townspeople had been won, but Sully couldn't answer why that mattered.

There existed a depth of loneliness so profound that once experienced, no matter how briefly, trust in life could not be restored. Sully took a knife and stabbed it in her gut just above her uterus then carved a large circle around the organ. She removed it from her body and dug a shallow grave with her hands, buried it there as she bled out. When she died, at least the others might be able to use the etherworld that had made her uterus into a portal.

"Sully!" she heard. "Sully!"

She had a feeling she was already gone, that she was hearing Ziza call her from the other side. There it was, that feeling Ziza described. Drowning.

Sully was cold and heavy, and she felt her body struggle to lift itself up. After a few seconds of trying, she gave up.

"No, no, no, no, no, no," said Ziza, grasping Sully's body, her voice fading until it was all gone.

Sully wanted to say sorry, but she didn't know words anymore. Was time passing? Was she wrapped in rope? Was the feeling of dying eternal? All these thoughts came as nightmare visions as she glided through a fog.

Forever passed by, then—

Sully felt heat. She felt water. She felt something squeezing her, choking her nearly.

Sully was being born.

She opened her eyes to find herself on a patch of dirt, Ziza above her.

"Oh, my Sully," Ziza said. She kissed Sully's face, a hot streak of tears wetting Sully's cheeks.

"I don't understand," said Sully. She looked around and smelled the air. It felt as if no time had passed. The scent of gunpowder poisoned the air.

"You were born again through your own womb," Ziza said, face stunned into a bewildered frown. She'd never looked so shaken. "You were only gone a minute. Then I heard the earth crying. I dug it up and there you were."

Miles came and tossed a blanket over Sully. A young man named Dominic carried her to her bed. Others doted on her. They brought her medicine. They brought her food. When the initial commotion of her birth had passed, she asked all but Ziza to go.

Sully expected her to say something like, "What makes you think I don't want to go, too," or, "Like I want to be here with your fool ass," but she hummed to herself in the rocking chair in the corner of the room.

What bothered Sully most about Ziza's relentless happiness was that it was not the result of obliviousness, naivete, or ignorance. It was a happiness that knew pain and had overcome it.

"How come you smile so much?" Sully asked.

Ziza walked to the edge of Sully's bed and took a seat, her bottom a few inches from Sully's feet. "Just always been like that," she said.

"I don't know how to feel nice."

"You're not a nice-feeling kind of person. I suppose that's not who you're meant to be. That's all right. I like you mean and crotchety," said Ziza.

"In another life I could've been sweet. I could've been just as happy and sweet as you, had it been different. Had everything been different. Had the world been different," Sully said, wiping a stray tear from the corner of her eye.

"We're already on our second lives. I don't think there's anything different," said Ziza.

Sully held a pillow tight to her chest. "I'm bored of hurting," she said. She thought of the ancestors she'd vesseled and brought back to life with the baptizing waters of her womb's amniotic fluid. With Ziza, she'd cultivated a small sanctuary for them on this farm, a sanctuary that would grow to include the nearby town. But it was not enough. She needed the whole world for them.

Before, Sully thought it was her lack of want for anything that made her feel so shapeless and void, but her relief at seeing Ziza upon her rebirth upended that notion. She wasn't numb for lack of want but for wanting too much. She was ravenous for the whole world. The sky and the oceans and the creatures in those oceans and the cities and heartbeats and Ziza and Miles and Bethie and Liza Jane and Nathaniel and the mountains and brass and harps and pianos and wildflowers and glaciers and brothers and sisters and cousins and picnics and the sun and telescopes and a treehouse and sausage and winter and the height of summer, when the air was so thick it stuck to your skin like pecan brittle in your back teeth.

Even as she imagined possessing all these things, she wanted yet more. It was strange, she thought, how limitless a void inside of a person could be. It was strange that a person could be killed, but not anything that that person had done.

Ziza scooted up on the bed and laid her hand on top of Sully's and hummed a hymn about battle. The pitches were low, and the key was minor, a haunting caress of song against Sully's skin. How many moments like this would it take for her raucous, angry soul to be soothed? How many songs? Were there enough in the world?

When the song finished, Ziza climbed into the bed with Sully and held her close. She sang yet more, no theme uniting which tunes she chose. Sully let a single hot tear fall onto Ziza's hand when she understood her spirit would never know true soothing, but wrapped up in Ziza, she saw pinpricks of true glory, a grace big enough to make it worth it. Perhaps there would not be peace, but there would be Ziza, and with Ziza, there was a future. Ziza hummed on, and in that moment, Sully was content just to listen.

In addition to appearing on the Stonewall Honor List and winning a Firecracker Award, **RIVERS SOLOMON**'s debut novel *An Unkindness of Ghosts* was a finalist for a Lambda, a Hurston/Wright, a Tiptree, and a Locus Award, and has been included in numerous best-of-the-year lists, including those from NPR, *Publishers Weekly*, and *The Guardian* (UK). Solomon's short work appears in *Black Warrior Review*, the *New York Times*, *Guernica*, *Best American Short Stories*, Tor.com, and elsewhere. Their second book, *The Deep* (based on a song by Daveed Diggs, William Hutson, and Jonathan Snipes) was published in 2019. They grew up between California, Indiana, Texas, and New York but currently reside in the United Kingdom.

THE THING, WITH FEATHERS

MARISSA LINGEN

Val had lost hope.

Routine carried her where hope had stopped: up the stairs to tend the lamp. Into the forest for wood, apples, berries, more rarely a deer or a grouse. Her stores of magic and wild rice came from the same place, though not from the same method: the smaller, murky inland lake, the one too small to need a lighthouse, only the canoes and the flat-bottom boats of the rice harvest.

Her neighbors were willing to sell her the rice; willing, too, to watch her pick her way carefully out to the middle in her canoe alone. They never asked her about summoning the magic, though she glowed afterwards with the overflow, and they had reason to distrust things that glowed, these last eight years.

In fact, they never asked her anything. Asking was rude. Sometimes they told her things: how much for the rice. What day there would be fresh corn in from the farmlands, if she wanted any. How they thought the winter would be. (Cold. Wet. Bad. Always bad.) Once, something funny the baby did—but only once, and that felt like too much.

Val told them things too. Mostly lake things. How the water was settling, what ships had gone by. Whether anything had come out of it they should watch for. Not so many things as they told her.

Then she went home, up the lighthouse tower, full of magic, bags of wild rice on her shoulders, and sometimes inland farm vegetables she'd traded for. Before she was more than a tall tree's fall into the forest, the deep silence had enveloped her, and she was home again.

The route home had gotten longer when the last of the old road crumbled and she had to pick her way through slough instead of walking over the concrete no one could make any more. It got shorter again when she and the neighbors combined their expertise to convince the nesting mallards to nest somewhere else so she didn't have to worry about the hissing remnants of their egg shards.

Someone else might have found that balance hopeful, but Val just nodded; things changed, not with a direction, just changed. The mallards were dissolving something else now; they had not returned to their pre-event waddling placidity.

It would have been easier with hope.

But the ships deserved not to run into the rocks, even if Val didn't expect anything much of the world or the people in it. The new things coming out of the lake often came in the dark, and they couldn't all see in it, and some of them—some few—deserved a light to crawl by. And where they would find another lighthouse keeper this late in the age of the world, Val could not begin to guess.

One fall afternoon, when the chill had bitten into the wind but the ice had not yet glossed even the small lake, much less the edges of the big one, a very small boat put in at the lighthouse pier. Val did not see it at first—fall meant longer nights tending to the light and more tasks to stock the lighthouse for winter. So instead of seeing the boat, she saw, at the very first, a pair of boots as she came out of the forest with her arms full of wood.

"Hello?" she said sharply around the wood.

"Hello, are you the lighthouse keeper?" The voice was scratchy, tenor, further east than the lake but not jarringly so. Cheerful.

Val set the wood on the woodpile, turned back carefully. She had no reason to be afraid. The magic of the lake was still strong in her for weeks yet, barring emergency, and the lighthouse grounds were her own. When she could see more than boots, the man's face was cheerful as his voice, a large pointed nose, spectacles of the wire design that were the only kind made, after. Dark curls touched with gray, a battered hat, smile lines. Few enough had managed smile lines, after.

"I'm Val, the lighthouse keeper. Yes."

"Lucian," he said. "Your old friend Mik said you might be able to help me. I've lost my hand connection to my magic. My wrist connection, actually. It's a bit awkward." He held his arms out, smiling.

He was not reaching for her. Val stepped back all the same. "Mik," she said, shaking her head. "I don't do that work anymore. Not for a very long time." Long enough, in fact, that Mik's name made her blink.

The stranger, Lucian, was undaunted. "But you *can* still?" he said.

"I don't know."

"Is there a guest house near here I can stay while we think it through, or a good sheltered spot to set up my tent?"

She wanted to tell him that there was no we here, no thinking to be done, only winter coming on to the big lake and its lighthouse, only chores to do and vanishing light to do them in. But he had not presumed upon her own space, which made her paradoxically more willing to share it. Even if it was only until the lake was clear to take him back again.

After all, he was a friend of Mik's. And she missed the time when that had meant something to her.

"There's a guest room on the ground floor," she said. "You can haul water for me. I don't promise anything."

He grinned, and the lines around his eyes deepened like they knew what they were doing. "Excellent. Mik said—"

"The me Mik knew was another person. Another life." She hesitated, but he had come by water, perhaps he would understand. "A river person, yes? I am a lake person. Don't think of what Mik said of me."

"Only of what you say." He nodded and shouldered his pack, keeping brisk pace with her into the lighthouse. She smiled up at him despite herself.

Supper was hollowed-out acorn squash stuffed with bacon, wild rice, dried cherries, sage leaves, hazelnuts, blueberries. Lucian scraped the squash skin clean.

And he asked *questions*. He had understood her right away, not to ask about Mik or the city or the days before. But that left more than Val had remembered there could be questions about. Birds, to her surprise and delight—the ordinary kind. She thought a great deal about the shorebirds but had said none of it aloud. No one had wanted to hear about trading the fall shorebirds for the winter-nesting ducks and gulls unless there was something altered about them.

"The ones with the little white apostrophes on their eyes," said Lucian, following Val up the stairs. "They're—" He stopped, both speech and action, and Val knew why.

She continued calmly up, taking the beacon oil trigger out of its housing. The dark would not wait. "Scoters. Yes, they're immensely more common since the event. I think they—well, there's something with the magic. I don't know what it is. They don't eat it in the sense of making permanently less of it. It might make their eggs stronger. They're the . . . the boundary birds, scoters. The boundary between the birds that were affected and the ones that weren't."

"That makes sense. About the eggs," Lucian said, watching her move with the efficiency of long practice. Val thought he was watching for a place where he could be helpful, but everything from wick to housing case was a step she had taken every evening, same fire, same wood, same glass, same magic, and was difficult to improve upon.

And she had mentioned the event, leaving him uncertain where her boundaries were, what he was allowed to say.

There was only one chair in the lamp room, but when Val had finished her evening ritual, she took pity on Lucian and said, "You can haul one up from the kitchen. If you like. Not the one I used."

He nodded and strode off down the steps, grateful for something to do. The chair scraped on the stone stairs, but they both emerged unscathed.

Val realized that she didn't do so much smiling on ordinary days. Tried to suppress it. Gave up.

They sat together at the big wooden table where Val kept her ship log—increasingly useless, she felt sure—and her private account of which creatures she spotted in the water—and of course her log of birds. In addition there were two stone game sets, of which Val had made solitaire game rules. She thought for a moment she might have to remind herself of the rules of playing stone games with another person, Mancala and the other one whose name she couldn't even remember.

But no, Lucian gently, shyly, asked about her private log. Not the birds that had kept their supper conversation so easy—but there had been that easy supper conversation, and so she slid the log across the table at him and stared out at the sun's last dying reflections across the water as he read silently.

He was perhaps thirty pages into her increasingly eccentric hand, and it full dark, when she realized that he had not turned any pages in some time. She glanced over. His chin was on his chest. She watched him sleep a moment—not looking young, exactly, still a grown man with a full life's experience written on his face. But unburdened. She wondered if she ever looked like that. She nudged his boot with her toe.

"Lucian," she said in a firm clear voice, when he didn't stir. "Lucian, I have to stay up the night with the lighthouse. You don't. Go on down to bed, I showed you where."

"Thank you for your indulgence," he murmured, his voice low and fuzzy with sleep. She waved him off impatiently and listened that he didn't break his neck on the stairs. It was odd having another person in the place, another breath and pair of hands, but not bad-odd. Nice.

It was only then that she realized she hadn't said a word about him leaving in the morning.

She stared at water and did not think of the work she used to do in the city.

Dawn ended Val's shift with the light, so it was late morning before she woke up again—an entirely ordinary time. For a moment she thought Lucian might have gone on his own, not finding what he sought from Mik's lighthouse keeper, and—relieved, disappointed—she sat up. But there was a reedy tenor humming softly in the kitchen. She reached for a sweater.

She found him contemplating a bag of gray powder in the pantry. "Good morning," he said. "I had travel supplies from my pack, but I'll gladly cook if you'll tell me—what's this?"

"Wild rice flour," she said. "Tasty stuff, but the griddlecakes you make with it come out looking like . . . well, you read through page fourteen before falling asleep."

"Page—oh." She watched him remember the tentacular beast that had climbed first the rocks and then the lighthouse itself before Val had ascertained that communication was either impossible or, at the very least, not desired by the other party. Lucian rallied. "Griddlecakes, you say. I can do that."

It turned out he could. And with hot butter and blueberry preserves on her fingers, Val was forced to ask herself why she had planned to send him packing so quickly in the first place.

She gave in. "Mik has never been up here."

Lucian looked startled but responded quickly. "I gathered."

"Mik has no idea what it's like."

He tapped her log book. "Well, no, although the river—"

"More basic than that. The light comes first. You understand? Anything else we do, the light comes *first*. You break both legs, I break both legs . . . we help each other crawl to get the light lit."

He thought about that. Nodded. "All right."

"Preparation for winter comes second, because when the lake ices over—the little one where I get my magic—and the trail snows in, I had better be stocked. Some winters I get shoveled out a few times. Not all."

"And if you're not prepared, you die."

She glared at him. "And if I'm not prepared, I die and *the light goes out*."

He flinched.

"So. We take care of these things. And then if we have any time or energy left—and if I have any ideas—we see about your wrists. Deal?" She sounded harsh to her own ears, but he was nodding vigorously before she had finished speaking.

"There are no guarantees, I know that," he said. "But even just the hope of something to help a little—"

She turned to the dishes so he wouldn't see her face. She was pretty sure he noticed, but he let her get away with not telling him about it, not having to have emotions right then, at least not openly. He didn't make her regret letting him stay.

It was a start.

The wood was a task Val mostly did without magic, so she could delegate that to Lucian right away upon discovering that he knew his way around an axe. She was not surprised, given his method of arrival, that he was also familiar with both catching fresh fish and tending to the salted ones in the drying process—but whether she should send him back out on the big lake in its current state without magical protections was another question.

Lucian was impatient with this response. "I got this far on my own without hovering," he protested.

Val gave him a flat look. "You wanted to read my logbook. Apparently you didn't want to think about it. You came this far to ask for my help—well, now you *have* asked. I'm not inclined to cast you to the harlequins for it."

"The harlequins!" he said. "What, the ducks?"

She pressed her lips together. "It's their lake now, and if you haven't the sense to know that, go gather blackberries until you've learned better."

The blackberries were near the end of their season, but he came back with so many apples—so many kinds of apple—to make up for it that she relented and started work on his wrists after supper, after the lamp was lit, before Lucian was ready to fall over in exhaustion.

She took each in her opposite hand, crossing them, which made him smile. Val remained serious. The smile dropped off Lucian's face. His wrists were thin but not spindly, solid enough. She dipped into her magic supply and washed it around them from the outside. No structural defect, nothing organic.

"When did this happen?" she asked.

"When?" he said, but it was not confusion—a hesitation, a play for time.

"What stupid thing were you attempting," she pushed.

His brown skin flushed pink.

"What pointless—"

"It wasn't pointless!"

She held his wrists in her hands. Waited.

"The slough, it, we were trying—"

She waited a moment longer, but from the way his mouth had twisted, he would need to be prompted again. "You and Mik."

"And Mik's friend Rhoda," Lucian went on, amiable as a child, and then stopped again, a child hitting a wall of nightmare. "Rhoda isn't . . . Rhoda couldn't make the trip."

Val did not let herself drop his wrists, but she closed her eyes and silently cursed Mik and his relentless hope and his apparently bullet-proof luck, that the things that came out of a unified slough never, ever came for him, but always for the person next to him.

She checked the lamp. First priority, last priority. It glowed steady and sure. While the waters of the big lake were rougher than the day Lucian had come in, louder, fiercer, nothing disturbed their surface but themselves. She could take the time she needed to start this.

She had no idea what time she would need to finish it. If in fact she could.

The power that she slipped into Lucian's wrists was cool and felt to her as myrtle smelled. She did not expect to ever be far enough south to smell myrtle again. Lucian hissed as it went down his elbows and pooled at the end of his arms, with no way for him to handle it.

She worked at it slowly, like pulling taffy that was uncomfortably cold to handle instead of burning hot. Lucian swallowed hard and audibly. Val shifted her weight from one foot to the other and persevered. Her magic dispersed into Lucian gradually, like a scent drifting out a kitchen window, like blood spilled in water. Lucian tossed his head like a toddler refusing to wake from a nightmare. She soothed the last bit of magic in.

Val broke off. "That's all for tonight. Go put them under the covers, keep them warm." She had been using such childhood metaphors to think of him that she half-expected the protests of a much-younger man, but instead he nodded thoughtfully and bid her good night.

And she was left with the question: what was she healing him *for*? If she repaired his ability to use magic, would she just be sending this man, who did his share of the cooking and understood when enough had to be enough, back into the thick of the idiotic intentions of Mik, or someone like him?

Would sending him back into the world as it was be any better if he had one less way to cope with it? or to try?

Damn Mik anyway, for not just quarantining that slough. Damn him for fighting.

She could have cheerfully damned Mik for the rest of the night, had the lake not interfered.

First there were the scoters: barely visible in the dark except when the lighthouse's beam caught the white punctuation of their eye-feathers. They marched the shore in a self-important and un-birdlike file. They kept silence and gave the lighthouse wide berth. Val noted them as best she could without looking away from the waters.

Then the water roiled and churned, as if it was boiling, but without the clouds of steam that had risen from the lake when sections had boiled the spring before. The water was unsettled. So was Val.

The hiss that rose from it was not the birds she was used to, nor the giant monster she had feared. It was a cloud, like midges but directed, angry, purposeful. She held her breath. But whatever their purpose was, it was out over the waters, not the lighthouse.

The lake calmed.

Val let her wholly inadequate defensive spells subside.

She cursed Mik's name once more for good measure.

The lamp needed almost an entire extra night worth of oil and magic, as though the insects had sucked it dry in their passing. Val pulled it out and started again. By the time she was done, she was too exhausted to be angry at anyone. Over the lake, somewhere, the flies remained, unless the birds had gotten them. She had at least three hours to stay awake until dawn, and Lucian's had been only the third water-craft since Midsummer. In the old days there would have been more than that in a night, more in an hour.

In the old days Val would never have kept the lighthouse to see them. She would have been down in the city, rushing around with city people, doing city things, choking on city air. In the old days, she would have hoped for a thousand trivial things, and several big ones, and not even noticed when one hope passed on into another.

She played a restless solitaire game with the Mancala set. Lost. Lost another. Started to juggle the pebbles in midair, without her hands, and made herself stop; who knew what magic she would need to heal Lucian, to deal with the birds and the flies and whatever else came out of the big lake. She might not have the time to harvest in the rice lake again in time. She couldn't afford to be profligate.

There was no reason to be resentful about a habit of mind she would have cultivated anyway. Nevertheless, she was.

Resentful felt better than fearful.

Dawn was not any later than usual, but it felt that way, with her knees tucked under her chin, coiled, waiting.

The next day, she didn't talk to Lucian at all until he came in from the woods smelling of ginger and glowing a bright orange. He had such a bemused look that although Val knew that these were very grave signs indeed, she burst out laughing.

"We need to talk about your turkeys," he said in tones of utter disgust.

"I think you've just found that they are not meaningfully *my* turkeys," said Val, snorting back another laugh.

"They seemed like—look, I've hunted pheasant before, down on the prairies."

The laughter drained out of Val. "How long ago was this? Are they still prairies now?" He opened his mouth to answer, but she raised her hand to stop him. "No. *No*. You have to—you haven't been listening. You went through whatever you did in the slough—you're not some callow child—and you don't talk to the locals about the birds? You just go after a turkey because it's sort of—it's *not* sort of like a pheasant, even before the event, it was nothing like a pheasant, how can you not know that!"

A small silence. "I do know that."

"Then how could you—"

"The protein on one of those things—"

"The *magic* on one of those things—"

"The *protein* on one of those things would have bought us time to work. Time to work with whatever magics you needed. It's not—I see how close you run things here. I see how tired you are."

Val sat down in her own chair, at her own kitchen table, everything familiar except the sense of being seen.

"Why are you so angry at me?" said Lucian gently, sitting down with her, his orange glow pulsing in a way that Val felt she should find ridiculous but could not.

"You are so determined to die," she said, and he pulled back in horror, but she continued: "So determined to fling yourself at things that *will* kill you. I can fix your wrists. Maybe. With time. I think I can remember how. I think what I'm doing will work. But that—that I can't fix."

Lucian was silent a very long time. Val got up and fetched a pitcher of lake water, uncleansed by magic or fine stones, and some dried violets. She crumbled the flowers into the water, briskly, and flicked it at him. He sputtered. She didn't laugh.

"I don't want to die," said Lucian.

Val got up and flicked the water at the back of his head, his back. She gave his shoulder a rough shove, and he obediently stood. She kept flicking. Circled back to the front. He pulled his spectacles off and let her douse him thoroughly.

"I don't want to die," he repeated, and finally the orange glow flickered and went out. He heaved a sigh and sank back into the chair. "That's not what this is, I'm not trying—look. You fight in your own way. You have this post, this lighthouse, it's your most important thing. I don't have a lighthouse. I just have to keep trying with whatever I find."

"The lighthouse," she enunciated carefully, "is not going to kill me."

"It might."

She folded her arms.

"There are fortresses, places where people like you—people like us—have built much bigger walls against—against what's out there. Then you have in the lighthouse. You could go live in one of those."

Val felt herself relaxing, almost against her will. "Ah," she said. She sat back in her chair across from him.

"So you do understand, it's just a matter of—"

"I don't believe in those."

Lucian nodded vigorously. "It's not right to lock yourself in while the rest of the world, the less privileged world—"

"I don't believe they'll work. Those places will be hunting grounds as soon as something wants them."

Val appreciated that Lucian didn't actually let his jaw drop, but his mouth did open slightly. "Then—you—"

All her anger seemed to have left her. "I would really prefer that you were not hunted with them," she said. "I would prefer not to put the time and effort into healing you only to have you hurl yourself into the maw of—of—turkeys. Or something that would like you to think it's a flock of turkeys."

"Which do you think it is?"

"I don't know."

They sat in a pleasant and companionable silence for long enough that he might have been one of the neighbors, long enough that Val wondered if she would have to break it to see to chores. Instead, Lucian said, "Why are you healing me?"

"I don't like for things to be broken."

He waited.

"There's very little I think I can do, but this—this is one. And I won't have you breaking it again."

"What will you have, then?"

"What?"

He stretched his legs out before him and gave her a long, challenging look over his spectacles. "If you don't want to heal my magic for use, what *is* it for?"

Val snorted out an exasperated breath and began to slam her way around the pantry, choosing parts of a meal she wouldn't have to focus on but could pretend to. "Sensible use," she said when the onion was chopped. "Not futile. Not risking yourself for nothing."

"It's not nothing."

"It is if you could have found out first."

"But there's so much to find out."

Val sighed and handed him potato after potato, loading them into his arm where it bent against his body. "I know."

When she went to work on his wrists again that night, she could feel the difference. There was still no flow-through, nothing like it—but she could feel everything was less raw, more human, more ready to grow.

Val was almost going to pull back—enough for one evening—when she felt Lucian's core reaching gently for her. Without access to his own hands, Lucian could do nothing . . . unless Val helped him. She had not thought of it until he was there, not pushing, just waiting to see what she did.

She let the two of them mingle their strength so it could flow smoothly out her hands. She did let herself pick up the game stones this time, with no better plan in place than to float them in the air. His sigh was barely audible, relieved.

She carefully, gently disengaged.

"How long?" she asked, quietly, but in the quiet that had fallen between them it echoed.

"Five months. And you?"

She did not pretend to misunderstand. "As many years. Go rest?"

There were no swarms that night, no line of fowl to point the way to a disturbance. The low hum that came from farther down the coast, to the southeast, did nothing to calm Val's nerves, but it helped her to stay awake. She was not properly grateful.

In the morning, Lucian was. Not only was there porridge, but he asked clearly about his foraging plan instead of charging off to offend the neighbors. He also asked rather than reorganizing her linen storage, but his idea was far better than the one she had inherited from the previous lighthouse keeper, and they did the reorganization together cheerfully and efficiently.

Val realized that he didn't remind her of anyone from her days in the city. Not a single person.

She already knew that she didn't want to be reminded of any of them.

Her shoulders relaxed a bit more, and she laughed at the expressive way he twisted his face when the shelves came loose. She watched his hands move. She watched how he tilted his head in consideration.

It had been a long time since consideration had meant anything different from contemplation.

There was cheerful work around the lighthouse, congenial quiet, the waves making peaceful and ordinary lake sounds, gulls being gulls without pretensions to anything more.

Val felt guilty for her conviction that it couldn't last.

It didn't.

The honking of the V of wild geese made her flinch and scurry for cover. The stone walls of the lighthouse felt flimsy, and there were so many geese. She could hear them even inside. It had been a long week already. No one needed geese. The honking continued. Val knew there must be a second wing of them coming, a third, more.

She looked around the interior of the lighthouse. Lucian was coming out of the bedroom she had begun to think of as his. She took a ragged breath to explain. "The geese are—"

"They migrate. I know them," he said. "The ones down in the city shift, do yours shift?"

Val nodded tersely.

"Not to human like the swans."

"No."

Lucian grimaced. "Wish there was something I could—"

"Stay inside. Stay safe."

He looked out the windows, at the skies darkening with wings. "I keep thinking, there has to be some reason it's geese. Whatever it is that's . . . transformed them, become them, whatever it is. They could have been crows or sparrows or something. Why geese?"

Val felt she should rush off to handle the geese, but the question stopped her. "They're strong," she said slowly. "And they flock . . . I mean, crows work together, back in the old days I saw them working to drive a marsh hawk off a meadow to take its eggs. I didn't know it was called that then, I didn't know what they wanted." Internally she cursed herself for the tangent, but Lucian was nodding.

"A lot of us didn't. The species, the names, we just . . . didn't. So when they turned like this, after the event—" She shook her head. "I have to deal with this now."

"I know, I know."

Val climbed to the tower, and Lucian followed without being

invited. Upon reflection she decided she hadn't asked him to stay out either. So that was all right. He was quiet, in the corner. Like a back-stop.

The geese were not. The geese were not flying on but circling around the lighthouse, blotting out the sunlight. Probably it was not personal, Val told herself. Probably the magic was like an odor. She made the place smell delicious.

It felt wrong to be in the lighthouse tower in the dark and not light the lamp. And yet that was not the good she could do now.

If there was any good she could do now.

Goose wings buffeted stone solidly. It had to hurt them, but they kept at it, pushed, perhaps, by the bodies of their flock. Then they slurped and shifted together, wing eating wing. Val felt more than heard Lucian's breath draw in, with the cacophony outside.

The merging goose flock thumped and squeezed the tower. The stones creaked. And finally, with no particular hope for it, Val released a spell out the window of the lamp.

The seething, grabbing mass that had been geese let out a thin honk and then a hum that modulated down to the noise of the night before. It jangled Val's nerves and made her teeth ache. The former goosemass buckled back in front of the lamp. Val wanted to think she was killing it, or at least driving it away, but though she kept the pressure on, she never punched a hole through, never saw daylight. There was always more goose mass to patch it with, and more.

The honking and humming was deafening. Her ears rang, popped, kept ringing.

Val let the spell fall, panting. Simply battering at them wasn't working. She remembered the days before the event, a creased science journal in a waiting room, when there were still waiting rooms, when waiting was something that didn't come with chopping and carving and mending. It said something about magnetic fields. She modified the spell to make one of her own, to interfere with whatever remained of goose in the mass outside the lighthouse.

The honk aligned itself in pain, fear. But the geese kept coming.

She could feel the magic she'd harvested from the rice lake

dwindling. Soon there would be only her own body's supply left, and what she would do to live, and light the lamp, after that, she didn't know.

Lucian's hand was on her wrist, then his other hand on her other wrist, from behind her, the entire length of him warm against her back. It would have been too much to ask of herself not to think of flinching—but she didn't *actually* flinch, and that was something, something that would have been beyond notable—huge—were it not that she understood what he was offering, and it was far beyond.

She wrapped his magic into her own and drew from his body instead.

Finally there was a pinprick of daylight—fading daylight, reflected setting sunlight—through the squeezing, squirming mass. The hum modulated into a dissonant chord. Val pressed their advantage, forcing the breach wider, longer.

With a shriek of scraping slates and a splash of ruptured organs, the goosemass went down.

Lucian let go of her wrists.

"Wood," Val gasped, and he understood her immediately, leaping for the stairs with such boneless alacrity she was afraid he would fall. She built the fire for the lamp's backup to take almost all wood, only the tiniest spark of magic, which she gave it and promptly passed out.

It was full dark when she awakened in her own bed. It had been so many years since she slept in the dark in her bed that it was terrifying to awaken that way. But Lucian must have put her there, she realized after the first moment's shock. She raked a hand through her sleep-mussed hair and padded up to find him.

"Does this happen often," he said, not turning away from the lamp. It burned hot and clear with the fire he was maintaining.

"Not precisely this."

"Imprecisely."

"You know it does."

He was silent a long time. "I had hoped that cities—the pollution—"

"Well, that's the thing about pollution, isn't it? It never stays in one convenient place. And farms and mines and logging concerns polluted plenty, back in the day. I don't know that pollution caused the event, but if it did, we're not safe here. Or anywhere."

The big lake made its deceptive placid lapping sounds against the rocks.

"I would like to stay here and help you," said Lucian in a low voice. "Once you've healed me. We work well together, if last night is any hint. I think we could work even better when I'm at full strength, and I think—forgive me—I think you could use the help."

Val looked for her indignation and found it missing. "I thought you wanted to fight in the cities."

"This is a fight too. And—you are a fight too."

She glared at him.

"We beat the geese."

"We did. There will be more." But for the first time, she could let herself think ahead, plan, even hope beyond the light. She flexed her wrists. "All right. I'm going to have to harvest magic again today. You might as well come to see where it grows. We'll see how this works out."

He didn't try to kiss her. She didn't move to kiss him. There was space that they might fill with that, or they might not. For the time, it could be filled with a magic harvest in the rice lake, and clearing a path to the forest through the goose corpses, and hope.

MARISSA LINGEN is among the top science fiction and fantasy writers in the world who were named after fruit. Her stories have been published in venues including *Analog*, *Beneath Ceaseless Skies*, *Fireside Fiction*, *Nature*, and *Uncanny*. She lives atop the oldest bedrock in the US with two large men and one small dog, where she writes, if not daily, frequently.

SOME KIND OF BLOOD-SOAKED FUTURE

CARLIE ST. GEORGE

Here's the thing about surviving a slumber party massacre: no one really wants you around anymore. All your friends are dead, and your mom is dead, and you get shuffled off to live with your miserable Aunt Katherine, who blames you for getting her sister killed because she's an awful human being like that. And you try to move on, but you don't know how because your nightmares are constant and therapy is hard, especially when a new killer arrives and murders your therapist with his own pencil. You survive that massacre, too—this one's on a field trip—but nobody cares that you saved some band kid's life because, clearly, you're cursed and should just leave town. Even the band kid isn't grateful, that pimpled little shit.

So, you leave town. But first, you rob your aunt blind.

Here's the thing about leaving town: you start getting scared everyone's right.

You're living in your car, which at first is pretty fun, right up until you realize you don't have a diploma or a GED, and your entire work history is three months at a shitty diner, a job you still had to have a home address and three personal references to even apply for. Also, it's four in the morning and you really have to pee, but it's pouring and you're alone, parked on some dark road near a forest full of howling things. Your only choices are either to brave the storm or finish the bottle of Gatorade and awkwardly squat over it in your back seat; you try the latter and end up with a mess, which means your car now smells like pee, which means your home now smells like pee, and you just want to give up, drive home, and admit defeat. Aunt Katherine would never take you back, though; you'd probably enter the foster system and get some abusive church lady, or, worse, somebody wonderful, someone who doesn't know how to cook and earnestly fails at slang and lets you cry on her shoulder whenever you wake up screaming. And a month will pass, then two, and you'll think *it's over, it's okay, we're safe*, until one day you come downstairs to find New Mom at the table, an ax in the back of her head and blood pouring out of her mouth and into her cereal.

You can't let that happen to another mother. You can't let anyone else die because of you, which means this is it; this is your future: alone, in a smelly car, until you run out of money and die. No. You have to do something. You have to make a plan. A five-year plan, just like in school, only cross out applying for scholarships or taking the SATs. Replace them with . . . replace them with . . .

You can only think of the things you stole from Aunt Katherine, especially the gun.

But you're not ready. You're so scared. You fought so fucking hard to live.

Eventually, you fall asleep. In the morning, you drive to a new town. Buy an air freshener. Drink some coffee. Spot a flier for tonight's frat party. Your dead friends would've loved a party like that, would've begged you to sneak in with them. Peer pressure isn't really your problem anymore, though, so instead you drive south for hours. You only hear the news days later: FRAT HOUSE MASSACRE, 14 DEAD.

It's terrible. It's a tragedy. It's evidence you aren't to blame, that there's slaughter in this world that doesn't solely belong to you. You didn't talk to any of these dead guys. You aren't responsible for any of this—

But you can't stop thinking about that band kid.

Jesus, what an asshole. What a typical Nice Guy turd, and you could've let him die, but you didn't, and there's *power* in that. Maybe you'd have saved more people, if you'd gone to that party. Maybe if you came across the killer yourself . . .

Well. You're not going to find out anything sitting here.

You drive back and it might be suicidal, but at least it's suicidal in an active way? That sounds suspiciously unhealthy, but you're too busy to consider it further: the frat's sister house is planning a memorial kegger because nobody ever learns anything, because the definition of insanity is who the hell knows, but the definition of *willful ignorance* is doing the same thing over and over and expecting different results. Whatever. The important thing is, you smell bad, so you sneak in a shower at some public gym before heading over to the sorority house. Can you pass for eighteen? Nope. But everyone's drunk, so they let you in anyway.

You try to find the killer before any of the girls die. It doesn't work: one gets smothered with her own sorority flag, while another is chopped in half mid keg stand. But you do shoot the killer right in his creepy doll face before a freshman gets disemboweled. Well. Okay. She gets a *little* disemboweled, but she's still alive when the paramedics come, and that means she'll be okay, probably. Anyway, that's still a dozen girls without a scratch on them. All psychologically scarred, sure, but there are limits to what you can fix.

One of the drunk girls hides you until the cops leave, and there, under the bed, next to a bunch of dirty clothes and—gross—a used condom, you think, *well, it's a reason, anyway. It's some kind of blood-soaked future.*

Altruism isn't putting gas in your car, though, so you make that drunk girl give you a hundred dollars and some fancy Juicy Couture shit to replace your gory jeans.

Here's the thing about your new future: it's hard and it's sad, but mostly it works.

You drive from town to town, looking for signs. Wild parties. Incompetent sheriffs. Fatal pranks one-to-five years prior. It gets easier to spot them. Easier to spot the girls, too, the ones killers gravitate toward: nice girls, good grades. Virgins, all of them.

You used to have good grades. Used to be nice, too.

Virginity, though, is still your superpower. It doesn't keep you alive, but it improves your chances. It means you can kill the monster, or die trying. It means you die last. It means you find the bodies.

Most people find that sort of thing traumatic, though, so you try and help them avoid it. Find the impending massacre. Track down the virgin. Get them the fuck out of town and slay the monster in their stead.

It's not a career for everyone. It's hard on the clothes, and you can never have sex. But honestly, that last part's a bonus, because you're ace as fuck, and it's really rewarding how your sexuality comes with practical benefits like this. Doesn't pay great, though. Some can't afford much, even when they're grateful. Others are just assholes you have to persuade with your gun. Your mom would be pretty horrified; she didn't believe in violence, so that ax to the head must've been an especially big shock. But you need that money: for gas and tampons and laundromats and weapons. Food, too, although there's not always much left for that. You almost get killed once by some asshole in a Dobby mask—a *Dobby mask*—because you haven't eaten in two days and get dizzy when you try to stab him in the balls.

You make friends with this kid, José. You try not to make friends, but it happens sometimes: not all research can be done from the library, and you have to infiltrate the school: walk around, pretend you're a new student, duck whenever a vice principal walks your way. You interrogate José for gossip because he looks sharp. He secretly follows you back to your car because, well, you weren't wrong.

José tries to help you save virgin Zoe and the entire Valentine's Day Court. The King and Queen are lost causes, but everyone else would've been fine if the bucktoothed sheriff hadn't bust in and arrested you for vagrancy, among other things. Considering you were holding a hacksaw at the time, you're lucky he didn't just shoot you. Still, by the time José breaks you out, the killer has resurrected and killed the sheriff, two deputies, Zoe's boyfriend, and Zoe's mom.

You decapitate the killer. It doesn't feel like a win. You have an overwhelming urge to get so drunk you can't even see straight. That's sure what José does. You force him to drink water, get him into bed. He grabs your hand when you reach for the light.

Stay, he slurs into his pillow. *Please.*

You shush him gently, tell him he's okay, but he shakes his head and almost rolls off the bed. *YOU*, he says loudly, pointing. *Don't go. You're not. Don't . . .*

No one's ever asked you to stay before. Maybe you cry a little, but he's too drunk to notice.

It's not safe to stay, though, and anyway, he's wrong; you're doing fine.

Here's the thing about never sticking around: the towns all blur into one another until one day, about ten months after you ran away, you're back in California. You end up in this two-stoplight town where a grave-digger somehow impaled himself on his own shovel, but that was just an unfortunate accident, and those missing teenagers? Playing hooky, obviously. Can't be anything more than that: this isn't the big city, after all.

You find the virgin almost immediately. Actually, she finds you: Joey Santiago, seventeen, named after Josephine Baker and Joey Guerrero, and, she tells you confidentially, Joey Potter, too. You're not sure what to do with that information since you don't know who any of those people are, but she's already handing you a water bottle as you put your last five bucks in the tank. Apparently, Joey and her mom foster a houseful of rescue dogs, and you're the human equivalent of a sad, hungry puppy with a broken tail. She insists you come home for dinner.

Mrs. Norwood is a pretty black woman in her late thirties: tall, muscular, very short blond hair. She delicately asks if you'd like to use the shower, and finds you absurdly long pink pajamas to wear, and loads up your plate with more takeout than you've ever seen. *Don't worry about the cost, honey*, she says. *Just eat up, and maybe we can discuss your living situation tomorrow.*

You desperately want to go along with it. These people are so kind, and you're so tired, and these empanadas are so fucking good you're about to cry . . . but you can't risk it. Mrs. Norwood is black, and Joey is black and Filipina, and all PoC, but especially Asian people, are way more likely to die in these scenarios, virgins or not. Not to mention they live in a converted barn with bad cell reception and six dogs, and the only reason the killer isn't already here is that Joey's half-sisters live an hour away with their dad. There just aren't enough victims for a proper slaughterhouse.

So, you give it to them straight and wait for the inevitable questions about your sanity. Instead, Mrs. Norwood takes her daughter's hand and says, in this house, we believe in masked killers. Global warming, too. And Joey's trembling, but her eyes are focused. Will he leave me alone if I'm not a virgin? Because that's a social construct anyway, and my boyfriend lives five minutes away. And Mrs. Norwood makes a face, but that doesn't stop her from asking will that work? Because I do have condoms, and you vow to yourself, here and now, that you will protect these precious people at all costs.

Unfortunately, that's when the doorbell rings and six teenage girls pile in with presents and a Safeway birthday cake. Joey's surprise party is supposed to be tomorrow, but one girl has to babysit and another has some cheerleading competition, and before Mrs. Norwood can make them leave, the lights cut out, and a dog, barking loudly, suddenly goes quiet. *It's too late*, you say. *He's here.*

Two girls immediately assume it's a prank. You tell them they're wrong, and they say shitty things about you and mental asylums. Joey goes off, which is delightful but also poorly timed, as it distracts you from stopping the panicked cheerleader from running out the door. By the time Mrs. Norwood calms everyone down, it's clear the party isn't going anywhere: every car has a severed fuel line and the cheerleader has a severed head.

Everyone screams a lot.

You get them all back inside. That includes the dogs, even the little black one who's definitely losing that leg but, shockingly, isn't dead yet. It's been a while since you could afford bullets, but you gather every knife in the house, all except the kitchen shears, which have mysteriously gone missing. Then you gather the girls in the living room, trying to make it to dawn.

You make it fifty-seven minutes, just enough time for two pieces of birthday cake and a ton of high school gossip: Madison, the blonde who was an asshole to you, used to date Joey's boyfriend. Charlotte, the brunette who was an asshole to you, hates Sam for beating her in girls' javelin. Sam, the only other brown girl, thinks Emma's basic; also, a slut. Emma, who wears both terms proudly, might be cool if she didn't constantly say things like *I don't mean to be racist, but*. And the baby-sitter, well. You don't even know her name, since she hasn't spoken since the cheerleader died. Joey's efforts to comfort her go pretty well until Emma, completely ignoring everything you've said, gets too close to a window. She's quickly impaled through the gut, her body pulled outside.

The babysitter half-faints. You seal up the window, but now someone else is screaming: a guy, somewhere out back. Charlotte says it's her boyfriend, Jake, or maybe Joey's boyfriend, Tyler; they were both going to sneak over with beer after Mrs. Norwood went to bed. *We have to help them*, Charlotte insists, and runs out the back door into the dark. There's a strange, gurgling sound. Then, nothing.

Soon, someone emerges from the fog.

It's Tyler. *They're dead*, he says, bleeding from a non-vital place. *Oh God, oh God, they're dead.* You want to kill him right now, but no one else will let you. They won't even let you tie him up, an obviously reason-able concession, probably because he insinuates you're crazy and lesbian-obsessed with Joey. Madison apparently believes in homicidal lesbians so much that she actually attacks you; you twist her arms behind her and yell, *Joey, why are you friends with these horrible people?*

No one has a good answer to that, but Sam does ask where Tyler's car is. Tyler doesn't think it matters. The killer probably cut my fuel line, too, he says, but that only makes Joey back up. *We never told you about the cars*, she says, and Tyler's all *whoops* before he pulls Madison from you and stabs her in the face.

This time, it's not just the girls screaming; Tyler does too because he's one of *those* types, maniacally laughing as he slashes forward like a drunk Robin Hood. You don't bother dodging much, just slide a boning knife straight into his heart.

Oh, Tyler mouths, and dies.

So. Easy.

Mrs. Norwood hugs Joey, and Sam hugs the babysitter, and you just stand there, looking at your left arm. It hurts like a motherfucker—

Tyler cut it up pretty good—but there's only minimal blood on your pants and shirt.

Too. Easy.

It's not over, you say but Mrs. Norwood doesn't hear you, opens the back door. I'll check on the others, she says, and you scream—

But someone's already stabbed her with the kitchen shears.

The killer is tall and narrow, wearing a dark robe and a devil mask. Mrs. Norwood collapses at their feet, while Joey screams and Sam turns and runs. The killer breaks a nearby broom across the countertop and launches it forward. It spears through Sam's chest into the front door. She slumps over, half-hanging and dead.

You look back at Mrs. Norwood. For just a second, you can't move. For just a second, you're not even in this house at all.

But then she gets up.

Her skin is ashy, her forehead beaded with sweat. The shears are still embedded in her shoulder. But she's on her feet, and when Devil Mask stalks past, Mrs. Norwood tackles them into the dining room. Immediately, she collapses again, but it's enough to snap your brain back into action. You kick Devil Mask in the devil mask; they grab a chair and knock you into the living room. Something squelches unpleasantly underneath you. You think of a body exploding into blood and cream, but of course it's just Joey's half-eaten birthday cake.

Hands around your neck, then. You reach for something, anything. You can't breathe. You can't—but your fingers grasp something, even as you knock away the mask.

Of course. Asshole brunette. Girls javelin. Ran outside to "check" on her boyfriend.

Fuck you, Charlotte, you wheeze and stab the plastic cake fork in her eye.

Charlotte screams and reels back. She pulls an actual goddamn machete, but Joey kicks her in the head soccer style. The machete flies up in the air.

Still coughing, you catch it and shove it right through Charlotte's fucking lying mouth.

Now. Now you're covered in enough blood for it to be over.

It hurts to move. You do it anyway, staggering over to Charlotte's purse as inexplicable sirens wail nearby. Charlotte has ten bucks, which isn't enough to repair your car by a long shot. Tyler doesn't have any cash at all.

He does, however, have car keys.

Honey, Mrs. Norwood says weakly. *Your arm.*

Your arm's nothing. It's fine. You can do the stitches later yourself. Mrs. Norwood doesn't seem assured by that and tries getting up again, but she's woozy from blood loss and almost passes out. Joey, squeezing her hand, bursts into tears. Neither tries to pull out the scissors. You love them impossibly.

But they can't want you, feral thing that you are, and even if they did . . .

No. You couldn't risk it. You won't.

The babysitter makes a small noise. Right, you forgot she was still alive. You should take money from her, too, since she hasn't done anything productive all night, but she wasn't actually shitty to you, and you feel bad, robbing some traumatized kid. You tell her it'll be okay. The ambulance is almost here. They'll all be okay, probably.

You don't have to leave, Joey says—

But you do. Of course, you do.

Here's the thing about leaving: you end up in a town ten minutes outside home because that's where Tyler's truck runs out of gas.

You hop out with some vague idea of making it to the gas station; instead, you end up at the cemetery where your mother is buried at. And your best friend. And your four other friends, and their boyfriends, too. You're still wearing the bloody pink pajamas from two days ago, but it's midnight and no one's around to notice. Anyway, the important thing is talking to your mom, but what can you say? Sorry you're dead, Mom? Sorry I'm everything you didn't want me to be?

You've never been able to risk getting drunk before. But right now? You need to get so drunk you don't even remember your own name.

So, you take your ten bucks and buy the cheapest bottle of whiskey you can find. The cashier is freaked out by your clothes, but he's also really high; plus, selling to a minor, so hopefully, he won't call the cops on you. You hike back to the truck and start drinking. It tastes like ass. You keep drinking. It doesn't taste so bad. You keep drinking. It doesn't taste like anything. You keep drinking.

Someone gets into the passenger seat. You're probably about to die.

The person becomes Mrs. Norwood. You think, anyway; her face keeps rippling. A hallucination, then. That's nice. You can tell the truth to hallucinations; they already know all your secrets, anyway. You try and tell her lots of things, like what fire axes can do to human skulls or how you see your mom in your dreams sometimes, but her head splits open wider and wider each time she says she loves you. And then Mrs. Norwood's drinking from the bottle, which, when did she get the bottle? And you're outside somewhere, throwing up, and Mrs. Norwood's telling you it'll be okay, and you're lying down in the back seat of some car, and you can't see her, but she's still saying it.

You're okay, now. You're safe. Go to sleep. Go to sleep.

So you sleep.

Here's the thing about passing out in a car that you may or may not have hallucinated: you don't know where the fuck you are when you wake up, and Jesus Christ, you feel like shit. There's water next to your bed with a note that says DRINK ME, and you should absolutely not do that, but you're thirsty, so. If you open the door and get stabbed to death by a man in a Mad Hatter mask, you'll only have yourself to blame.

You open the door and are immediately attacked by six scrappy mutts. The smallest one only has three legs. You pick him up carefully and go downstairs.

Mrs. Norwood is in the kitchen, moving slowly. Carrying your drunk ass around couldn't have been any good for her shoulder. She serves you a plate of hangover food and only adds more each you time you protest. Eventually, you give up and eat it. *Where's Joey?* you ask.

At her Dad's, Mrs. Norwood tells you. *We're probably going to move. You're going to come with us.*

You almost choke on your food.

You tell her she doesn't need to do that. She gets you another bottle of water. You tell her she can help pay for your car. She says your car smells like piss and should be sold for parts immediately. You tell her you're fine. She says you're full of shit. You tell her you're dangerous. She says your Aunt Katherine's full of shit, too, and everyone else from your hometown, blaming a child for monsters in the night. You tell her you're eighteen, which is a year and three months from the truth. She says you're a child and retired from this life of chasing killers, at least until you graduate college. You tell her it was your choice to leave, your choice to fight, your choice to live the way you've been living. She looks at you real close and asks *was it?*

You start crying.

She lets you sob on her shoulder. *You're staying*, she tells you firmly, and eventually, you swallow and say, *okay.*

Here's the thing about sticking around: sometimes, it's hard not calling the shots. Sometimes, Mrs. Norwood's rules are stupid. Sometimes, you and Joey fight over the dumbest things. And killers do come back, occasionally: you go to some Christmas party and find a dead body underneath the tree, but Mrs. Norwood breaks through the door with a chain saw, and Joey's aim with the rifle is really improving, and all you have to do is make cocoa and wipe blood off the presents. Sometimes, you're scared to touch your new family; sometimes, you think you should run away for their own good. But mostly, you institute Friday Movie Nights and eat whenever you want. Mostly, you get hugs before going to bed. Mostly, you keep adding to your five-year plan.

CARLIE ST. GEORGE is a Clarion West graduate from Northern California. Her stories can be found in *The Dark*, *Nightmare*, *Strange Horizons*, *Sword & Sonnet*, *Lightspeed*, and other publications. St. George also writes essays about various movies and television shows on her blog, *My Geek Blasphemy*. It is entirely possible that she has spent a bit too much time analyzing superheroes, *Star Trek*, and *Teen Wolf*.

READ AFTER BURNING

MARIA DAHVANA HEADLEY

I t is crucial to remember that magic is unpredictable. Old magic, new magic, all magic. Magic has its own mysteries and rewires itself according to mood, like weather discovered between streets, rainstorms dousing only one person, or like a blizzard on the skull of a soldier, a brass band on the deck of a submarine. War magic exists, and wedding magic. Love magic and murder magic, spells for secrets kept forever, and spells for dismantling structures. Magic itself, though, sometimes ceases to exist in moments when it's most necessary, and even when you've memorized the entirety of the history of spells and sacrifices, there are always ways to fail and invent, to combine traditions into something else entirely. There are ways to shift the story from one of ending, to one of beginning.

All this happened a long time ago, before the story you know. You were born in a world that wasn't ending. This is a story about how that re-beginning came to be. It's about the Library of the Low, about books written to be burned, and about how we brought ourselves back from the brink.

I'm old now, but old doesn't matter. How many years have humans been looking up at the stars and thinking themselves annotated among them? How long have the stories between us been whispered and written and lost and found again?

This, then, is a story about the story: It's about librarians. It begins on the day of my father's death. I was ten years old. I knew the facts about blood; all ten-year-olds do. Do you? You do.

I knew this fact, for example: There was no stopping blood until it was ready. Sometimes it poured like magical porridge down the streets of a village, and other times it stood up on its own and walked out from the ground beneath an execution, a red shadow. There were spells for bringing the dead back to life, but none of them worked anymore, or at least they didn't in the part of the country I was from.

I don't need to tell you the long version of what happened to America. It's no kind of jawdrop. It was a tin-can-telephone apocalypse. Men hunched in their hideys pushing buttons, curfewing the country, and misunderstanding each other, getting more and more angry and more and more panicked, until everyone who wasn't like them got declared illegal.

When the country began to totally unravel—there are those who'd say it was always full of moth bites and founded on badly counted stitches, and I tend to agree with them—my mother was at the University on a fellowship, studying the history of rebellion. My daddy was the Head Librarian's assistant.

The Head Librarian was called the Needle. She'd been memorizing the universe since time's diaper days, and I never knew her real name. She was, back then, in charge of rare things from all over the world. Her collection included books like the Firfol and the Gutenbib, alongside manuscripts from authors like Octavia the Empress and Ursula Major. The collection also included an immense library of books full of the magic of both the ancient world and the new world. Everything could turn into magic if it tried. The Librarians had prepared for trouble by acquiring secrets and spells. They knew what was coming.

If you asked any of the Librarians from my town, they'd tell you their sleep went dreamless long before the country officially declared itself an *oh fuck*. They squirreled books and smuggled scholars, as many as they could, which wasn't many. Some made it to Mexico. Others got to Canada. A few embarked on a ship loaded with messages in bottles.

The Needle, though, had plans for saving. She stayed, and my parents stayed with her. They spent the first years of the falling apart sitting at a desk deep beneath the University library, repeating everything the Needle told them, making memory footnotes alphabetically, in as many languages as she could teach them. She started them off small and got bigger.

"Ink," she told my parents, "is not illegal," and so they started making ink out of anything they could find. They made it out of burned plastic. They made it out of wasps harvested while eating the dead. They made ink in every color but red: blue and black, brown and gold. Red reminded the Needle of things she didn't care to remember. My parents sharpened tools, started making plans, married each other in the dark of a room that had been reserved for books damaged by breathing.

The first tattoo the Needle gave was to herself.

The men in charge wanted people to forget penicillin and remember plague. They shut down the schools, starved out the teachers, and figured if they gave it a few years, everybody but them would die of measles, flu, or fear. Citizens ended up surviving on Spam and soup. No medicine. Little plots of land and falling-down houses. Basically conditions like those much of the rest of the world had faced for many years, but no one here was used to them, and so a lot of the population dropped dead due to shock, snakes, spiders, and each other. I was born four years into all of this. My mother died in childbirth, because by that time there were no doctors left in our city. The last one had been executed.

None of the magic worked that time.

The Needle delivered me, and she closed my mother's eyes when it was time to close them.

You can call me Enry. That's what my daddy named me. He said there was no *H* to be had in a world where hell had spit up this many fools and holy was this much in question.

I was not an unhappy child. The world withering above me was the only world I'd ever known, and to me it was a beautiful one.

Every few days a murmuration of soldiers came through town and said no one had any right to rights. Whenever they came, I hid myself in a knowledge shelter with the rest of the children born since the end of the world, and we waited for the soldiers to pass.

The rest of the time, we learned languages and studied history, farmed with sunlamps, and guarded the books. We were taught to read on medieval fairy tales about weather and Victorian poems about ghosts, on books of code in thirty-four languages, and magic books dating to long before Christianity. We were taught myths from Libya and poems from Andalusia and Syria, spells from Greece and gods from the land we hid beneath. We were taught about genocide but also about making the land bear fruit. We only came aboveground at night. We were not supposed to exist.

The adults, though, had to show their faces on the surface to get water rations and to be censused.

When I was ten years old, my daddy went aboveground one morning and didn't come back by nightfall.

I found him on his back in the center of the old marble floor in the University library. Someone had decided he was smart enough to kill, or maybe he'd just walked in the path of a bullet. These were bullet years, and they flew from end to end of cities like hummingbirds had, before the hummingbirds had fled. Bullets wanted to feed. We all knew it. We'd been warned.

My daddy pointed at his chest and fumbled at his collar. I loosened his tie. I unbuttoned his buttons. I opened his shirt.

"You have to burn this," he said. "Some books, you can only read after burning. Do you hear me? Do you understand?"

Blood was making a lake around us, and my knees were wet with it. My daddy's breathing slowed, and his hands froze like winter had nested inside him. He was the only parent I had.

I had no spell to keep him from dying, though there should have been spells. Everyone talked about magic, but no one had all the magic they needed. That was another thing you knew if you were ten years old and living beneath a library, if the world had started ending long before you were born and now you found yourself alone in it.

There was never enough magic to save everyone. Sometimes you only had enough for yourself, or you had the wrong kind entirely. I had almost nothing in the way of spells back then. I knew how to make a dragonfly out of sonnets and a bird out of ballads. I could bring a little beam of light to life in my hand and watch it glow, but it wasn't hot and it wasn't a heart. I had nothing for my daddy and no way to refill him from my own soul, no way to split it, no way to share.

It is crucial to remember that life, when it is long, is full of goodbyes. I had a husband once. You are the child of one of the children of my children's children. My husband was a man who could walk on water and whose veins ran with poems written six centuries before anyone insisted on religion. By the time I met him, I had enough magic to fill anyone with light. I could read in the dark, and the books of my family were written all over the world.

You are the *amen* of my family, and I am the *in the beginning* of yours. This story is the prayer, or one of them. This story says you can live through anything and that when it is time to go, when the entire world goes dark, then you go together, holding on to one another's hands, and you whisper the memory of birds and bees and the names of those you loved.

When it is not time to go, though, this story says you rise.

This is what I whisper to you now, so that you will carry the story of the library, so that you will know how we made magic and how we made books out of burdens. This is to teach you how to transform loss into literature, and love into a future. It is to teach you how to make a book that will endure burning.

Hours after my father's body went cold, the Needle found me huddled beside him.

"Will we get revenge?" I asked her. The hole in my daddy's heart hid half a sentence, and I wanted to cut it from the skin of the person who'd killed him.

"It's a long revenge," she said, with some regret, and I was unsatisfied. I wanted urgency, murder, fury.

The Needle had white hair to her knees, and the ends were stone black. She carried an ax and kept it sharp, but that wasn't what she gave me. The Needle gave me a bath and made me a sandwich, went back out in her night camouflage and hauled my daddy in.

"Before revenge," she said, "is ceremony."

"Do we have to go through the alphabet?" I asked, but the Needle had nothing to say to me about the letters between *C* and *R*.

The Needle kept the contents of all of her books in her head, though most of them had been burned ten months into the end. On her desk there was a heavy gold medallion she called the Old Boy, because on the back of it there were three men holding hands and declaring themselves brothers. In the winter she warmed it beside the fire, wrapped it in a towel, and used it to heat her feet. When she needed to send a signal, she used it to catch the light.

She called to all the Librarians in the area, and we went down six flights to her brain bunker. The stainless cubbies down there dated to years before the mess seized power, when somebody'd had an idea about keeping rare books safe in case of disaster.

Soon we were standing in the Needle's knowledge shelter, around the table that held my daddy's body. There he was, stripped naked and covered in tattoos, all of him made of words except the hole in his heart. I'd never seen him undressed before. In our house, he'd worn a darned suit, buttoned to the neck, none of his ink visible.

"Man needs a hat and tie at all times," he'd say to me. The rest of him was startling to me. My daddy specialized in invisible ink, and the tattoos between the lines, he'd told me when I was little, would only show up if you shone a candle through his skin. I'd never seen them; there was no way to see them on someone who was alive.

Read after burning, I thought, and couldn't think it anymore. I stood beside the table, at the level of my daddy's head, put my hand on his cheek, and felt the stubble of his beard poking through his story.

"Sharp, Volume One," barked the Needle, and we brought out our knives.

* * *

I was the one who was meant to cut the first page of the book of Silas Sharp. That's what you did if the book was your parent.

The Librarians rolled up their sleeves. Arms tattooed in a hundred colors and designs, the secret history of the former world. They had shaven skulls beneath their hats, and their heads were wrapped with Ada Lovelace and Hypatia and Malcolm X, with the speeches of Shirley Chisholm, with Chelsea Manning, with the decoded diagrams of the Voynich Manuscript. Their arms were annotated with Etty Hillesum's diary of life before Auschwitz, with Sappho's fragments, with Angela Davis, with Giordano Bruno, with Julian of Norwich, with bell hooks, with the story of the Union soldier who began as Jennie Hodgers and volunteered to fight as Albert Cashier, with Bruno Schulz, with Scheherazade, with Ruth Bader Ginsburg, with Danez Smith, with Roxane Gay, with Kuzhali Manickavel, with the motions of the planets, with the regrets of those who'd dropped bombs, with the sequencing of DNA, with the names of the dead, with almanacs and maps, with methods for purifying water, with primers for teaching letters, with names of criminals, stories of pain, dreams of better things.

None of this was categorized as magic, but it was magic nonetheless. All of this was the daily light, the brightness, the resistance, and refusal of intellect to endure extinction.

"What's that?" I asked one old man, dark skin and a silver beard, his text luminous in the shadows of the bunker.

"Dictionaries, Enry," he said. They were tattooed in pale ink. "Glow-in-the-dark microscript," he said, and smiled at me. "I made it out of worms. This arm is Oxford English, but English isn't all there is. There are words here that've never been defined."

"Which should be the first page of my daddy?" I asked him.

"I'd say you should start there, with Silas's heart."

"But there's something missing," I said.

"There's always something missing," said the Dictionarian. "Usually the missing sections aren't marked as simply as they are on Silas."

"I can't decide," I said.

"We've never been a simple people, Enry," said the Needle. "Nowhere, nohow, nobody. This decision isn't simple, but you have it in you to make it."

I lifted my scalpel and started to cut. He'd still be warm on the inside. He'd only been dead two hours. But skin degraded quickly. You had to cut fast.

I touched my daddy's heart. I looked for the words that were missing, that had been driven down into him. I'd seen my daddy dress for the bindings of other Librarians and come back into the house salt-scrubbed and drunk on moonshine. In those early mornings, my daddy would tell me about the books.

"There've been many books made this way," he'd say. "Long ago, books were made of animals. There were pocket bibles made of vermin—mice and rats—and fables made of rabbits. There were histories written on the skin of foxes, and there is at least one book in the world—or was—that was said to be bound in unicorn. There's a sea volume, a tremendous novel calligraphed on vellum made of the skin of a blue whale."

"A whale?" I asked.

"No one has seen a whale for a long time," my father said, "but when I was a boy, I went on a ship and saw a whale blow, and then its tail as it dove, and that was story enough for me. This very library, the University's, had a serpent's story, inked into a seventeen-foot snake-skin, accordion-folded. The history of written words is, at least in part, once, and now again, a history of skin."

"What about the skin of people?" I asked.

"There've been other versions of this kind of library," he told me. "Lampshades and wallets. There've been bodies stolen throughout the history of humans, but the books bound into the Library of the Low are made not of stolen bodies but given ones. There's nothing unholy in turning your own body into a bible for the living."

"How do *you* know?" I asked him.

"I don't," he said. "But I studied under the Needle, and what I know about the world's words, I know from her. We make our bodies into things that can last. We are not destined for coffins, nor for crypts. Our bodies will live on in the library, and one day, maybe, the world will change because of us."

"But they're only books," I said.

"There's magic written into them. The Needle taught me some old things."

He pointed at his chest, at a line of text, and around the line, for a moment, there was something else, a brightness—calligraphy made of fire. Then it was gone.

Now my blade went in there, beside the word *beginning*. This was my job too, to read out the first page of Sharp, Volume I. I would, one day, be Sharp, Volume II.

"In the beginning," I whispered, "time started in secret."

"Long before the stories said it started, and long after," said the Needle.

"This is how we bury our dead," I said. That was the line assigned to me. "This is how we find a path to heaven."

I sliced down the page, a rectangle. The room exhaled Silas Sharp's name, and I was done with the part I had to do, the start of the book.

The Librarians would scrape and stretch gently, to keep the pages from tearing. They'd be the ones who'd tattoo and inscribe the rest of my daddy, his bones and his fingernails, all night and into the next day, turning flesh into future. They could make pages that were thin enough to see sentences through, and the book of Silas Sharp, in the end, would contain at least a million words, written on every part of his body. His skull would be sliced into transparent coins, and his hair would be woven into the threads that would hold the binding. The muscles of his heart would be the toughest pages, inscribed with words my daddy had given to the Needle long ago. All Librarians gave their dedication to her.

I went back to the Needle's house to cry. Even if this was how the world was, I would have traded all the knowledge in the universe for my daddy telling me a bedtime story, for him sitting in our kitchen in his hat, humming to himself as he tattooed an animal in iambic pentameter.

We'd had plenty of words in the history of humans, but still, it was easy to take them away. Thousands of years of progress had been obliterated by the time I was born. Knowledge couldn't keep everything bad from happening; that was my first story, and it was a true one.

Knowledge wasn't enough.

I had never known my mother, but her book—unfinished—was about how to build bombs out of normal household ingredients. Her back was tattooed in formulas for Greek fire, and her cheekbones with love songs. They were part of the book too.

She had all this knowledge written on her skin, but still she died.

On the day my father was killed, I thought that knowledge was no use to me, that we would have been better off warring, running outside and fighting the soldiers. They were murderers, and I wanted revenge. Instead, I had a story I couldn't understand, the invisible ink of my father's tattoos, unreadable, useless. I raged in the basement, my own skin free of words, my heart free of forgiveness. Love was not enough, and neither were words. Nothing was enough to replace him.

I imagined myself to sleep: the men in charge, and the way I'd slay them, paring their skin from their bones, twisting their hair into ropes. I'd use their skeletons for my bed frame, and their hearts, I'd throw on the fire. They wouldn't be dedicated. They'd only be dead.

Yes: This is how we did it in those days. This is what we'd, from some angles, been reduced to, and from others, evolved toward. Books were written to be read, and we were writing them, making them, creating them, in a treeless place.

When the Needle got the idea to make the Skincyclopedia, it was because paper had gotten banned to everybody but the bodies willing to swear they'd never ever write anything wrong as long as they lived. Then paper got rendered illegal in favor of just a few things you could yell, four or five words at a time. There was a decree saying you weren't allowed to teach your babies to speak anymore, or to teach them to read. You were allowed the slogans, and beyond that, they'd show you pictures and films of how they wanted you to be.

The Needle remembered a time before all the books were banned, a time when even the crumbling scrolls were digitized and available for viewing.

"I can't hear a word you say," the Needle'd said, legendarily, when one of the men in charge came to her door, asking her to be their translator.

The men in charge were afraid of encrypted communication among the rebels and wanted someone who knew things about codes and cabals. Knowledge had become frightening to the powers that were, and they'd decided to make it invisible. The Needle didn't understand their logic.

Written history was filled with men like them, calling themselves heroes as they destroyed everyone else. The Needle told them she was fixing to die out like a dodo anyway and that she'd gone and forgotten everything but a recipe for piecrust. She went back into her house and closed the door in their faces.

"Are you writing down all the books you know?" my daddy asked the Needle when he first began to do the library with her.

"No," the Needle said. "I'm making a new story out of the old stories. This story"—she called out the name, something about mice, something about men—"this one has a wife, killed for no reason. This one too. And this one. This one has a boy hung up in a lynching tree. This one has an eleven-year-old girl narrated into existence by the man who rapes her. This one has a scientist dying of cancer, her husband getting credit for her discoveries. This one has dozens of people trying to swim across a river and shot from the banks. This one has a child dying because his family can't afford medicine. This one has a boy murdered because he loves boys."

"You're writing down the American collection again?" my daddy asked the Needle. Those stories sounded like the way the world was.

"No," said the Needle. "There are some stories here that are holy. Others, I think, may benefit from being remembered differently."

That was how this started.

By the time my daddy was murdered, the Needle and her Librarians were fourteen years into the Library of the Low. There were no margins, not on most of the first generation of Librarians, and not on any of the animals either. One of our goats was tattooed with a version of *The Odyssey* in which Penelope and the witches were the heroes, and another wore the secrets of manned flight, starring Amelia Earhart, Carlotta the Lady Aeronaut, Sally Ride, and Miss Baker—the first American monkey to survive weightlessness. There were shelves and shelves of stories.

"Knowledge," said the Needle every Sunday, when we met to pray over poems, "is the only immortal. We leave our words behind us. It is our task to pass them properly."

"*Holy!*" she said, reading from one of her own arms, quoting one of the poets. "*Holy! Holy! Holy!*"

"*Holy the eyeball,*" the children echoed.

"*Holy the abyss,*" she replied. This was not the only poem the Needle quoted. She had a hymnal of her chosen poets, but this one was a simple one, an annotation of things the world was trying to render obsolete.

"*apricot trees exist, apricot trees exist / bracken exists; and blackberries, blackberries,*" she said next, quoting another poet, Inger Christensen. There was an alphabet of lines tattooed on her other arm. "*fig trees and the products of fission exist; / errors exist, instrumental, systemic, / random; remote control exists, and birds; / and fruit trees exist.*"

"Amen," we said. "Amen."

It is crucial to remember, and it is the history of stories, that even the righteous resort to wrongs. That even the magical can be frightened, and that even the revolutionary can fail when they curl into comfort. There are many nights in a lifetime, if it is long, and some of them must be spent sleeping. It is crucial to remember that even in groups of the good, humans are still humans, and bodies are still fragile, that uncertainty can take over and that when it does, there is no option but shouting strength back into the crowd. There are stories about perfection, but those stories are lies. No one ever made the world better by being perfect. There is only mess in humans, and sometimes that mess turns to magic, and sometimes that magic turns to kindness, to salvation, to survival.

* * *

Every Sunday, when the Librarians met at the Needle's bunker, there was a vote taken on what to do, but the vote always came down on the side of staying secret.

"There is a long history," said the Needle. "Of monks and nuns guarding the books instead of joining the war. And yet, the time may come. Is it today? Have we done enough to preserve? Is it time to rise?"

The hands went up. It was not.

I visited my parents in the library and put them on the table in front of me, memorizing their contents, filling in their gaps. I read the rest of us, the dead I'd never met and the dead I knew. I read stories about love and about murder, stories about farming and about revolution. I read the library end to end, books from the immigrants who'd come from the south and the ones who'd come across the oceans, books from the people who'd been born here on this ground and died here too.

I pressed my hands to my parents' pages and turned them. There was a full-page illustration of a woman warrior with a sword, and I looked at that most often. My mother's book. My father's book had a full page of my mother herself, wearing her glasses, working on the bibliography of rage and weaponry for the gone, for the America I'd never encountered, one full of dirt roads and donut shops, unplundered graveyards and grocery stores, skyscrapers and sugarcane. Police cars, pummeling. Immigrants, ICE agents. Hunger and hunger and hunger. Hurt.

"Holy," I whispered. "Unholy."

In the early mornings, the world was lost in translation, a language the soldiers and the men in power didn't speak. There was fog, and in the night there was a warming river, and we brought people over it. There were babies born and new stories written, but we stayed the same, hidden in the Library of the Low, keeping knowledge from being burned, while the rest of the world caught fire.

I got my first tattoo as a copy of something from my mother's book, a katana down my spine, and my second tattoo from my father's book, a pen down the center of my chest, the same size as the sword. This was my family tree, quill and blade, ink and metal, the same importance, the same time. The back cover and the front. Who knew what my pages would contain? Who knew which of these things was mightier?

I didn't remember the past, and I couldn't imagine the future. I held off on more tattoos, and though everyone wondered, they didn't force me. There was no forcing a generation without memory of libraries. We had not memorized paper books. We had not touched trees.

Read after burning, I thought, and went to my father's book, and looked at it in the dark, but I couldn't burn it. It was all I had of him, his book and his bones, the words he'd chosen.

I held a candle to the page with the hole from his heart, and there was nothing of wonder on it, nothing magic.

Out there, in the rest of the country, people shouted their slogans and were rendered speechless. We farmed under lights we'd made and hoarded knowledge because there was no way to share it. We kept electricity on Earth. When we died, we were meant to pass the knowledge on our skin forward, not lose it on a battleground.

When I went to sleep at night, I could smell the towns around ours being burned: smoke full of story, secrets drifting overhead, but we took no action. We had a tiny world of our own, and that world was filled with our rituals and ceremonies, with our history, with our books made of the people we'd loved. We thought, for a time, that it was enough to save ourselves.

This was not the Needle's plan."

What is anyone's plan? The idea that the world will remain viable, that there will be no clouds of poison, no blight, no famine, is an optimistic one. The idea that one's children will survive even birth? Also optimistic. And yet.

When I was sixteen, one of our books got out into the world, the pages thin and the text intricate, and someone made up a story about it. There was a whisper that we were making books out of babies, converting them into the thinnest paper, tattooing their soft skin and turning it into a history of lies. These weren't even babies that had been born, the story went, but babies we'd preempted from birth, to turn into pocket bibles of revolution.

The soldiers charged the Librarians with resisting the arrest of everything. We were, they said, worshipping idols and insisting on sentences. All of the Librarians were taken but the Needle, who was so old by now that they decided she'd die on the road.

The men insisted that the babies were everywhere, that they'd been born to women in their seventies, and nothing the Needle said could dissuade them. They'd inherited knowledge too and believed it as firmly as we believed ours.

"Who had a baby?" she shouted at them. "How can you think this is a town full of baby killers, if there's no one of an age to give birth to them?"

Our Librarians were put into a wagon, some screaming, some shouting slogans other than the ones allotted us. The Needle and the children of the town were left behind, all of us hidden for our entire lives.

"It's time to change the color of the ink," the Needle said, when they were gone. "Sometimes bloodstains are the only writing you get to leave behind. Many of my people left nothing but red." She looked at me, her eyes narrowed. "We'll leave more than bloodstains. We'll leave char."

The Needle took us back down into her bunker, hobbling on the stairs.

"What are you willing to die for, Enry?" the Needle asked me. "You don't always get to choose, but this time, you do. You, boy, you're the one I'm talking to."

I didn't know.

"Open that door," she said.

I unbarred it. It was a room full of vials and metal, as secret as the rooms full of books, but different from them. Maybe not different. This was a room full of things that could catch fire or slice strangers.

"There is nothing holy," the Needle said, "about tradition. No tradition. Not mine, not theirs. Anyone who's ever thought so has ruined things all over again."

"But," I said, "we made the library. We have to protect it."

"We made the library because they tried to crush knowledge. We will fight because they tried to crush us," said the Needle. She trembled, but not with fear.

"I'm ready to burn, Enry Sharp," she said.

We loaded all the books of the Library of the Low into rolling carts, and we took the elevator, using power we normally saved. We rose up from the inside of the earth, beneath a stolen University, and when we came to the surface, we were a small army of young Librarians, and one old woman carrying a knife made of a melted medallion.

We marched.

The Needle once told me that we couldn't fix everything with love, even though some of the books said we could. Some of the poems said it was the answer. Some of the anatomical diagrams of hearts showed them full of certainty. I thought about my father's heart and the missing words inside it.

We marched for our parents, with them beneath our arms. We carried their skin and hair. We carried their words. We marched down a dirt road, and on both sides there were places consumed by smoke.

"Holy," we said.

High above us there was a swallow spinning, and below us seeds were still germinating and we were walking in boots we'd inherited, carrying daggers forged of our parents' wedding rings and jewelry.

"There aren't enough of us," I said to the Needle, as we arrived in the City. Walls of windows, broken. Buildings crumbling, but behind them I could see movement.

"There are," she said, and unbowed her lace collar. I could see words beginning to be revealed there, round and round her throat. The Needle's eyes were blacker than her ink, and her skin shone silver.

We stood in the center of the road and looked at the house, white columns built on the backs of Americans. Graffiti on its sides and trees from which bodies had been hanged. Some people had thought this was a beautiful place.

I opened a book in each of my hands, the book of Silas Sharp and the book of Yoon Hyelie Sharp. Beside me, the rest of the Librarians opened the books of their parents, and the ones whose parents had been taken readied their implements.

The doors began to open and there were soldiers coming for us. We saw men standing there, old as the Needle. The Needle stood at the head of our formation, tall and unbound, her shirt open, and in her hand she held a torch.

We all knew that we were about to die. There was nothing in us that was stronger than the guards here, and there were only a few of us to begin with. There were good ways to die, and this was one of them.

"READ AFTER BURNING!" we screamed, and we set fire to our dead.

I set fire to the book of Silas, and out of it rose my father, and I set fire to the book of Yoon, and out of it rose my mother.

The Needle set fire to herself and we closed our eyes at the light she made, the way her body blazed and hissed, words made of magic, words made of the Needle's own rage and reading.

This was the Needle's analysis of civilization, and this was her love, given form. This was what magic looked like at this point in the history of the world, a surge of stories transmitted in smoke.

I had never seen my parents together until I saw their books. I watched their skin insist on change and the spells contained within their volumes spitting fire. What can you see in firelight? More than you can see in the dark. I watched my mother's sword and my father's pen stand at attention, and then I watched them switch instruments.

I felt my own living skin warming in the light of the people I'd come from, the library that had raised me thus far, the stories that had been altered to show something other than quiet.

The Needle rose over us, a cloud of words, and she rushed at the men who'd decided America belonged to them. With her rushed the rest of the Librarians, resurrected to revolution, brought back to life with the magic of burned libraries and belief.

The old men stood, looking up, five of them, skinny, pale, and blinded, as the words of my people circled them, closed in on them, and redlined them out of the story. I watched as the Needle edited. I watched my daddy and my mother making a study of this part of our history, shredding them into fire and then into ash.

These are the parts of our story that, while alive, are also at rest. The lies entwined with lives, the magic used for shrinking the span of knowledge rather than encouraging it to grow.

My hands were open, and in them were flames. I kept my hands open as I fought. My hands were full of story.

Our knives were used too, bloodied on the living, but the living soldiers were surrounded by the words of the dead, and we were stronger than we thought we were. An army of children, but we'd been raised on something better than this.

I was the one watching when the Needle finished them, her hair flying up in the wind, each strand a sentence. I watched her words rush into their throats, filling them with stories they were not a part of. There was char, and an old white house on fire, and smoke filled with forgotten things.

I didn't know the world before the end of the world, but I knew it when it began again, out of dust and dark, out of whispers and bones.

There were twelve children, and then there was rain.

Was any of this magic? Not more so than the magic made in spring, and not more so than the spinning of the seasons. It is crucial to remember that none of this is certain, that even when joy is proximate, sorrow might be walking beside it. Indeed, it is crucial to remember how to extend your hand to someone different from your own self.

Magic is unpredictable. That's for you to remember. Kindness is too. It is all part of the same continuum, just as you and I are part of the same line. It would be years yet before I met the man I would love, and years before you would be born to a child of a child of his, crying in the arms of the midwife, fingers spread. This would not be the only revolution. There's never just one. This is how it begins.

"Enry," my father said as his smoke faded. By then it was dawn, and we were standing on the lawn of this building built to show what glory looked like from a distance.

"Henry," my mother said, as her embers died down.

The two of them looked around, and I could see their tattoos glowing like birds might, if the world was a world where birds lived, or like whales might, deep in the sea and looking for love, calling out in song to others of their kind. Not everything was gone. Some things were invisible, and other things had been in hiding and were coming out again.

"What does this word mean?" you ask me, and you touch a word on my skin, red ink, because after the world began again, we used red instead of black, to say that we had blood flowing and that nothing was fixed in forever.

"What do you think it means?" I ask. The meanings change along with the words. The text on my skin is a new story daily, and here is what I know.

I wake up every morning, and the world has changed overnight. I can feel my father's blood and my mother's magic, and I can feel the Needle, her body blowing apart.

When do things change entirely, you wonder? When do they get better? When will it be possible?

It is possible now.

You're built to open your fists, and show me your palms, and to pass food from them into the hands of others. You're built for comfort and for fire, for battle and for poetry, and you are a child of my family, and my family was made by the world.

Here we stand in the dark now, and I'm old and you're holding my hand and walking me from the bed to the window. We're looking out at all of it, the wonder and the danger. There are voices and the sun blazes, and everything is bright enough that if I were reading the letters on your skin, I wouldn't be able to parse them.

Now look at your own hands and the wrinkles in them. Those wrinkles are what happen when you clench your fists. You were born for this resistance, for this preparation, for this life. You were born to fight.

MARIA DAHVANA HEADLEY is the *New York Times*–bestselling author of six books, including the novels *Magonia* and *Aerie* and, most recently, *The Mere Wife*, a contemporary novel adaptation of *Beowulf*. Her new verse translation of *Beowulf* was published in August 2020 by Farrar, Straus and Giroux. Headley's work has been supported by the MacDowell Colony and by Arte Studio Ginestrelle, where the first draft of *Beowulf* was written. She was raised with a wolf and a pack of sled dogs in the high desert of rural Idaho and now lives in Brooklyn, New York.

OTHER RECOMMENDATIONS FROM 2019

I usually don't do a recommended reads/honorable mentions list because I invariably forget to include some great stories. And, of course, I can't read *everything* published. (Or even know it exists.) This year, although recognizing those faults, I'm giving it a shot. Those with an asterisk (*) are *highly* recommended.

Novellas

Ballingrud, Nathan: "The Butcher's Table" (*Wounds: Six Stories From the Border of Hell*)

Bear, Elizabeth: "A Time to Reap" (*Uncanny #31*)

Bestwick, Simon: "And Cannot Come Again" (*And Cannot Come Again*)*

Clark, P. Djèlí: *The Haunting of Tram Car 015*

Cooney, C. S. E.: *Desdemona and the Deep*

Langan, John: "Natalya, Queen of the Hungry Dogs" (*Echoes: The Saga Anthology of Ghost Stories*, ed. E. Datlow)

Moore, Tegan: "A Forest, or a Tree" (Tor.com)

Sharma, Priya: *Ormeshadow*

Smith, Michael Marshall: "The Burning Woods" (*I Am the Abyss*)*

Solomon, Rivers (based on the song by Daveed Diggs, William Hutson & Jonathan Snipes): *The Deep*
Tantlinger, Sara: *To Be Devoured*
Warren, Kaaron: *Into Bones Like Oil**
Wise, A. C.: *Catfish Lullaby*

Stories

Aliyu, Rafeeat: "58 Rules to Ensure Your Husband Loves You Forever" (*Nightmare #77)*
Arkenberg, Megan: "It Is Not So, It Was Not So" (*The Dark #51*) "The Night Princes" (*Nightmare #81*)
Barnes, Steven, and Tananarive Due: "Fugue State" (*Apex #120*)
Bear, Elizabeth: "Lest We Forget" (*Uncanny #28*)
Bermudez, Amanda J.: "Totenhaus" (*Black Static #68*)
Bestwick, Simon: "Below" (*Terror Tales of Northwest England*, ed. P. Finch)
de Bodard, Aliette: "A Burning Sword for Her Cradle" (*Echoes: The Saga Anthology of Ghost Stories*, ed. E. Datlow)
Braum, Daniel: "How to Stay Afloat When Drowning" (*Pareidolia*, eds. J. Everington & D. Howarth)
Broaddus, Maurice: "The Migration Suite: A Study in C Sharp Minor" (*Uncanny # 29*)
Bruce, Georgina: "The Lady of Situations" (*The Lady of Situations*)
Buckell, Tobias S.: "N-Coin" (*Apex #120*)
Carroll, Siobhan: "The Air, the Ocean, the Earth, the Deep " (*Echoes: The Saga Anthology of Ghost Stories*, ed. E. Datlow) "For He Can Creep" (Tor.com)
Cataneo, Emily B.: "The Longest Night" (*Black Static #72*)*
Chan, L.: "The House Wins in the End" (*The Dark #50*)
Chronister, Kay: "Roiling and Without Form" (*Black Static #68*) "Thin Places" (*The Dark #50*)
Cisco, Michael: "Their Silent Faces" (*Spirits Unwrapped*, ed. D. Braum)
Coen, Pip: "Second Skin" (*F&SF*, May/June 2019)
Coles, Donyae: "Breaking the Waters" (*PseudoPod 666*)

Das, Indrapramit: "A Shade of Dusk" (*Echoes: The Saga Anthology of Ghost Stories,* ed. E. Datlow)

DeLucci, Theresa: "Cavity" (*Strange Horizons* 7/8/19)

DeMeester, Kristi: "A Crown of Leaves" (*Black Static* #70)
"A Song for Wounded Mouths" (*PseudoPod* 64)

Dines, Steven J.: "Pendulum" (*Black Static* #70)

Elison, Meg: "Hey Alexa" (*Do Not Go Quietly,* eds. J. Sizemore & L. Conner)

Files, Gemma: "The Puppet Motel" (*Echoes: The Saga Anthology of Ghost Stories,* ed. E. Datlow)*

Ford, Jeffrey: "The Jeweled Wren" (*Echoes: The Saga Anthology of Ghost Stories,* ed. E. Datlow)
"Sisyphus in Elysium" (*The Mythic Dream,* eds. D. Parisien & N. Wolfe)

Fu, Angela: "Tansy" (*The Dark* #44)

Gardner, Cate: "The Mute Swan" (*Terror Tales of Northwest England,* ed. P. Finch)

Goodfellow, Cody: "Massaging the Monster" (*Black Static* #70)

Goss, Theodora: "A Country Called Winter" (*Snow White Learns Witchcraft*)
"How to Become a Witch-Queen" (*Hex Life: Wicked New Tales of Witchery,* eds. C. Golden & R. A. Deering)

Greenblatt, A. T.: "Before the World Crumbles Away" (*Uncanny* #27)

Hodge, Brian: "One Last Year Without a Summer" (*Skidding Into Oblivion*)

Howard, Kat: "Curses Like Words, Like Feathers, Like Stories" (*The Mythic Dream,* eds. D. Parisien & N. Wolfe)
"An Invitation to a Burning" (*Hex Life: Wicked New Tales of Witchery,* eds C. Golden & R. A. Deering)

Huang, S.L.: "As the Last I May Know" (Tor.com)

Huerta, Lizz: "The Wall" (*A People's Future of the United States,* eds. V. LaValle & J. J. Adams)

Johnstone, Carole: "Deep, Fast, Green" (*Echoes: The Saga Anthology of Ghost Stories,* ed. E. Datlow)*
"Skinner Box" (Tor.com)

Johnstone, Tom: "The Wakeman Recreation Ground" (*Last Stop Wellsbourne*)*

Jones, Stephen Graham: "This Was Always Going to Happen" (*Terror at 5280'*, ed. Anonymous)*

"The Tree of Self-Knowledge" (*Echoes: The Saga Anthology of Ghost Stories*, ed. E. Datlow)

Kim, Alice Sola: "Now Wait for This Week" Alice Sola Kim (*The Cut* 1/17/19)*

Laben, Carrie: "The Crying Bride" (*The Dark* #45)*

Langan, Sarah: "The Night Nurse" (*Hex Life: Wicked New Tales of Witchery*, eds C. Golden & R. A. Deering)*

Lansdale, Joe R.: "The Senior Girls Bayonet Drill Team" (*At Home in the Dark*, ed. L. Block)*

Lauryn, Inda: "Dustdaughter" (*Uncanny* #26)

Leckie, Ann: "The Justified" (*The Mythic Dream*, eds. D. Parisien & N. Wolfe)

Lewis, L.D.: "Moses" (*Anathema* 4/19)

"Signal" (Fireside 8/19)

Liburd, Tonya: "Bootleg Jesus" (*Diabolical Plots* 6/17/19)

Lore, Danny: "Fare" (*Fireside* 8/19)

Lombardi, Nicola: "Striges" (*The World of SF, Fantasy and Horror, Vol. IV*, ed. R. N. Stephenson)

Lothian, Jack: "They Are Us (1964): An Oral History" (*Twice-Told: A Collection of Doubles*, ed. C. M. Muller)

Lu, S. Qiouyi: "As Dark as Hunger" (*Black Static* #72)*

Mauro, Laura: "In the City of Bones" (*Sing Your Sadness Deep*)

"The Pain-eater's Daughter" (*Sing Your Sadness Deep*)

McHugh, Maura: "The Boughs Withered: When I Told Them My Dreams" (*The Boughs Withered When I Told Them My Dreams*)

Miller, Sam J.: "Shucked" (*F&SF*, Nov/Dec 2019)

Mills, Samantha: "Adrianna in Pomegranate" (*Beneath Ceaseless Skies*, 2/19)

Mondal, Mimi: "Malotibala Printing Press" (*Nightmare* #80)

Morrow, James: "Bird Thou Never Wert" (*F&SF* Nov/Dec 2019)

Ness, Mari: "The Girl and the House" (*Nightmare* #79)

Ogden, Aimee: "Blood, Bone, Seed, Spark" (*Beneath Ceaseless Skies* #271)

Ogle, L'Erin: "The Girls Who Come Back Are Made of Metal and Glass" (*Metaphorosis* 6/28/19)*

Okungbawa, Suyi Davies: "Dune Song" (*Apex* #120)
"The Haunting of 13 Olúwo Street" (*Fireside* 10/19)

Osahon, Ize-Iyamu: "Therein Lies a Soul" (*The Dark* #49)

Palmer, Suzanne: "The Painter of Trees" (*Clarkesworld* 6/19)

Perry, Steve: "I'm With the Band" (*Pop the Clutch*, ed. E. J. Guignard)

Peterfreund, Diana: "Playscape" (*F&SF*, Mar/Apr 2019)*

Pueyo, H.: "An Open Coffin" (*The Dark* #47)

Read, Sarah: "The Hope Chest" (*Black Static* #72)*

Rebelein, Sam: "My Name Is Ellie" (*Bourbon Penn 18*)

Rickert, M.: "Evergreen" (*F&SF*, Nov/Dec 2019)

Roanhorse, Rebecca: "A Brief Lesson in Native American Astronomy (*The Mythic Dream*, eds. D. Parisien & N. Wolfe)

Saab, Sara: "The Wiley" (*The Dark* #48)

Sen, Nibedita: "We Sang You as Ours" (*The Dark* #49)

Shearman, Robert: "I Say (I Say, I Say)" (*Tales from the Shadow Booth: Vol. 3*, ed. D. Coxon)

Sheil, Steven: "The Touch of Her" (*Black Static* #70)

Slatter, Angela: "Widows' Walk" (*Hex Life: Wicked New Tales of Witchery*, eds C. Golden & R. A. Deering)
"Wilderling" (*The Dark* #48)*

Srinivasan, Shalini: "Road: A Fairy Tale" (*Strange Horizons* 5/20/19)

Strantzas, Simon: "Antripuu" (*Nightmare* #82)

Stufflebeam, Bonnie Jo: "Every Song Must End" (*Uncanny* #27)

Swanwick, Michael: "Ghost Ships" (*F&SF*, Sept/Oct 2019)

Swirsky, Rachel, and P. H. Lee: "Compassionate Simulation" (*Uncanny* # 29)

Tem, Steve Rasnic: "Snowmen" (*Everything Is Fine Now*)
"A Sudden Event" (*The Night Doctor and Other Tales*)
"The Woman in the Attic" (*Everything Is Fine Now*)

Theodoridou, Natalia: "The Summer Is Ended and We Are Not Saved" (*Black Static* #70)

Tremblay, Paul: ~~"Ice Cold Lemonade 25¢~~ Haunted House Tour: 1 Per Person" (*Echoes: The Saga Anthology of Ghost Stories*, ed. E. Datlow)

Watt, D. P.: "Our Second Home" (*Petals & Violins*)

Westlake, Jack: "Looking" (*Black Static #72*)
"Pomegranate Pomegranate" (*Black Static #69*)

White, Gordon B.: "Birds of Passage" (*PseudoPod 663*)

Wise, A. C.: "The Ghost Sequences" (*Echoes: The Saga Anthology of Ghost Stories*, ed. E. Datlow)
"How the Trick Is Done" (*Uncanny # 29*)

Wolfmoor, Merc Fenn: "Sweet Dreams Are Made of You" (*Nightmare # 84*)

Yap, Isabel: "Windrose in Scarlet" (*Lightspeed* 10/19)

Zahabi, Rebecca: "It Never Snows in Snowtown" (*F&SF*, Nov/Dec 2019)*

ACKNOWLEDGMENTS

S pecial thanks to John Joseph Adams, Andy Cox, Ellen Datlow, C. C. Finlay, Diana Fox, Lane Heymont, Rene Sears, Jonathan Strahan, and Jarred Weisfeld. Also to Ohio Governor Mike DeWine and Ohio Department of Health Director Dr. Amy Acton who made me (indirectly) stay home to finish this on time. All stories are reprinted with permission of the author.

"A Strange, Uncertain Light" © 2019 G. V. Anderson (First publication: *The Magazine of Fantasy & Science Fiction*, July/August 2019)

"About the O'Dells" © 2019 Pat Cadigan (First publication: *Echoes: The Saga Anthology of Ghost Stories*, ed. Ellen Datlow)

"The Fourth Trimester Is the Strangest" © 2019 Rebecca Campbell (First publication: *The Magazine of Fantasy & Science Fiction*, May/June 2019)

"Hunting by the River" © 2019 Daniel Carpenter (First publication: *Black Static #69*)

"Conversations With the Sea Witch" © 2019 Theodora Goss (First publication: *Snow White Learns Witchcraft*)

"Read After Burning" © 2019 Maria Dahvana Headley (First publication: *A People's Future of the United States*, eds. Victor LaValle & J. J. Adams)

ACKNOWLEDGMENTS

"Nice Things" © 2019 Ellen Klages (First publication: *Uncanny #28*)

"The Thing, With Feathers" © 2019 Marissa Lingen (First publication: *Uncanny #26*)

"Thoughts and Prayers" © 2019 Ken Liu (First publication: *Future Tense 1/26*)

"Haunt" © 2019 Carmen Maria Machado (First publication: *Conjunctions 72*)

"Phantoms of the Midway" © 2019 Seanan McGuire (First publication: *The Mythic Dream*, eds. Dominik Parisien & Navah Wolfe)

"Shattered Sidewalks of the Human Heart" © 2019 Sam J. Miller (First publication: *Clarkesworld #154*)

"The Surviving Child" © 2019 Joyce Carol Oates (First publication: *Echoes: The Saga Anthology of Ghost Stories*, ed. Ellen Datlow)

"His Heart Is the Haunted House" © 2019 Aimee Ogden (First publication: *Apparition Literary Magazine Issue Seven: Retribution*)

"The Coven of Dead Girls" © 2019 L'Erin Ogle (First publication: *PseudoPod*, episode 651)

"Logic Puzzles" © 2019 Vaishnavi Patel (First publication: *The Dark #54*)

"The Blur in the Corner of Your Eye" © 2019 Sarah Pinsker (First publication: *Uncanny #29*)

"Burrowing Machines" © 2019 Sara Saab (First publication: *The Dark #44*)

"Some Kind of Blood-Soaked Future" © 2019 Carlie St. George (First publication: *Nightmare #85*)

"In That Place She Grows a Garden" © 2019 Del Sandeen (First publication: *Fiyah #10*)

"The Promise of Saints" © 2019 Angela Slatter (First publication: *A Miscellany of Death*, ed. Mark Beech)

"Blood Is Another Word for Hunger" © 2019 Rivers Solomon (First publication: Tor.com 7/24/19)

"Boiled Bones and Black Eggs" © 2019 Nghi Vo (First publication: *Beneath Ceaseless Skies #275*)

"A Catalog of Storms" © 2019 Fran Wilde (First publication: *Uncanny #26*)

ABOUT THE EDITOR

Paula Guran is an editor, reviewer, and typesetter. In an earlier life she produced the weekly email newsletter *DarkEcho* (winning two Stokers, an IHG Award, and a World Fantasy Award nomination), edited the magazine *Horror Garage* (earning another IHG and a second World Fantasy nomination), and has contributed reviews, interviews, and articles to numerous professional publications.

This is, if she's counted correctly (and she often doesn't), the forty-seventh anthology Guran has edited. She's also edited scores of novels and some collections. After more than a dozen years of full-time editing, she is now freelancing.

Guran has four fabulous grandchildren she would be happy to tell you about.

She lives in Akron, Ohio, with her faithful cat Nala.